ISLAND SPIRIT

A Novel ▪ Kay Hadashi

Honolulu ▪ Los Angeles ▪ Seattle

The Island Breeze Series

■ ■

Island Spirit.
Book One of The Island Breeze Series.
Kay Hadashi. Copyright 2014. © All Rights Reserved.
2nd Edition, January 2021.

In this second edition, portions of Chasing Tradewinds have been
included into this version of Island Spirit.

ISBN-10: 1499559461
ISBN-13: 978-1499559460

Cover art by the author.
Image from shutterstock.com. Original image by Tugol.
Book design by Kay Hadashi Novels.

www.kayhadashi.com

An Expected Surprise

June Kato lay in bed, staring at the ceiling, her eyes wet. What had started as a romantic evening had somehow turned deadly during the night.

Looking around the room, it occurred to her it was one of the few places they had shared a bed. The things that filled his life were all around, the heavy wood furniture, photos of friends and acquaintances on the wall, a few prized mementoes on shelves. They were items of pride, reflections of the past and signs of the future. It was in that room where the final argument had started in the middle of the night.

Their relationship hadn't started with romance and laughter. Instead, it began with her performing his life saving surgery. Somewhere along the way, physical exams gave way to phone calls, then meetings for coffee, and eventually the occasional dinner at her home, always accompanied by security agents. On a rare moment when they were on the same coast at the same time, and had time to spend together, they met at his desert house to consummate their relationship. That was three years before, and since then, true romance was always nearby, but never quite within reach.

After two years of developing a long-distance relationship, he hit the campaign trail, once again running for President. She watched and worried as their romance continued in fits and starts, June barely fitting into his busy life. The closer he got to winning his campaign and the race for presidency, the more she felt like a groupie in his life. Hours would be spent trying to figure out where he was at any given moment, just so she could meet with him for a day or two. Now, here she was in his private Brentwood home bedroom, waiting for the inevitable to happen.

Jack Melendez was a tough nut to crack, the toughest June had ever met. Looking at him objectively, she knew he was the perfect candidate to lead the nation as President, even if he was in a different political party from what she followed. He would also be an excellent husband and father, if it ever came to that. But deep down inside, she knew starting a marriage and ostensibly a family right when he was moving into the White House would be far less than ideal. June also knew that leaving her hometown of Los Angeles and moving to Washington DC was not in the cards for her.

As a child, she'd never fantasized about marrying a powerful man, living in a dream house, or being wealthy. Even now, living in her old house in the LA hills and running a busy career as a neurosurgeon, she'd reached beyond what anyone might've expected. Her sister had worked just as hard in her fashion career, reaching supermodel status early. Both had been labeled as over-achievers since childhood. Now, here June was, looking at over-achievement once again, this time potentially serving tea in the White House rose garden, attending state dinners, and meeting the leaders of the world.

She didn't want that, though.

Once again, they had argued about it during the night. Almost any woman in America would jump at the chance to live the fairy tale life of being First Lady. But not June. She wanted nothing of politics, or politicians. In fact, she was the first to join a public protest, refuse to vote if a proper candidate wasn't on the ballot, and gripe about misuse of her hard-earned tax money. So when Jack proposed marriage the week before and June accepted, her family and friends were shocked. The idea that she would soon pack her bags and move into the White House was so far out of character for her, people worried. But things had changed in the week since.

Blotting the tears from her eyes, June lifted her left hand in the air. The large diamond sparkled as brightly as ever, almost mocking her decision. There was the slight tremor that had been plaguing her the last couple of years, something she'd been able to control. Looking at her right hand, the tremor was even worse. It was a grim reminder that her career as a neurosurgeon wouldn't last forever. So far, she'd been able to control it during surgery and no one else had ever noticed. Maybe it was a matter of nerves and nothing more.

Knowing she would have to face the inevitable, she went for a shower, dressed, and found Jack in the courtyard garden. Breakfast was just being brought out, perfect timing for her arrival at the table as always.

"I love that two-headed shower, Jack," June said, breaking the ice. She settled down at the small bistro-style table across from him. Trying to ignore the two Secret Service agents that stood in the shadows of the garden, she took a drink from one of the glasses of pulpy orange juice he'd poured. It was all a delay before getting to what was in her heart.

"Waste of water," he said.

"Maybe so. But for a shower like that, I don't mind so much."

He put a muffin on her plate and pushed the butter across the table. "June, I need to apologize for last night. I never meant to…"

"Jack, let me talk for a moment." Her appetite gone, her mood plummeting, her soul feeling as if it were being crushed, June tried to smile anyway. It didn't work. "I can't go to DC with you."

"I knew this was coming."

"Please, just let me finish. This is hard enough as it is." June nervously rubbed the engagement ring on her finger with the tip of her thumb. "You know I love you deeply, and nothing will ever change that. But I just can't play the role of First Lady. Seriously, can you see me serving tea and crumpets to a bunch of stiff, over-dressed political wives in the Rose Garden?"

"No, but I can see you taking a swing at the first Secret Service agent that got in your way."

"Probably so," she chuckled. The mirth didn't last long. "It's just too much politics, too much game playing, too much slime that I just can't be a part of. I'm sorry, but I don't want to be famous."

"You already are."

"Maybe in some small way in the world of neurosurgery, but I don't want my life in the White House residence to be the topic of conversation every time there's a slow news day in the West Wing."

"That's a deal breaker for you? Life in the White House for four years?" he asked.

"Or eight years."

"One term at a time. What's so bad about being in DC for a while?"

"Giving up my position here in LA, moving to a place where I have no friends or relatives, leaving my career and family behind, only to pretend to be somebody I'm not. I know it's some sort of old-fashioned idea to care about one's reputation, and rather egotistical to even think about it, but I've worked hard all my life to develop a good rep in the world of neurosurgery. I'm pretty reluctant to toss that aside, just to play White House hostess. I'm not willing to take the enormous risk of marrying into a situation that we both know could turn out to be a massive disaster."

"You downplay your reputation, June. You're huge in the world of medicine. That's why the Navy and Secret Service came to you to perform my surgery. Docs at Balboa and Bethesda all knew you were the only one who could help secure any chance for my survival. The mere fact that the surgical technique you used was one you spent several years developing. It's even named for you, the Kato approach to third ventricle surgery, or something like that. People from all over the world come to you for help."

"And I'm reluctant to let them down. Once I step into the White House, all that would end. Oh sure, officially I'd have a staff position at some grand Maryland medical center, but how much would your agents allow me to work? As First Lady, I'd have to have a Secret Service agent in the room before doing an exam, and the only way patients could get in to see me is after they'd been thoroughly vetted for security. Once again, I'd spend my time playing hostess to people I don't know nor care about, and not doing surgery." Her hands hidden in her lap, her thumb was rubbing the ring on her finger faster than ever.

Interrupting them was kitchen staff coming to take away their plates. Nothing had been touched by either of them. June knew a signal of some sort must've been passed without her noticing, purposefully giving them both a reason to take deep breaths.

"I'm sorry you feel that way," Jack said once the meal had been cleared away.

"I'm sorry. I shouldn't have let it get this far."

He refilled their cups of coffee. "Neither of us should have."

June slipped the diamond ring off her finger and looked at it one last time. She set it on the table between them and looked up at Jack's face. Somehow, her eyes had remained miraculously dry.

"I know I've let you and your family down. A wedding, newlyweds in the White House, a whole new rendition of Camelot for America."

"Well, America never knew of the engagement, and hardly even knew of you. That's how you wanted it right from the beginning, to remain anonymous." Jack set his napkin on the table. "We've had planning sessions on how to manage the relationship, and the announcement to the nation about the engagement. It was going to be a few weeks after the inauguration, with the wedding in the spring."

"Ha! And then I stumble in and kick dirt all over everything. But that's something I don't want, to have my life planned, managed, rehearsed, and orchestrated for me. If I had some idea that your Chief of Staff wouldn't meddle in our private lives, I'd think about it more. But as it stands…"

"Leon is a putz. He's going to make a mess of things anyway. Are you sure you don't want to be a part of the three ring circus that's surely coming to town?"

"I truly am sorry, Jack. My best wishes for the inauguration, and for your presidency."

***

June had never felt so bad when she let herself in the front door of her home. At the last moment, she turned and waved as the large sedan pulled away from the curb. The glint of morning sunlight off the polished car flashed in her eyes, and she couldn't see if there was a wave in return through the tinted windows. As the car rolled down the street, the companion car with it followed closely. Once the cars had rounded the corner, she closed her door.

June kicked off her shoes, set her overnight bag on the floor, and tossed her purse on the desk. When she dressed after breakfast for the ride home, she had combed her hair and quickly, dabbed on a bit of makeup, but knew she still looked haggard. A half hour of crying did that to a girl. She looked at her hands. Something was missing, her diamond engagement ring. Four carats of sparkle and promise were nowhere to be found.

She tried rubbing away the pain of the missing diamond ring. Unsuccessful, she sat at her desk, flipped open the Yellow Pages and searched until she found the number she wanted. She still had another week of vacation time and was going to put it to good use. In possibly the most impulsive thing she had ever done, she called the airlines and bought a very expensive airline ticket to Maui for that very afternoon. It was the week of Christmas through New Year's, and she was surprised at the available seat, but not at the cost of the ticket. No matter the cost, there was one thing she knew: she wasn't spending the holidays at home bawling over a broken engagement.

She made another call, and knowing she was interrupting her sister's busy morning, she called in a favor.

"Amy, you have time to give me a ride somewhere?"

"Can't your new Secret Service buddies give you a ride? What's the point of having those guys hanging around if they won't take you places?"

"Come on, I need to be somewhere."

"Where?"

"LAX."

"Jack's making you fly commercial and not on his private Lear?"

"Sis…" June sighed. "Okay, first, there's news about Jack. Second, I'm not spending the week with him, but going somewhere alone."

"Uh oh," Amy said.

"Uh oh is right. I'll explain later. Just come pick me up at home."

As soon as she was showered and dressed, she dumped what was in her overnight bag, still clean and unworn formal clothes meant for a week with Jack, right into the hamper. If whatever she took to Maui wasn't enough for a week, she could buy something there. She wouldn't need much on her sudden, new vacation. All she wanted were daily long runs, punctuated with just as many naps.

Checking her hastily written notes for the flight, she still didn't have a room or a rental car. All she knew about Maui was that the island was ringed with resorts and rental cars were everywhere. Almost as if it were too much to bear, making those arrangements could wait.

She heard a car horn toot and peeked out the front window to see her sister waiting. There had been a rainsquall while she was in the shower, but it had already settled, the sun peeking out again. She grabbed a medical journal from her coffee table, stuffed it in her purse and left, locking her front door behind her and setting the alarm.

Amy seemed impatient watching June buckle her seat belt.

"What?" June asked.

"Why am I taking you to the airport?" June's twin sister asked. "I thought you were spending the week with Jack?"

"I'm being impulsive today," June said back.

"I should say so." Amy put the car in gear, drove down out of the hills above LA, and got out into mid-afternoon traffic. "Why the airport?"

"For a flight. Why else?"

"To?"

"Anywhere but here."

"What about Jack?" Amy glanced at June's hand. "There's something missing from your outfit, by the way."

"Oh?"

"Yeah. Big, shiny, four carats of 'I love you' written all over it."

11

"I gave that back," June said as matter of factly as she could. Her mood wasn't holding up as well as she planned. "It didn't seem to fit the way an engagement ring should."

"When did you break up? Because I never knew something was wrong," Amy asked.

June finally let the dam burst, rambling away. "This morning at breakfast. All I ever heard about was the campaign, the election, how easy it would be for me to move to Washington DC, how I could get a great staff job at Bethesda, be belle of the ball every weekend. Like I'm supposed to give up what I have here in my life just so I can be a part of his life there. I'm not interested in being someone's little woman."

"Don't want to be his trophy wife?" Amy asked.

"More like honorable mention at the county fair."

"Unbelievable," Amy said. "Who else but June Kato has the balls to break it off with the President-elect. He's a nice guy, for crying out loud! Even Mom and Dad voted for him!"

"Most of America voted for him. But most of America doesn't have to live in the White House and have their personal lives monitored by federal agents and their schedules managed by some stressed-out jerk named Leon."

"You're stressed out enough all by yourself, Babe. But what happened?"

"Don't worry. I was polite about it," June said quietly, pointing her finger at an open lane on the freeway. "There won't be anything in the newspapers. No big scene in public dragging the Kato family name through the mud. Just a lot of blubbering all over his shoulder in the backseat of a limousine."

"Oh, well, now that makes it better." Amy got into the fast lane. "But why am I taking you to the airport if you aren't going away with Jack?"

"Like I said, I'm being impulsive. I'm learning how to throw caution to the wind and have fun. I have a week of vacation, and I plan to do something with it besides pull weeds in the back yard or paint the kitchen."

"And…" Amy led.

"A week on Maui sounds like a fantastic idea. I even have an airline reservation…" June looked at her watch. "…which takes off an hour from now, so snap it up."

Amy gave it some gas and got into her usual tailgating position. "Do you have a place to stay?"

"That's something that still needs to be resolved."

"I must admit, this is a side of you I've never seen before. Everything has always been thoughtfully planned out years in advance, everything from your weekly menu to how long a pair of socks will last."

"Any idea about Maui hotels? You've stayed in them."

"Utmost of comfort, highest quality service, fabulous in every way. Also expensive, budget breakers, especially for a brain surgeon who does way too much pro bono work." Amy angled her sedan toward an off ramp, getting a couple of honks along the way. "I might know of a condo you can stay in, if you don't mind me interfering in your fun? Or at least pay for a room at a resort?"

"I can pay my own way in life. There must be a budget place I can find when I get there."

"Budget? On Maui?" Amy laughed. "No convents for you to stay at like your last trip to Hawaii?"

"My vacations are a little under-whelming. That's why I'm splurging and staying where real tourists stay. Only on a budget."

"Let me arrange something while you're on your flight. I wouldn't worry about you so much if I knew where you were staying."

"I'm a big girl, Sis. I can have madcap Hawaiian adventures all by myself."

"Yeah, and that's what I'm worried about. Remember what happened the last time you went to Hawaii? And I'm not so sure you know how to be spontaneous."

June sighed audibly, a habit she had been trying to break. Criticism over her occasional sighs of mild exasperation had led to their argument the night before. It was odd to her how little effort was needed to get the ring off her finger. But right then, it felt good to sigh away a few invisible tears.

"Okay, fine. You win. But I'm paying you back."

"Do you have a back-up plan, just in case hotels are full? It's the holiday season, and Hawaii gets busy at this time of year."

"Sleep on the beach if I have to."

Amy laughed. "My sister. From the White House to homeless, in one short day!" She pulled the sedan to the curb at the airport departures terminal. June grabbed her overnight bag, her only luggage. "Packed light, I see."

"Impulsive, remember?" June stepped out the luxury sedan and looked back at her sister. "Kiss the girls for me, okay?"

June slammed the car door closed and watched Amy drive away, wondering where she would sleep that night. Amy had been right, that being spontaneous was one thing, but acting impulsive could be a problem. She wondered if she should wait another day, just to make better arrangements. But when she saw the hustle and bustle of the busy airport, she let a sense of adventure sweep through her. Maybe it was the unplanned breakup from the night before, but she had the idea something new was starting.

After the earlier rain shower, a rainbow had formed in the direction of the coast, a jetliner headed directly for it.

***

By the end of the long flight, June was exhausted. She had spent the previous evening in passion, then the night in tears, followed by the entire day in mourning. She barely got off the plane in one piece, just the small overnight bag in her hand.

On her way out of the Maui airport, she stopped in the terminal to check messages on her cell phone. She had half a dozen from Amy. The first two were warnings to be careful, the next two were to have fun, the next included directions to a time share at a resort on the opposite side of the island, and the last was a combination warning to have fun but be careful.

She gave her sister a call. "What am I supposed to be careful about?"

"Rebounding."

"A rebound relationship?" June laughed. "You know me, Sis. I go years between relationships."

"They have a way of sneaking up on you. Just be careful."

"Who? Guys or rebound relationships?"

"Both. Did you get the address I sent?" Amy asked.

"Yes, Mommy. I have it pinned to my shirt, Mommy."

"Hey! You know what?"

June laughed and ended the call.

She stopped at the first rental car agency she came to and got their cheapest car. After getting a tourist map of the island thrust into her hand, she asked the young woman for directions.

"Napili Winds Resort?" the agency clerk verified. "Yeah, that's actually in Ka'anapali, even though it's called Napili Winds."

"What does that mean to me?" June asked.

"Never been here before?"

"It's all foreign language to me." June tried smiling her apology. "Look, all I know is that I'm on a small island in the middle of the Pacific Ocean. I don't know anybody here, I don't know one place from another, and I'm not even sure of what time it is. If you could just point on the map where I'm supposed to go to find the bed that has been assigned to me, I'd really appreciate it."

"Yeah, sure." The rental clerk jabbed her finger at a spot on the island about as far from the airport as someone could drive. "Right here, just a few miles from Lahaina Town. Classy place. My sister and I go shopping in the boutiques there all the time. Never buy nothing, though. Too expensive."

June forced out a benevolent smile, too tired to care if it looked sincere. She had the girl draw a line on the map of the best route to get to the tourist area.

"Hard to get lost. Just drive that way, follow the highway through Wailuku Town, then go until you see the ocean. Turn right and drive along the beach for a while until you go through a little tunnel. In a little while you'll go past Lahaina Town on the left, and a few miles past there's the new hospital on the right."

"Great, but I don't need a hospital. I need a bed. Where's Napili Winds Resort?"

"First signal past the hospital, turn left and there you are! Not much beyond there except golf courses. If you see those, turn around."

"What happens if I drive past those?" June asked.

"You'll end up back here after taking a lap around West Maui."

June looked at the map of Maui as if it were a miniature version of Los Angeles. "I don't need better directions that that?"

"Lady, it's an island, and not very big. You can't get lost."

The only times June had ever been to Hawaii were for a quick fashion model job many years before on another island, and for an epic failure of a vacation, also on another island. All she knew of Maui was its fame for beachside weddings at resorts, world famous surfing, and sunsets.

Once she left the city area of central Maui, she passed through a tunnel and found mostly rural countryside as she drove along the coast. On one side were the surging ocean waves, and on the other were rocky green mountains, with white clouds tumbling over the peaks. The few towns she passed through were small, with mom and pop businesses slowly turning to tourist activity centers, with large resorts along the coast.

The Napili Winds Resort was easier to find than what the rental agency woman made it sound. Walking into the open-air lobby, June discovered it was half timeshare condos and half tourist resort. What she found next at reception check-in truly surprised her.

"We have you in one of our beachside cabana rooms, Miss Kato," the pretty receptionist told her. She wore a sleeveless Hawaiian-motif dress in subdued colors and a small gardenia behind one ear. June knew of some myth about a flower behind one ear meant a woman was spoken for, and behind the other meant she was available, but had no idea if it was true. She was polite and cheerful, and handed over a key card to a room with a bed, which was all that mattered right then.

The receptionist looked over the counter to where June was standing. "I can have a porter help with your bags, Miss."

Evidently Amy had booked the room under June's name but hadn't given her title of doctor, which was also fine with June. Along with solo runs and lonely naps, some anonymity was in order. While most of her relationship with Jack Melendez had been kept quiet, there had been a few media stories about the woman he was dating, along with pictures in tabloid magazines, with growing speculation as to her identity, including being a surgeon. All it took was a nosy receptionist or housekeeper at the resort to recognize June and her secret would be out. With another quick glance at the wood, tile, and tropical plant décor of the lobby, June knew her wealthy sister had booked her in a five-star resort instead of a borrowed condo or cheap inn, most likely for the discretion.

"No bags. But I didn't personally make the reservation. Has it been paid for already?"

"Paid in full through next Saturday night." With a new smile, the receptionist slid another card across the counter, Napili Winds Resort Services emblazoned across the front. "This is a gift card for any of our services, massage, salon, boutiques and restaurants. Whoever made the reservation certainly wanted to be sure you enjoyed your vacation!"

June took her cards, and with her carry-on in hand, followed the porter to her room. It was late evening by then, with warm tropical breezes blowing through the open floor plan of the hotel. While the porter used the keycard to let her in, she dug through her wallet for a tip. All she had were a few coins.

The porter flicked on a couple of lights and opened the sheer curtains hiding the floor to ceiling windows. It was a full suite, with a large living room and separate bedroom and kitchen, resembling a luxury apartment.

"Ma'am, you can manage your air conditioning with this," the porter said, giving her a simple remote that operated the A/C.

"Is there a patio? I'll probably sit out there most of the time."

He opened large sliding glass doors that led out to a patio with a table and chairs, along with a chaise lounge. The sound of gentle waves breaking indicated the beach couldn't have been more than a few steps away. Small lights illuminated a walkway outside, with benches here and there aimed for a view of the ocean.

Back inside, June looked at the porter, arranging a gift basket on the kitchenette counter.

"Don't get too involved in that," she told him, still poking through her bag for a tip that might not insult him. "I have nothing to give you." She tossed her bag down on an easy chair. "Are you on duty tomorrow?"

"Yes, Ma'am."

A gentle breeze blew through the room, making the sheer curtains wave about, while another wave broke on the beach outside.

"Okay, tell you what. Whatever you were expecting tonight, I'll double it tomorrow. But you have to promise to never call me ma'am. Just call me June."

With a twinkle to his eyes, he smiled and let himself out. Just after he was gone, she threw the security hasp, set the deadbolt for the door, and turned out the room lights. She collapsed into an easy chair, with a banana from the fruit basket and a can of Japanese brand aloe juice from the minibar. The warm breeze that came in through the large door swept through the room, bringing with it the scent of the ocean.

"Somehow, I have to pay Amy back for all of this," she mumbled into the dark room.

Taking a deep breath, she let her eyes close, jumbled thoughts of a very long and painful day washing through her mind. She was close to a sobbing breakdown when sleep rescued her.

***

June wasn't sure of the time, or even where she was when she woke. The chair was soft, and she felt comfortable curled into a ball. Making the few steps to the bed seemed pointless. But when she turned over in the chair to snuggle in better, something sharp snagged her wrist.

"What was that?" she mumbled. Her eyes only half open, she held her arm up for a look. That's when she felt a tickling sensation on her hand.

She jumped up, instantly awake. She flicked her hand in the air, then a second time, watching as a large brown spider fell to the carpeted floor and rushed off toward a dark corner. It wasn't a tarantula that she occasionally found in the hills around her home, but something with long, skinny legs.

"Oh no you don't!"

She grabbed the glass she had used for juice and trapped the spider. Leaving the spider inside the upside-down glass, June went to the bathroom.

"You bit me, you little…"

She washed the bite mark on her wrist, tried squeezing the wound to force out any venom that might've been injected, and washed it again.

On her way to the kitchen, she stopped to look down at the spider turning circles in the glass, trying to find a way out. It was big enough to reach from one side of the glass to the other without having to stretch its legs. She tapped a fingernail on the glass. "Vacation, you know? I just got here!"

She wrapped some ice cubes in a bar towel and held it on the bite. Using a paper coaster from the minibar, she trapped the spider inside the glass, grabbed her wallet and keycard, and went to reception.

"Miss Kato, you're not asleep yet?" the same receptionist asked.

June set the glass on the desk. "Can you do me a favor? Stick some tape on that so my little pal doesn't get away." She held up her wrist to show the woman the bite mark. It was already beginning to throb and turn red. "Any idea if these things are poisonous?"

"Ugh. Looks like cane spider." The young woman grimaced, her voice reverting to a local pidgin accent from the more formal five star resort tone she had used earlier. "Can be poisonous if they really sink their chompers into you. Usually they just run away rather than bite, kinda shy like that. But I'm so sorry!"

"Is there a clinic here at the resort?"

"Only during the day time. You should have that looked at by a doctor at the hospital. Please be sure to have the bill sent to us."

June got the directions to a local hospital only a couple of miles away. "I think I saw a sign for it when I was driving here."

"It's a new place, private, nice," the receptionist told June. "They'll take good care of you."

June made the quick drive in the dark of night and went into the Emergency Room entrance. Quiet, only one other patient was there, a young guy that had taken a solid wallop to his nose. He had blood down his face and on his shirt, his badge of honor for losing a fistfight. Apparently, closing time at the bars on Saturday nights was the same everywhere.

June was shown to a curtained exam cubicle and took her pet spider with her. It took only a moment before someone came in to see her.

"Let's see," the man said. His nametag indicated his name was Henry and he was a nurse. He was about her age and spoke with an accent that was more mainland than Maui. Dressed in hospital scrubs, he would've been good looking in the daytime. He had a paper chart in his hands. "June Kato has a spider bite. Is that correct?"

Sitting on the edge of the stretcher, June shook his hand and held up her wrist still wrapped in a wet towel with the remnants of ice cubes. She picked up the glass with the spider still in it, now curled into a ball on the bottom. She held it out for him to take.

"Meet Marvin. He's been fed," she said. Lifting the cool wet towel away from her wrist, the redness was expanding and a lump had formed.

"Oh, yes, we see these from time to time here. We call them cane field spiders. The one's still small. Have you done anything to the bite?"

"Washed and iced it. Scolded Marvin relentlessly. But that thing is considered small?"

A Filipina in a white lab coat showed up. Dr. Cabrera, her nametag indicating she was the Emergency Room doctor. She did a quick exam of June's wrist.

"Yeah, cane spider bite. Not really poisonous, just painful. My parents used to get these all the time working in the cane fields." She ordered some antibiotics and an antihistamine to reduce the inflammation. She looked at June again. "Tourist, yeah?"

She had the same local accent as a friend June had met a couple of years before on a different island during her failed attempt at taking a vacation. "Yep."

"No worries. You can still suntan on the beach every day." With a yawn, Dr. Cabrera picked up the glass. "I'll get rid of this thing for you. When you find these, just squish them with a shoe."

"Uh, no, that's okay. Maybe we can just put him outside where he belongs," June offered.

Both Henry and Dr. Cabrera looked at her inquisitively.

"I don't like to kill things," June offered as her explanation.

Henry smiled.

"He just bit you!" the ER doctor said.

"It doesn't mean he deserves execution."

When Dr. Cabrera wandered off with a shrug, Henry took charge of the glass. "I'll let him out at the far end of the parking lot."

June waited for Henry to return. When he got back, he had a syringe in his hand.

"That must be the antihistamine," June said, looking at the syringe. She pushed her shirtsleeve up.

"Your antibiotics are coming from the pharmacy. The sooner I give this antihistamine to you, the sooner the inflammation goes away. It hurts less in the butt than in the arm and gets into your circulation faster."

June eyed him for a moment. As a doctor, one thing she knew about was administration of medications, and she had to admit he was right, that a shot in her butt would hurt less. She just didn't like the idea of pulling her pants down for a stranger. Amy's voice floated through her mind, warning her about getting naked with the first guy she met.

"Unless you're shy about it?" he asked.

"In my rear end is fine." She stood and began undoing her pants button. It was the same jeans she had been wearing all day, almost twenty-four hours by then. Henry turned away and yanked the curtain closed around them for privacy.

"Most people put up a fight about that," Henry told her.

"My butt's been seen before," June told him, referring to her bygone days of fashion modeling. She wasn't telling him that, though. She just wanted the shot and to get back to a bed in a hopefully spider-free hotel room.

With her pants down, June stretched out on the stretcher again, letting Henry tug at her panties a bit. She felt his fingers quickly check for the proper landmarks before wiping with the alcohol swab.

"Okay," he said.

June felt the pinch of the needle, something cold, and then her panties get tugged back up again, all in one fluid motion. She pulled her jeans up after he explained the bottle of antibiotic pills, June nodding the whole time.

"You seem to be pretty familiar with our routines, Miss Kato," he said to her.

"Yeah, actually, it's Doctor Kato. But please call me June."

"Oh? What's your specialty?"

"Neurosurgery. My practice is in LA."

"Oh really? I worked at Good Sam out in the San Fernando Valley after nursing school. What hospital are you at?" he asked, rolling a gauzy dressing onto her wrist.

"Mercy downtown," she answered. The conversation was just delaying her bedtime. The hand on the clock on the wall had just rotated past two in the morning. Adjusting the time for LA, it was right about when she would be getting up for a run in the hills around her home.

"Oh, downtown. Knife and gun club stuff. Freeway trauma."

"Keeps us busy." June rubbed her face with her hands, half to push away the late night cobwebs, and to politely signal she was tired.

"Okay, you got your antihistamine, and the antibiotics pills, and Herman..."

"Marvin," she said to correct him.

"And Marvin is once again a free range spider. Anything else?"

June slipped off the stretcher to stand on the floor, gathering her things. "Is it safe to go for runs around here?"

"Not on the highway. Too many distracted drivers. But all the way from Lahaina through Ka'anapali until you get to Napili there are side roads. And you have the beach to run on first thing in the morning, before too many sunbathers show up."

Back at the hotel, the only thing she did in her room was check the bed for spiders, pull off her clothes and dive in.

***

There was no mistaking the sound. June's cell phone was ringing with the Pet Shop Boys' *Opportunities* ring tone. It was Amy calling already.

She grabbed the phone off the nightstand, blindly tapped, and held it to her face. Sprawled face down on her bed, she didn't want to move or even open her eyes.

"This better be good."

"Hi Babe. How was the flight? Is the room okay?"

"The flight was a cesspool of influenza, and the room comes with pets." She rolled over onto her back. "But the hospital is close."

"Hospital? Pets? What's going on?"

"Got bit by a spider while sleeping last night, so I went to the ER. Got a shot in my ass and a bottle of antibiotics, along with a whopper of a bill. Otherwise, so far, so good."

"What is it with you and vacations?" Amy asked, laughing. "Can't you stay out of trouble for even one day?"

"Apparently, vacations hate me as much as I hate them."

"Yeah, I guess so."

There was a pause, but June knew the interrogation wasn't done.

"What else, Sis? I know you want to ask something."

"Did you hear from Jack?"

23

June looked for messages on her phone.

"Nada."

"So…"

"It's done, Sis," June muttered into her phone. She undid her bra and tossed it aside, leaving her almost naked in the warm room. She rubbed a knuckle into the spot where she got the injection on her rear and pulled the sheet over her again. "I'm here being attacked by spiders from Maui, and he's five thousand miles away preparing to rule the world, which is just fine with me."

"But…"

"And you know what? This is the first I've thought of him since getting off the airplane yesterday."

"That's it then?"

"That's it. Jack Melendez is ancient history, and all the meetings and the security and the politics and the crap that went with him."

"What now?"

"I get several more hours of sleep, make some long distance calls checking on my patients at Mercy, and find a smutty romance novel in the hotel gift shop to read. That should fill the remainder of the day."

"No, I mean, what are you doing with the rest of your life?" Amy asked.

"Now that I've got a blank slate of a social life to work with? I don't know. Maybe it's time to make some changes, you know? Forty is staring us in the face. Time to have a little more fun before it's too late."

"Not getting a tat, are you?"

"Ha! Maybe a flashy one on my rear end. When the nurses at work see that in the locker room, they'll have something to talk about." She rolled over onto her back. "What are you guys doing today?"

"Try and get both kids dressed at the same time, then the mall. Dinner with Mick. The usual." June listened as her sister gave directions to the nanny about making the girls dress themselves. "But, hey. Eat something today, okay? No starvation diets."

June made calls to the hospital back home in LA to check on her patients. One of her colleagues was watching over them while she was on vacation, but she could still obsess about them. She learned, as always, that they were all as well as could be expected. No reason to worry, or an excuse to go home.

Once again, her troubles were her own.

***

Finding nothing on the lunch menu she had an appetite for in the resort restaurant, she got toast. The waitress brought a stainless steel tray of jams for her to use. June gave each a sniff. One smelled strongly tropical, with pineapple, orange, and something else, which became the winner. Finishing the meal by washing down her antibiotic pill with mango juice and coffee, she found a paperback book in a gift shop.

After nine pages and a long nap, she showered and went for a walk. It was almost time for dinner, but she wasn't going to eat at the hotel again. Instead, she turned her back on the touristy beach area and went off in the direction of the nearby town. Breaking into a sweat and still feeling too jetlagged for much walking, she cut over to a smaller residential road that ran close to the shore.

She found an old timey grocery store, a white sign with scuffed blue lettering labeling it as Fujitani Grocery, where she went in for something to drink. Only further along was a public beach, where she sat at picnic bench in the shade, draining half the bottle of water.

June watched as waves slowly rolled in, one small set after another. She knew Maui was famous for surfing and water sports, and wondered where those beaches were, if this was one of them. She watched a few surfers carve long boards through shallow waves, turning back to deeper water at the ends of their rides. One of them looked clumsy, wobbling more than standing erect.

"And that would be me."

Some of the other picnic tables were piled high with food, surrounded by families, barbecues burning meat, barely-dressed kids running through the little park. A pickup truck pulled up, kids jumping out the back, the driver delivering a large cooler to his friends. It was Sunday evening at a beach park, Maui-style.

The sun was getting low over the horizon, and the last of the surfers paddled in to the beach near her. The clumsy one took his board to an old van, dried off, and drove away. The last one out of the ocean stowed his board in a pickup truck before going to the outdoor shower. It was almost dark by the time he was done drying off, making the slow walk back to his truck, letting the water drain from his body. June couldn't be sure, but something seemed familiar about him. So far, she had met no one on the island except the rental car clerk, the resort receptionist and porter, and two people at the hospital.

His face was unmistakable when he got near her table.

"Hey, Henry," she called out to him, smiling. All he had on were his board shorts and a dark suntan. She had a hard time keeping her eyes on his face as he got closer.

"Yeah, hi," he said back.

Instead of the travel blouse and pants she'd worn to the hospital the night before, she had dressed for comfort in a black tank top and jogging shorts. The breeze tousled loose locks of hair across her face, which she ignored. She held up her left wrist with just a small bandage on it. "Remember me? June Kato? Brutally attacked by a vicious island resident?"

"Oh yeah!" He walked over with a large smile on his face. "We called you the spider lady for the rest of the night."

"It's not like my name is long or difficult to spell," she said.

"You sure it's you? You look different."

June wondered if she did look that different, without the travel clothes or her hair hidden in a bun. She also wondered which way she looked more attractive to this easygoing island guy, tidy and well dressed, or more scantily clad with her hair fluttering in the wind. "Need to see my rear end for positive ID?"

He chuckled. "No, your front end looks good enough."

She crossed her arms. "Oh really?"

"I mean…let me try again. How's your arm?" he asked.

She motioned him to sit at the table with her. She pushed aside the gauze bandages for him to see. "Better. Should be gone in a few days." She looked at the water he just came out of, the sky over the ocean a deep purple, just a few clouds glazed red and orange hanging low over the horizon. "So, you surf well. I was watching for a while."

"Pretty good. I learned when I was a kid, but never had the time to surf much when I lived in California. Not ready for that big surf stuff they have up at Peahi or Ho'okipa, though."

"I've never heard of them," June said back.

"Maui north shore, good surfing, big sets."

"That means it has big waves?"

"Too big for me in the winter. I might be able to handle Girly Bowl in the off-season, though."

"Girly Bowl?"

"It's a place…never mind."

June finished her bottle of water while he spoke, wondering what a girly bowl might be. The only reason she got the rental car was to get from the airport to the resort and back again. As far as sightseeing went, if she didn't see it while out on morning runs and afternoon walks, it wasn't worth finding, making the rental worthless.

"Maybe I'll drive there sometime. But you make it sound like you're not from California originally?"

"Maui built." He jabbed his thumb toward the highway. "Grew up in town. Went to the mainland for college, worked for a while, and when this new hospital opened, came back here."

"That's why you don't have much of an accent?" she asked. Henry was definitely fit, something June couldn't help but notice. She tried her best to not check him out by keeping her eyes trained on his face.

He laughed a gentle chuckle, completely different from Jack's hearty hoot. "Accent comes and goes, when I'm at work I talk one way. Around old friends or local people, talk local way. Honestly, I don't really notice."

The scent of meat on the barbecue hit her again, something heavily spiced with garlic, food she wouldn't eat as a vegetarian. But her stomach rumbled anyway. "Hey, is there a cheap place to eat at around here? Or am I stuck with ten dollar pieces of resort toast for the next week?"

"Already clean out the minibar of chips and beer?"

"Still working on a fruit basket."

"Oh yeah. Nothing says resort like a basket of stale fruit shipped here from the mainland."

June was instantly defensive of her stale fruit. "I got it from my sister. Anyway, you never answered my question."

"Not really. Unless you like noodles. There's a place called Uncle's Saimin just a couple of blocks up the street. Otherwise, it's just takeout musubi from the little grocery store."

"Ramen and saimin are my comfort foods. If I get a big bowl of salty broth and noodles, I'm a happy girl!"

The breeze had become steady as they talked, and a pile of napkins blew from the family picnic table to where they sat, a little boy sent to collect them. June watched him run back to his mother with the napkins waving around in his hands.

"So, would your wife scratch my eyes out if I bought you a bowl of noodles at Uncle's?" June asked him, standing. "I mean, it would be as thanks for not groping me last night when you gave me the injection."

"Yeah, I missed my chance, didn't I?"

"Sure did. Although you would've pulled back some broken knuckles had you tried."

"Good injection though, huh?"

"Barely felt it. You want the noodles or not?"

He grabbed his shirt from the van and put on an old pair of rubber slippers for the short walk to Uncle's. It had only a few tables, a little on the greasy side, but it was the kind of place June's parents would like, and her too. Even her highbrow sister would admit to liking the place if someone pressed her hard enough for the truth. It was mostly different kinds of noodle plates, and several styles of musubi, rice balls with toppings held on with strips of nori seaweed. As soon as she walked in the place, she could smell pork frying.

After ordering at the front counter, they sat at a small table in the corner next to the front window. June had her back crowded into a potted ficus plant slowly taking over the front of the café.

"You never did answer my question," June said to him, straightening the plastic tablecloth.

"I did. I came here for the noodles, right?"

"Not about the noodles, but about your wife scratching my eyes out if she found you here with me," she said.

"Oh, her." Henry looked her in the eyes for a moment, maybe searching for an answer of his own. "Women actually do that to each other?"

"Some of us. So, you are married?"

"Nope."

June did her best to hide her smile. Maybe that rebound relationship was heading in her direction after all, in the form of a fling.

"But you made it sound like you do when you said, 'Oh, her'."

"Engaged."

"Which is even worse. Here I am throwing myself at you, and she's at home assembling a herd of attack spiders to defend her man. When's the date?"

"Two weeks."

June sat back. "Yikes! This close to the wedding, I doubt she'd bother sending spiders and go for broke with a full-on attack of…whatever Maui has that's worse than Marvin."

"Giant centipedes. Anyway, you're safe. She's off the island right now. In Honolulu for girl stuff, whatever that is," he said. "Apparently, you're not married?"

"I was engaged until recently," she said.

"How recently?"

June looked at her watch. "Not quite two full days."

"And you're already out cruising guys at the beach?"

"I guess it looks that way, huh? But I came here to Maui just to get away and think for a while. I have a week off, which I was originally planning to spend with him."

"But something happened and here you are, eating dinner with a stranger about to take the plunge."

June slumped in her chair. "Wow, that really is pathetic."

"Let's see. What I've read in women's fashion magazines is that most of the time when a man breaks it off with a woman, it's because she's psycho about something."

"You read a lot of women's magazines?" June asked, wondering if she'd found something to tease him about. Since he was spoken for, he was also fair game to tease.

"It gets slow at night sometimes. At work, I mean."

"What do the magazines say about when a woman breaks it off with the man?"

"That she doesn't like his job, has no future, that sort of thing."

"Ha! Yeah, that rings true, I suppose."

"He didn't have a good job?" Henry asked.

"More like not having a career progression that I could see myself being a part of."

Their bowls of food came, June's saimin with tofu and Henry's ramen with fake crab.

"And now you're here on Maui to soothe your broken heart?" he asked.

"More like celebrate the fact I got out of the deal with my ego intact."

Henry slurped a few noodles. "It works that way for a lot of women. They have an ugly breakup, and come to Maui to soothe their trodden soul with pitchers of booze and sunburns. After running up a tab, they go home to sue their soon-to-be-ex for as much as they can get."

"Wow. Not too much of a misogynist, are you, Henry?"

"Go for a walk along the beach tomorrow at your resort. Every lady by herself with an umbrella drink is likely drinking away her man troubles."

"What about the ones drinking beer?" she asked.

"Craft IPA or union made?"

"Union."

"They're near the end of their visit and have switched over to drinking beer instead of booze."

"And craft IPA drinkers?" she asked.

"They're the ones who've come back to live, ready to make lifestyles changes."

"Changes as in…"

"Right. They're the ones men have to be careful around." He slurped a few more noodles. "Look, you asked me a question the other day about why I came back to Maui. Sure, I could've stayed in LA and earned a bigger paycheck that would've gone a lot further than what I earn goes here. There's tons of stuff to do there, the ocean, the mountains, desert, endless entertainment in the city. Depending on the part of the city, LA's a great place to live."

"But?" she asked.

"But there's something special about Hawaii, and about Maui most of all. There's a spirit here that can't be found anywhere else. It's something that connects the people to the land. Even though the ancient Hawaiian ways are mostly long gone, Mauians still feel as though we're connected to the place through that spirit." He looked at June for a moment. "Maybe you have to be born here to understand."

"Maybe so," she said. What he said sounded a little out there, but she had to admit that since she'd arrived, she felt as though she was changing, even if it was calming down a little from the stress in her life.

"How long were you engaged?" he asked.

"One whole week." June held up her left hand as if she were looking at the engagement ring and stuck out a pouty lip. "Nice ring, though. Kind of miss seeing a sparkly satellite dish on my hand."

"What happened, if you don't mind me asking?" he asked.

"Yeah, actually, I do mind. Maybe some other time, okay?"

"You're here for only a week. We might not meet again."

"Tell you what," she said, chuckling. "If you see me sitting around the beach drinking craft IPAs, I'll be ready to talk about it."

She finished her noodles and watched him eat his. He handled his chopsticks naturally, as if they had been in his hand all his life, the way they had been in hers. Once they were done, she tossed some cash down on the table as a tip and they left.

"Working tonight?" she asked. She forced a slow pace to their walk back to the resort, if only to enjoy his company. Unlike most emergency room people she knew, he had a calm way about him.

"I have the next four nights off. Three twelve-hour shifts on, then four off. I pick up extra shifts sometimes for the cash."

"You like working nights?"

"Extra pay, fewer bosses."

Ever since their conversation about her broken engagement, her ring finger had itched. Rubbing it one last time before forcing her hands apart, she looked at Henry and provided a nervous smile.

"Okay, you win. But it might be the silliest story you've ever heard."

"About the guy whose heart you broke?"

"Yeah, him, wise guy. And I have an idea he'll be a little too busy to notice he has a broken heart."

She had no idea of how to start, or what to tell him, that it was all so new to her also. Not just the broken engagement, but that she had been engaged at all, and to whom. In a way, it felt like a therapy session, giving her the chance to get a few things out of her system. "So, he'll be President soon, and if we got married, I'd have to give up my neurosurgery practice in LA and move to DC. I would've got a staff position at Bethesda, but in name only. I doubt there would've been opportunity to do any surgery. More likely I'd be hosting luncheons in some fancy dining room. None of that is particularly appealing to me."

"President of what?" he asked.

She smiled at him. "The United States."

"Did I give you the wrong meds last night?" he asked. "Did the spider venom go to your brain while you slept?"

"And that's why I didn't want to bring it up," June said back quietly. "Because the story sounds so goofy."

They walked quietly for a few minutes before getting to the edge of her resort.

"You're serious? You mean Jack Melendez?" Henry asked her, stopping in his tracks.

"The very same."

"But he got in that trouble...he missed out on his inauguration when he needed that..."

"Emergency brain surgery. Then he started the relationship with his surgeon, which not only did the media love, but his campaign manager, also. Yes, that was me."

"You're the woman doctor I've read about in the newspaper?"

"The unnamed woman doctor, yes. And please don't bring up the ethics of a surgeon and a patient dating. We never got to that point in our relationship until long after his recovery was complete. In fact, as soon as I had his incision closed and port-op orders written, I was shoved aside and his care was taken over by Navy doctors."

"And you guys were officially engaged?" he asked, scratching his head.

"That's what made it so difficult." She reached up and wiped a trickle of sweat from her brow. "Then yesterday morning at breakfast I gave the ring back, went home, had a good cry, and bought a plane ticket to Maui. And here I am with a week off and a spider bite on my wrist, eating dinner with a stranger getting married in two weeks."

"And you're not drunk?"

"Sober as a temperance meeting."

"This is like tabloid news stuff, something they put in racks at supermarket checkout stands," he said.

"If you don't mind, I'd appreciate it if you kept it under your hat, at least as long as I'm here on the island."

"And of course, once you leave, if I tell anyone the story of how I met the President's ex-fiancé, nobody will believe me and I'll have no way to back up my claims."

"Exactly. As it stands, if the tabloids get a hold of any of this, America will be disappointed they don't have a White House wedding to watch on TV, his approval rating will plummet, and I'll be labeled as the President's mistress. Kind of a messy deal all the way around."

Henry grinned. "What's it worth to you for me to keep it quiet?"

June smiled back, hoping he was kidding. "And what's it worth to you for me not to send some big, ugly thugs to your home the day before the wedding?"

***

After hemming and hawing for a few minutes, June and Henry had made a date for the next day, agreeing to not call it a date. June had tossed and turned all night, wondering how she could contact him, purely to cancel. Standing him up by not showing up just wasn't the kind thing to do. When she woke in the morning, she knew she had no other alternative but to meet with an engaged man for a date that wasn't really a date.

Instead of continuing with the rat's nest her hair had become in the last few days, and no makeup, she was going to fluff and primp a bit for her non-date. It also meant she would need some clothes. The only decent clothes she had was the outfit she wore on the plane, and that smelled rank. And she wasn't going out with the guy in jogging clothes again.

For lack of time, she canceled the massage she had previously scheduled. She found some things to wear in a boutique, something that wouldn't break her budget. She was employed full-time as a physician, but she worked at a county hospital where reimbursement was never very good. In fact, she wasn't making much more than some of the older nurses made at the hospital. But between washing her clothes in the bathroom sink, pressing her new outfit, and getting a nap, she had just enough time to shower and dress before rushing off to the lobby.

"What am I doing?" she muttered under her breath. She followed shady pathways from her cabana room to the lobby in a separate building. "I'm here for two days, and I'm already dating a guy? He's engaged, for crying out loud. What's wrong with me?"

Somehow, she got turned around in the vast resort and found herself at the beach. Backtracking, she hurried.

"This is the rebound trap Amy warned me about. And I walked right into it."

Henry was already in the lobby waiting. Seeing him in a polo pullover and chino shorts, she felt overdressed in the new skirt and pressed blouse. She gave him a hurried peck to the cheek, barely stopping to say hello before they left.

"Sorry, I shouldn't have done that," June said, as they left the parking lot.

"Done what?"

"Kissed you."

"It's not like we made out."

"But still."

"Let me worry about Karen. You have enough on your mind," he said.

"That's her name? Does Karen work?"

"In the tourist industry. Nothing special right now, just in a convenience store at the same resort you're staying at. She's going to school, hoping to start a career in tourism."

"When does she get home from Honolulu?"

"Not till next week. Our little affair can continue for a while."

June's cheeks flared red with what he said. "Affair? Look, Henry. I'm not coming in between an engaged couple. I have enough trouble of my own right now."

"Yanking your chain, June. After all, I've already seen your butt."

June breathed a sigh of relief. "And that didn't win your heart?"

"Sorry. But I'll add your name to the list if things don't work out with Karen."

Earlier in the day she had studied a tourist map of places to eat in the old whaling town of Lahaina. Front Street facing the harbor looked to be touristy, with many of the small eateries in town. She got a little of the history, discovered some interesting restaurants, and found there would be decent shopping. For a rare moment in her life, she felt like being a tourist.

"What did you have in mind for dinner?" she asked once they were parked on the edge of town.

"Play it by ear, I guess. There're some New Age vegetarian places in town we can try."

June ate vegetarian for the health benefits and as a personal philosophy, but didn't consider herself even remotely New Age.

"Be tourist guide for me, Henry. While leading me to a place that serves more than noodles, tell about the town."

They turned a corner where he took the lead. "When the tourists hit, bam! It gets pretty lively, especially in the evening. Boutique clothing stores and tourist stuff, little restaurants all over, good bars if you're feeling more adventurous than last night?"

"I think my alcoholic adventures will consist of red wine and dark chocolate, in the privacy of my room where I can have a good cry. But I'll take a glass of iced tea."

There was a brightly lit joint on the intersection of two small side streets just off the main walking district, the front door aimed at the corner. Left over from bygone years, it had a rough clapboard exterior and a second floor that looked like there were tiny rooms for rent. The sign over the door said 'Lahaina Nuthouse'.

It was busy inside, mostly with the twenty-something-year-old wannabe surfer crowd. Sunburnt college coeds too buxom for their bikini tops and sari skirts were jammed around tables, making rank jokes about guys at the opposite side of the bar. There was only one small table situated between some red-faced Australians and a group of tipsy women, and it looked like the war between the sexes wasn't going well right then.

"Let's sit at the bar," June suggested, dragging Henry by the arm. She made sure to keep space between them, giving her stool a nudge away from his. It was a wood-top bar that had seen plenty of use, and June leaned her elbows on the smooth surface. The bartender tossed down cardboard coasters, Henry getting a Heineken, June having iced tea. "How'd this place get its name?"

"This was the mental hospital many years ago," Henry told her. "It was still open when I was a kid. We could walk by and hear stuff going on, and some pretty crazy stories drifted around about what went on inside."

"I bet. I noticed it's conveniently located across the street from the old prison. That would've been handy." They clinked their drinks with an unspoken toast. "So, tell me about your hospital. Does it stay pretty busy?"

"Not yet. There are several resorts around here, so at any given time maybe half our patients are tourists. Chest pain from old guys drinking and eating too much after playing golf under the tropical sun. Snockered women with twisted ankles from wearing flip flops to the bar. Drunk driver car accidents. Pretty vegetarians with spider bites."

She elbowed him playfully. "I see a common thread in there."

"Unfortunately, with tourism comes alcohol and all its side effects."

"I suppose." She wanted to change the subject. Her otherwise good mood might crumble with too much shoptalk. "Why'd you come back to Maui, Henry? You mentioned your parents have passed, so you could go back to LA to a bigger hospital and more challenging patients. I mean, don't you miss the bigger paychecks in California?"

"That's why I put in so much overtime, at least one or two nights a week. We're short-staffed anyway, and sixty hour work weeks for nurses is nothing unusual in Hawaii." He took a swig of his beer, swirled the foam at the top, and took another swig. "But you can't beat the climate. And if you like water sports or doing anything outdoors, you can find it here."

June sipped her pale iced tea at a much more leisurely pace than Henry was going through his beer. The tea had a sweet pineapple flavor, with some other fruits, more of a cider flavor than brewed tea. That's when she realized all she had to eat that afternoon was an orange from the fruit basket, why hunger pangs were beginning.

"You like to surf?" she asked.

"Still getting back into it. I go once a week or so. What about you? Are you a water sports kind of gal?"

"I can stay afloat, and even get from one end of the pool to the other without help from a lifeguard."

"Wouldn't it be more fun with the lifeguard?" he asked, winking.

"Maybe I should give it a try sometime. Nothing to lose at this point."

Henry mentioned that pool lifeguards were easier to chat with than beach guards.

"I'll keep it in mind. Mostly, I like to run. Somehow, it's become my way to escape all the silliness of life for a while. Sort of meditative for me. Something else I would've been forced to give up had I married what's his name."

"Better than booze, I suppose."

"Way better than booze."

She took another sip of her drink, tasted the heavy-handed fruit sugar in it that time, and nudged it away. She was done with it.

"I have an extra board, if you want to go out with me sometime?"

"Surfing?" She reminded herself the vacation had been hastily arranged, and impulse was meant to be the theme. She also reminded herself it wouldn't be a date, to go surfing with him. So far, however, all she'd done is get a spider bite and go on a date with an engaged nurse. All she wanted was a way to get Jack out of her system, and a tryst with a man would be perfect for that. The first man she met was attractive, charming, and easy to be around. But in some cruel twist of fate, however, he was about to walk down the aisle. She could easily have obsessed about it, something she was learning not to do. Amy's words came to her, about being too uptight and not having enough fun. "When?"

"Tomorrow morning should be good. There's a place just up the coast that gets decent sets and has a sandy bottom. Nothing to eat around there, so we'll have to take a cooler. And sunscreen."

"You said Karen gets home next week. Have you told her about me?"

"What about you?" he asked.

"That you're hanging out with a single woman while she's on vacation."

He held up fingers to count on them, one by one. "First, just like all tourists, you're going home at the end of the week. Second, nothing is going to happen between us. Third, your butt did absolutely nothing for me."

She nudged him with her elbow. "That's so insulting! I have a perfectly acceptable butt, even if it is almost forty years old!"

"Remember that wine and chocolate you mentioned earlier? Guess where it's all gone?"

June glared at the side of Henry's head as he took another pull from his glass. Telling an ex-fashion model she has a large rear end is right up there with telling her she has a bad complexion or boring hair. If he had said the same to Amy, the date would be over and Henry would be wearing his beer down the front of himself.

"In spite of what you've just said, and with the sword of Damocles hanging precariously over your head, I'm willing to squeeze my overgrown fanny into a swimsuit and give surfing a try."

His glass was empty by then, right about the time the waitress returned with the news of a bigger table in the back of the restaurant. June left her half-finished glass of tea behind.

Henry got a fish meal, something with a Hawaiian name June didn't recognize. She ordered the largest salad they had and asked for no meat but extra cheese, hoping it would turn into something filling. She stuck with another iced tea.

"I hope you don't mind, but I called a couple of the docs I work with and asked about you today," Henry said. "Interesting past."

June wanted her meal to arrive so she'd have an activity to hide behind instead of answering questions.

"Which part is interesting?" she asked, before launching into what might turn into long explanations and lame excuses.

"You were a model before becoming a doctor?"

"Oh, that. Ancient history. It was a good way to pay for college and med school. But where did you hear about that?"

"Dr. Cabrera remembered who you were not long after you left the ER the other night. You name rang bells for the medical journal articles you've written, and she remembered seeing your face in fashion magazines a long time ago."

"Yep. Some of those old pictures still show up in new issues every now and then."

"Just like your sister."

"Not quite like her. She has style and pizzazz, which earned her a lot of fame and money. Now she has a fashion garment business that's taking over her life. Her things are getting recognition from Shanghai to Florence. All I ever had to offer the fashion world were a dimple and six pack abs, which required endless sit-ups to maintain. Which apparently has been replaced by a rear end the size of a Buick."

"I was just teasing about that. Don't take it seriously."

"Ego's a little fragile right now, Henry."

"Let me see if I can build it back up a little. You've been carving out a reputation as a neurosurgeon. I stopped in at the hospital library and read through several articles you've published on third ventricle access procedures, but I didn't see where very many other docs are doing the same thing."

"In the world of neuroscience, some people consider me a dinosaur. With so many new chemotherapeutic agents coming along lately, oncologists take center stage with cancer treatments. That means there's less call for surgeons like me."

"But in the articles I read, you indicated not every third ventricle disease can be treated medically or chemotherapeutically, that sometimes surgery is required."

She was impressed he had read so thoroughly about her career. "That's why I developed that procedure. Benign growths can be removed, and even large tumors can be debulked, requiring less chemo and a smaller spectrum of drugs. Oncology may no longer be in its infancy, but it's still in its childhood. We'll always need surgeons."

Their meals came. Over the food, she told Henry about her career-long quest to find better and safer access to points deep within the brain that few other surgeons were willing to risk. Much of her reputation had been built on that, and patients from all over America were sent to her clinic for related illnesses. It was because of her and other younger doctors willing to advance their specialties that Mercy Hospital was able to grow and flourish while other LA facilities barely clung to life.

"Our hospital needs a few more docs like you," he told her. "We don't even have a neurosurgeon right now. There's only one on the island, and he's over at the bigger facility in town. Because of that, all the neuro patients go there, and almost all of the spine patients, or over to Honolulu."

"That's a ton of revenue you're missing out on. Is the hospital trying to recruit someone? Maybe they can get someone right out of training?"

"I've heard they push the island lifestyle as much as they do the job or hospital when they recruit."

"I guess someone would have to expect to be busy enough to earn a living. It's pretty expensive here, Henry. And for someone just coming out of training, they'll have huge med school tuition loans to repay, plus the cost to set up a private practice clinic. That right there costs as much as buying a house."

"I guess. I don't know much about it. As a nurse, I just mind my own business."

It sounded as though his mood was sinking, that maybe deep down inside there was a part of his career that hadn't gone the way he'd expected. It was a story often told, how someone had set sail with their hopes and dreams, only to have them dashed on the rocky shores of life. Even though she didn't know why, June felt for the guy.

"Maybe you can take me on a tour of your hospital sometime? From what I saw, it looked very modern and up to date."

"Cutting edge, by golly!"

That got a smile from both of them. The words 'cutting edge' had long been over-used by hospital administrators in advertising and community promotional efforts.

It got to the end of their meal and Henry was quick to reach for his wallet. Outside, she convinced him on taking her for a stroll through town instead of the planned movie. Walking along the main shopping street, the sidewalks were busy with middle-aged tourists looking for bargains, and younger ones looking for budget bars to stretch their booze money.

They wandered for several blocks until they got to a small fashion boutique. June couldn't help but stop to look in the window. She recognized some of the spring-themed clothes on mannequins.

"Looks expensive," Henry said.

"They are," June confirmed. "Much of it is from my sister's collection, last year's stuff."

She dragged him in, where he stood almost stationary while she looked through a few blouses, mostly at the tags.

"Big mark up," she whispered when she went back to him. She looked at a few more garments before remembering she was on a non-date and not out shopping. Henry still looked uncomfortably stiff and she went back to him. "Come on. There must be an ice cream shop in this town somewhere."

She took him by the hand and led him outside. When he turned her up a street toward a small mall, she forced herself to let go of his hand. Still, the empty silence between them on the two-block walk to the ice cream shop dragged on for far too long.

"Sorry, I don't know what I was thinking when I held your hand."

"Forget it. Were those nice clothes?" he asked. "I asked because Karen likes going there."

"They are, but maybe I'm biased. A lot of that stuff was from my sister's line."

"Oh, it's true what you said about her?"

"Next time you go in, look at the tag. If it says it's from Miko Fashions, its Amy's."

"Seems expensive. Karen doesn't buy much of it."

"Well, tell me her size and basic skin color and I can have some things sent. She could consider it a wedding gift from your mistress."

In the ice cream shop, she found her old favorite mint chip and got a scoop in a cup, watching Henry try to decide on chocolate or vanilla. He paid and joined her at a little table.

"Not much of an ice cream eater, Henry?" She watched as he struggled to eat his selection of a bland vanilla.

"Not much of a dairy kind of guy."

"What's this? No milk? No yogurt?"

"Karen is lactose intolerant and she's convinced me to give it up also."

She set down her plastic spoon. "And yet, here you are on an evening date with a lactose-friendly woman while your lactose intolerant fiancé is out of town." She started eating her mint chip again.

"Yeah, the other woman on the side, or whatever they're called."

"Sorry, that was uncalled for." From the tone of his voice, June knew she'd hurt his feelings with what she said. He was turning out to be her only friend on the island, someone she felt comfortable palling around with, if only for a few days. Revising her earlier ideas about Henry being the perfect vacation romance, he was turning into the perfect vacation friend. "Most of our conversations seem to involve me apologizing to you."

"Already forgotten. Still going for surf tomorrow?" he asked, pushing his unfinished cup of melting ice cream away.

"I'd love to give it a try. That's what this vacation is all about, to do a few impulsive things and forget about what happened with Jack, even if I look foolish while doing both."

"Just like skiing or snowboarding, everybody looks like a clumsy oaf the first few times they try surfing."

"Where am I dropping you?" she asked when they got back to her car.

"I can get home from here," he told her. "This is closer to home than to your hotel."

"Not going to invite me in for coffee or a nightcap?"

"Might be pushing the limits with Karen."

"Oh yes. The fiancé. How could I forget?"

***

In the morning, Henry came to June's hotel where she was waiting in front of the lobby, simple clothes over a swimsuit. She had already hit a sportswear boutique for sunscreen and a rash guard, a thick shirt that protects skin from coral and rock scratches, along with several bottles of juice and water.

"How big are the waves at the beach we're going to?" June asked as they drove along.

"Not too big for a beginner."

"Henry, I don't want to die on vacation. Impulsive fun is one thing. Risking life and limb is something else entirely."

"West Maui swells are one to three today, and I have a tanker you can use."

"Foreign language to the girl from the mainland," she said. "What's a tanker?"

"Surfboard big as a battleship."

"Floats good?"

"Better than you will."

While Henry drove, June looked at the front page of the local newspaper that she had got at her hotel room.

"What's this?" she said, tapping her finger on the newspaper headline.

He glanced. "Yeah, another shark bite. Used to be only once a year or so when some dope would paddle out way too far. But lately the sharks have been coming in closer to the reef to feed. These days, Maui gets maybe three or four bites a year."

"So, you're taking me out to feed the sharks?" She bit her lip, still reading the article.

"Sharks don't come around this side of the island. Not the hungry ones anyway."

"You know who you have to answer to if I get eaten by a shark, right?" she muttered.

"The President?"

"No, my sister, and she's a lot tougher to handle than an elected politician with a law degree."

"Funny thing, though, about you getting bit by a spider."

"Why?"

"You're a twin, right?" he asked.

"Yeah. So?"

"There's an old legend here in the islands about twin princesses named La'ieikawai and La'ielohelohe. Their father was a chieftain, and demanded that his firstborn child be a son, even threatening to kill a daughter if one was born first. Well, sure enough, twin girls were born. Their grandmother immediately separated them and stole them away in the middle of the night. La'ieikawai, the older one, was raised in a cave near the coast, with the only way in through a deep pool of water. When she got older, people began to realize the girl was of royal birth since a rainbow often formed outside the cave where she lived."

"What happened to the younger sister?" June asked. She was the younger between her and Amy.

"Raised by a priest in the mountains, I think. The older La'ieikawai had to be moved to other islands to keep her safe from men sniffing around for a bride all the time. They tried to hide her on the Big Island, and then here on Maui. But then a chief from Kauai heard about her and started pursuing."

June took a sip from her takeout coffee. "It's always the same thing. The older one always gets the good stuff. Nobody ever cares about the younger kid."

"You haven't heard the half of it. The story goes that she was taken care of by supernatural birds with beautiful feathers, and they even came together to make a bed for her to sleep on. When she finally grew up and lived in a regular house, it was made entirely of feathers."

"At home, I have a down comforter. Does that count for anything?"

"Ha! Yes, June Kato, it does."

"But what does any of that have to do with my spider bite?"

"Come to think of it, not all that much. The older twin got married to a god of some sort. But the husband heard about a beautiful woman on Earth and came down her to see her. It was the younger twin, La'ielohelohe, and they quickly fell in love. There was some trouble..."

"Of course."

"And the husband lost his god rating and had to live on Earth for the rest of his life. But the older twin came back to Earth when she felt sorry for her sister and lived in luxury with her and several maidens."

"Cute," June said. She was beginning to wonder why he was telling her an ancient Hawaiian love legend. "What's that got to do with the spider that bit me?"

"Well, right now I can't remember exactly. But one of the maidens went up to Heaven to look for someone that could help the twins with something."

June made a point of sighing impatiently.

"The maiden rode a lizard into the sky until they got to a giant spider web."

"Don't tell me, the maiden got bit by the spider and had to go to the hospital in Heaven?" June asked, trying to wrap up the story.

"Not exactly. The maiden climbed the spider web to get all the way up into Heaven, and met her long lost parents there."

June finished her coffee. "Henry, does this story have an ending? Please tell me the younger sister eventually finds a husband."

"Well, unfortunately, the story just sort of ends there."

"I figured as much."

A few minutes later, they parked at Olowalu Beach. June pulled her new, pink and black rash guard over her bikini top, took off her jogging shorts, and took the giant surfboard that Henry brought for her. She watched as he tossed the keys for the pickup on the floor and covered them with the rubber floor mat.

"Watch your step," he told her as they walked passed a row of trees toward the water. "Kiawe trees have sharp thorns."

"What kind of paradise is this place? Poisonous spiders, drunk drivers, man-eating sharks, and thorn trees. And I have to wear a bullet proof vest when I go in the ocean." She walked quickly through the loose sand to keep up. "It would've been safer to stay home in LA, put on a plaid shirt, and go for a long walk in South Central."

They got to the edge of the water and watched the waves for a moment. At least Henry watched the waves, and June looked at the deadly waters of Hawaii, certain a dorsal fin would pop above the surface at any moment. Small waves rolled in every thirty seconds or so, gently curling over about fifty yards from shore.

"You do know how to swim, right?"

"Yeah. The waves don't look so big, I guess."

"Done complaining about paradise?"

"Done whining." She looked along the length of her board, almost twice her height, and seemed as wide as a bed mattress. "But I reserve the right to piss and moan if this thing doesn't float."

He pointed to a wave, and did some dry land teaching. "It's all about balance. Just let the energy of the wave push you along. The more board you can get into the face of the wave, the faster you go and the longer the ride."

The sun was shining full force by then, and June felt hot under the rash guard. Looking around the beach, more tourists had shown up, some snapping pictures of palms, the waves, even of her and Henry. Getting her attention back onto the task of surfing, he showed her how to adjust the leg tether, and led June into the water.

Ten minutes later, June took her first wobbly ride on the buoyant surfboard. When the wave died behind her, she crouched down and slipped off one side. Standing tiptoe on the sandy bottom, June wiped the water from her face. Turning the board in the water, she struggled back on top and paddled out again.

She joined Henry, who was straddling his board, waiting. "Kinda fun, huh?"

"It is! And not so hard, I guess."

They bobbed up, then down, as a tidal swell passed beneath them.

"Judging from that big grin on your face, I'd say you're having some fun on your vacation," he said over the sounds of waves and wind.

June tried scooting her board through the water closer to him but almost fell off. Henry effortlessly turned his board so they were closer together. She felt like kissing him then, and because of his status of being engaged, forced herself not to. Another swell rose below them and sent her tumbling into the water. She came up, spitting ocean water. Wiping her face, she couldn't help but grin.

"Yep, having fun!"

***

Driving back to the hotel, June felt a little sorry she'd made friends with Henry so quickly. Her heart was still being yanked in the direction of romance, something she couldn't allow happen. She also knew that taking up with him was simply a way of hiding from the fact she'd just broken up with Jack. So, when Henry offered to take her hiking the next day, she had to put on the brakes.

"You'd love it up on Haleakala, June. Fantastic views, perfectly clear skies in the afternoons, and some of the most inspiring scenery anywhere in the islands."

"Sounds nice, and thanks for the offer, but I can hike on my own."

"Still worried about Karen?" he asked.

"More like worried about me."

He chuckled. "Oh, falling for my charms?"

"Maybe a little too much." June went from watching the scenery out the window to looking at him. "I still have a ton of stuff to process about Jack. That's half the point of being here. And I really should call and make sure he's okay."

"If you're feeling uncomfortable, maybe it's best we don't spend any more time together?"

"That would be the wise thing. Karen should be on your mind, not taking a tourist out on non-dates. As much as I hate the idea, I have to say goodbye to you." June muscled out a smile. "By the way, what day is the wedding?"

"Next Saturday at noon. At one of the churches in town."

"Well, I wish you both the best. Would it cause too much trouble if I sent a gift?"

"I'm not sure how I'd explain something from a name she didn't recognize."

"I suppose there would be a few uneasy questions to answer."

Henry pulled into the resort parking lot and parked. "You really are the mystery surgeon the media talked about?"

"Unfortunately."

"That means I almost dated someone really famous?"

June leaned over and kissed his cheek. "Henry, if you want to remember our time together as dates, it's okay with me. Just don't ever tell Karen my name."

When June got back to her hotel room, she had the usual aches and pains leftover from trying a new sport. Before getting into the shower, she called the resort spa to see if massage times were available. Finding they had time in an hour, she hurried through her shower and went to the spa.

Like the rest of the resort, the spa had the usual Hawaiian décor, with lush plantings, stucco walls painted in pastel colors, and a few tiki torches along the path to the front door. Inside was much larger than she had expected, being an upscale salon with boutique spa services. The place was busy and every chair looked as though they were filled with women on vacation. The pretty receptionist smiled politely.

"I have an appointment for a massage with Dalene."

"That's me. You're June?" a tall brunette asked walking up to June, extending her hand. Loose curls tumbled down her shoulders, more than a few of which were highlighted blond. Her short painted nails gleamed, and she wore a tropical blouse and loose pants, befitting her job at the resort. Her smile was cheerful but had a hint of shyness in it. June was instantly comfortable with her massage therapist.

"Yes, June Kato. Thanks for taking my appointment."

June was led down a hallway to a vacant massage room. The lighting was dim and the scent of incense was in the air. A tabletop fountain tinkled in one corner. Otherwise, the only furniture was the long bed used for massages. "I hope you like the room. I helped decorate it."

Dalene had a suspiciously California accent, something June was familiar with as a native Californian herself.

"It's lovely. Very peaceful."

"Are you looking for anything in particular? Deep tissue, relaxation?"

"Maybe a little of both. Mostly just to work some of the kinks out of my muscles. I got some exercise this morning that was more energetic than what I'd planned."

June was left alone to disrobe. Climbing on the table, she stretched out on her belly and pulled the sheet up to her shoulders. There was a gentle knock at the door and Dalene came back in.

"I use an eucalyptus-scented oil, if that's okay? It's a very light oil and washes off easily."

"Should be fine. But I must warn you, I might doze off."

Dalene pulled the sheet down to expose June's back and spread warm oil across her skin. "You're very fit. I can't imagine getting exercise would leave you with sore muscles."

"Oh, I went surfing for the first time." She winced when the massage therapist found a knot next to a shoulder blade. "But I seemed to spend more time falling off than riding waves."

"I've heard it's fun but I've never tried."

"Maybe someday."

"Are you a visitor here?" Dalene asked.

"Yes, my yearly vacation. Never really seen Maui before, so here I am."

"Be careful. I came here for a week a few years ago and instantly fell in love with the place. Before I knew it, my house back home was sold and I was packing my bags."

"You still like it?" June asked.

"With each new day, I love it a little more. The cooing doves in the morning, the gentle breezes, and the sunsets are to die for. Have you seen one yet?"

"I'm still trying to get over jetlag and I've been sleeping at all different times of the day."

"Maybe this evening."

"Do you recommend a good place to watch?"

Dalene began working on one of June's legs. "It sets on this side of the island. Anywhere along here. In fact, the resort has some large lawns with walking paths and benches. Just find a place to sit that faces the ocean and you'll have a front row view to the best sunset anywhere."

"Sounds like a plan."

"What other plans do you have for Maui?" Dalene asked, beginning to work on the other leg.

"Well, if this weather, clean air, and pretty scenery continue, I might just find a room to live in."

"It's already starting. That's how it started with me."

"Just kidding. Tomorrow, I'm hiking on a place called Haleakala. I think I said it right."

"That's the big volcano on the other side of the island. Take sturdy shoes and wear something warm if you go all the way to the summit. Check the weather reports before you go. It's been known to snow up there at this time of year."

"That would be fun. Are there things to do on Maui for single people, but not meat markets, if you know what I mean?"

"In town, it's all about family stuff. In the resort area called Kihei, it's singles heaven. I like your idea of hiking up the mountain."

Dalene had June turn over onto her back and began massaging her shoulders.

"The mall in town also has a lot of fun shops, if shopping is something you're into."

"Not really. About the only time I ever go to the mall is with my nieces."

"Oh, you don't have kids of your own?"

"I'm just about as single as a person could be."

"Don't have to be married to have kids."

June laughed. "A man helps in that regard."

Dalene began massaging an arm and hand. "You don't want kids?"

"At this point in my life, it's not a matter of wanting or not wanting them. Forty is hurtling toward me like an out of control train. It's beginning to look as though I've run out of time."

Dalene started working on June's other arm. "Well, nature has a way of providing kids to people, whether they think they're suited to parenthood or not."

"I'm really not so sure how good of a parent I'd be. Pretty wrapped up in my career. I just can't imagine myself raising kids. I'd probably leave them in the supermarket and never realize it until I got home and had all the groceries put away."

"Everybody makes mistakes. When I raised mine, I figured if they went to bed in one piece and weren't crying too much, it was a successful day of child rearing."

June laughed. "My philosophy would be the beatings will continue until morale improves."

"That works, too!"

The massage therapist went to the head of the massage bed and pulled June's hair back to work on her face. "Your hair is very pretty."

"Thanks. A little rough right now, from the saltwater."

"This is your natural color?"

"Yep. About as black as hair can be, except for those pesky white ones that show up now and then."

"You should try some color. Maybe have highlights done while you're here, a fun souvenir to take home with you?"

"Not so sure of what I should have done. It definitely needs something. I'm not sure how much longer I can pull off having long hair."

"Well, maybe when you move here, you'll go a little wild."

"What's wild on Maui?"

"Live in a funky house near the beach, get a new wardrobe, do something flashy with your hair, maybe even start that family you're afraid of."

"The rest I can see, but I'm not so sure about my family being here. We're a little too dedicated to living in Los Angeles."

Dalene finished the massage with one last gentle press to June's forehead. "Keep an open mind and wonderful things will happen."

***

Early the next morning, June went for a run outside the resort. Following along the highway, it was quiet in the pre-dawn cool. Seeing an old driveway with a House For Sale sign but no houses around, she jogged up.

A hundred yards up was an old house, obviously abandoned. Small, it looked like other houses she had seen on Maui, leftover from the sugar plantation days, with simple clapboard siding, a corrugated metal roof, and a covered porch that spanned the front of the house. The landscaping was overgrown, the roofing was stained, some of the clapboard siding boards were coming loose. At least the windows were intact and the front and back doors were locked. There were no other houses within sight, giving the old place a haunted feeling.

June rubbed patches of grime from windows and peeked in. It was empty inside, with old appliances and fixtures in the kitchen and bathroom.

"Three little bedrooms, one bathroom, and a tiny kitchen. Probably more than a few critters living in there. Someone would have to knock it down and build new."

She started back down the driveway but turned to look back.

"Great location, though. So far off the road, nobody else around. All that open countryside in back would be great for kids."

***

The rest of her week on Maui was filled with one mini-adventure after another: hiking into the crater of Haleakala, discovering an old trail through ancient lava fields, snooping through resort boutiques, finding beaches for naps and suntanning, and going on long runs each morning. It wasn't until Friday that she had the courage to call Jack.

"How's DC?" she asked.

"Lonely."

"Jack, please."

"Sorry. It's just hard getting used to the idea you're not going to join me here."

"Believe me, I've thought about coming there a million times since last week."

"Why don't you?" he asked.

"You know why. And I don't want to start this argument again."

"Your mind really is made up?"

June knew she had to be strong. "Yep, sorry. You'll have to run the White House on your own."

"It won't be nearly so much fun without you, June."

"If there's one thing that I would never put on a list of fun things to do, it would be living in the White House."

"What will you do now?" he asked.

"Oh, back to work on Monday morning. I have patients waiting."

"I mean with your life?"

"As in find another man? That hardly seems possible after being with you. Any man that ever came near would be held up to your standards. I seriously doubt anyone else could ever measure up. Unless magic strikes, it looks like I'm a career woman until retirement."

"It doesn't sound like much of a life, June."

"Oh, after spending a few days on Maui, I've discovered the value of vacations. I've also discovered the value of taking things a little easier, of not having so much stress in my life."

He laughed. "This is June Kato speaking, the Queen of Stress?"

"One in the same. Believe it or not, I haven't clamped my molars in consternation together all week."

"Unbelievable. It sounds like you're already changing."

"And there's going to be a lot more changes coming."

***

With nothing but memories, a rash guard, and real estate magazines to pack as souvenirs, getting ready to go home was easy. Maybe too easy. Checking out of the hotel was simple, hardly anything to sign for, and never once having to produce a credit card to pay for anything. June found the porter that had helped her with maps and driving directions, and handed over a healthy tip.

Driving back toward the airport on the opposite side of the island, she slowed when she got to the short tunnel, heeding Henry's warning. She took it slow and easy the whole way back, not wanting to end the vacation quite yet. Compared to the one and only other vacation she had ever taken, also to Hawaii but to a different island, it was a smashing success.

Instead of going directly to the airport, she took herself on a driving tour of the small towns that made up most of the population in central Maui. The mall and the larger hospital were easily found, along with older commercial and business areas. One part of the city was laid out in an organized manner, an older subdivision of sorts, and June wondered if that was where Henry had grown up.

One of the last streets she drove along was a small commercial area in the older but quainter of the two towns. If her parents saw it, they'd think it would be an ideal place for one of their flowers shops. As she drove, chicken skin rose on her arms. One block in particular caught her attention, her eyes going to an empty storefront. A *For Lease* sign sat in the front window. An eerie sense of dread developed as she looked at the small shop.

Trying to shake off the peculiar sensation, she gave the car some gas, ending her ad hoc tour.

Mid-afternoon dragged at the small Maui airport. She dearly wanted coffee, but couldn't risk a full bladder for a long flight. Instead, she read a magazine left behind in the main waiting area outside security. Checking the time, she decided the line to get through security was short enough to stand in. She collected her two small carry-ons and started the next leg of her long journey home.

With a few more minutes to wait at the gate, June got out her phone. Since halfway through her vacation, something had been at the back of her mind, a sensation she just couldn't shake. Hoping she had memorized the number correctly, she called a real estate office.

"Yes, I'm curious about a little house in Ka'anapali. I'm not sure of the exact address but it's only about a mile or so from the new hospital."

"That old cane plantation house?" the woman real estate agent asked.

"I think so. How much is the owner asking?"

"First, you need to know there are a lot of restrictions on that property."

"Such as?" June asked, now almost sorry she'd called. She had little experience dealing with realtors, but knew they could be tricky

"First, the original house must remain intact, including the interior, because of its historical value."

June lost most of her interest. In California, anything labeled as 'historical' meant twice as expensive. "I see."

"Also, no other buildings can be built on the property, even though the parcel is large."

A large parcel of property in Hawaii meant the price doubled again.

"But repairs can be made, and additions can be made to the sides or back, as long as the original style remains intact as seen from the front. Even the paint color schemes on the exterior are restricted."

"Can't really see it from the road, though."

"That's what everybody else has said. The good news is that it's on county water supply and electrical, and everything in the house works, at least when the water and power are turned on. It's been fumigated and inspectors have found very little dry rot."

"How long has it been vacant?" June asked.

"Let's see. If I remember correctly, old lady Medeiros passed away about two years ago."

"And she was the last resident?"

"She passed away in the house. One of those sad stories, where the old person lived alone and nobody ever went to visit. When no one heard from her in a while, a police officer was sent to check. I guess she'd been that way for a while, if you know what I mean."

June cringed at the idea of living in a house in which someone had died. She believed in ghosts just enough to give her chicken skin. "So, who owns it now?" June asked, rubbing warmth back into her arms.

"Her family. They're on the mainland and just want to get rid of it. It sounds like they're never coming back to Maui. Would you like to take a look inside? I'd be glad to show it to you."

June looked at the time on her watch. "Unfortunately, I'm headed to the mainland in a few minutes. But just out of curiosity, what's the asking price?"

When the realtor mentioned the price, June was shocked. "So little? I'd have thought that a place like that near a resort would go for a lot more?"

"The thing is, not much can be done because of its historical significance to the island and developers can't touch it. Most people that have looked at it thought there would have to be a lot of hard work put into it and they lose interest. Plus, there aren't many employment opportunities along that part of the island, at least not for several more years. That, and the family just wants to be rid of it."

"And there haven't been any offers?"

"In two years, nothing."

"Thanks. I'll think about it." June's flight was called, and she needed to end the call. For some odd reason, she felt compelled to leave the realtor her name and contact number in LA.

Saying Goodbye

Walking through LAX arrivals terminal, June sent a text to Amy.

Here now.

With only her small carry-on, June got out to the terminal loading zone in only a few minutes. Amy arrived five minutes after that in her sedan. The first thing she did was take June's left hand in her own.

"What?" June asked.

"No more engagement ring. It really happened."

June took her hand back to snap her seatbelt. "Yeah, it happened. Get over it."

"How'd it go on Maui?" Amy asked as soon as they were headed out the airport. "Tell me about the guy."

"It was a vacation. Good to be back...I guess. What guy?" June turned in her seat to look back at her nieces. A tug of war was going on between them with a stuffed dinosaur doll. "Hey girls! Having a fun day off with Mommy?"

June was amused as they kept at their battle.

"Koemi has assembled a gang of thugs at the park, and Ruka has been waiting impatiently for your return."

June looked at Koemi again, the older of the twins. She had the remnants of a shiner on one eye, the prize from one of her frequent wrestling matches. Ruka had grass stains on her clothes.

"That was us at that age," June said as Amy got the car up to speed on the freeway. "What is Ruka waiting for?"

"She wants you to go shopping at the mall with her. She's decided you're her best friend."

"It'll have to wait. I'm on call at the hospital for the next three weekends. Maybe on Thursday if I get out early enough."

"Can you do me another favor?" Amy asked. "Watch the kids for an hour or so? I need to check on something at one of the flower stores."

"As long as they don't mind watching crabby Aunt June do laundry and clean the house."

"What about the guy?" Amy asked.

"What guy?"

"There's always a guy."

"There is?" June asked, confused.

"You went on vacation, by yourself, to Maui, and didn't hook up?"

Henry's face flashed through June's mind. "Uh, no. It seems everyone on Maui is married, except co-ed dropouts living at the beach, and angry New Age divorcees."

"You didn't look hard enough."

"I found what I needed. Or at least a hint of it."

"Another one of your little mysteries that the rest of us will have to solve," Amy said. "Have you told Mom yet?"

"About Jack? Sort of afraid to. Dad's been excited, I think more about knowing Jack than me getting married."

"They'll get over it. But you better call her soon because she knows."

June tried glaring down her sister. "How'd that happen?"

"It might've slipped out."

"Yeah, slipped out."

No sooner were they in June's house that the girls dashed off to the spare bedroom to play. It had been set aside when they were babies as their special bedroom, decorated for kids, with toys in the closet and clothes in drawers. It had also been the same room June and Amy used as kids on sleepovers at their grandparents' house, the original owners. Long before June and Amy came along, their father used it as his bedroom growing up. Now years later, a new generation of Kato's were using the room.

After an hour of cleaning and laundry, June called the girls to the dining room. It was an early lunch, since June hadn't eaten since leaving Maui the evening before. Getting pressure from the girls to tell about her vacation, she turned the story into a fairy tale.

"Well, once upon a time, a princess grew very lonely and very sad. So one day, she asked her favorite unicorn to take her far, far away."

"Where'd they go, Auntie?"

"To a little island way out in the middle of the ocean. It was called The Island of Pretty Sunsets. She lived in a little house, and there was sunshine and flowers everywhere. But there was a big, ugly, scary monster on the island, and it would chase the princess sometimes. And guess what?"

The girls' eyes grew large.

"The monster bit the princess and she almost died!"

"But someone saved her?"

"Oh, yes. A handsome young prince came along and rescued her, just before the monster bit her head off!"

"How did he save her?"

"He gave her the magic elixir and the monster never came back."

"Then what?" they asked in unison.

"The ocean was nearby, and every day the princess would run on the beach and play in the waves."

"Was it dangerous?"

"It was very dangerous, until the prince came along again. He gave her a magic carpet to ride when she was in the water."

"Maybe the prince liked the princess?" one of the girls asked. She giggled. "Or the princess liked the prince?"

"What was his name?" the other added.

"Prince Henry."

"Was he handsome?"

"Oh, yes, very handsome. And then one day…"

"What did he look like, Auntie?"

"Do you want to hear about the princess on the island or about the prince?" she asked with a smile.

"Both!" one of the girls shouted.

"Did the princess kiss the prince for saving her from the monster?" the other asked.

"Oh, well, maybe once."

The girls giggled and squirmed in their seats. June couldn't help but chuckle with them.

Amy was just coming in the front door as the giggling settled. She made the same sandwich the others had and sat at the table with them.

"Tell us about your vacation," Amy prompted. "How was the room? Sounds like it came fully furnished?"

"The room was great. I really owe you a ton for that. And never mind about the furnishings."

"What was the deal with the spider?"

June held her wrist up, but the bite mark was long gone.

"Was the spider the monster?" Koemi asked.

"Auntie, was the spider big and ugly?" Ruka asked, examining her wrist.

"Yeah, honey, but it hardly hurt. You don't have to worry about spiders, okay?" June said, pushing her half-eaten sandwich away.

"Got some sun on you, anyway," Amy said, looking at June's dark complexion. She pushed the sandwich back again.

"Went for a run every morning. Learned how to surf, too."

"My sister the surfer chick," Amy said. "Who taught you that?"

"Some guy."

"The one that furnished the room?"

"Unfortunately, the room wasn't furnished that way." June had to change the subject. "It's so pretty there. The ocean, everything blooming, the clear air."

The girls finished eating and were dismissed from the table. "Who was the guy?" Amy asked once they were gone.

"There wasn't a guy."

"A guest at the resort?" Amy asked.

"There was no guy."

"You said someone took you surfing. What was his name?"

June picked up her sandwich again, trying to think of an answer. She hated her sister's interrogations, because she never won the battle for privacy. "I don't know. He gave me surf lessons. Mister Surf Pro, I guess."

"Did you go jogging with Mister Jog Pro?"

"People staying at resorts don't typically get up at five in the morning to go for runs."

June collected the empty plates and took them to the kitchen. Amy wasn't far behind.

"Well? What else?"

"It was a vacation. I went for a run each morning, drove up to the top of some volcano, caught up on sleep."

"Caught up on sleep? What kind of vacation is that? You were supposed to lose sleep, Babe, with Mister Surf Pro, if at all possible."

June went to the small pantry and moved wet clothes into the dryer. "It was a vacation, okay? I did all the things you and Mom have been harping at me about for years. And yes, as a matter of fact, I did enjoy it."

She slammed the dryer door closed, turned the machine on, and brushed past Amy. In the kitchen, she began washing the lunch dishes.

"I might even go back there the next time I have time off."

Amy dried dishes and put them away. "It took a five-star resort, but you finally relaxed?"

"Yes, Sis. Five-star relaxation was had by your uptight little sister."

"But who was the guy that taught you to surf?"

June glared at her sister, changing the subject again, tipping the scales of conversation in her favor. "How's Mick? That's why you went to the flower shop, right? From what I've heard, the stores are still making good money, even if you're not involved in their management these days."

Mick had been June's love interest off and on for many years, but Amy had recently stepped in the middle. Newly retired from the military, Mick had been hired to manage one of their parents' five flower shops, the Kato family business, and it hadn't taken long for Amy to swoop in for the kill.

"He's fine. He was over for dinner last night."

"Did he stay over?"

"Why?" Amy asked.

"I've heard he stays over on weekends. Every weekend."

Amy looked at her daughters in the living room playing a reading game on an electronic device.

"You think they're spying for you, but I have them working as double agents for me, too," June said.

"Triple agents," Amy muttered back. "Mom has them on her payroll, also."

"Probably pays them better than us."

Amy got her bag, digging her car keys out, ready to leave. "Cookies will always get information out of kids."

"Better than the rice crackers I give them."

After the girls were corralled and herded out to the car, June waved from the sidewalk.

Amy rolled down her window. "Don't forget Ruka on Thursday."

***

June heard a chiming sound, and couldn't quite pick out what it was. She opened her eyes and looked around the dark room, expecting to see the tropical motif of a resort room.

When she realized she was at home again, not at the resort on Maui, she sat up and rubbed her face. Grabbing her phone, she tapped the front when she saw who was calling.

"What, Sis?" She had wanted to make a smart remark about how she was supposed to be in bed with Mick by then, but held her tongue.

"Who's Prince Henry?" Amy asked right off.

"Who?"

"The girls told me your fairy tale, of how you met someone named Prince Henry while on vacation."

"How'd they…it was just a story to keep them occupied." She had to change the subject. "Is Mick still there?"

"Don't change the subject. Spill it, Babe."

"Just a guy I met."

"Who? The surfer?"

June flicked on a light. "He was the nurse at the hospital that first day. The spider bite, remember?"

"And?"

"Then I bumped into him the next day while out on a walk. He was just coming in from surfing." June turned on her side and shoved the pillow under her head, knowing she was going to be on the phone for a while. In a way, it felt good to talk about her close call non-romance on vacation, and for once not Jack. "He walked by and I said hello."

"Which means he's good looking. What else?"

"We got together once or twice. He took me surfing, had dinner, that's about it."

"How many times did you go sightseeing at his place?"

"Never."

"And in your room?"

"Amy…"

"Give it."

"Never!"

"I'm supposed to believe that?"

"Yes."

"Why didn't you hook up with him?"

"Because he's getting married in a few days."

"Well, rats. That changes things," Amy said. "He wasn't willing to, you know."

"I wasn't willing. But I need to call Mom. I've made her wait long enough."

"Babe, I have one question, now that you and Jack are done."

"What's that?"

"How's he in bed? I mean, is our next President a stud?"

"Are you working for the tabloids now?" June asked.

"No, just curious. Come on, spill it, June."

"Okay, answer me this first. How's Mick in bed? Oh wait, I already know!"

June hung up and called her mother.

"Hi Mom."

"Dear. Why haven't you called sooner?"

"Did Amy talk to you?"

"Of course. But that doesn't answer my question."

"I didn't call because I wanted some time to think."

"You've had plenty of time to think for several months, years even. Now, all of a sudden, one week after getting engaged, you decide to break it off with Jack? Or is it just cold feet?" her mother asked.

"It's way bigger than cold feet. It was having to change my entire life just to be with him. I'm not so sure it would've been worth it."

"Changing your life, or being with him?"

"Either," said June. "Jack's a great guy, and I love him, I think I do anyway. But we just never had any time together. And we wouldn't have time together, at least for the next few years. What kind of way is that to start a marriage?"

"Yes, well, the fact that Amy and I both talked to you about that months ago doesn't need to be brought up. But what about Jack? Have you talked to him lately? He must be hurting also."

"I doubt he even knows I'm not in the same room with him."

Her father took over the call. "You need to call him and make sure he's cool with it, June. It wasn't just you and your career on the line. You've left him with a mess to clean up."

"Since when are you friends of the establishment?"

"I don't know if you've watched the news lately, but Jack's campaign manager has been doing some damage control while you've been vacationing on Maui the last few days."

"What's so bad about me going to Maui for a quick vacation?" June asked.

"It was on the news, about the breakup and how the ex-fiancé went on vacation while Jack tackled international conflict from the Oval Office. There were pictures of you with some other guy, at the beach and again in some little town one evening. Is that what my daughter does? Break it off with one guy to go on vacation with another the very same day?"

"No!" June was confused. It had to have been Henry her father was talking about. She was also pissed. She hadn't watched much television while on vacation, but she never would've guessed her break up with Jack would make the media. For all she knew, the engagement and the relationship were still unknown publically. She did have to admit, however, that it would've looked as though she was with another man right after breaking it off with Jack. His Chief of Staff, Leon, had to be behind it. "He's not just a guy I met on vacation. I had a spider bite and needed to go to the ER for treatment. He was the nurse who treated me. If the media would've done some fact checking, instead of dreaming up some tabloid story, they would've known that."

"What I saw on television didn't look like a nurse treating a patient in the ER. It looked like a date."

"Oh, for goodness sakes. We met just a couple of times."

"Pretty selfish, June," her father said. "Not a kind way of treating someone you care about. For either of them."

"Don't give me that hippie crap, Dad. It's become stale. I'm sure you and Mom made a mess or two along the way."

"When we were twenty. But you're not a kid anymore. You know better. And we weren't involved with people that had a lot to lose."

"Dad, nothing ever happened between Henry and me. He showed me around a couple of places and taught me how to surf. That's all."

"I believe you, but will the media?" he asked. "You need to consider Jack's career, not just your own."

"And now you're friends with politicians? It's not like you're a stalwart of the establishment!"

"Jack's a good man. We both voted for him a few years ago, even before we met him, and we did the second time." Her dad stalled for a moment, but he wasn't done. "The guy on Maui might have a lot to lose too, if he gets mixed up in something that doesn't belong to him."

June let it go. She wasn't going to argue politics or lifestyle with her father right then, especially since her politics were very similar to his. "Something tells me you wouldn't vote for me right now."

"Not till you make things right with Jack," he told her. "With both of them."

"But…"

"You don't have to make up with Jack. Just make sure his world is good, that you haven't done any harm. And if you need to, make things right no matter how hard it might be."

After hanging up, June was too tired to cry.

***

June sat in her office in the Mercy Hospital neurosurgery clinic, waiting for her first patient of the day. She was passing the time by checking her weekly schedule on the computer when there was a knock at the door.

She hoped a patient was ready to be seen, to finally get the long week started. "What?"

"Hey, just wanted to welcome you home. Have a good time?" Fred Towns, the head of neurosurgery at Mercy Hospital, said.

"Thanks. Busy week, Fred?"

"Manageable. How was the vacation?" He smiled benevolently, and for a change, he hushed his voice. "Finally get that grand tour of Washington DC from your VIP fiancé?"

June lifted her hands from her lap and set them on the table, staring down at her naked ring finger. "Last minute change in plans. Went to Maui instead."

Fred looked down at her hand. "I see you lost some weight."

"Yeah, four carats."

"Want to talk about it? I have time," offered Fred.

Tears welled in her eyes, and Fred pushed a box of tissues across to her. She wasn't surprised by the tears, since they were long overdue. It was, however, an inconvenient time to shed them. In the end, she won the battle and held them back.

After heaving a settling sigh, she started. "I'd have to quit my job here and move there, and everywhere else Jack went in the future. DC, Sacto, Chile, and God help me, Brentwood. I'd be his Number One groupie, serving tea to stiffs in the garden, smiling brightly, saying all the right things, being Little Miss Diplomat in all things politic."

"It wouldn't last forever. Four years, eight tops. What's wrong with that?"

"And then another election or appointment or position after the White House, and another and another. I'd never be June Kato again, but Mrs. Melendez, the First Lady…or whatever."

"Well, I have to tell you, I'm a bit relieved. I was trying to figure out how to replace you. Neurosurgeons with your talent don't come along very often."

"Thanks. Looks like you're stuck with me for a while."

As soon as Fred left, there was another knock at her door.

June sighed, not wanting another interruption. "Yes?"

The door swung open. "Hey! How was Washington DC?" asked Becky, her office manager. "Wow, you got a tan!"

Silently, June held up her left hand, displaying her empty ring finger.

Becky's smile dropped into a frown as quickly as she sat in a chair. "What happened?"

"Life." June shut down her computer and looked up at Becky. "Life happened."

"Do I want to know details?" Becky asked with a cringe.

"Do you want a blubbering fool in the office all day?"

"That bad?"

June leaned back in her chair. "Not really. It just wasn't going to work out. So, I gave the ring back. Surprising how easy it is to put a ring on your finger, but how hard it is to pull it off again."

"You stayed home all week? You should've called me. We could've done something."

"I went to Maui instead. That very same day, as a matter of fact." June continued to rub her ring finger. "My sister even paid for me to stay in a resort."

"She can afford Maui. Wish I could've gone with you," Becky said.

"Wish you had come. Evidently the tabloid news figured out who Jack's mystery woman was and got a few pics of me on vacation. It's been on the news. You never saw?"

"I saw something but the sound wasn't on. It just seemed like another fluff story."

"I've become famous, whether I want to be or not." June twirled a pen on her desk. "It seems like everybody in my family has seen it."

"What was the story about?" Becky asked.

"Oh, that I met this guy and we hung out right after I broke up with Jack. All we did was have dinner in some cheap place, went for a walk, and went to the beach. Apparently, some journalist recognized me and made a hobby of following us around and taking pictures with a telephoto lens. But nothing happened. So stupid."

"And of course, they were able to get pictures of the two of you making it look like something was going on, right?"

"I haven't seen them but my dad said they were pretty condemning."

"Did they name you? Or just get pictures?"

"I have no idea. All my Dad said was that he saw pictures of me on the news, doing stuff with a guy in Hawaii, and the networks tried to build it up into some big thing that included Jack."

"Maybe if they never used your name, nobody will know?" Becky offered.

"It's Jack and his reputation that we're worried about."

A nurse came to the door, letting June know her first patient was ready to be seen.

"I'll check the tabloid newspapers on my break to see if I can find anything," Becky whispered when she left the office.

At lunch, June finally had time for a break. Troubled all morning by what her father had said about the news, Henry, and how her vacation 'activities' might affect Jack and his presidency, she closed herself in the office and dialed her phone.

"Hey, Jack. This is June."

"June. I'm swamped. What's up?"

"Just wanted to say hi. And…"

"And what? I don't have much time."

There it was again, not enough time for her.

"I was wondering if I've ruined your office by being stupid?"

"What?" he asked.

"Did me going to Hawaii mess up things for you?" she asked with a more reasonable tone. "The pictures that were taken?"

"You mean the pictures of you and the guy at the beach? No, not at all. If anything, my Chief of Staff thinks it might've made us look more interesting. He's able to put a positive spin on it."

"Good for you, and Leon. But..."

"June, as far as anybody can tell, the news carriers never learned your name or anything personal."

"I wasn't thinking of that. But how did they know it was me? And in Hawaii?"

"Someone must've recognized you from earlier news reports, either at the airport or at the resort. Did you fly first class?" Jack asked.

"Yeah. I had to splurge on the ticket."

"And you stayed in that classy resort where celebrities stay. Paparazzi are good at spotting people flying first class and staying at five-star resorts."

It ended up being either her own fault, or her sister's for being recognized. "I should've known. That was Amy's idea, for me to stay at that specific resort."

"They snapped a few pictures, sold them to the tabloids, and made a few bucks. No big deal, June."

"So, you're not mad?" she asked after a moment.

"About tabloid press? Never. Anyway, I didn't do anything newsworthy, to the tabloids anyway."

"I just want you to know that nothing happened between me and that guy." That was the real reason she had called, also the reason her father had badgered her about.

"I know. You aren't like that, June. Frankly, I'm just too busy right now to notice anything other than dealing with something in the Middle East. It looks as though I'm inheriting a bigger mess than what I figured. But I got to go. Keep in touch, okay?"

The call ended as quickly as that.

After hanging the phone up, she gave it a glare. "Sorry to interrupt your day."

There was a knock at the door. June sighed and called them in.

"Going to lunch?" Becky asked, poking her head in the office.

They went across the street to the taco truck, their usual stop if they had time on clinic days.

"Good news," June told Becky while poking at her spicy tofu burrito. "Evidently no one at the tabloids ever knew my name."

"You talked to him?" Becky asked, meaning Jack Melendez, June's recent fiancé.

"Yeah, and they even think it might've helped their reputation, in some sort of weird way."

"You're off the hook, then."

A man stepped over to their table and asked if he could share. Becky nodded him to the opposite end.

"Yeah, off the hook."

June noticed the man was watching them, but tried ignoring him.

"Sure was a pretty ring."

"You know it. Something about four carats of sparkle on your finger that perk up a girl's attitude," June said, looking at her empty hand.

"But you gave it back?"

"Couldn't keep it. What would I do with an engagement ring and no fiancé?"

"Now I know why you look familiar!" the man at the table with them said. "You're that woman on the news lately, the one that blew off that Melendez guy!"

"No, that's someone…"

"I gotta tell yah, he was no good anyway. Good for you to break up with him. I didn't vote for him before, and I won't the next time either," he said.

Becky gave a mini-eye roll to June.

"Oh?" June asked, still not looking at the guy. "Why not?"

"Never much liked his politics. Always talking about the little guy, but has the snooty place in Brentwood, the fancy apartment back East, and that ranch out in the desert. Like he knows what it's like to be a little guy."

"I guess along the way, someone in his family learned how to make money."

"Maybe the wealthy people could learn to share with the rest of us."

"I'm with you there, sir. And in more ways than one." June smiled. "But that wasn't me."

He looked intently at her face. "Are you sure?"

"Would the recently ex-fiancé of a soon-to-be President be eating lunch at a taco truck?" she asked.

He took one last look at her face. "I guess not."

They got up, and with a polite smile to the man, went back to the clinic.

"It sounds like a lot more people saw those reports than your parents, June."

"They're recognizing me, too."

"Not much you can do for damage control now," Becky muttered.

June thought of the recent conversations she'd had with both Amy and Jack, about relaxing a little and enjoying life a little more. In one of those conversations, the idea of change had come up.

"Not much can be done about it. I certainly can't wear a disguise everywhere I go."

***

By the time Tuesday's surgical schedule was done, June was exhausted. After rounds with her resident, she stopped in the cafeteria for something to eat, knowing full well she wouldn't make something if she waited to get home.

Becky followed June to her office, watching her change out of her light jacket and into her clinic lab coat.

"Everything okay? Not having a meltdown?" Becky asked.

"As in coming apart at the seams? No. I had one last cry last night and now I'm over the breakup. Over Jack, over chasing him around the country on my weekends off, over being some sort of politician's groupie. Time to get back to work and save the world, one brain at a time."

"You're more than that, June. And you know it. Quit feeling sorry for yourself."

"Yeah, you're right."

"You never did tell me what you did on Maui," Becky said to her after closing the door.

"The first day I was there I got bit by a spider and went to the hospital. That's how I met that guy. He was a nurse at the hospital."

"Nothing could come of it?" Becky asked.

"Getting married soon, as in next week, soon." June shrugged. "He took me surfing one day, for two hours, tops. After that, it was mostly a little sightseeing, going for runs, and reading smutty romances. I guess that's what people do on vacation."

"You really did have a nice vacation. Now it's time to start planning the next one."

June's first patient of the day had a rather complex history. She had been seen at a hospital in another state, then sent to other hospitals, never getting the answer she wanted to hear. Finally, she landed at Mercy. Somehow, she had got lost in the shuffle there, never getting in June's clinic until that day. She had a large tumor in the center of her brain, a place few surgeons would touch. Before chemotherapy could start, the tumor would need to be removed if there was any hope for the patient to survive. Since June was the surgeon that had devised the difficult technique years before, the patient had been steered to her.

"And that's why we need to move as quickly as possible on your procedure, Mrs. Henderson. Between the size of your tumor, and the need for chemotherapy, I need to get to it as soon as possible. A certain amount of healing needs to take place before the chemo can start, so the sooner the better. And tomorrow is best."

"Tomorrow?" the woman asked. She sat frozen in her chair, getting the bad news all over again from yet another doctor. He husband sat next to her, just as frozen.

"It's a long surgery, but I can do it in the afternoon and evening. I have all the scans I need, and the basic blood work has been done. I can have you admitted right now, and get all the rest of the labs and paperwork done this evening."

"What exactly is the hurry?" the husband asked. "Nobody has explained things the way you do, Doctor."

June went to the small X-ray view box on the wall in her office and jammed two films up, the light flickering to life.

"This white area is your tumor, quite large. So large, in fact, that it's crowding for space inside your skull. That means there is pressure on your brain stem, something vitally important. So far, you've had very few symptoms, something I'm rather surprised about." She took down one film and jammed another up. "Here's the scan from only a few weeks ago. Now, compare that to the one from yesterday, and you can see how much growth there's been in just a short time."

June put up another scan, this one of the vascular system of the woman's brain while the middle-aged couple watched.

"You can also see where the tumor is highly vascular, which is why it's growing so fast. Frankly, it'll be pretty difficult to do the case, but I'll take it slow and easy." She looked at the husband, noticing him turning pale. "It will be a long day for you, Mister Henderson."

She took the films down and put them back in their sleeve.

"Okay, tomorrow it is," the patient said.

As her husband gripped his wife's hand, he asked June a question. "We've been wondering, well, you seem to look like that lady we've seen on the TV news lately."

June knew what he meant. In the last couple of days, the so-called 'White House mystery woman' had been relabeled as the 'Presidential Mistress', and with each passing day, more images would pop up in the media. What had started out in the tabloid news was beginning to appear as a human-interest story on mainstream local news programs. There had even been a couple pictures of her in LA, in public near the hospital, always with the speculation of who she was. Since the pictures had been taken from a distance with telephoto lenses, they were just blurry enough for her to not be recognizable.

"I know who you mean and no, that's not me. I sure wish it was, though, because I would love to live in the White House!"

***

The week ground on slowly, with June watching the evening TV news intently. With each passing day, there were more stories about the soon-to-be President's mistress, with blurry images taken by telephoto lenses. Her name was never divulged, likely because it had never been learned by the media. But every network had their own theory of who the mystery woman was, and speculation on an upcoming wedding was the biggest part of every story. They were getting close, too close.

She'd also been on call each night that week, making up for lost time while she was away. All three nights, there had been shootings in LA, Mercy Hospital getting several of the victims. She had worked on three of them, one each night, losing all of them after epic battles against death. That was something that was taking as much toll on her vacation-refreshed mood as the media attention was. Now that she had a moment to take a breath, she knew she couldn't keep working at Mercy forever.

Mercy Hospital had treated her well, for the most part. But it was a county hospital, a place notorious for poor reimbursement, gang-banger patients, and too much work. As LA grew ever larger, the hospital got busier, and so did June's practice. With each passing year, she was spending more time at work, and no respite was on the horizon.

"There's got to be a better way of living a life than this."

By Thursday afternoon, she'd had enough and promised to never again watch the news. Seeing the TV playing in the OR employee lunchroom showing a local gossip program, June went off to a small waiting area to read the text message she got from Amy.

Have time for Ruka today?

"I forgot about her."

She sent a text back to Amy confirming she would be there on time. When a family came in to wait for someone in surgery, June retreated to somewhere else for privacy. In the locker room, June found the number she wanted in her phone and made a call.

"Hi, Elaine? This is June Kato. I called about houses on Maui a few days ago."

"That little cottage in Ka'anapali, right? It's still available."

"That was a little rough around the edges for me. What else is there in that price range?"

"Nothing. Not even close. I have some lovely new construction on the beach, if that sounds interesting?"

"It would if I was a millionaire. What about in town? In Wailuku and the other one. I can't think of the name right now."

"Kahului. Those houses don't come onto the market very often. Families move in and never leave."

"What about a condo?" she said through a sigh. "Something near the hospital?"

"I have quite a few listings in that area. How about I email you something?"

June gave the realtor her email address as a pair of nurses came into the locker room. Her next call was to Amy.

"I'd forgotten Ruka wants to go shopping." June looked at the time. "What time should I pick her up?"

"Don't bail on me, June. She's been driving me nuts all week about wanting to go to the mall with you."

"Does she need anything in particular? Why is it so important that I go with her?"

"She has something she's keeping a secret. Probably just a play date with her newest best friend."

***

Parking outside Amy's Orange County house, June went through the courtyard to the kitchen entrance. Ruka and Koemi were in the backyard wrestling over a soap bubble maker when June got there.

"Ever figure out Ruka's secret agenda?"

"Who knows?"

77

The backdoor opened then banged shut again. "Auntie!" both twins shouted in unison.

"Auntie June is here, Ruka. It's time to share your secret," Amy told her.

Ruka only stared up at June, nervously fidgeting.

"Well, Ruka?" June asked.

The little girl waved June to bend down to tell her secret. "I want to look different than Sister."

"I see. That might be pretty hard. Do you have any ideas?"

The girl pantomimed getting a haircut.

"What kind of haircut do you want?" Amy asked.

"Whoosh!" the girl said, swinging her hand over her head.

"Short?"

The girl nodded and indicated the length.

"Why so short?" June asked.

"Cause I like it and it's different than Sister's!"

"I can do it, too!" Koemi said.

"No you can't! It's my idea first!" Ruka said, starting a standoff.

"You really want it?" Amy asked. "Or just because Koemi doesn't have it?"

"I really want it!" Ruka nodded her head. She had half a dozen metal barrettes holding her hair back from her face.

June looked at Amy one last time for further instructions, getting only a shrug of the shoulders in return. "Go ahead and play mommy for the rest of the afternoon. Ko-chan and I have some errands to do ourselves."

"Honey, are you sure you want short hair?" June asked her niece when they got to the mall. They held hands as they walked to Kiddy Klips, just a few shops inside the door.

"I want to look different than Sister!"

"Oh yes, that's important, huh? Well, we better do something about that."

Ruka pantomimed with her fingers getting a haircut as they walked.

"You know, it doesn't have to be really short to look different than Sister. Maybe something at your shoulders would be cute?"

"Made up my mind, Auntie."

With a sense of dread, June pushed the children's salon door open. The last thing she wanted was to get halfway through a haircut on a screaming child, and not even her own kid.

After getting schooled by the six-year-old on what she wanted, the hairstylist took the girl by the hand.

"Last chance to change your mind, Ruka."

The girl crossed her arms over her chest.

"Stubborn, just like your mother," June muttered, nodding the go-ahead to the stylist.

The stylist led Ruka away by the hand. She turned and looked back at June. "Maybe you should come with us."

June grabbed a storybook from a play table and followed. Other kids were in chairs nearby, a couple of them wailing their lungs out, their mothers trying to settle them midway through haircuts. She didn't know what else to do to keep her niece quiet and sitting still, but coercion wasn't out of the picture. Just as Amy had said, June was playing mommy for the rest of the day.

She leaned in close to Ruka after the cape was secure around her neck. "Honey, you need to sit still and be quiet so this lady can do her work, okay?"

"I promise."

"Good girl," the stylist said. She removed the barrettes, handing them over to June, and began to spray water into the little girl's hair, combing it through. She wore an apron with comical cartoon characters of dinosaurs on it. "This sure will be fun."

"Pretty soon, Koemi won't look like you at all! And at the end, we get to go shopping for shoes."

"Koemi will have icky hair, huh?"

"Well, it might not be icky, but I bet she'd cry and cry if she was here. But you're not going to, right?"

"Okay."

June hoped the bribery worked. The last thing she wanted was a dramatic scene with a six-year-old in public. The stylist wisely turned the chair around so the girl was facing June instead of the mirror. She looked at June one last time. "Should I start?"

"Ruka?" June asked her niece.

The girl pantomimed one last time.

The stylist started in the back where June couldn't see.

"Auntie, tell me a story."

June looked through the storybook in her hand.

"Tell me the story about the princess on the island."

"Ooh, that sounds like a good story," the stylist said. "Was there a prince also?"

"Yeah. He was tall and handsome, and he killed the monster!" Ruka explained.

June closed the book, wondering how to proceed with the story. The stylist was busy at the back of the girl's head, long strands of hair falling to the floor.

"Did I tell you about the big white castle the princess visited?" June asked her niece.

"How big?"

"Oh, so big! Well, one day, the prince asked the princess if she wanted to live in the castle with him."

"They hafta get married first."

"Sure do. Well, the princess decided not to marry the prince after all."

"Then what happened?" the girl asked.

"The princess went home and was very lonely for a long time."

"She never went back to the big castle to see the prince?"

"Not right away." June leaned closer. "But guess what? One day, she went far, far away, all the way to the castle to see the prince again."

The girl squirmed with excitement. "Did they kiss?"

"Mmm, maybe once. But there was big news!"

"What?"

"The prince had become a king!"

She squirmed even more. "Was he still handsome?" the girl asked.

"Oh, wow! The most handsome king there ever was!"

"And they got married?"

"They sure did!"

"And then she was the queen!" Ruka giggled. "Did they kiss?"

"Maybe once more," June said.

"Just like Mick kisses Mommy?"

That stung June a bit, but she continued on. "Even better than that!"

The hairstylist moved to the side of the girl, starting there, June cringing at the little girl's makeover.

"What'd they do after kissing?" Ruka asked, hardly even noticing what the stylist was doing.

"Yeah, what did they do after kissing?" the stylist asked with a sly smile on her face.

"Well, they had a wonderful honeymoon."

"What's that?" the girl asked.

"They went on vacation."

"Then what, Auntie?"

"Well, since the queen was so important in her own land, she had to go back there."

"Oh, that's so sad," the stylist said.

"You don't know the half of it," June muttered.

"The queen left the king? She didn't love him anymore?"

June looked at the small metal clips in her hand, one bent out of shape from her gripping it.

"She loved him very, very much, honey."

"Did she ever go back to him?"

"Every chance she got."

The girl smiled sheepishly. "Did they have babies?"

"Oh, I don't know the whole story, Ruka" June said, watching hair fall away from Ruka's head. The stylist was making short order of the girl's haircut, even while other children in chairs nearby wailed.

"Yeah, what's the fun of being married to a king if you can't make babies?" the stylist said.

"Maybe someday, huh, Auntie?" Ruka said.

"Yes, maybe someday. But sometimes kings and queens don't always have baby princes or princesses."

"That would be sad."

"It sure would be."

June was watching the haircut, trying to ignore the crying kids around her. Mothers were distraught, taking pictures of their kids, collecting souvenirs from the floor. June just wanted to be done with the fairy tale.

"Hey! Maybe since the queen lived so far away, they loved each other even more, and had a baby anyway?" Ruka asked. Other women in the salon were now listening to the fairy tale. "What do they call it? Nonsense makes the heart grow bigger?"

June and the stylist chuckled as she started on the other side of the girl's head. "Something like that."

"Will the queen have a prince or princess?" Ruka asked after a moment.

"A baby? Which would be better?" June asked her.

"Well, a prince would be king someday and rule the land."

"What about a princess?" the stylist asked.

"Oh, well, a princess can do anything she wants! She can pretend to be a prince and slay dragons, and fight warriors, and someday have a castle of her own."

"That's very ambitious, Ruka. Is that what you'll do someday?"

"Someday, when I get bigger!" said the little girl. "What about you, Auntie? Will you have a prince or princess someday?"

June went back to nervously picking at a fingernail. "I don't know, honey."

"Just like the queen and the king. They don't know either."

"I hope they do," the stylist said, putting the finishing touches on the haircut.

"You too, Auntie. I hope you have a beautiful princess in your castle someday, to be a part of your story."

"I hope so, too. I just don't know the end of my story yet."

A few minutes later, Ruka had a bowl cut, something that suited a little girl. While other mothers led their kids away in tears or with haircuts half complete but abandoned in the middle due to dramatics, Ruka hopped down from her chair and took June's hand. June overpaid, leaving a healthy tip for the stylist.

"You know, this whole time I thought you looked familiar," the stylist said. "Are you someone on TV?"

"Um, no."

"Auntie's on the news."

"No I'm not, Ruka."

"Oh, you're that lady who…"

"Not me," June said, shutting down the stylist.

"Sorry, my mistake," the stylist said as June hustled Ruka out the door.

"You look pretty, Honey," June told her once they were out in the mall. "And you didn't cry at all. What do you want to do now?"

"Castle Town!" the girl said, pointing to where other kids were playing.

June let her loose to join the other kids, quickly finding someone she knew. June took a seat outside to watch and pulled her cell phone out. It had chimed with a text message at one point during the fairy tale.

It was from Amy. *Well?*

June called her. "Just finished."

"And?"

"It's cute. It seems to suit her face. "

"What's it look like?"

"Pretty much the same as what Mom did to us when we were that age but it looks professional."

"Did she cry?" Amy asked.

"Nope."

"She sat still for it?"

"Better than I did. But I bribed her so she wouldn't fuss."

"Babe, if you can manage that, you're ready for motherhood."

"Ha! As if that will ever happen!" June watched as Ruka raced through a part of the plastic castle while a mother micromanaged her kids. "What are you guys doing?"

"Looking at dresses. Their little friend has a birthday party coming up."

"Does Ruka need anything?" June asked.

"She could use a pair of sneakers. And she likes cheese pizza these days. She won't eat much of it, so you could probably share a slice with her in the food court."

"When do you need her back?"

"Maybe you could take her home? You know, keep her. Until she goes to college, anyway."

"As much as I'd like to, you'd miss her after a while."

"I'd pay you."

"Tell you what. I'll drop her at Mom's house. They have the time to raise her."

"Never mind. Hey, what's with you being so secretive about your weekend plans? Mom said you're going out of town. Did that Maui vacation spoil you?"

"No, just taking a breather," June said.

"Going to Vegas?"

"Maybe."

"Who're you taking?" Amy demanded.

"No one! Just getting some rest. Isn't that what you and Mom are always nagging me about? It's been a busy week, and I just want some peace and quiet."

"Something's going on, and I'll get it out of you, one way or another."

"I'll tell you about it when I get home. Promise."

June made another call, checking on her flight the next afternoon.

"Auntie, can we have pizza now?" Ruka asked when she got to June.

She put her phone away. "Yeah, honey, I'm hungry. And we have new shoes to get."

As soon as Ruka was home and turned over to her mother again, June collapsed in a chair at the kitchen table. After calling to check on her morning patient, she watched as Amy poured two glasses of wine.

"She looks like an entirely different kid," Amy said.

"They look just like us when we were that age." June took a sip of her wine and pushed the glass away. "Is it always so exhausting?"

"Being a mother?" Amy asked. "You had one kid for only a few hours. Try twins, twenty-four/seven."

"Whatever you pay your nanny, it isn't enough."

"You seem more tired than usual. Not getting sick again, are you?"

"I'm fine." Sensing a tremor kicking in, June massaged the muscles in her hand. "I had a long case this morning, and a long week. Doing those things are starting to take more out of me."

"Neither one of us are getting any younger. Do you have to do all those big, deep brain things you do?"

"As crass as it sounds, that's what pays the best. There's almost zero reimbursement for trauma or gangster stuff. I earn my living on tumor cases and spines."

"And that's the most stressful stuff, right?"

June nodded, still rubbing stress from the thick muscle at the base of her thumb. "Not making things any easier is all this stuff on TV lately about Jack and his White House mistress."

"The tabloid paparazzi has discovered your routine, where you go, the times of day you're most likely to be somewhere. It was the same way for me in Italy. It won't get any better, Babe."

Paparazzi was something Amy knew about, as an ex-supermodel.

"Any suggestions?"

"Wear a big hat and sunglasses when out in public. For you, it won't last forever. They'll get bored and move on. Most of them, anyway."

"What if I came out and told the truth?" June asked.

"In a press conference? Better pass that by Jack and the people managing his career. Personally, I think it would stir up even more interest. Those guys in the media have no end to the questions they can ask, and in the most awkward situations." Amy took a sip of her wine. "No, better to continue to deny everything, wear a hat, and limit the amount of time you spend outdoors. Otherwise, find a disguise."

June knew what had to be done. "Yeah, disguise."

"Hey, still babysitting this weekend, right?"

"I'll be over right after work tomorrow afternoon, just so you start your weekend adventure one evening earlier."

"Thanks."

"Who's this little weekend fling with, anyway?" June chanced asking. She already had a good idea of who the mystery man was.

Amy turned away. "Don't worry about that. Just show up, okay?"

Letting herself in the backdoor to Amy's house, she went to the smaller, private kitchen, the one most often used by the family. Every time she got there, she was impressed all over again. If it hadn't been in a neighborhood inside a gated community, it would be called a mansion, or even a villa. Just as she was tossing down her bag and briefcase on the kitchen table, Mick came in.

"June, you're here early."

"Hey, Mick. Is Amy around? She's having me watch the kids while she goes out of town this weekend."

"I know. I'm the one going with her."

"You?"

"I'm sure you've figured that out by now, June."

June turned away, only wanting to go for a run before taking over babysitting duties. "Figured out what?"

"Look, I've been wanting to talk to you about this for quite a while, but you never seem to be in one spot for more than a few seconds."

"Talk about what?" she asked.

"I'm asking Amy to marry me this weekend."

June grabbed her bag without saying a word, aiming for the powder room off the kitchen.

"You don't have anything to say?" he asked.

Two minutes later, she came out dressed in exercise clothes. "I'm going for a run. Want to come? Or are you preserving your knees for when you bend done on one in some big romantic gesture?"

"I think I could keep up." He was already in jogging shorts and an olive drab shirt with USMC in red letters across the chest. "I'll get my shoes on and we'll go."

"No need for shoes. I was headed down to the beach to run there. It's only a few blocks."

They were out the door and set off down the sidewalk to leave the gated community behind. Within minutes, they were on the beach, jogging through a cool fog barefoot.

"How far are we going?" he asked.

"Until I tire you out."

"That could be a while."

June picked up the pace just a bit faster than she would normally go. It had been a long time since they had gone for a run together, and it felt good in a way. She listened to her own breathing, and compared it to his. From the sound of it, he was moving along through the soft sand as easily as she was. She counted the number of lifeguard stations they passed, trying to gauge how far they'd gone. In the loose sand, the distance felt twice as long as if they were on asphalt or grass. They got to where a beach ended at a cluster of restaurants and condos, and stopped at a drinking fountain.

June dried her face on the front of her T-shirt, forgetting she didn't have a jogger bra on underneath. Just as Mick was leaning up from taking a drink, June pulled her shirt back down, wondering if he got a glimpse of her chest. Not that it mattered; he had seen it too many times before.

They started up running again, the sun just beginning to peek through the fog along the way.

"So, Amy huh?" June asked as a leading question.

"Yeah, Amy. Is that going to come between you two?" he asked between slow, easy breaths.

"Shouldn't. She's pretty busy, you know."

"She has time on weekends."

"What about the girls? You get along with them?" June asked. She knew the answer, that the girls adored him.

"Seem to. They don't start crying whenever they see me, anyway."

"That's always a plus. But you do realize it's a family plan if you get married? She's been married before, and she doesn't want any more disasters. Neither do I, or our parents. We want her to have something a lot better than what she had with Jasper. You need to live up to our standards, not just hers."

"And we'll decide what those standards are, June, not you or your mom and dad."

"Mick, she's not going to settle the way I…never mind."

"The way you settled for my behavior when we were married?"

June stopped running. "You promised never to bring that up."

"But we were. You can refuse to think about it, but we were married once."

"A long time ago, for about ten minutes."

"Twenty years ago for six months."

"Yeah, some marriage," she said, starting to run again. "Crappy little apartment on Slauson in South Central. I was paying for everything, including undergrad tuition, while you were out doing your gangster stuff. Then you landed in court one time too many, and the judge gave you the choice between prison or the military. Out the door you went with the recruiter, leaving me behind to get a divorce. Yes, our little secret."

"Everybody got what they wanted. I got a respectable career, and you got another reason to hate the military and war."

She felt as though she'd been purposefully shut down from the topic, and accepted it. She jogged off to the side, up to the edge of the gently breaking waves that were washing in. Mostly she was hoping Mick would continue on without her, that she could run alone for as long as she had the energy. Instead, he joined her.

Coming to a stop when she was shin-deep in the cold water, he stopped near her.

"What happened with Jack?" he asked.

"Just not the right guy for me, I guess. It was a decision I made, not you or Amy or anyone else."

"What's going on, June? What's with all the hostility?"

"Nothing, Mick. I'm not any more hostile than anyone else on this stupid planet."

"Come on…"

She turned to look at him. A wave of water splashed against her legs and spread across the beach, pebbles tumbling against her ankles as the water drifted back out again. Because of the fog and the hard run, she'd worked up a heavy sweat, and she slicked her short hair back.

"Come on what? You're with my sister, that's what!"

"And it used to be you. So?"

"I don't believe you just said that! Do you even care about her? Or is she a prettier and wealthier replacement for me?"

"That's pretty low, June. You had all your issues, a protest for this, demonstrating against that. Then there was the cop, and another cop, then a politician. You were always breaking up with me just as I was deployed, with the excuse that you were too busy. And when I got home again, there was some new guy." He stood his ground as another wave came in, heavier that time, washing through their legs up to their waists. "I finally gave up and moved on. You want to know the reason why? Amy's a lot easier to get along with than you are."

"Screw you, Mick. For your information, I was never with either of those cops. And as far as Jack goes, he was a done deal before it ever got off the ground. He's looking for a trophy wife, and I ain't no kind of trophy, am I?"

"Not right now, you're not."

She couldn't help but laugh.

***

Everywhere she took the kids that weekend, people seemed to recognize June. A few even came over and asked if she was the woman on the TV news shows when they were at the park. Her only escape was to wear Amy's clothes, a large hat, and sunglasses. By the time Amy and Mick got home on Sunday, June and the kids were holed up in the house, even on a sunny day.

While Mick stood back, Amy flashed her new engagement ring, and June properly oohed and ahhed. She hung around for a while longer, just so she wouldn't look as though she was making a jailbreak for the door.

"The inauguration is this week," Amy said at one point while unpacking.

June watched. "Yep, Thursday."

"Going?"

"I'll be at work, knee deep in a brain tumor."

"Not going to stand by your man at his proudest moment?" Amy asked.

"Not my man, and really don't want to be a part of that moment."

When Thursday, the day of Jack's inauguration, rolled around, June had a gap between surgical patients mid-morning. She had been surprised by a call from Leon, Jack's Chief of Staff, inviting her to the inauguration, and again by Jack. Both times, she politely made up excuses why she couldn't. She had no intention of watching, either in person or on television. But when she went to the OR lunchroom for coffee, the TV was on with the sound turned down, tuned in to the inauguration, which was just starting.

June leaned in the doorway, watching. There Jack was, standing with the usual crowd of people in stiff suits and overcoats in front of the Capitol building. Just as he was putting his hand up, she was nudged. It was Becky, standing there with her.

"Something's missing," Becky muttered.

"Yeah, the sound's turned down," June muttered back, taking a sip of her coffee.

"No, I mean a person."

June looked at the space next to Jack, the place where a wife would stand while he was sworn in. She saw herself there, in a stiff, gray suit, a hat on her head, its small ribbon fluttering in the chilly wind. She would be wearing a wool overcoat, a fashion statement making a declaration about Amy's winter line of clothing. She would be smiling, and smile even more when Jack put his hand down, giving him a congratulatory kiss on the cheek. It was what America wanted to see. "Not me."

Everyone in the room watched the moment in silence, until the TV station broke for a commercial interruption. But before an advertisement was shown, the station went back to their anchor newscasters in the local studio, once again showing images of June that had been captured by photographers only that morning, still harping on the mystery woman who hadn't shown up for the inauguration. These were the clearest pictures yet of June, something that could finally be used to identify her. When several of the nurses glanced at June, she turned away, going back to her room, taking her coffee with her.

***

At the end of the day, June made a phone call on her way out of the hospital. When she left, she had to force her way through rush hour traffic to get to the south end of Los Angeles. Parking and hurrying in, June got to her appointment at Verna's salon just in time. While Amy went to the most expensive salon in Orange County, June still went to the same place in south LA she'd been going since she was a teenager, when she first started her modeling career.

"Been a while since you've been in, June. Use to be that you'd be in here all the time, hair, nails, sumptin'," Verna said, picking through a few snags. "Not avoiding me, are you?"

"You? Never. I'm just so busy anymore."

"Got yourself a new guy keepin' you busy?"

"Ha! I wish!"

Verna held long hair to each side. "Not taking care of this like you always did before."

"Not modeling anymore, so there's no reason to."

The stylist let the hair drop. "What am I doing with it?"

June gulped, wondering what was coming. All she knew was that she was tired of being recognized and accused of being the President's mystery mistress. "I need something new, different."

"Oh, I know what it is. It's all that stuff on the TV, all the gossip about you lately!" Verna said, a little too loudly.

There were customers in chairs on each side of June, a young Asian woman with blonde hair who looked like she street-walked downtown nightclub districts, and a black woman getting her natural style fluffed to the maximum. They looked at June, along with their stylists.

"Yeah, that stuff on TV," June muttered. "Everywhere I go, people ask if I'm the President's mystery mistress, or whatever she's being called today."

Verna walked to in front of June and faced her. As the stylist nodded her head slowly, June knew she was had. Verna knew her secret. June shrugged and raised her hands in a pleading gesture.

"Uh huh," was all Verna said, going to her place behind June again. She scooped and lifted June's hair, letting it hang like drapery. "What are you thinking?"

"Time for something different, but I'm not sure what. What ideas do you have?"

"It's time to shake things up, Girl."

June had come in specifically to change her appearance enough so that she would no longer be spotted by the media. Now, she was faced with the decision of how different she wanted to look. "I...well..."

Verna leaned close to whisper. "I can make it so them news people don't bother you no more."

June smiled and nodded her head. "That's why I'm here."

"Y'all got time?"

"As much as you need."

Verna beamed from ear to ear. "Let's get started. Y'all shoulda had a glass of wine, though."

"I've been through worse," June said

"One thing's for sure. Ain't nobody will mistake you for that other girl."

After being shampooed and the cut started, the other two customers left, leaving them alone. Verna stopped cutting and leaned in close. "Tell me the truth. That's you, that girl on the TV, right?"

June sighed. "Yep, it's me. And no, I'm not answering any questions about how we got together or why we broke up. And no, I didn't leave him to be with a man in Hawaii. I just couldn't deal with the lifestyle of politics."

"Can't blame you for that, Girl," Verna said, going back to her task of creation. "I don't see how anybody survives that place."

"The White House? Either do I," June said. "I know I wouldn't have."

"Good for you for sticking to what's real for you."

"That's just it. I'm not so sure what I have now is what's best for me. I mean, I'm good at what I do, and for the most part enjoy it. But it's so stressful anymore here in LA."

"Stressful how?" Verna asked.

"My hours at the hospital are getting longer, payment is getting worse, my clinic gets more crowded by the day with people with problems I can do nothing about, but they beg for help anyway. Half of them got themselves into trouble by being stupid, demand I fix them, and then don't bother paying the bill. Don't get me wrong. I love LA. It's been my home all my life. But there's got to be something better."

"Can't take yourself some time off and recharge the batteries?"

"Just did not too long ago. That's when I saw how much different things are for other people."

"It sounds like there's a but coming," Verna said.

"Yeah." June collected a lock of her hair and examined it for a moment, curious as to why she wasn't anxious about the haircut. "I'm just not real happy about life. It seems like something is missing or I need to make some change."

"A baby is what's missing, Girl."

"Maybe. But I knew that wasn't going to happen in the White House, and it's not like men are standing in line for dates with me these days."

"Can you have a baby, start a family without a man? Can you-know-who supply some of his you-know-what?"

June blushed. "I guess I'm too old-fashioned for that."

"The real thing would be a lot more fun that the turkey baster!" Verna said, laughing.

June blushed even more. "I think with as busy as I am, I'd have to hire a live-in nanny, something Amy can afford but I can't."

"Those grandparents are sitting around looking for something to do, right? Can't get better nannies than grandparents."

With most of her hair gone, June watched as Verna collected a different set of sheers used for thinning.

"Have them live in the same house as me and the baby? I don't think so. There's a reason why kids move out. When the door hit me in the butt on the way out, I wasn't the only one happy about it."

After a quick blow, Verna began on painting in colorant for highlights and applying foils.

"Girl, it's not about them, or Amy, or the nanny, but about you and the baby. If you want a baby, you'll find a way of having one. Then you find a way of raising it. Then find a way of educating it, finding it a job, a college, and a career. That's your job as a mother. Forget about the sniffles, the drama, the violin lessons, and the soccer games. Raise them up to be a decent kid with a good outlook on life, and you've been successful. If you need a turkey baster and to move to another place to do that, and if that's what you feel is missing in your life, you do that."

"At this point in time, I'm not sure which would be easier, having a baby or starting over in a new place. One thing's for sure and that's I'd never survive doing both."

"All I know, June, is that when some girls get pregnant, they fall apart. They think everything's gotta change. And maybe for some of them, it should. You know, like turning over a new leaf. And other girls, they just add having a kid to the list of things that need to be done that week. After four kids of my own, I'm still not sure what it is, only that it's a little of both. Being prego is a good time to make those changes that need to be made, because in a few more months, there's gonna be someone relying on you. But if you take it all too seriously, nobody'll survive."

"Yeah, survive."

"Survival of the fittest out there, June. What you need to ask yourself is if you want to be in the game, or just watch from the sidelines."

That hit home. June knew she'd been watching Amy raise the kids, and was only pretending to be mommy on the occasional weekend. She needed to decide the extent of the game she wanted to play.

An hour later, June looked at her new hairstyle, a heavily honey blonde highlighted pixie. While they waited for the highlights to process, she'd had her brows plucked and shaped.

"Well?" Verna asked, taking off the cape.

June felt her soft hair, short bangs and a delicate fringe around her ears and neck. "Why didn't we do this a long time ago?"

***

Weeks passed, and the media sensation died down over the identity of the President's mystery lover, and why she wasn't at his side in the White House. June figured it was because new stories had come along, and not the change in her appearance. One thing she had done was start exercising again, not just running. One form of that exercise came in her return to the Sunday afternoon self-defense classes she had enjoyed so much in the past.

Carrying her bag of workout gear into the gymnasium, June went straight for the restroom to change from hospital clothes to workout clothes. She saw Mick on the other side of the open gym, already sparring with the teacher of the self-defense class that would start in a few minutes.

It was a warm spring day in LA, and she left off her usual sweat pants, wearing only jogging shorts and a sweatshirt. Back out in the gym again, she stretched her arms and legs.

"Hey, I wasn't sure you were coming today," Mick said when he got to her. All he had on was a T-shirt, shorts, and thin sparring gloves.

"I need the workout," she said back, without greeting him. She strapped on the padded chest protector, and pulled on sparring gloves. Mick helped with her padded head protector. "Looks like a new group of students."

"First class. Jukey wants to know if you'll do a demo with me?"

"You mean he wants the new class to see how a sissy girl brain surgeon can kick a Marine's ass?"

He laughed. "Something like that."

They turned for where the group had assembled and Jukey, the teacher, was starting the class.

"Well, you might want to put on some protection. Especially below the waist."

"Oh, yeah?" he asked with a smile.

"I'm sending you home to Amy in pain, and I strongly suggest you protect all body parts that can't be sacrificed."

Jukey introduced June and Mick to the group, and explained the demo they would give. It was a simple rushing attack from the rear.

They went at it half-speed, Jukey explaining about leverage and technique, while June gently slammed Mick to the padded floor.

"Okay, that's great," a woman said with her arms crossed. "The skinny lady can defend herself when she knows she'll be attacked. But what about full speed?"

For the demo, June took up a stance, pretending to talk on a phone, allowing Mick to rush her from the side. At the sound of his last footstep, she was able to turn, duck slightly, get a hold of him, and sent him sailing several feet away, all by using leverage. Even though that part of the demonstration was done, she didn't stop there, however. June went to Mick, still just getting up. With a rapid, sharp kick to his hip, she sent him tumbling.

She still wasn't done.

With only two quick steps, she was on him before he even came to a stop. He tried fighting her off, but she had the best of him since she was the one on top. A decade of serious training all rushed back into her arms and legs, of how to subdue an aggressor with an arm lock. Straddling his back, June got one of his arms pinned behind his back, and an arm lock around his neck. Pulling back hard, they both let out grunts.

Jukey rushed over, trying to pull June off. She had got much more involved in the demo than planned. Once he had her pulled off Mick, Jukey gave June a push back.

"Well, that's what a skinny woman can do to a full-sized Marine, if she's had the training," Jukey said, trying to laugh it off. Most of the small class was looking at June, still breathing hard, staring down at Mick.

Mick got up, and returned her glare. "Really want to spar with me, June?"

"Not afraid of you, Mick. There's nothing you can do to me that can hurt me more than what you already have."

"Okay, maybe we should get the class…" Jukey began to say, trying to interrupt them.

"Not right now, Jukey," June mumbled.

Mick had already balled his large hands into fists and had taken a practiced stance, slowly stepping forward toward June. She wasn't waiting, though.

June threw a quick jab at his face, but only as a ploy. The jab was quickly followed by a kick to his crotch, followed by a spin and an elbow to Mick's chest. It had worked perfectly, a technique she had developed herself. The only difference between using it in a class and in real life was that her elbow connected with his chest instead of his throat.

He coughed sharply but stayed up. Too close to kick, she landed another punch, that time to his belly. But it was too little, too late.

Just as fast, he had her on the floor, much of his weight on top of her. Ground grappling was a death sentence for anybody not as big as their opponent, and June knew it. Weight and size almost always won a ground fight. Being outweighed by fifty pounds, June tried squirming away, but she was caught under him, fighting off his attempts to reign in her flailing punches. Just as he got one of her arms pinned at her side, she arched her back, her last resort in getting away.

By then, Jukey was yelling at both of them to stop, trying to separate them.

It took all her strength, even more than what she thought she had, but she was able to tip his weight off her body. That gave her just enough space to fight. She alternated between slamming hammer strikes into his chest with crashing her free knee into his groin. Keeping it up as long as she could, June began to black out from the headlock Mick had got on her.

It was all she could do to stay focused. Quitting the hammer strikes, she reached up to his face, found his eyes, and sent a thumbnail across one eye.

He grunted again, and his arm loosened around her neck. She groped his face until she found his other eye, her fingers poised to inflict more pain.

"Want more?" she grunted out.

"Go ahead."

Instead of his eye, she shoved her hand down into his shorts and found his organ. Giving it as hard of a squeeze as she could, she didn't let up until Mick let loose of her neck. Once his body weight was off her, she let loose, drew her fist back, and crashed it into his chest. Finally, with some separation between them, she was able to get her leg bent, and sent her foot into his belly.

She scrambled up, but remained bent over, panting. She looked at him a few feet away, ready to send another kick or punch or hammer strike if he looked like he'd attack.

"Now you can marry my sister," June said once Mick was up again. She turned and limped away. "But if anything ever happens to her or the kids…" She nodded over to where they had just fought. "…that's only a hint at what I'll do to you."

Several weeks passed, and June never did hear from Mick, and even more surprisingly, Amy. She was sure she would've been scolded endlessly by her sister for the fight with Mick. What had started out as a training demonstration for how a woman could defend herself from a larger man, had quickly turned into a real fight. June no longer cared, though, and she hadn't been back to the gym for training since.

In many ways, she had found some peace with the situation between her and Amy and Mick, or at least some closure. No longer did the situation haunt her. She knew Mick was a good man, and would take care of Amy and the kids. What better husband and father could there be for them than someone that was a part of the family business and could defend them?

***

To prove to herself that she was dedicated to finding a healthier lifestyle, June returned to Maui for another week, this time in secret. She stayed at the same resort, only in a cheaper room. On her last full day there, she met with the real estate agent she'd been talking to for the last several months.

"Well, that's four condos we've seen, Doctor Kato. You don't seem terribly enthused about the condo lifestyle."

"Maybe because I've always lived in a house. I hate the idea of giving up on having a garden to putter in."

"Well, Hawaii can be a gardener's paradise. What sort of gardening do you do?"

They were driving aimlessly down the highway when June saw the hospital out the window. It was another place she needed to go while she was there, if only to walk the halls to get a feel for the place.

"Well, I inherited my grandfather's home, and he had a traditional Japanese garden in the back. A little teahouse, pruned azaleas, bamboo, stone path, that sort of thing."

"You could certainly do something like that here."

They passed by the driveway that went up to the abandoned house she'd looked at one day on her previous visit.

"Tell me, do vegetables grow well here? I have a little organic farm in LA. I'd like to try doing something like that again."

"Oh, Maui onions are quite famous. Almost anything that can be grown on the mainland can be grown here also, and with a year round growing season, farmers get several crops a year. It has something to do with the volcanic soil. It's all small scale, though."

June looked back at the slope where the old house was, trying to see if she could spot it.

"Elaine, do you happen to know if that old house is still available?"

The real estate agent smiled with a twinkle to her eye. "I thought you'd ask about that place. I just happened to bring the keys for it. Want to go take a look?"

"I came this far. There's no reason not to."

Elaine made a U-turn in the middle of the highway and went back to the house.

"Don't get your hopes up too much with this place, Doctor Kato," the realtor said, unlocking the front door. "It's seen better days."

They went in. Elaine tried a light switch but nothing happened. The house was light enough from windows to see their way through. For being essentially an abandoned house, it was surprisingly clean inside.

"You said once it's been inspected?"

"By the county. They rated it as livable."

June paid close attention to the hardwood floor, something she'd learned before she came. If the floor was stained by water, it meant there were problems with the roof. If the wall plaster was falling away, there could be a problem with the plumbing. There were other things to watch for, scorch marks around electrical outlets, loose floorboards, the smell of dry rot.

She took a marble from her pocket and set it in the middle of the living room floor.

"What's that for?" Elaine asked.

"If the marble rolls away, it means the floor isn't level and that could mean there are problems with the foundation."

When the marble didn't budge, she tried the same thing in other places, along with on windowsills throughout the house. Pushing the door into the only bathroom, they both looked down at the antique toilet.

"I'm told it works," Elaine said.

"Are there hardware stores on the island?"

"In town about an hour away. Someone would have to fill the back of their truck with things for the house to make the long drive worthwhile."

June went to the kitchen last.

"If it were me, I'd start with the kitchen. Maybe gutting it would be best," Elaine said, swiping her fingertip across the stovetop, giving the grime close scrutiny. To June, it looked like it needed a thorough cleaning, but if the plumbing and the stove worked, all she needed to do was replace the ancient refrigerator.

Scrub this, paint that, repair something else. Her mental list of things that needed to be done with the house grew with each room they inspected. But that wasn't the only thing bothering her.

Each time she went down the central hallway, she got chicken skin on her arms. Each room seemed to have a personality of its own, and not just from the old paint schemes or a creaky floorboard. Maybe in some ways the old house wasn't that much different than hers in LA, that several generations of one family had lived there, all leaving an indefinable but indelible mark on the place.

Being left alone to snoop, June heard a floorboard squeak at one point, in the hallway just outside one of the bedrooms. Going into that room, it was small, painted in colors a child would enjoy. Sunlight came in the window, shining down on the place where a bed would be. Even though it raised chicken skin on her arms, she didn't feel fearful.

June toured the small house again, trying windows and doors, knocking on walls with a knuckle, picking at paint with a fingernail, looking through closets. "It's still the same price as what you told me last year?"

"Should be."

They left the house, Elaine locking it up. June went around the outside of the house, looking at the roof and eaves, the windows and siding. The last thing she did was dig a handful of dirt to inspect its potential for a pea patch. Even though it wasn't wet, it packed together the way quality dirt should, a benefit of being agricultural land in the past.

June tossed the dirt way and rubbed her hands together. "Think the family would go down on the price if they were offered cash?"

"Cash, as in one payment?"

"That's the idea."

"I'd have to make some calls from my office. Are you one the island much longer?"

"I go home tomorrow. Just call me at that same number you have for me when you get an idea of their final price."

***

On Monday morning, June realized she got more sleep during her quick trip to Maui than she had in ages. She was beginning the week feeling refreshed for a change, and as soon as she parked her car at work, she got a call on her cell phone from Elaine about the final price on the house from the family.

"That's the lowest they can go?"

"That's actually a special offer to you, Doctor Kato. When the family heard a doctor wants to move from the mainland to work at the new hospital, and about the story of how you live in your grandparents' old house, they wanted to make it easier for you to join the community. Honestly, I doubt anyone else would get the same deal."

"What happens now? Do I put earnest money on it?"

When June got the amount and learned it could be a personal check sent by mail to Elaine, she got out her checkbook, wrote the check, sealed it in an envelope, and took that to the hospital mail drop.

Slipping the envelope through the slot, she kept it pinched between her fingers. Taking it back out, she checked the address and made sure the flap was sealed. She took a long look at it, wondering what to expect, if she would change her mind in a few weeks and the money would be a loss. Instead of mailing it away, she put it back in her pocket. Before she did that, she needed to talk to someone first.

Settling at her desk in her office, she made a quick phone call. After that, she got on an internet site for booking travel reservations, just as Becky came in and joined her.

"How was your week off?" she asked.

"Never better," June said with a smile. "Yours?"

"Sucked. Had a date but he never showed. And there's something wrong with the plumbing in my house."

"Oh?"

"Flush and it never goes away without lots of plunging. Something is dripping under the kitchen sink, and forget about the tub draining anytime this week."

"Get it fixed yet?" June asked.

"I'm not sure it's worth it. You've been there. The place is falling apart faster than Rodney and I can keep it propped up. I seriously don't know what I was thinking when I bought it." Becky leaned forward to look at the computer screen. "Already making plans for another trip?"

"Just a long weekend."

"Where?"

"DC."

"As in Washington DC?"

June clicked on something, booking a flight. "Yep."

"As in the White House?"

"Yep."

"So..." Becky said hesitantly.

"I don't know yet. That's why I'm going, to find out."

Becky slapped her thigh. "I knew it! When I saw your dreamy face while you watched the inauguration a while back, I knew you still had a thing for him!"

"Just relax, okay? I'm just going to see what's up between us. It'll likely be nothing and I'll come home complaining about the waste of money I spent to buy a ticket to get there and back. Let's not start any gossip that might spiral out of control like last time."

June clicked to another website, this time for real estate.

"That looks like your house," Becky said.

"Sure does."

"Why is it listed for sale?"

"Because it is."

Becky looked at June. "Huh?"

"For sale, as is, looking at all offers."

"Why is it for sale?"

June clicked on another page, bringing up images of the old house on Maui. "So I can buy this."

"But that's on Maui."

"Right." June looked at Becky from her computer. "I have to sell mine to buy this."

"Your what?"

"My house," June told her. "I don't have enough cash to put a down payment on the Maui house unless I sell my house first. Want to buy it?"

"Seriously?"

"You just said you're tired of taking care of your old place. Mine is in great condition, and I'm listing it at a decent price."

"You're thinking of leaving LA? You're moving?"

June turned off her computer. "Consider my luck these last few years here in LA. That's continuing with my sister marrying my old boyfriend. Do you really think I can just sit around and watch them play house?"

"Yeah, that is pretty harsh. But you're going to move?" Becky leaned in close to whisper. "You'd move into the White House, just so you wouldn't have to see your sister married to Mick?"

June put on her white lab coat, ready to get the next part of her day started. "I'm done with driving all over creation to babysit kids, go to work, go to the farm, go here, go there. Tired of traffic and smog and gangsters and greedy hospital administrators. Time for a change, and I finally know where to go for it."

June was thoroughly glared at by Becky each time she went out to the front of the clinic that day, right up until they went across the street to the taco truck for a late lunch. It had been one of the places where her picture had been taken by paparazzi and the tabloid media, but in the weeks since her new hairstyle, her picture hadn't been on TV news. Her scheme of making the change in her looks had worked.

"You're seriously thinking of leaving town?" Becky asked as soon as they sat.

"Yeah. It's time for me to move on."

"But the media isn't hassling you, we have a couple of new surgeons in the department, and you're getting more time off. You don't have to sell your house just because you want to leave Mercy. Go back into private practiced downtown. They'd love to have you."

"Before you tell me all the reasons why I shouldn't go, just know it isn't easy for me. My family, my job, my reputation as a neurosurgeon, my house, all my friends. You. I'd have to leave everything behind. But I'm good with it, you know? I mean, how much bad luck can someone have in just a few years. My poor little Guardian Angel has been working overtime to keep me going lately. It's time, overdue, really."

"If it had been me, I would've left years ago, June. But what finally made you decide to leave? Did you get a job offer somewhere that you couldn't pass up?"

"In a way, I suppose."

"And you need to sell your house here to be able to afford one there. It's your family's home, though. Are they okay with it?"

"It belongs to me, fair and square. They can have their family meetings at Amy's house for now on. Anyway, my mom and dad are okay with it, even encouraged me."

"What about Amy? She must be heartbroken."

"Amy doesn't know. And she's not going to know, at least until I can figure out the right time and place to tell her. That's probably the hardest part of this thing, leaving her and the kids behind."

"Did you talk to Fred yet?"

"I told him I'm thinking of leaving. Plus, I found someone to take my spot, and someone else for a year from now."

"Who?"

"Remember Jeremy Goldstein? He's already signed on fulltime starting soon, and Lane Marich will join you guys a year from now. Which means Fred only needs to find a replacement for himself, something I can't help with anyway. But I just need to talk to him again, and send off a letter to Mercy administration and the university to formalize my departure."

"I want to see that letter before you send it off." June and Becky finished eating, and headed back for the clinic across the street. "That's why you're going to see Jack, to see what he thinks?"

"I can make up my own mind without the help of a man. I'm going to visit him to see if the flame is still burning for either of us. If it is, I'll stay there and play White House hostess for a few years."

"And if not?" Becky asked, when they left their picnic bench behind to return to the hospital.

"I have a few ideas up my sleeve. Nothing firm, yet."

"Is that house on Maui one of your ideas?"

"It's the best one."

"You still need to sell your house," Becky said.

"That's where you come in. You said you weren't satisfied with your house. What about mine? The commute isn't bad, and Rodney would have the back garden to do with whatever he wanted."

Rodney was Becky's younger brother, in his young twenties, and slightly autistic at a high functioning level. As it was, he took the bus everywhere and had become very familiar with June's house and garden. He even worked at the small organic farm June owned out in the valley.

"If he took over back there, nothing would ever change. Ten years from now, you wouldn't notice a single leaf in difference."

June pushed open the clinic door, letting Becky in. "That's what I'm counting on. If anybody could take care of Granddad's little garden, it would be your brother. The thing is, I just don't have the time anymore to do it justice. He would, though."

"Are you selling the nursery?"

"No. Believe it or not, it actually turns a profit for me." June shrugged a shoulder. "And Rodney needs a place to work. If I sold, someone would turn it into spec houses."

"He truly is your biggest fan. If he hadn't met you, he'd probably sit at home every day and watch TV."

"And I'm his. Nobody works harder than that guy."

A nurse flagged down June to let her know a patient was waiting.

"But think about it." June took a slip of paper from her pocket and stuffed it in Becky's hand. "That's what I need, and I'm pretty sure you can afford it."

***

At the Maryland airport June flew into, she was met by Secret Service agents and taken directly to the White House. If the routine of getting through levels of security was difficult before, it was downright mind numbing at the White House. Jack had been in office for a few months, and from what June saw in the media, it had been going about as well as any other new Presidency. When she called him and asked if she could come for a quick visit, she was surprised he said he could make time for her, that the cherry trees along the mall were in full bloom, and they might even be able to go for a stroll to view them. After nearly an hour of security processes and being shown to the Queen's Bedroom on the third floor in the residence in the east wing, she was issued a lanyard with ID that permitted her in most of the Executive Residence, the original central portion of the White House. She had a few minutes to inspect her room, before freshening up and changing into clean clothes. Finally, a female Secret Service agent June had met a few years before came to escort her down a broad set of stairs to the ground floor. They went past groups of visitors on tours, staffers hurrying from one place to another, and officious-looking people in expensive suits carrying briefcases. At one point, she thought she recognized someone from TV news talk shows. As different as medical centers were from ordinary society, she knew she was entering an entirely new world to her.

"Doctor Kato, inside the Oval Office are priceless antiques and gifts from other nations. Please do your best to not handle things."

"Sonia, please just call me June."

The pretty blonde smiled. "Not in this building. We're rather formal here."

"I'm meeting him in the Oval Office? I thought he had a private office where he did his real work?"

"He has time for you now, and at the moment he's in the Oval."

When June was let in, she saw him behind the famous Resolute Desk, arguing with someone on the phone.

"Maybe this isn't a good time?" she whispered to the agent that remained with her.

"He's almost done."

June almost jumped when Jack slammed the phone down. When he looked up, he seemed to notice them for the first time.

"June! Please, come in and make yourself comfortable."

"Hi, Jack. Sorry, Mister President."

Jack looked at the agent. "We're fine, Sonia. I'll be going to the residence soon."

The agent nodded and left them alone in the official office of the President, speaking into her cuff on her way out.

Jack went out from behind his desk to greet June. Expecting a handshake, she got a bear hug instead. She closed her eyes, and let that same old feeling sink in, of wanting his body next to hers in bed.

Looking into his eyes, June couldn't help herself. Leaning forward, she kissed him. When she pushed back, she turned around to look away. "I suppose we're on camera, being watched by a technician in the basement?"

"We're on several cameras, being watched by several agents in the room just through that door over there."

She turned back to face him. "Great. Why aren't they rushing in to tackle me, before leading me off to some dungeon?"

"They have other orders. Instead, they're waiting to escort you to the residence. You are staying here while in DC, right?"

"Sonia already has me in the residence. I hope that's okay?"

"Perfect. And as far as what to call me, it's Jack when we're alone or when Sonia or Carl are with us, and Mister President when others are around. Which I doubt will be very often. Otherwise, Sonia has been assigned to you while you're here in DC."

"Assigned as in my protection or your protection from me?"

"Her job is to assure everyone's well-being while you're here."

June smiled, trying not to laugh at the exact answer she expected to get while in the White House, one of the many reasons why she didn't want to marry into it. "You're sure it's okay that I stay the night?"

"You mean will the agents and house staff gossip about the mystery woman visiting the President late at night?"

"We ran into that problem last year," June said. "I'd rather not have it start again."

"The agents are sworn, and the house staff in the residency is paid far too much to risk their jobs over gossiping."

"Well, human nature being what it is," she said, taking herself on a quick tour of the famous room. He went along with her, his hand pressing gently on her back.

"You've changed your hair. Looks nice."

"Thanks. I found it easier to look different than try to duck the paparazzi everywhere I went. I just had it touched up a few days ago. It's much shorter than what I've ever had before. Maybe I went a little nuts with this low maintenance pixie with all these honey blond highlights." She stopped suddenly and looked into his eyes. "Where did I lose you?"

"Somewhere around touched up. Looks great, though."

"Thanks. I'm surprised Amy didn't freak out when she saw it."

"I read about her upcoming wedding. I had my secretary send something."

"She mentioned it. Thanks for that."

He pressed a button on his desk. Almost immediately, the office door opened, with two agents waiting outside. June went out first, as she had been told earlier by Sonia, and found two Marine guards posted there also. In near silence, she and the President were led down a hall to an elevator, which took them up to the residence. She was given a quick tour, and they went to the dining room for a late meal. The cook himself brought it out to serve.

"It's all vegetarian, June," he said. "Cliff here has assured me of that."

A bottle of California red wine was opened and decanted.

"Cliff, this is wonderful," June told the chef about her meal. They made small talk for a few minutes, and she forced a promise for the recipe from him. Once they were alone, she looked across the table at him. "Jack, this place is gorgeous."

"Tell me about this visit, June. A sudden change in heart?

"I don't know about a change in heart, but we do need to talk."

"Are you getting married? Because you're not wearing a ring."

"No, nothing even remotely like that."

"Are you ill?"

She put her hands in her lap to massage the muscle at the base of on thumb, feeling the every-present tremor. Somehow, Fred Towns had never noticing when they worked together in surgery that a tremor was starting.

"No, I'm fine."

"What could be so important that you've come all this way?"

"No better way than to just tell you. The thing is, I've closed my practice in LA and I'm moving to Maui."

"Oh, well that's good news, right? There wasn't trouble, was there?"

"Nothing like that." She pressed out a smile, wondering how to proceed. In a way, she was surprised he didn't already know. She'd been rehearsing her little speech since before getting on the airplane, weeks in fact. "Last year, when I left you and went to Maui, I discovered how little joy I was getting out of life. I think when I backed out of our engagement, that was in some weird way the first step for me in looking for a better life."

"Looking back at it now, I think you did the wise thing, June. I know now how prescient you were then about seeing this place, and whatever we might've called a marriage, much more objectively than I ever did."

"Well, after that, I started taking a hard look at everything in my life. Work, home, my social life, everything. Nothing brought me any pleasure at all. I tried pinning all that negativity on you, when it really belonged to me all along."

"And moving to Maui is the answer?"

"It's a start. It's better there for me than LA. My mom sat me down one day and laid it on the line. She said that I needed to make some changes or I'd end up having a heart attack. And she was right."

"And buying a plane ticket to paradise was the answer?"

"It took a lot more than just a plane ticket. I've found two surgeons to replace me at Mercy, the Kato family home is up for sale, been credentialed and licensed to work at the hospital, and have found a house there that I can afford. But I can't buy that house until I sell the house in the hills. All without my sister finding out, who by the way is getting married to one of my old lovers."

Jack laughed. "And I thought I had a stressful year moving in here!"

***

After June showered and dressed for bed, she took a book off the shelf to read. Climbing into the king-sized bed, with its fine cotton sheets and down comforter, she left only one small lamp burn next to her. She had only two nights before leaving, but scanning what was called the Queen's Bedroom, she wished she could stay longer. She didn't know what to expect in the residential home at America's most famous address, but it was eerily silent.

Until there was a gentle knock at a door she hadn't noticed before. It barely even looked like a door, but more of a wooden panel built to be hidden within the wall. When there was a second, more forceful knock, she couldn't ignore it.

"Yes?"

The door eased open, the hinges silent, the bottom just breezing over the carpeting. The face that looked in was just a silhouette. "Still awake?"

June pulled the comforter up to her chin. "Who is it?"

A man stepped into the room and closed the door behind him. June flipped a switch on a control box on the end table, trying to turn on another light. When nothing happened, she quickly hit all the switches until several lights came on in the room.

"Oh, Jack." He was still dressed, but no longer in his suit jacket or necktie. "I wasn't expecting to see you until morning. If even then. Did I forget something? Was I supposed to check in with agents before going to bed?"

"No, you're fine. I was checking to make sure you're comfortable. Find something interesting to read?"

She opened the cover of the book she'd selected. "First edition of Hemingway's 'The Old Man and the Sea'. Seems expensive for a bedroom shelf."

"Those are probably all first editions or at least rare editions. All gifts from somebody throughout the years. Please don't steal it."

"This comforter might go home with me." June swept her hand over the soft fabric. "I was just wondering who else has slept in this bed."

"You can check the archives tomorrow, if you like. I'm sure they even have records of when the mattress and linens were purchased, and for which guests they were used. The historians here like to keep track of those sorts of things."

"And that means my fanny will be added to the list of all the other fannies that have perched on that particular seat in the bathroom?"

He sat on the edge of the bed. "Now there's a list the American public should never see."

"And from what I've read in the newspaper, a lot of rear ends, also." She reached out to take his hand. "Is that why you really came in here? To discuss first edition fannies?"

"Mostly. Just as a reminder, Secret Service is always in the halls, and cameras are always on in every room."

"Even this one?" she asked, pulling her hand away from his.

"Even this one. But for some reason, not in mine. All the security in this building is meant to keep me safe, but in the one place where I'm most vulnerable, no cameras or agents."

June let the comforter slide down her chest a little. "You feel vulnerable in your bedroom?"

"With you in the building, yes."

"I'm pretty harmless these days, Jack." June cleared her voice. Wearing only a tank top and undies, she wasn't sure if she was over or under-dressed for the room. "You're in there by yourself?"

"The only way for you to know that is to come for a visit later."

"Oh, now that wouldn't look suspicious at all, when a female guest sneaks down the hall in the middle of the night and lets herself into the President's room."

"If you used the main corridor, yes." He nodded in the direction of the door he just came through. "But that door leads to a smaller hallway the public knows nothing about. Only two agents are in there at any given time, both of whom are on my personal detail, handpicked by me. A visitor would have to follow it around, something of a maze to get to the opposite end of the building where my bedroom is located."

"Well, as intriguing as a midnight visit in the White House sounds, I'm sure you have a busy schedule in the morning. I'll leave the back hallway shenanigans to your next guest."

He gripped her hand and smiled before leaving through the same door.

June tried reading the book, but thinking of the value, she carefully returned it to the shelf. Wearing a heavy bathrobe, she snooped around the room, looking at a few of the treasures that decorated every nook and cranny, before looking through the desk. Finding official white House stationery, she took a sheet and envelope to put in her bag as a souvenir. She figured taking anything else would be considered theft.

She zipped closed her bag, securing the sheet and envelop inside. "June Kato, White House shoplifter."

Turning off most of the lights and pacing another lap around the room, she could still pick up Jack's scent in the air.

"Why in the world did I come here? Just to tell him goodbye in person? Am I that silly?"

June looked through the books on the shelf again, more as a distraction than to find something to read.

"I spent a lot of money on a ticket to come sleep in the White House. This idea of coming here was so stupid."

She took another book off the shelf. Looking inside, she discovered it was a signed first edition of Faulkner's *The Sound and the Fury*. She quickly put it back and decided to touch nothing else. Instead, she flapped air beneath the heavy bathrobe, wondering if the heat in her room had been turned up.

"What did he say? The back hall is empty except only two agents? Was he insinuating something with that?"

She went to the bathroom and swept a comb through her hair a few times, and pinched her cheeks. Opening the robe, she dabbed on perfume. Wondering what White House protocol was for women in the President's bedroom, she snugged the robe tight around her waist. Looking in the mirror, she tried to smile.

"Now what? I smell nice, look okay, and I'm not a neurotic mess this week."

Leaving the bathroom, she flicked off the last of the lights in her room. Instead of getting in bed, she went to the door Jack had used.

"Well, tabloid news agencies, here comes your next story."

Once again, the door silently swept open. She peeked out to see an agent seated near her door. Upon seeing her, the man stood.

"Good evening, Ma'am."

She looked the length of the narrow hallway. The lighting was dim, no furniture was along the wood paneled walls, and plush carpeting covered the floor. Looking at the agent a second time, he smiled politely for a brief moment.

She ducked back into her room, closing the door again.

"Okay, that didn't look stupid."

June paced another lap trying to get her courage up.

"This is like being a teenager and sneaking a boy into the house."

She took a book down, looked at it, and put it back again. It had a signature that looked like one of the earliest President's.

"Except this is the most famous house in the world and the boy is the President. That's a different kind of trouble than if Mom would've caught me."

She straightened the comforter on the bed for some reason.

"Actually, it's the exact same kind of trouble."

She returned to the bathroom, tried to use the toilet, pinched her cheeks again, and brushed her teeth. She went back to the door and grabbed the doorknob.

"Come on, you big sissy."

She swung the door open and stepped into the hallway, closing it behind her. She nodded at the agent again. That's when she realized she didn't know which way Jack's bedroom was. Taking a chance, she turned to the right. After only two steps, the agent smiled and pointed his finger in the opposite direction.

Feeling her cheeks blush, June turned around. Heading the opposite way, she hurried when she passed her own bedroom door. It truly was a maze, with several corners to turn and closed doors to pass, all of it while dressed only in a bathrobe and barefoot. When she closed in on another agent outside a double door painted white, the Presidential Seal woven into the carpeting just before it, she hoped she found the right place.

"Yes, hi," she said to the agent. "Sorry, I forgot to put on my lanyard and ID. I'm…"

"Good evening, Miss Enwright."

"Miss Enwright?"

"That's the name of the person using the Queen's Bedroom tonight, and you are the only guest in the residence right now."

"I see." If there was one thing June Kato didn't look like, it was someone named Enwright. She went along with whatever charade was being played. "Is Ja…he…the President available?"

"The President is expecting you."

The agent swung the door open to let June in. As soon as she was, the door closed softly behind her. Jack was just coming out of the bathroom from showering, only a towel around his waist, the scent of his soap strong in the air. When their eyes met, June felt as though she was caught in the act of something.

"June." He went straight for her.

When he opened his arms, she fell into them, pressing her body against his, her face against his chest. "Jack."

After kissing, she nudged free from him. "I, uh…how many laws or policies or protocols am I breaking right now?"

"None. Would you like a glass of wine? I have that San Luis Obispo chablis you like so much."

"I've mostly given up on drinking, except for red wine and dark chocolate when I'm stressed out." She watched as he put the bottle down without decanting any. "Keep it handy, though. I might need some later."

Jack put on a bathrobe and motioned June to sit on a couch with him.

"What are we doing here, Jack? What's going on between us?"

"Two old friends and lovers. You came for a visit, and it seems in a very literal sense, right into my bedroom."

"But between us?"

He put his arm around her and held her close. "June, I still love you. I'm sure I always will. That door you just passed through isn't a revolving door as the media tries to imply. You're the only woman who has been in here since I moved in."

"Your love life is as…"

"Sad as yours, yes."

"Maybe you call yours sad, I just call mine pathetic."

"You went out with a realtor a few times last year."

"You know about that?" she asked, pushing away from him. "You're keeping tabs on me?"

"No, but certain agencies do. They have to. The Service, the CIA, the NSA, they're all paranoid that spies are everywhere in a President's life. Even if I tried ordering them to leave you alone, they'd still keep an eye on you. They call it national security."

June tried not to sigh as she leaned into him. "Well, regardless of what your spies have told you, nothing happened between that realtor and me."

"I never asked, they never told. There really are some things that need to remain personal."

"Like me being in here tonight?"

"Exactly. Which begs the question, are you staying the night?"

"In the official Presidential bedroom?" She snuggled her face into his chest, letting his scent swirl through her nose and into her mind. "If I'm not tossed into the castle dungeon in the morning."

"I find it comfortable."

June untied the belt to her robe and let it slip off her shoulders. Her top came off right after. With the softest of nudges from him, she fell back onto the bed.

***

When June woke in the morning, Jack had already started his day, leaving the bed next to her empty.

"And this is what I didn't want…" she said, rolling onto her back and pulling the sheet up to cover her chest. "…waking up alone in a White House bedroom."

She put on her robe and stuffed her undies in a pocket. She peeked out into the hall, trying to straighten her hair. A different agent was stationed there.

"Good morning, Miss Rostovich."

"Yes, hi." She closed the bedroom door behind her and hurried down the hall toward her room where another new agent was stationed. "Pardon me, just exactly how do I find breakfast here?"

"You can have something brought to your room, or join the others in the dining room."

"Others?"

"A small brunch is being served for a Congressional caucus. You might be more comfortable having something brought to your room. If you ever need something brought from the kitchen, just dial three on your room phone."

***

After finishing her breakfast and watching as the room service trolley was being taken away, June wondered how she was supposed to spend her time that day. Jack would naturally be busy, and she had made plans to go shopping while in DC. Fashions on the East Coast were much more formal than California, and especially Hawaii, but an addition to her wardrobe might be in order. If she were to eat dinner with him in a formal dining room, she'd need something better than the simple pants suit she'd traveled in.

Dressing in the best outfit she brought, she took her wallet, hung her lanyard around her neck, and left the room into the main hallway. It was business as usual, with staffers and White House employees headed in every direction. Opposite her door was a young woman seated on a chair. She stood when June came out.

"Miss Rostovich, welcome to the White House. My name is Jennifer, and I'm here to make sure you are comfortable. Think of me as your personal assistant during your stay."

June looked at the name on her own ID, and sure enough, it was a new card with a different name on it. All she could figure was that someone had been in her room during the night. They got a few pleasantries out of the way.

"Do you have plans for the day?" Jennifer asked.

"I'd like to say hi to the President, if that's possible. Otherwise, I was planning to go on a little shopping spree."

Jennifer made a perfectly practiced expression when she looked at her watch. "I'm afraid the President is busy until mid-afternoon. We might be able to get you in then. But I'd be happy to give you a tour of the building before getting a car and taking you shopping."

"I haven't seen much, just, well…"

"Is there something in particular you'd like to shop for?"

"I guess I feel a little underdressed being here. A little out of my element, I suppose."

"I know the perfect place for us to go."

June was surprised by how busy the White House was, with numerous people carrying briefcases and stacks of papers, tour groups, and what appeared to be Secret Service agents and Marine guards stationed at corners and intersections of hallways. Getting a personalized tour was interesting, allowing June to see some of the behind the scenes places that ordinary tours didn't get. After two hours of wandering from one end of the White House to the other, Jennifer called for a car to be brought around to the back entrance.

"We have to go with agents?" June asked as the rear door was opened for her and Jennifer.

"I'm afraid so. But once we're busy shopping, I doubt you'll notice them at all."

Inside, June found Sonia was joining them. They took the chance to catch up on each other's life as they drove along. It was a warm spring day, early afternoon when they went outside. Not just one car but two had been brought, driven by large men in sunglasses and wired earpieces. As if guided by Jack's promise, the pair of vehicles went along a street famous for its cherry trees, tiny pink petals fluttering in the breeze. Apparently, that's a stroll along the mall for people living in the White House.

"You sound like old chums?" Jennifer asked.

June and Sonia looked at each other, sharing a smile. "We spent a very interesting day together a few years ago," June said, hoping she wasn't breaking a rule or divulging a secret.

"Jennifer, in many ways, Miss Rostovich is responsible for this President being in office."

"Oh?"

"Talk to one of the historians. They can show you something in the private archives."

June didn't know what the private archives were, but figured it was White House lingo for something secure and inaccessible to the public.

"And Miss Rostovich, your real name has been expunged from the record, replaced by another."

Instead of being mostly invisible, agents were constantly under foot as June tried on dresses and business suits at the classiest department store in town. Even though she was constantly checking messages on her phone, Jennifer played the role of sister and co-shopper, giving approving or disapproving votes on outfits. When June found a beige suit with an open jacket and a pencil skirt, something she could still pull off, it fit perfectly. She showed it to Jennifer.

"I don't know when I'd even wear this."

"It looks tailor made to your figure."

Even though Jennifer sounded like a junior politician, June decided to wear the suit, along with a new white silk blouse, out of the store after paying. Back in their SUV with their federal agent guards, they wound through the city on the way back to the White House.

Jennifer checked her watch. "By the time we get back, the President will have some time available to see you."

Sure enough, June was escorted directly to the Oval Office once they were back. After sending away Leon Moretti, the White House Chief of Staff, Jack closed the door and kissed June's cheek.

"Thanks for seeing me. I hope I'm not interrupting anything?"

"I have an hour or so. I hear you went shopping?"

"I got this," June said, sliding her hand down the front of her outfit. "Not sure why. Not really my style anymore."

"You look fantastic."

"Thanks. Jack, about last night…"

"Already regretting what we did?"

"No, not at all. I just need to make it clear this isn't going anywhere. I'm not moving in here with you."

"Does that mean you came all the way to DC to have a one night stand with the President?"

"No. I was hoping for two nights," June said.

He opened the drawer to the Resolute Desk and took something out. Opening the lid to a small jewelry box, he set it on the desk aimed at her. It was the same four-carat engagement ring she'd worn for a week.

"I wish you'd reconsider."

June could hardly take her eyes off the sparkle of the ring. "It's been months, and believe me, I've reconsidered probably a thousand times since then. I'm still just as conflicted about it as ever."

"Maybe not as conflicted as you think. You made the decision to leave your practice in LA and move to Maui, starting all over.

That suggests you're leaving me even further behind than when you took the ring off."

"No, Jack. I'm never going to leave you behind. I love you, I truly do. If it was any other circumstance besides being trapped in this ridiculously over-done building, I'd jump with no hesitation at all."

"What if there was a way?"

"A way for what?" she asked.

"For us being married, you going to Maui, and me remaining here?"

"Come on, Jack. Think about what you're saying. You want us to get married and then immediately separate? You don't really think that's a solution, right?"

"Why can't it be?"

June paced a lap around the Oval Office. "To what end? I come here twice a year for quickies with the President, and you come to Maui for a week-long working vacation?"

"Would that be so bad? Once I'm out of office, we could be together permanently at the Brentwood hacienda."

"Me, in Brentwood?"

"It's not Dante's Hell, June."

"Not exactly a place a Kato would live." She went to a small statuette on a shelf for a closer look. "What would the media say? How in the world would Leon spin that to make it look good?"

"The media doesn't have to know."

Seeing Russian writing on what was likely a gift, she carefully put the statue back where it belonged. "There's no way guests would keep quiet. Just planning something like a President's wedding and the news would be all over the headlines by the end of the day."

"Unless we did it right now, right here, today."

"Don't be absurd, Jack. We're not teenagers."

"I'm serious, June. I don't want you to slip away again. You have no idea how much I think of you, of how much I miss you."

"I'm not sure I like the idea that thoughts of me are distracting you from running the country." June had to admit she felt exactly the same way, of Jack always being in her mind. He wasn't being the President right then, but her lover. The words, the expression on his face were exactly what she'd wanted from him since the very beginning. "But today? We would need a license, wait the required amount of time, and I have a flight tomorrow morning."

Jack opened the desk drawer again, this time taking out a sheet of paper. June tried reading it from where she stood but couldn't quite see what it said.

"What's that?" she asked.

"Marriage license. It's the same one we almost filed last year."

"You still have it?"

"One in the same."

She took it from the desk to read. "It can't still be valid."

"No expiration. All it needs is signatures."

June felt slightly numb. It was one thing being asked to marry him again; it was something else altogether in these surroundings. "Wait, our marriage license has been in the Resolute Desk?"

"The first thing I put in there after moving in here."

June had to think. It was either the silliest marriage proposal of all time or the most romantic. What woman could say no?

June paced a lap around the room before putting the license back on the desk. In some odd way, she liked his idea of being married but from afar. It would cut back on their arguing, and once he was out of office, they could be together full time in homier circumstances. If he became a two-term President, she could retire and they could live on Maui, albeit in a place a little more luxurious than the house she was moving into. In some fantasy princess fairy tale that she might tell her nieces, it made sense.

Just then, there was a knock at the door and Leon stuck his head in. He looked back and forth between June and Jack. "Mister President, there's something I need to speak to you about."

"Not right now, Leon," June said to him.

Leon stepped into the room. With just a glance at June, he looked at Jack with a begging expression. "Rather important, Sir."

June glared at him. "And this is more important."

"Discussing something rather personal right now, Leon," Jack said.

"This is of national importance, Sir."

June set her eyes on a man she really didn't like. "You know what, Leon? This is critically important to me, and right now, I'm running the show in the Oval Office. Once I'm done managing America's number one problem, I'll be glad to let you have the show back again. Capisce?"

"Yes, certainly." Leon left the room, quietly closing the door behind him.

June turned her sights on Jack again. "What are you thinking?"

"I'm thinking I should let you run the country while I go to Maui."

"Don't tempt me. The first thing I'd do is fire that guy." June paced another lap around the room. "This isn't a fairy tale, Jack."

"No, it's real life. A real wedding and a real marriage. Just not conventional."

"Nothing between us has even been conventional, not from the very moment we met."

"Then, what's the hold up?"

"I'm supposed to get married without my family, my mom or my sister to see?"

"Do you see anybody from my family hanging around here?"

"A wedding is something a girl dreams about all her life. She wants to look her best, have her family and friends watching, flowers everywhere. Not in some roadside chapel. We're not teenagers eloping."

"Might I remind you, you've been married once before."

She narrowed her eyes at him. "How'd you know that?"

"CIA, NSA, remember?"

She clenched her molars, thinking. "That was a very long time ago and barely lasted a few months. It would be best for you to leave that part of my life alone."

"Once I'm out of office, we'll plan a real wedding, with the flowers and the dress, the works. Whatever you want. We could have it at the Brentwood house. Or even Maui, if that's what you want."

She tapped her finger on the marriage license. "So, this would be a place holder? A way of making sure I didn't escape your grip?"

"Or me escape yours."

June went to the desk, grabbed a pen from a desk set, and scrawled her signature at the bottom of the license. She tossed the pen down.

"Up to you, Mister President. Time to make an executive decision."

He used the same pen and signed in giant letters next to her signature. Picking up his phone, he made a call, leaving it on speaker.

"Margie, find the White House chaplain and have him come to the Oval, ASAP. Also, are there any gardenias in the building today?"

"I saw some in the Blue Room."

"Have those brought to the Oval, please."

"What are you doing?" June asked after the call was done.

"Arranging a wedding. We need a chaplain, and you need flowers. Gardenias are still your favorite, right?"

"Well, yes, but…"

"You want to get married or not?"

The blood drained from June's head, making her feel a little dizzy. Having a wedding all of a sudden was playing havoc with her heart. "Yes."

"It looks like you'll be going to Maui alone for our honeymoon while I stay here. I'll do my best to come in a few weeks."

June was still stunned, barely following what Jack was saying to her. "Don't we need witnesses?"

Jack made another call. "Margie, get Sonia in here, and Leon."

"Not Leon," June said.

"Forget Leon. Get Carl Masters in here, but tell him it's not trouble, only that I need to ask him a question."

"Right away, Sir."

"Where are we having it?" June asked, hardly getting the words out. "Is there a chapel in the White House?"

"Right here in the Oval Office. We have the location, the flowers, the minister, and the witnesses. And a bride that looks quite lovely today."

Feeling her legs get weak, June sat in a chair.

Within a minute, Sonia came into the Oval Office, followed closely by Carl Masters, both Secret Service agents on Jack's personal security detail. June had known Agent Masters for as long as she had known Jack, even longer, and found him to be a kind but stern man.

"What's going on, Sir?" Masters asked.

"Just wait for a few minutes. We'll need both of you for something as soon as the chaplain gets here."

"The chaplain, Sir?" Masters asked.

Sonia's face broke into a smile and she took June aside while Jack talked with the agent.

"I saw the license on the desk. Are you and the President getting married?"

"As soon as the chaplain arrives, apparently. Do I look okay?"

Sonia led June to a small bathroom just off the Oval Office. Using the little bit of makeup that was in there, June swiped on some eyeliner and peach lipstick.

"This is so exciting," Sonia whispered.

"Or insane," June whispered back, stroking a comb through her hair a few times.

"I've always seen how much you love him in your face every time you've visited. It's the right thing to do, June."

"Is it? Honestly, I'm a little numb right now."

When they returned to the office, the chaplain had arrived. He held two small books in his hand, grinning from ear to ear. Masters stood waiting, a stern look on his face as always. Jennifer had been called to the room also.

"Jennifer, as one of the White House historians, has a wedding ceremony ever been performed in the Oval Office?" Jack asked.

"No, Sir. There have been quite a few weddings at the White House, in the Blue Room, the East Room, and in the gardens, but never in this office." She looked at the group assembled. "Oh my goodness!"

Leon stepped up to face the young woman closely. "You will need to keep absolutely quiet, understand?"

"Yes, Sir, of course."

"Not just with the public, but throughout the White House, including the residence." Leon looked at both agents. "That includes the Secret Service."

A staffer brought the small batch of gardenias, which Jennifer fixed into a bouquet with a rubber band and wrapped the stems with tissues. When June took the small bouquet, she gave them a sniff and fixed a few of the petals.

"Are we ready?" the chaplain asked.

"I am," June said, looking up from her flowers. "Jack, ready to be a family man?"

***

When June woke the next morning, gardenia petals were everywhere, on the comforter, in the bed, on the floor. What was missing was clothing, but at least her groom was still there.

It was well after six o'clock and Jack was still in bed with her. She stroked her hand across his chest, tugging at a few of the hairs. "Not up running the country already?"

"I think I can stretch our honeymoon until seven. When do you leave for Maui?"

"No definite timeline. I still need to find a buyer for my house so I can make a down payment on the one on Maui."

"What if I bought it?"

"Which? The house in the hills or the Maui house?"

He shrugged. "Both. It could me my wedding gift to you."

June sat up, searching for her camisole that had been flung aside several hours before. "See, that's exactly what I don't want, is you buying my love. I can buy my own house and manage my finances just fine."

"Okay, answer this. Once you sell your LA house, will you have enough to buy the Maui house outright?" he asked.

June found her camisole and slipped it over her head. "Just barely, but it doesn't leave me with money to fix some of the problems with it, or to open an office at the new hospital on the island."

"I suppose a personal loan would be out of the question?"

"A loan between husband and wife?" Saying the words shocked her for a moment.

"Is there anything in the house to make it livable?"

She lay down again, resting her head on his chest. "You could barely call it livable. I'd need to ship my furniture and belongings, which takes three weeks. Otherwise, I have a ton of scrubbing, sanding, painting, and replacing to do to make the place decent. Amy's wedding is coming at the family faster than a speeding bullet, and I'd like to be moved in by then. She's still under the impression I'm going there strictly to be her bridesmaid."

"You haven't told her you're moving there?"

"All of this moving business of mine came about right at the same time she was planning her wedding to Mick. There was no way I was going to steal her limelight by announcing my move."

"But everybody else in your family knows, right?"

"Everybody within a three thousand miles radius of Amy knows, including Mick. In some feat of magic, nobody has let on about me. I just don't want to wreck the fun for her."

"And now you have a second secret to keep from them?" he asked.

She craned her neck to look at him. "What's that?"

He lifted her hand, the one with the diamond ring.

"Oh, that. That's going to require some diplomacy and tact, something I'm not so good at." She watched the sparkle of the ring. "I could tell her I didn't want to upstage her wedding. That would work."

"I don't know if that's the most unselfish thing I've ever heard or the dumbest," he said.

"More like the dumbest. I rue the day I have to tell her, though, which I'm saving for after the wedding and as close to the time of her departure as possible."

"What still needs to be done with the house?"

June began counting on her fingers. "New roof, repair the siding, paint the entire exterior, scrape the windows so they work again, repair the front porch. That's the exterior." She started counting in the other hand. Power sand and refinish the floors, repair a few places in the plaster walls, paint everything, gut, rebuild, and paint the kitchen, and do something with that nasty bathroom."

"All this work will be done by one woman?"

"I plan on drinking a lot of coffee. But I have a home repair how-to book. If it doesn't get done, I can work on in my spare time, one room at a time. The kitchen and the morning throne are the top priorities."

"Mind if I make a suggestion?" he asked.

"Live here in the Residence? Because I'm almost sold."

"What's holding you back?"

"The bathrooms. Honestly, I'm a little disappointed with the quality of the bathrooms. What was your suggestion?"

"Hire someone to do the exterior work to get it weather proof while you work on the interior. Do the bathroom and kitchen first, followed by general repairs, and leave all the painting for later."

"With my budget right now, 'hire' is a four letter word."

"You know, I'm not without funds, and we are married now. Would it be insulting if I were to help pay?"

June stared at the ceiling. "Maybe a little. I'm selling my grandparents' home so I can make this move. I'm pretty much all-in when it comes to making this move on my own."

"No reason to be stubborn about it, June."

"It's less about being stubborn and more about proving I can do it. All my life, I've had everything laid out in front of me years in advance. I knew how much tuition would cost, projected rent and car bills, and worked just enough to pay for it all. Sure, I had to struggle to make ends meet a few times, but for the most part, it all came together pretty easily for me."

"Because you planned it all out ahead of time."

"Partly, yes. But I want to make this move work, under my own power, just to prove to myself I'm an adult. I see so many young doctors struggle to start their practices and I've always said I was glad it wasn't me. Well, it's my turn to find out what that's like."

"You don't want any help at all, even if someone came along and helped out?"

"You're not coming to Maui to scrape paint, Jack. You have a country to run."

"Well, there's always a way of getting things done. You never have shown me any pictures of the place."

June brought up pictures on her phone of the old house. "You can see where the landscaping is mature but overgrown. I don't have much choice about the paint scheme, since it's a historical place, so the exterior needs to be green with white trim and a light-colored roof. For the interior, I'm mostly allowed to do whatever I want."

"Can you send me those pictures?" he asked, looking at them closely. Once he was done, he gave the phone back. "I imagine Amy's wedding is huge?"

"Massive. Old friends from everywhere are coming, even from Europe. It'll be standing room only at one of Maui's largest beach estates. The rental on that place is a budget breaker."

"Any other preparations before you go? To live there, I mean."

"Sell the house, buy the other house, have a final family get-together, walk through Granddad's garden one last time, and say goodbye. Surprising how much more complicated it is than that, though."

"June Kato living on Maui." Jack put on his robe, the signal their first morning of marriage was coming to an end.

"You're not expecting me to become Mrs. Jack Melendez, right? Or even June Kato-Melendez?"

"Nobody in their right mind could ever expect something like that from you."

June listened as Jack showered, and watched as he dressed. She wasn't sure of what to expect, but a President, at least this one, put on his pants one leg at a time. When he was done, he reminded her of the back hallway, and kissed her goodbye.

"Yep. Making lots of changes."

***

On her way out, June was able to stop in Jack's private office to say a quick goodbye.

"As fabulous as this ring is, I should leave it here," she said, fluttering her fingers, watching the diamond sparkle.

"Breaking up with me already?"

"No. It's just that it will lead to too many questions if I wear it, and it will be so much safer here with you than in my possession. If I leave it with you, I can wear it whenever I come for a visit."

She slipped the wedding ring from her finger.

"Are you able to keep the band?"

"I could wear it on another finger." She put the simple platinum band on the ring finger of her right hand and gave Jack the diamond ring. "Don't lose that. You promised me a real wedding someday."

When June got home, her phone rang even before she was out of the airport. Knowing who it was from, she answered.

"Well, hello there, Mister Kato! What took you so long to call your bride?"

"Hello, Doctor Kato? This is Marvin Stone, of Stone Real Estate. This is June Kato, right?"

She'd almost made a terrible mistake. She thought it was Jack to check on her getting home okay. Instead, it was the realtor that she found to sell her house. "Yes, this is June."

"There's good news. I have a solid buyer for your house. They're willing to pay full asking price, also."

The timing was just a little too suspicious. "Who's the buyer, if you don't mind me asking?"

"They've asked that their name be kept private until escrow and paperwork are complete."

"Yeah, that's what I figured. Let me call you back in just a moment, okay?" Sitting in her car at the airport parking lot, she called Jack. "Hey, I told you this morning that I don't want your help in buying my house!"

"I don't know what you're talking about. June, I'm pretty tight with time right now…"

"You didn't buy my house in LA?"

"No. You told me not to, so I didn't. Why? Is there a buyer?"

"Yeah. I just got a call from my realtor that there's a buyer willing to pay full price. I thought it was you."

"I haven't had five minutes all day to even think about it."

Hearing something about a problem in a faraway land, June ended that call and called her realtor back. While she listened to it ring, she thought of her house in the hills, and how this could be one of the last times she ever drove up the canyon road to it.

"So, take their offer of full price?" Marvin asked.

"They're solid for the money? Because I don't want any surprises. I'm relying on that to buy something else and I have no wiggle room at all in this deal."

"Everything checks out. All we need are signatures on paperwork and it's a done deal. Honestly, I've never seen a real estate deal go through as quickly as this one. The buyers barely wanted to look at the place before making their decision. This has been no stress at all."

"No stress for you, anyway," June said, after ending the call.

A month later, escrow closed and June held her last family meeting in the house. Everybody came for one last dinner. In spite of the big news, Amy had been left out of the loop, and decision made by all the rest of them, just so her looming wedding wouldn't be upstaged by June's change of residence and job. As it was, June had a plane ticket to get to Maui only a few days before the wedding, and was hoping she could get a few jobs done on the house before the wedding. One of the biggest problems was that she couldn't pack too many things to be shipped until after Amy left the house that evening, leaving her to rush around later.

Over the years, the Kato family dinners had gone through cycles, from large meals to quick get-togethers, and back again. Rotating through the three homes in the Los Angeles area, the monthly gatherings were often conducted as business meetings rather than just simply meals. Just planning a time and place that all of them could meet was a logistical nightmare. But on this particular Sunday, June needed everyone at her place. It would be the last time for them, and she knew it. With only twelve hours before her one-way flight to Maui, time in her own home was running out.

"Thanks for bringing Auntie, Mom. I just didn't have time to go pick her up today."

"She grew up in this house with your dad. It'll be the last time she'll ever be here."

"And she knows that, right?" June half-whispered.

"She knows. Since the stroke, she hasn't been able to get around so much, but she's glad you invited her."

"She's as much of a part of this family as anybody. Why wouldn't she come?" June took a batch of biscuits from the oven and set them aside to cool. "You're sure Amy is bringing the kids...and Mick?" June asked her mother as she hurried through the last of her preparations.

"They'll be here. But does she know..."

"No, they don't know, and it's going to stay that way. Mick might be suspicious of something, but I haven't said anything to him. Amy's wedding is coming up, and whatever is going on with me isn't going to take away from her wedding. Understand?"

"You have to tell her eventually that you're staying on Maui."

"Yeah, Mom, I will. The day after the wedding. Just let me manage it, okay?"

"So many secrets between the two of you lately. Neither of you have ever been that way before."

"What other secrets are there?" June asked, wondering if somehow they had learned of her wedding with Jack the month before.

The front door opened, and Amy, Mick, and the kids came in, instantly energizing the house. Amy chattered on with their aunt about the wedding preparations, while Mick and their dad played hide and seek in the back yard with the girls. June and her mother set the table with bowls and trays of food, maybe the largest family dinner June had ever prepared.

June watched out the back window at the others playing for a moment, trying to take in the scene. Thirty-some years before it was her and Amy who were playing in the same garden, their grandfather acting as master of ceremonies. It might be a new generation there now, but the scene played out the same.

It was when the realization that it would be the last time Katos would play in that garden, June fought back a tear.

"Amy, get the girls in here and washed up. Dinner is ready," June barked at her sister. She knocked on the window to get her father's attention, wagging her finger to come in. "Mom, help Auntie to the table."

"Amy, do you need anything else for the wedding?" their father, Tak, asked over dessert of mint chip ice cream.

"Not much, Dad, unless you've learned how to sew?"

He waved her off with a smile.

"Don't ask that klutz," Mabel said.

"It's mostly just details, little stuff. That's why June's going a little early, to manage things there."

June tried to smile as everyone at the table looked at her. They all knew of her plans but for Amy.

"Once we get there, I might need some errands run and some crowd control. We need to keep a lot of people busy for a day or two before the wedding, and I might need you to take guests back to the airport the day after. Otherwise, there isn't much."

"You're holding up okay?" her mom asked.

"I'm a little on edge right now, Mom," Amy said, settling down one of her daughters. "As long as something doesn't come along and jam up the works, I should be fine. But I really can't handle any bad news right now."

Several pairs of eyes shot in June's direction, while she slumped in her chair, picking at a fingernail.

"It'll be fine, Sis. Nobody is doing anything to disrupt. Just let us know if there's anything at all you need."

As the grandparents took the dishes to the kitchen, the girls ran for the back yard again. When Amy turned for the living room to join their aunt, June steered her away.

"Mick, why don't you watch TV with Auntie," June told him, dragging Amy to the back door. "I just need to talk outside with Amy for a few minutes."

"What?" Amy asked. "I really don't want to talk about the wedding, Babe."

"No, we won't. I just thought it might be nice to come out here and play with the girls."

"Yeah, sure, whatever. Sounds like you're nesting, though."

June sighed. "Just playing with the girls. Nothing more sinister than that."

They started a new game of hide and seek with the girls, staying under the patio overhang with Amy for a moment. Once she was done counting to twenty, June led her sister along the stone path that had been there for over fifty years, pretending to look for six year olds.

"When was the last time you were out here with them? Or just the last time you were out here in the garden at all?" June asked.

"Oh wow, I don't know. That photo shoot for the department store a few years ago?"

"Buck got some good pics that day, remember?" June asked with a smile. It was her last real modeling job in her fashion career, and it took place in her back garden. The advertising images that came from it were also some of her favorites. "I heard he died a while back."

They got to the little teahouse and sat on the large granite stoop in front of it, listening to the girls inside giggle.

"Between him and Bobby, they made our careers."

"Okay, ladies, we need to keep on schedule today," June said in a falsetto voice, imitating Bobby, a set director that raised them in the world of fashion modeling. "Amy Kato, have you eaten yet today?"

"No, Bobby, not yet." The both laughed when Amy took over the imitation. "June Kato, have you been getting any sleep?"

"I have finals coming up soon!"

"Well, I don't want either of you girls passing out when you're on my set," Amy finished, ending the parody of one of their most beloved workmates from their fashion careers.

The sliding door of the teahouse opened slowly behind them.

"Mommy, who was that?" one of the girls asked.

Both the girls came out of the tiny house and sat on Amy and June's laps.

"Oh, just a lady we used to know a long time ago."

"Do I know her?" Koemi asked.

"You met her once, but you were just a baby then. Right here at the house, in your guy's room."

"Can we meet her again?" Ruka asked.

"Mmm, maybe someday. But not right now."

The girls dragged June and Amy up to their feet for more play, June glad for it. She wasn't sure why, but she wanted Amy to go on one last play date at the home. It was the third generation of Katos to play in that garden as children, and the fourth to be there. And very soon, it would come to an end.

In the morning, June went for her last run in the hills, even before sunrise. She was sure to hit every landmark—Rattlesnake Woods, Hunter's Pond, Eucalyptus Ravine, and Dead Oak Grove, all of them family names—before making the last leg of the journey home. After a shower and filling one last box for the move to Maui, she took her five bags of clothes and essentials to the front porch.

She couldn't leave without one last walk through the house and garden. Pressing on a loose floorboard to make it squeak, jiggling the toilet handle, setting the time on the old over clock barely filled five minutes while she waited for her ride to the airport. She knew she had to go out one last time to the garden, and did it hesitantly.

Going out to the patio, more memories than ever flooded her mind. Amy's kids playing there the evening before; her and Amy's coming-of-age party while wearing kimono; the fashion photo shoot a few years before; the sight of her grandfather twisting wire onto an azalea branch; a romantic liaison with Jack in a dark corner. There had been more than a few of those over the years, with both her and Amy, and their father too, if the truth was told. But all that was done now, at least for the Kato family.

Not knowing what else to do, and maybe to hide one or two tears that were threatening, she got the hose and turned it on to mist the mossy areas. A few tiny weeds were pulled and tossed in the compost bin. She swept the patio with the old bamboo broom that her grandfather had made decades before. Leaning the broom in the tool shed for the last time, she went back to the sliding glass door into the house and slid it closed.

She didn't know why she slid it open again. The new owners weren't supposed to move in for a few days and she was supposed to leave the place locked and her keys in the mailbox. Leaving the door open, she took a step back and bowed deeply.

"Kato-ka ga koko ni aru kotode arigato gozaimashita. Kore ie wa subarashi desu. Tsugi no riyosha ni shinsetsu ni shite kudasai."

Leaving the patio door open, she hurried to the front door and held it open to let the breeze blow through. It was an old-fashioned custom, to air out a home when leaving for the last time, to blow out the old spirits that might still be around, and allow space for the next family to enter. But when she got to the porch, she got a surprise.

"Becky! Rodney! What are you guys doing here?" She closed and latched the door behind her. "We've already said goodbye half a dozen times. You're even thinking of visiting Maui in a few weeks."

"Hi June," Rodney said. "Sorry you're going away."

"Thanks, Rodney." June set her sights on Becky. "What's up?"

Becky swept her foot over the stone porch. "Yeah, you see, we're the ones who bought the place."

"Oh." June almost felt as though her friend had been a traitor. "Oh! Well, I just said goodbye to a few old ghosts and was going to wait at the curb for my taxi." She stuck her house keys in Becky's hand, four sets altogether. "You'll have to wait a few more hours to move in. The mover isn't supposed to be here until later today."

"Is there anything we need to know?" Becky asked.

Becky and Rodney had been there a hundred times, at least. They knew it as well as anyone. Just as June was about to take them on a quick tour of the house and garden, pointing out a few problems that had been painted over during the last few decades, her taxi pulled to the curb.

"No, not really. Everything works, mostly. I just sprinkled the moss. There's a baby jackrabbit living in the tool shed. Just give it leftover salad so it doesn't eat the landscape plants..."

The taxi driver tooted his horn.

"Yeah, I gotta go."

After giving them both hugs that were meant more for the house, June took her bags and hurried down the walk to the taxi, and a new life.

Starting Over

When June got to the airport on Maui, she had four large suitcases and her maid of honor gown in a luggage bag to contend with. Instead of going to the rental agencies, she had to get a taxi into town where her new pickup truck was waiting. The trick was getting into a taxi before everybody else did.

On her third attempt she was beaten to a taxi, she griped as it left with a businessman who out-sprinted her for the passenger door. "Yeah, thanks a lot. I have a maid of honor dress here! We're all in trouble if something happens to it!"

An old shuttle van rolled up to her, the driver tooting its horn.

"Kihei resort?" the driver shouted over the noisy exhaust and his loud music.

"Just into town."

"Where in town?"

"The car dealership near the mall."

He tossed his head toward the door. "Get in. I can drop you."

The longhaired young man remained behind the steering wheel while June loaded her bags into the van, hanging her dress on a hook.

"With all that, you look like you're going to a Kihei resort."

June sat on a bench. "Just into town to the Maui Motors dealership."

"Cheaper to rent a car on vacation than buy one," he said.

"How much is it for the trip into town?"

"Fifty bucks."

June started getting her things off the van again and waved at the next taxi coming along. Once again, it was grabbed by someone else before she could get her bags to it.

"Hey, you owe me for waiting."

"Forget it. You never did anything." She turned away to look elsewhere while he sat there in the van, letting the engine idle pungent exhaust out the back.

He opened the door again. "Twenty bucks!"

"I can practically walk there."

"Not with all that stuff you can't."

"Too bad for you that you'll never find out."

"How much?" he shouted.

He must've seen the same security guard coming down the terminal curb, headed in his direction, just like June did. That gave her leverage.

"Ten."

The driver kept his eyes on his rearview mirror, watching as the guard got close. "Okay, fine. Just snap it up and get your stuff in here."

When June dug a ten-dollar bill from her wallet, the driver started up with her again.

"Here for a vacation?"

"Wedding."

"Yours?"

"Sister's."

"Bridesmaid?"

"Maid of honor."

"On the beach?"

"At a house."

"That big one next weekend everyone is talking about?"

"Yep."

"Can I come?"

"Nope."

Five minutes later and ten dollars lighter, June was at the dealership, talking to a sales agent. In another twenty minutes, the paperwork was complete, her new pickup was brought around, and the sales agent helped her load her bags in the back. The gown was hung in the front, where it wouldn't get wrinkled. June was barely able to suppress a yawn when she adjusted the seat position.

"Pardon me for asking, but what's a nice looking lady like you need a pickup truck for?"

She started the truck. "I've been told I have a lot of baggage in my life."

June knew very few of the roads on Maui, mostly the main highway that led to the south shore of West Maui, where she would live and work. Amy's wedding was also in the area, within jogging distance of her new home.

First, she had to make a stop in town at a chain grocery store where a large order of wine was waiting for her to pick up. Loading several crates of wine for the wedding reception into the back of her pickup before covering it with a tarp, she felt like a moonshiner.

"Okay, one last stop before going home."

Hearing her own voice say the word 'home' in this strange town sounded odd. She had spent less than two weeks total on Maui, spread over two trips months apart. Knowing little about the island, and not entirely sure she could even find her house, it didn't feel any more like home than Kansas. In a way, she felt like a woman without a home, which brought an overwhelming sense of dread with it.

"Once I get a few things set up and get some sleep, I'll feel better," she muttered as she parked in front of the realtor's office.

Elaine was at her desk, jangling a set of keys when June went in.

"Wow, new home town, new house, and a new truck to go with them," she said, putting the keys in June's hand. No paperwork needed to be completed, as that had been done by mail. It had taken several trips back and forth across the ocean in a mailbag until all the Ts were crossed and Is dotted, but June didn't owe anyone a penny for anything once the deal was done.

"I can't believe today finally came." June rubbed the keys with a thumb, feeling the notched edges. "I'm more in disbelief that I survived!"

"Your sister's wedding is next week, right?"

"Don't remind me. That's been an even bigger survival test than me buying the house."

"We've all been following the wedding plans in the newspaper. Almost every day there's another item about it. Really a big deal."

It almost sounded as though Elaine was angling for an invitation. "Well, the wedding is a closed ceremony, but I hope you come to the reception. It should be fun. You never know who might be looking for a place to buy on Maui, right?"

June got some maps and directories for services on the island from the realtor, along with reminders on how to find the house.

"I must say, you have some very nice friends, Doctor Kato."

What sounded like a cryptic message June took as a compliment. "I do?"

When Elaine's phone rang, June took the chance to leave. She still had some driving to do and only wanted to get some peace and quiet. After jotting a promise note to invite the realtor to an open house once the house was livable, June left.

She drove along the shoreline route to her new hometown of Ka'anapali, a resort area with a growing residential and commercial base. She passed the new hospital, the signal the house was only a mile further along. She found the driveway easily because someone had done some pruning of the overgrown shrubbery, but when she got to the house, a surprise was waiting.

Two pickup trucks and a van were parked at the house, and several men were busy at work carrying tools, lumber, and buckets of paint. Two men were on the roof, hammering nails through painted corrugated steel sheets, fixing them to fresh plywood, most of the surface covered. Others were working on loose siding. They weren't dressed like regular construction workers, with hard hats or tool belts, but more like just a bunch of friends had shown up to work on a buddy's house on a weekend.

Stepping out of her truck, she got out her cell phone, wondering what number to dial for Maui Police. One of the men nodded at her as he went by carrying roofing material to a ladder.

June waved down one of the men. "What's going on? Who are all of you?"

He simply pointed to another man, coming in their direction. "Talk to gunny."

"Doctor Kato?" the other man said, reaching his hand forward. "Welcome to Hawaii."

"You are?"

"Gunnery Sergeant William Jacobs. I'll introduce my crew when we take a break."

June knew a gunnery sergeant was a Marine rank, since Mick had held that rank for many years. "You're Marines? Why are Marines working on my house?"

"We're from Kaneohe Air Base on Oahu. We were given a furlough to come here to work on this house. That's why we're in civvies rather than utilities." He pulled out something that looked like a work order only on military stationery and showed her what was to be done to the house. With it were several photos of the house, before and after concept images. "Remove and replace roofing; repair and replace as needed clapboard siding; remove, scrape, paint, and replace windows. Repair and paint interior walls as needed, remove original kitchen flooring and replace with…"

June took the list and read it quickly. "Who gave you this?"

Some of the other Marines gathered around them.

"Came direct from base commander. You weren't expecting us?"

"I just got off a flight. I had no idea this was happening. Who said you could do this?"

"Ma'am, I'm sorry. We're just following orders. Are you asking us to stop?"

June had a pretty good idea of where their orders originated. "Are you allowed to take a break while I make a phone call?"

The gunny waved the others into the shade while June sat in her pickup to make a call.

"Jack, sorry to interrupt your day. Something has come up."

"You must be at your house?" he asked.

"Just got here. Lo and behold, there's a squad of Marines taking apart the house."

"Are they putting it back together again?"

"Hopefully. Do you know anything about this?"

"June, you knew there was no way you could do all that work on your own, not in a year. And both of us know you'd never hire someone to help. All I did was find an economical and feasible alternative to assuring you'd have a good home to live in."

In a way, she found the gesture very charming. She was also steamed he did it without asking for her permission. "Jack, I don't need your help."

"Do you have enough money to pay subcontractors to do the work? Do you have any experience in functioning as a general contractor for a remodel, in a state and building codes you're unfamiliar with?"

"No."

He hushed his voice slightly. "Well, since we're married now, I went ahead and made an executive decision, to make sure you lived in a good house."

"What's that make me, junior executive in the deal?"

"CEO."

"More like Chief Bottle Washer." She noticed the gunny get his squad working again. "Did you have to send in the Marines?"

"I called in a favor of their base commander. According to their pre-enlistment files, they all have experience in construction. Even though they're doing work on a furlough, they're staying in nice rooms at the resort across the road," he said. "Grunts don't get that very often."

"Something I'm footing the bill for, I suppose?"

"I know you're good for it. I have your ring as collateral. It's a win-win deal all the way around, June."

"So, that's how deals work in the White House? Trade a sparkly bobble for a squad of Marines?"

"If only it were that simple. I'm told they should be done by the end of the week. Keep it under your hat, though."

"They're certainly working hard. I don't know how to thank you for this."

"June, thank them instead. I have to go to a meeting. I'll call at the end of the week."

With that, the line went dead.

Amy had arranged a room at the resort for June since she was going there early to manage some of the details for the wedding, giving her a place to stay for the week. Amy still didn't know June wouldn't be returning home with the rest of them, and June was still trying to figure out a way of telling her she would be staying behind permanently. Too tired to think about much of anything, she went across the highway and checked into the resort hotel to get some sorely needed rest.

***

The room was dimly lit when she woke. After a long yawn and stretching her arms over her head, June went right to her cell phone. She had a number stored in it from the past, and right then, there was no more important contact listed.

June stared down at the number and wondered if it was worth it. There would be a tremendous amount of physical pleasure, and with Jack five thousand miles away, physical release of anxiety wouldn't be coming to her any time soon. Beyond the animal gratification would be a sense of satisfaction in her place in the world, a return to a deep level of calm she hadn't felt in a while.

"I shouldn't waste my money."

She set the phone aside, flicking on the television. There were local news stories of increased airline traffic through the airport, a highway repaving project somewhere, a new organic farm opening upcountry, wherever that was. Upon hearing about the little farm, she had a sudden and unexpected pang of nostalgia. Television wasn't going to fill the void.

Wrapped in the bed sheet, she poked through her suitcases, and found what she was looking for. Back in bed, she opened her paperback romance novel to the bookmarked page and read.

Stopping, she flipped back through earlier pages. "What did Trey look like again?"

With a sigh, she stuck the bookmark at page one and tossed it in a drawer of an end table. Her phone sat there, beckoning her.

"This could be the start of a bad habit," she said to herself, picking up the phone.

She found the number and tapped on it, waiting. She had needs that evening, and she couldn't get them satisfied by sitting alone in the dark reading cowboy romance.

June made an appointment for a massage for an hour later, hurried through a shower, tossed on simple resort clothes, and hurried to the spa.

"Sorry to keep you here late," June said, stepping into the room. Dalene's spa room had been repainted in deep blues and emerald greens, a splash of pale gray swirled around the room, something of a stylistic ocean wave. Soft slack key guitar music oozed from hidden speakers, a mild scent of fruity incense in the air. Seashells in baskets and burning candles decorated the simple furnishings in each corner. It was geared toward women with a strong New Age effect, something that normally turned away June's interest. That evening, however, she was all for it.

"I remember you," Dalene said, starting the massage. "You were here a while back."

"Good memory. Almost a year."

"You were on that quickie impulse vacation, right? Hadn't you just run off from some guy?"

June wanted to laugh over the idea President Jack Melendez would be labeled as 'some guy', or that she had run off from him. "Something like that."

"I noticed you're not wearing a wedding ring, so you must not have gone back to him."

"We stay in touch. He lives five thousand miles away, so not much can happen between us anyway, right?"

"Five thousand?"

"Oh, I took your advice and made the big change. I moved here and he moved back east. I checked and it comes to exactly 4,779 miles."

"Hey, congratulations. Very exciting. How long have you been here?"

"Twelve whole hours. I'm staying here at the resort while some work is being done on my house."

Dalene had June turn over onto her back for the second half of the massage. "Have a job yet?"

"At the hospital down the road. I start next week."

"Good to have a solid employer. I hope they're paying you well."

"I'm a doctor, and opening a new practice here on the island has been a little frightening. But the hospital administration has assured me they'll do everything they can to help me find patients."

"I need a checkup. Maybe I could be your first patient?"

"Actually, you should hope you aren't one of my patients. I'm a neurosurgeon. I do surgery on the brain, spine, and nerves."

Dalene laughed. "Yes, it might be best to stay out of your office."

"I just hope I can make enough of a profit to survive. I hate the idea of going back to LA with my tail between my legs, trying to get my old job back again."

"Just don't go back to the guy that gave you so much trouble."

June thought about Jack. It had been several days since she'd seen him and a few hours since talking to him on the phone. She'd given back the diamond ring all over again, but this time she was officially married. It was about time she started to miss him. "Not right away, anyway."

"Don't worry about him. You'll be fine. Just find a guy to show you a good time, buy you a few meals, maybe help do some of the work on your house."

"In my case, that will probably be my father. They're coming this week and I have the idea they're planning on staying with me for a while. Otherwise, I think my dating days are over."

"Why? You're attractive, have a nice body, starting a good job. Seems like men should be standing in line for a date with you."

"Very few have stood in line for a second date. That's always been the problem."

"Well, you were engaged, so you must have something going for you."

"I can't spackle the crow's feet at my eyes much longer and apparently my butt has become, well, flabby. I'm rushing toward forty like an out of control freight train."

"You look thirty."

"Thanks. I know you're lying but I'll take any compliment I can get these days."

"Your hair is cute. Sexy."

June reached up to her hair and stroked her fingers through. It was shorter than ever before in her life, and blonder since her last visit to Verna a week before. She still got a mild surprise whenever she looked in the mirror. "Thanks. Sort of an impulse thing a while back. Just had it touched up a few days ago for my sister's wedding."

"Best wishes to her. When is her wedding?" Her hands paused again briefly. "I assume it's here on the island?"

June smiled again. "Next weekend. At that beach estate just down the road from here."

"That big thing I've read about in the newspaper? All of Maui is talking about it."

"Which is exactly what my sister wants. If the paparazzi doesn't show up, she'll be disappointed."

The irony of how Amy wanted the media and how June had recently shied away from it wasn't lost on June.

Dalene continued to work. Finishing with her hands and arms, she uncovered June's chest. "She was that famous supermodel and that makes you the twin?"

And there it was, once again playing second fiddle to Amy, her twin older by only five minutes, internationally known and extravagantly wealthy. As prominent as June had become in the world of neuroscience, it would never compare to Amy's world.

"Yes, the sister and the maid of honor."

"Lucky guy she's marrying. Do you know him well?"

June took a deep breath and exhaled it as a sigh. The massage was turning out to be a therapy appointment. "Pretty well. We used to date."

"Oh, ouch. Was he the one you were engaged to but ran away from, and then she stole him away?"

June stared up at the ceiling, wondering if she should continue. "Engaged? No. But we were married briefly, a very long time ago."

"Starting to sound like a soap opera. One twin married to a guy and then the other."

"In a lot of ways, our family is like some nutty group you'd see on TV. All we need is an unwed pregnant woman and we'd have a hit."

"You'd need a celebrity, an entertainer or politician with a secret mistress to make it perfect. But you have to tell me the story of this guy that's coming between you and your sister."

"Oh, not really coming between us. I'm good with him marrying Amy. He'll be a good father to her children."

"She has kids? The plot thickens."

"Even more than what you think. I have a pretty good idea he's their father and not the man everyone thinks is their father."

Dalene's hands began working more slowly. "You better start at the beginning."

"Well, as kids, the three of us were good friends. Then as teenagers, we both dated him, back and forth a few times until my parents put an end to that. Once I started college, Mick and I started dating more seriously, until we had a quickie wedding, something nobody ever knew about, even Amy. He was still trying to find his way in those days, but was finding more trouble than solid work. Well, one day he was in court and the judge gave him the choice between going to jail for a while or enlisting in the military. Maybe the smartest thing he ever did was talk to the recruiter that was in the courtroom that day. It just happened to be a Marine recruiter."

"What about your marriage with him?"

"The last remnants of it crumbled while he was away, and he agreed to a simple divorce. I was still in college then and didn't have the time or energy to follow a soldier around the landscape. But the thing was, I was still terribly in love with him, and whenever he had furlough, he'd some for a visit. We dated off and on for years, at least until I found the other guy I told you about."

"The one you were engaged to?"

"Right. That's when Mick retired from the service and got a job working for my parents. Then, just like you guessed, Amy worked her magic on him."

"But what about Amy's kids?"

"Oh, she was married for a while, right when the kids were born. Everybody thinks Jasper is the kids' father, but they look too much like Mick."

"Let me get this right," Dalene said, pausing the massage for a moment. "After you divorced Mick, you still dated him whenever he was in town. And when Amy was married to Jasper, she also got with Mick, who might be the father of her kids."

"Right. And as soon as I met my guy, Amy and Mick hooked up again, only secretly, thinking I never knew. But by then, her little girls had become fountains of information, and spilled everything that went on in Amy's house for the price of a cookie."

"And now she's marrying Mick while you have a broken engagement. Somehow, that doesn't seem fair."

"Not so bad. I don't have to be married to either one of them, so it works out pretty good for me!" June said.

"What do your parents think of all this?"

"Oh, they're ex-hippies. All this spouse swapping stuff is pretty ordinary for them, even though they both talk a pretty good morality line these days."

Dalene laughed. "Well, it's good thing you'll be living here on Maui and the rest of them on the mainland. Otherwise, fur might fly."

June thought of some of the workouts she and Mick had done together, and the overly-aggressive outcomes. "Or blood. But Amy really is my best friend. I'm going to miss her and the kids."

"Well, our time is done," Dalene said, covering June's body with the sheet. "I hope the wedding goes well."

***

Twice a day, June checked on the progress on the house, and saw big changes each time. To her eye, the whole thing was being dismantled one stick at a time, scraped, cleaned, and painted, before being reassembled. Even the carport was being worked on.

To show her appreciation, she brought a cooler of beer each time she visited, filling it with Mick's favorite union-made beer. If it was good enough for a retired grunt, it should be good enough for young ones, she figured.

While Marines on furlough worked on her house, she ran errands for Amy's wedding, collecting more wine, making final arrangements for flower displays and decorations, checking in with the caterer, and visiting the church and minister. Mostly it was a matter of making the final payments to each, using Amy's credit card. When Friday rolled around, her private squad of Marines handed over the keys to her house. They even had a ribbon cutting ceremony at the front door.

Gunnery Sergeant Jacobs took June a few steps away, ostensibly to take a picture of her standing in front of her new house.

"Ma'am, I'm sorry, but we did our best with trying to find that creak in the floor."

"I've heard it a few times also. Do you know what room it's in?" she asked. Of everything about the house, the one thing that annoyed her were the creaky floorboards.

"We always seemed to be on the opposite side of the house when we heard it. Maybe in the hallway. When you do find it, just crawl under the house and put a few screws up between the gap to close it. That takes care of most noisy floors."

"Thanks."

"There's something funny about this whole deal, Ma'am."

"Oh?"

"We generally don't do things like this. The resort, the extra furlough time, the coolers of beer. You must have some pull with someone."

"I suppose I do. But let's just leave it at that. Just know there's a lady on Maui who appreciates everything you guys have done, a lot more than what you realize."

They took one last look at the house as the men packed up their things. "Well, it'll be a nice place to raise a family."

"Family? Fat chance on that ever happening," June said to herself as the Marines drove away.

She went back to the house for another inspection tour. Getting her phone out, she called Jack.

"How does it look?" Jack asked on the phone while she was inspecting each room.

"It's perfect. They did an amazing job."

"Everything works?"

"The water runs, the toilet flushes, the outlets work, the lights come on. They even got rid of all the old junk in the carport and the old appliances. I just need something to sleep on."

"No furniture yet?"

"My stuff is supposed to get into port a few days from now, and appliances are coming from town next week. Amy and her entourage got here yesterday."

"How is she?" Jack asked.

"Surprisingly calm. Once she knew all of her micromanaging had paid off, she found a shaded chaise lounge and ordered a bottle of wine."

"Which is what you should be doing. Not many days left until you start work there, right?"

"Hey, you really have been paying attention to me. But yes, I've gone to the hospital a few times to make sure they have everything they need from me. That's almost got lost with everything else going on." June's sense of missing Jack right then was strong, almost a sense of isolation, being so far from him. She knew she was wasting his time with the call but just couldn't bear to be the one to end it. "I should let you go run the country."

"Today I seem to be running the world."

"Anything you can tell me about?"

"It'll be in the news by tomorrow. Nothing to worry about, though."

After the call, June went from room to room, mentally filling the house with the furniture that was still on its way. While standing in the living room, she heard a noise from down the hall, as if someone was stepping on a loose board. She looked but nothing was there, just an empty house, sunlight coming in through windows.

"Maybe not a family, but at least I'll have a ghost for a roommate." The creak happened again at the other end of the house. "Yes, my own little island spirit."

***

After Amy arrived on the island, along with her parents, nieces, Mick, and the other bridesmaids, June made it to each of the scheduled family meetings and dinners. Somehow, June's secret of moving to Maui had remained intact. Now that the time had come, June almost wished someone would've spilled. She could tell that her family was busy trying to jockey her and her sister into a position so they could talk, but she made one excuse after another.

It was the day before the wedding and Amy had deemed the preparations a success, telling everyone to relax and take life easy. June was about to burst, though, and was even feeling physically ill from the anxiety of withholding her news from her sister. She decided she needed to have that talk now if she was to enjoy any part of the wedding. But Amy had beat her to it by calling for a private meeting between them.

June found Amy already set up in her private cabana chaise lounge near the beach. Another covered lounge chair had been turned around to face in the opposite direction, both lounges pushed up against each other with only a small table between them. On the table were two drinks, an obvious mimosa in a champagne glass close to Amy and an empty glass waiting for June. There was also a plate of muffins and butter. In an ice bucket was the open bottle of Champagne waiting to refill Amy's glass.

"Amy, celebrating early?" June asked after settling into the shade of her lounge. She gave her empty glass a look but held off on filling it.

"You're not the one getting married tomorrow."

"And the booze is to keep you from backing out?"

Amy took a drink and set the glass down. "For such a big resort, there's a lot of togetherness here."

"Um…"

"Not you. I told you to meet me here, remember?"

June finally poured some juice, and began picking apart a muffin. It was still early enough to consider it breakfast. Something else she had done during the week was get daily runs to sweat off a few pounds, hoping her gown would fit better for the wedding. That also meant a few meals had been skipped, and the sweetness of the muffin and juice was strong. "So…"

"Between every one of our aunts, uncles, and cousins, and half the people I've ever worked with…"

"Most of whom are here on your dime."

"And Mom, Dad, and the girls…"

"It won't be much of a honeymoon."

"Right." Amy took a sip of her mimosa.

"What's this about a honeymoon?" a man asked. He leaned down and kissed Amy on the cheek, while June looked off into the distance. Even after so many years, it still stung to see Mick kiss her sister. "Somebody else is planning my honeymoon for me?"

"Hey Mick," June said, still avoiding looking directly at him. She smiled and waved at the little girls that were holding his hands. At some point in the last few days, Koemi had received the same haircut as Ruka, making them twins again. "No, what you guys do on your honeymoon is up to you. Not that I know anything about honeymoons."

The two little girls went to June, and promptly got their faces covered with kisses.

"Auntie, we're going to the beach!" one of the twins said. She was dressed in a red swimsuit with white polka dots, the other in an all-black thing with a tiny skirt. The scent of sunscreen was strong.

June aimed a warning finger at them. "And you won't go in the water unless…"

"Daddy holds our hands!" the other girl said.

The words stung June's heart, but she smiled. "That's right, honey. Be careful in the water and make sure to hold his hand really tight. A big, big wave might knock him over!"

Both girls giggled before tugging Mick toward the beach.

She watched as they walked away, her nieces holding the hands of the man in the middle, the man that had once held her hand, the man who had come in between her and Amy. June grabbed the muffin again and tore it in two. Once it was crushed into smaller pieces, she tossed bits into her mouth one at a time.

"You okay?" Amy asked after half the muffin was gone. She filled June's orange juice glass with Champagne.

June stared out toward the sea. "Never better."

Amy set her magazine aside. "He is their daddy, you know."

"Mick and the girls?"

"Yeah."

June took a sip of the Champagne and set it aside. She picked up a magazine, flipped it open, then tossed it down.

"Did you hear me?" Amy asked.

"I heard you!" June griped back. She stared out at the ocean again. Her mind hot with profanity. "I've always figured as much. They look more like Mick than that Jasper idiot you married. And they have Mick's eyes."

"When did you figure it out?" Amy asked quietly. "I don't think Mom ever has."

"Mom's not dumb. If I can figure it out, so can she."

"You've known for quite a while?" Amy asked.

"Maybe from the very beginning. I knew for sure a couple of years ago when I saw the three of them standing together. Pretty unmistakable." June took another sip of the Champagne, something she rarely drank because she never had liked it. Right then, any booze would work. With the second tilt of the glass, she finished it. "And by the way, Dad has it figured out, too."

"Which means I'm the family fool."

"Not at all. Maybe you were when you married Jasper, but as a family, we've decided to overlook that. You were dieting then and weren't thinking right."

The plummeting mood between them broke with their shared laughter.

"But seriously, you're good with it?" Amy asked after blotting her eyes with a napkin.

"Yeah, Sis, I'm good with it. Nothing could ever change how I feel about the girls. Anyway, their daddy will be raising them."

June refilled their glasses with Champagne.

"What about you, Babe? Ever gonna make one of your own?"

June ran her hand over her belly, feeling the surgical scars under her tank top. "You know there's not much chance for that. Only half the equipment necessary and I'm not so sure it's working right anymore."

"Takes a guy anyway. Unless you do the test tube business."

"The old-fashioned way is more fun. The problem is finding someone that can put up with me."

"Done deal with Jack?" Amy asked. "Have you talked with him lately? He must be thinking of you since he sent a gift."

"He's a little too busy these days to chat on the phone with a commoner like me. But yes, we talk every now and then."

"Well, I say move on. Out of a million or so eligible men in LA, you can't find one?"

The opportunity had finally come. Amy had opened the door for June. All she had to do was take advantage of it.

"Not looking there anymore." June emptied the last of the bubbly drink into her glass and swallowed it down.

"Well, let's see," Amy said. She started enumerating on one finger at a time. "There was the male model in Japan. Then the car washer that suddenly moved to San Diego. The over-worked firefighter. The married detective. Then the other detective that lives three thousand miles away from you."

"Not to mention one or two creepy guys along the way."

"And don't forget America's President."

"Yeah, him." June slumped down in her chaise lounge. "Quite the collection."

"At least you got a ring from him."

"And it looked dang nice on my hand, too! For a whole week, anyway."

She wasn't going to dig up long buried skeletons to mention her first marriage to Mick. It was hard enough to keep secret her current standing of being married to Jack.

"But you have a better idea?" Amy asked.

June turned on her side to face her sister. Her head spun a little from the first booze she'd had in far too long.

"Since we're on the subject…"

"Spill it, Babe. Something's been on your mind ever since we got here. We haven't talked in weeks, and I know something's on your mind."

"I'm branching out to here."

"Here? To Hawaii? That's a long way to…"

"Just let me finish. This is hard enough, you know? I would've told you sooner, but I didn't want to upstage your wedding."

Amy looked at June, but remained obediently quiet.

"I'm moving here, Sis. I already have a job at the new hospital here in town, and bought a house. I've already started remodeling."

"You're moving? Here? But what about…"

June ignored her and kept talking fast enough to not get interrupted. "I've resigned at Mercy. I already have medical licensure and credentials at a hospital here on Maui, plus two other islands. The new hospital here needs a neurosurgeon and made me a good offer. I'd be in private practice again, but for the time being I'd be able to use one of the hospital clinics. At least until I get office space of my own." June looked Amy in the eyes. "I start next week."

Amy sat up. Not much rattled Amy, but this did. "Next week? Moving? What the heck?"

"Already moved, actually. I'm here to stay. I won't be going home with you guys." June gulped some air, wondering what to expect.

"I don't understand. You never said anything."

"Remember when I came here a while back?"

"You finally took a decent vacation. So?"

"Kind of fell in love with the place. No one knows it, but I've been back to look for a place to live and to check out the hospital. It's taken almost a year to get things arranged. Now, as soon as the wedding is over, I move on with my life here on the island."

"But…"

June interrupted. "The climate, the slower lifestyle, the clean environment. You and Mom have been harping at me to get some control over my life and health. It turns out Maui is the control valve that I need."

"But that dinner at your house last week. I saw you there, your furniture, everything you own," Amy said.

"That was my last night there. All that has been packed into a shipping container and is on its way here."

"And that's why you dragged me out to the garden. You wanted one last moment of us being out there together."

"Kinda sentimental about it," June said quietly.

"You could've told me so I could've said goodbye, also."

"Look at how blue the sky is, how clean the ocean water is, the green mountains all over the place. Have you seen any of this island?" June wanted to go on about something Henry had told her months before, something she was just getting a peek into, about how the island had a spirit of its own. "Same temperature every day, steady breeze, and when it rains, nobody cares because it's not a cold rain."

"You're moving here because you like the weather? Nobody throws away everything they've worked for because they like the weather somewhere else. June, you're not a teenager!"

"I just want to start over with something new, something all my own."

"Something all your own? Babe, everything you've accomplished in your life has been by your own doing. You've had two fantastic careers, fashion and medicine, and even built that organic farm with your own two hands. And I mean literally with your own hands digging in the dirt. How is that not being successful?"

"Because it has all ground me down to a stump, or at least my soul, anyway. Somewhere along the way, all I learned how to do was work. I'm absolutely clueless as to how to have fun. I couldn't attract men because of being too grumpy and now that I'm nearly forty, I'm afraid having a family has passed me by. I'm not willing to give up anything else." She tried picking up her glass of

Champagne but her tremor kicked in at the worst possible moment. "I just want to enjoy what I have in front of me. Whatever that might turn out to be."

Amy drained her glass and poured another. "Well, this is upsetting."

"This isn't easy for me, either"

"But you bought a house? And how can you afford to buy something on Maui? That county hospital doesn't...didn't exactly overpay you. Why didn't you come to me about the house? I could've bought the old place to keep it in the family."

"Think about it, Sis. Did we ever meet there anymore? Granddad and Grandma left years ago. Even Dad and Auntie didn't want the place. Sure, they grew up there, but they've moved on. And it'll be another twenty years before Ruka and Koemi would be interested. You would've had to rent it out, and who knows to who?" June shrugged. "The last time we were there, I had to drag you out to the garden. It was time to move on."

"You loved that place. The garden, Granddad's garden. Nobody will ever take care of it the way you did."

"I didn't have time for it any more. As much as I loved being in it, the garden had become just another chore."

"But..." Amy began. For a change, a tear was coming to her eye first. She waved down a waiter passing by and ordered a bottle of locally made wine.

June waited until the waiter had left with the empty drink glasses and ice bucket. "The buyer will keep it up."

"They'll dig it up with a shovel the day after they move in."

"You remember Becky, my office manager? She's the one that bought the place. After her parents passed a while back, she inherited some money. Between selling her place and using the inheritance, she didn't need much of a loan to buy my old house."

"I would've thought she'd come with you. But what about her brother, Rodney? Don't they live together? And what about your little farm?"

"He moved in with Becky. And I'm keeping the farm, mainly so Rodney still has a job. He promised to take care of Granddad's garden, and I trust him." June had already convinced their parents of the plan, and for the most part, herself. Amy was proving to be tough about it. "But none of that matters."

"It does matter!" Amy said, just as the waiter poured two glasses of wine for them before he left. "You're half my life! How can you leave me?"

"You have Mick, the kids will be in school soon, and you have your own businesses to keep you busy. I have to schedule an appointment through your personal assistant a month ahead of time just to have lunch with you."

"Babe, come on."

"I have to do this. In fact, it's been overdue. For almost forty years, I've been doing what everyone else expects of me. I put myself through college and medical school on the money I earned as a model. And as a model, I grinned at so many camera lenses that I lost track of when I was sincerely smiling or just hamming for an advertiser. Now I spend half my time grinning at fathead hospital administrators that use me as a tool to earn them money. Or picking bullet fragments out of gangbangers' skulls and spines. Isn't that something you're always griping at me about? And you've got to admit, my dating luck these last few years hasn't been so good."

"But…"

"But here, none of that crap would exist. My past would finally become history. A small hospital where I could take care of people that need my services rather than just want them. It's warm and sunny every day of the year. Fantastic places to go for runs."

"And maybe meet a guy to fall in love with," Amy said back quietly.

June thought of her simple wedding with Jack, and the promise there would be a real one in the future. That little secret would be too much to spring on Amy right then. "One hurdle at a time."

While Amy poured wine in her own glass, June switched over to juice, the wine turning a little sour in her stomach.

"Well, I don't know about you, but I got all day to sit here and get drunk while you tell me about this new lifestyle you're developing."

"We have your wedding rehearsal later, remember?"

"And we can stagger in together."

They clinked their glasses together and swallowed. June wasn't sure if it was too much mango pulp, or simply the excitement of the moment, but her stomach flipped again.

***

June was sharing her parents' room for the night before the wedding, just to spend time with them. Her parents were getting older, the family was changing, and everyone wanted one last piece of yesterday.

On her way back to their room after an evening run, she stopped in the resort's convenience store and went right to the feminine hygiene section. Finding what she needed, she paid and went back to the room. Her parents were out for a walk on the beach, so she had some time to herself. In the bathroom, she used the device and set it on the counter, turning the indicator side away so she couldn't watch. She sat on the toilet seat humming the *Jeopardy!* theme song several times until she thought enough time had passed. She looked at the stick, tapped it on the counter, and looked again before wrapping it in toilet paper and hiding it in her luggage. Checking at the time, she had just enough time to shower and dress before her parents got back from a sightseeing tour.

Other than the bridesmaid dress she would wear the next day, the linen outfit she'd bought on her recent trip to Washington DC was the classiest thing she had to wear to Amy's rehearsal dinner. After all the running and the slight nausea she'd felt all week, she had lost a few pounds, allowing the dress to fit more modestly than before. With the small jacket off, half the back was open, and it was time to show it off. A sleeveless silk blouse with an open back and a hem on a pencil skirt that barely made it to her knees would be perfect for a balmy evening on Maui. And with matching beige canvas flats, a bit of makeup, and some shine in her hair, she looked as good as she could get. The last thing she put on was a

South Seas golden pearl necklace Amy had given her as a birthday gift the summer before.

It was a night for making impressions. Everyone at the dinner had known June all her life, including top models from around the world, advertisers and European fashion designers, and a horde of others that had been a part of Amy's fashion lifestyle. One last time, June wanted to show off she still had a figure and could knock dead any camera lens aimed in her direction.

Looking at the fit of the dress, reality set in. She knew she was five pounds too heavy for it. Just as she was considering changing clothes, there was a knock at the door.

"Yes?"

The door cracked open. "Dear?"

"Yeah, Mom. Come on in."

"We're ready to go to dinner."

"Close the door."

She sat on the bed next to June. "Feeling sad it's Amy's wedding and not your own?"

"Maybe at first, but I'm over it. Seeing the girls so happy with Mick makes it worthwhile."

She held June's hand, something unusual for them. "What is it then?"

"Have I been stupid, moving here?"

"We've been over that. I thought you were settled about it? You have your Dad and me convinced, and Maui is a nice place. Amy is planning to visit every year at Christmas and wants to send the girls here in the summer. From what I've heard, you and Mick are back on good terms. What's to worry about?"

"Things are going to change."

"You knew that, Dear, even before you moved here."

"No, I mean more than what I expected…or planned for." June got up from the edge of the bed and went to her suitcase. Retrieving what she hid there earlier, she took it to her mother, unwrapping the tissue from it. She gave it one last look, before handing it over.

A pink plus sign still appeared through the little window in the stick.

"It's yours?" Mabel asked.

June sat on the bed next to her mother. "Today, about an hour ago."

"Who is it?"

"Remember I disappeared for a few days a while back? I went to Washington DC to see Jack," June said. A smile formed and quickly spread across her face, which instantly hopped to Mabel's face. June took the stick back and wrapped it in the tissue again. "But I need to check it again before I get too excited. False positives are pretty common with these things."

When they were done hugging, Mabel dried June's face. "What are you going to do?"

"Start a family. Funny, Amy just accused me of acting like a teenager. It seems that I am."

"No, you're not. You're just in love with a man that's impossible to marry."

June was bursting to tell her mother about the quick wedding held in the Oval Office, but kept it corralled. "Seems like it."

"The timing is certainly…"

"Interesting?" June said to interrupt. She continued to blot her wet eyes.

"When will you know for sure?"

"In another month. I need to find a GYN here, and with my history, who knows what might happen." June looked at her mother, full of seriousness now. "But please don't tell Dad, and especially Amy. I've already upset her wedding enough. I doubt she could take much more from me."

They hugged again, until there was another knock at the door.

"Yeah, Dad, we're coming."

June wiped her face one last time, before applying more makeup. With so many people from the fashion world at the dinner, puffy eyes just wouldn't do that evening.

***

After gossip was shared, the toasts were given, the speeches made, and the dinner eaten, the party broke up. If there was one thing Amy brought home from modeling in Europe for a decade, other than a massive bank account, it was how to run a social scene. It took Amy almost no time or effort to get people out of the resort restaurant dining room that had been reserved for them, and back to their rooms. It had been an eclectic group of old friends, close family members, and the groomsmen and bridesmaids. June could tell Amy had had enough as she shook hands one last time with the guests before the next day's ceremony.

"Go for a walk? Seems like a nice evening for a stroll on the beach," her father said to June when they were outside and dismissed by Amy.

"Sounds good, Dad. Just don't force me into a sappy father-daughter talk. I've had enough heart to heart talks lately to last me a lifetime."

To June, it would've been the perfect time for a romantic walk beneath the palms with Jack. Handholding, flirting, and promises that would never be fulfilled. Her father would have to do. When they got to there, they carried their shoes in their free hands.

"You look great, by the way," he told her.

"Thanks. It's always nice to get a compliment from a man. I'm not sure how much longer I can pull off looking great."

"Keep eating right, get exercise, and your figure will turn heads for years to come."

"And it's a little weird hearing that from my own father, Dad. Anyway, the figure is about to go out the window."

"Maui food is more fattening than at home?"

"No." Was it time to break the news to her father? "I made a little discovery this afternoon."

"What's that?"

"You might be a grandfather again."

"Amy's pregnant?"

June sighed. "Not that I'm aware of."

He stopped walking. "You are?"

"Good deduction, Dad. But it's not certain yet, and I'm not so sure how viable the pregnancy will be if I am."

"Is that good news?"

"Ordinarily, yes. The timing isn't so good, though. I've got a ton of new stuff on my plate to deal with. Being pregnant is a giant helping of something rather unexpected."

"Your mother knows?"

"I told her right before dinner. Nobody else, though, and I'm keeping it that way."

"That's why she kept smiling at you all throughout dinner, giving you more to eat from her plate. Do you know…"

"Jack."

"Oh."

"Mom will fill you in on the details once you're home and out of earshot of Amy. That's the critical thing here, that Amy doesn't find out until weeks after she's home from her honeymoon. Capisce?"

"Got it." He gave her a thumb's up and started walking again. "When you said viable, what did you mean?"

"That's a medical term used in describing the potential survivability of a fetus." June went on to explain to her father about the rape she'd suffered a few years before, how it had resulted in a tubal pregnancy, and emergency surgery had been required, resulting in the loss of one ovary and tube. "Because of that, the probability of me bringing a pregnancy to full term is pretty low."

"Is there anything you can do to help increase the odds?"

"Like stand on my head during a full moon? Not really. I have to be careful with getting exercise but not overdo it. Eating right, no booze, low stress, staying positive, getting in to see a high-risk obstetrician is about the best I can do. Once an ultrasound is done to see if it's tubal, then I'll know how to proceed. Until then, keeping our fingers crossed, and keeping Amy out of the loop so she doesn't try and micromanage my health, is the best we can do."

"Yes, she definitely would do that. What's tubal?"

"There's a tube that goes from the ovary to the uterus. Occasionally, conception happens there and the fertilized egg gets stuck in the tube rather than dropping to the uterus, the womb. That's what happened to me before, and I never knew it until the tube burst and turned into a mess."

"I never heard about that," he said.

"Something else Amy managed in my life. Mom never knew until a while back."

"Any other secrets the rest of you are withholding from me?"

"Wow, Dad. How far back do you want to go?"

"Maybe I shouldn't know. What's the deal with Jack? Is he going to do the honorable thing and marry you?"

"Well, you may as well be the first to know. We already are married."

He stopped dead in his tracks, a gentle wave washing over their feet. "You and Amy are quite the pair, considering the mischief with men you've gotten into over the years."

"You don't know the half of it."

"And just exactly when was this wedding?"

"Last week. I went to DC for a couple of days. I just wanted to tell him in person about moving to Maui, and offer something of an apology for how I treated him the year before."

"From the sounds of it, he accepted."

"Dad, please. But one thing led to another, and the next thing I knew, I was saying 'I Do' in the Oval Office."

"How romantic."

"Well, he's promised a real wedding once he's out of office."

"Do the two of you really expect to carry on a long distance relationship for that long? Four years could easily turn into eight, and everyone knows you won't move into the White House and he won't quit at one term."

"We're taking it one day at a time, just like any other marriage. And this is something else Amy doesn't need to know about until the right time comes, which I will deal with in my own way."

"Have you given any thought to how you're going to manage your schedule at the hospital and having a baby, and then raising it alone?"

"I've only known for a few hours, and right now I'm trying my best to not freak out. I just want to get through Amy's wedding tomorrow and everybody home safe and sound before I start worrying about something new."

They stopped to sit on a bench that faced the ocean. In the dark, June could see little of the great body of water, but the sound of the gentle waves lapping at the shore gave the moment a peaceful feeling.

"You know, I have an idea," he said.

"I thought you would."

"Once the house is ship-shape and you've settled into your routine at work, your mother and I could move in and help out."

"Oh, now wouldn't that be nice. A single pregnant girl living with her parents."

"It wouldn't be like that, June."

"It's exactly like that."

"Your mom could help with the pregnancy and I could do some work around the house."

"It sounds tempting. Jack's wedding gift to me was to find some guys to do a quick remodel on the house this last week." June took a deep breath. "It's such a little place, though. Tiny bedrooms with no space for a true nursery in the same bedroom as me. I'm already thinking of adding on a room. Is that something you could help with if I found a builder?"

"I could do it myself."

"You're not a carpenter, Dad. You're a retired florist."

"I'd have nine months. It would save you a lot of money."

They left the bench when a soft sprinkle began to fall. "We'll talk later. I can't start any more projects right now. As it is, I'm barely holding things together."

***

The next morning, June was up early. She had something to do that morning, and she couldn't put it off any longer. During their meeting the day before, Amy had suggested—in a very strong way—that June talk to Mick.

"For what?" she had asked.

"You guys never did break up formally."

"Break up? Amy, I haven't dated Mick in years. There's nothing between us. He's all yours."

"That's what he said. But I'm not so sure you've said it to each other. I want the two of you to break up with each other."

"Amy, do you know how psycho that sounds? You want your sister to break up with a guy she dated a long time ago, on the day of her wedding."

"Is it any more psycho than anything else right now?"

And so the time for it came. It was one of those moments in life that couldn't be avoided, a simple scene that would only become more complicated with each passing word. June would never again feel Mick's strong arms holding her; never again would their lips meet; never again would his masculine scent be left behind on her pillow. It was gone forever, and somehow she had to put a lock on both their hearts.

She put on a pair of jogging shorts and a favorite old T-shirt. Stuffing her feet into sneakers at the door, she went out to find Mick already waiting in the resort parking lot.

"How far you want to go?" Mick asked as they jogged up the driveway.

"Down through the little town. There's a public beach down there with a drinking fountain." Because of her big news from the day before, June still needed the exercise, but needed to tone it down a little. That meant shorter distances, easier paces, and better hydration. "That's become my turn-around point."

Mick set the pace, just slightly faster than what June wanted. She forced him into an easier gait, and was even able to spit out a few questions as they ran.

"Big day. Holding up okay?" she asked.

"I'm surprised Amy hasn't freaked out."

"She has everything planned out to the last detail, and somehow it all came together."

"Like always."

They got to the park and June slowed to a stop at the drinking fountain. Instead of drinking, Mick only watched the ocean nearby.

June wiped sweat from her face with the back of her hand.

"Just like old times," Mick said, looking at her. "Working each other into a sweat on a Sunday."

June smiled. "That was good training. I learned a lot from you, and Jukey."

"As if fighting like a Marine will ever do you any good."

"It already has. You have no idea how much." She muscled out a smile. "Actually…"

"What?" he asked.

"I have to apologize for what I did the last time we sparred."

"Both of us got kind of aggressive that day. Don't worry about it."

"We always worked well together, didn't we?" she asked, a sharp pang in her heart over what was coming next. It wasn't just coming, but tumbling out of control.

"We did. In a lot of ways. We were good together…when we were actually together."

They stood looking at each other. Mick seemed eager to get going again.

In the past, she would've wanted to take him back to her house, hide him away, to spend the day in passion with the man that had been on her mind and in her heart for so many years. He had broken her heart so many times, and she decided it wouldn't happen again years before. Anyway, Jack filled her heart to over-flowing. She really was over Mick, except for saying those last few words.

She listened to the tug of war between her heart and her mind. It got out of control once her soul got involved. Pushing it all aside, June looked in his eyes, desperately hoping he would understand what she was about to say.

"But it can't be that way any longer, Mick."

"What do you mean?"

"You're marrying my sister in a few hours. You and I have gone our separate ways."

He shrugged. "So?"

"No more Sundays at the gym, no more runs, no more time alone, no more anything."

"Whatever you might be thinking, I'm over you June, and have been for a long time."

That pang of hope or jealousy or sorrow she had felt only a moment before suddenly turned to anger. Or self pity. It was hard to tell right then. Too much was crashing together in such a short time. "You have no clue of how much that hurts me, do you?"

"Can't hurt too much, especially since you took up with a President, someone just about impossible for any other woman to reach. I heard about the quick little wedding in the Oval Office."

"Does Amy know?"

"Not yet. In your family, it's only a matter of time. I know a lot more than what you realize."

June's face flashed red, not from embarrassment, but anger that people had been talking behind her back far too much. Right then, she wondered to what extent. "What do you know about it?"

"Big wedding plans for the future. You'll be marrying into wealth. Or you already have. I also heard about the squad of grunts that worked on your house."

"How'd you hear about that?" she asked.

"That gunny in charge of it was an old buddy of mine. He put the Kato names together and gave me a call. It seems Jack has a lot of pull in a lot of places."

"Oh? Does that hurt you, knowing some other man is paying attention to me?"

Mick finally went on the defensive. "How many times did you wander off to someone else, just as we were getting close?"

"Me?" June couldn't believe what she was hearing. "How many times were you shipped out to some rocket crater behind enemy lines? And every couple of years, you re-enlisted for more instead of staying home and being with me. Do you have any idea how many times you broke my heart? Do you have any idea how many nights I couldn't sleep, wondering what might be happening to you at any given moment? And that was when we weren't even together!" She turned to face another direction.

"Until I got out."

"And you immediately went to Amy."

"Come on, Babe…" he started. It was the nickname Amy and Mick had for June since childhood, and they were the only two allowed to use it.

"Don't Babe me. Don't ever call me that again."

They turned away from each other when a van parked, and waited for a surfer to carry his board to the beach.

"We should get back," he said. "Busy day."

"You go ahead. I'm going to wait for a few more minutes."

She wanted to have a good cry, something long overdue.

Mick reached to her, touching her arm. She shook him off.

"No."

He ran off, back in the direction of the resort. It took a monumental effort, but she didn't watch him recede into the distance.

She ran for a few minutes until she found a nearby bench that looked out at the ocean. Feeling a light breeze kick up, she listened to the palms shudder and gentle waves wash across the beach. As much as she wanted them, the tears never came.

"They deserve each other."

She set her hand on her tummy and thought of Jack.

"I've got something better."

***

June's maid of honor gown was a sleeveless pale peach taffeta, with a high waist, a white crepe bodice, and a hem that reached almost to the floor. She wore a pair of diamond stud earrings, a gift from Amy to the bridesmaids, June's just a bit larger than the other girls'.

Her phone rang just as she and her parents were about to leave for the ceremony. Answering while climbing into her father's rental, she learned that a truck was available to deliver the container of household furnishings she had shipped from LA.

"You have to deliver it today? I'm a little busy this afternoon."

"Look, lady, the container is already loaded onto the truck's trailer. You want it taken off and delivered another day, that'll cost you extra. Then we put you at the end of the list, which means in a week or so. You want your stuff or not?"

She finagled a deal to have them call her when they got the shipping container to her house. It was only a five-minute drive away from the site of the wedding reception, and it would be easy enough for her to dash over and sign delivery papers. All they really had to do was leave the shipping container somewhere near the house.

"Good news," she said to her parents after the call. "My stuff is here a few days early, and they can deliver it today. I can finally move into my house. Yay!"

"All you need are appliances, right?" her mother asked while they rode along.

June touched her tummy. "Appliances, food in the fridge, stuff for a nursery. I don't know how I can make it work."

"If anyone can find a way, you can, Dear," her mother said, gripping June's hand.

They got to the estate, the site for the wedding. It was surrounded by high lava rock walls, with abundant flowering plants and trees, the ocean just beyond the house.

Tak whistled. "Some place."

"I'm surprised Amy didn't buy it," June mumbled.

"What a lovely setting for a wedding," her mother said.

"Can't get any classier than this for a wedding," Tak said.

'Getting hitched in the Oval Office wasn't so bad, either,' June thought.

While her parents mingled, June went around shaking hands, kissing and having her cheek kissed, and smiling to old friends from the fashion business for probably the last time. Guests were being seated by ushers, bridesmaids and groomsmen chatted near a gazebo covered with flowers, but after an hour Amy and her mom were nowhere to be found. After a quick search, she found them in the house, still trying to get the dress just right.

"Mom, go see if Dad needs something to drink. Babe, deal with this bodice, will you?"

Once their mother left them alone, June went to work on Amy's dress.

"I heard you and Mick talked this morning."

June worked on the folds in Amy's gown, getting them arranged just right. "You don't have to ever worry about us going anywhere near each other, Sis."

"So I heard. You're cool, calm, and collected, right? A fistfight between the two of you isn't going to break out at the altar in the middle of the ceremony?"

"Only if he starts something."

One of the bridesmaids came in to let them know the minister was ready to get started.

"The gown's fine, Babe. Do something with this bodice."

June reached in to adjust Amy's breasts to get the fit perfect. "Okay?"

Amy touched her head. "This flower thing on my head okay?"

"It's fine. The dress is fantastic, your makeup is perfect, and the flowers couldn't be fresher. I think it's time."

"Yeah, time," Amy said, shaking nerves from her hands.

"Unless you're having second thoughts?"

"About marrying Mick? No. It's just that every prominent fashion photographer is out there, including several from bridal mags."

"So I saw. Makes me a little nervous also."

"You'd think the two of us wouldn't be nervous before having our pictures taken for a magazine spread."

"Of the few million times shutters have opened and closed with us in focus, I never got used to it."

They went to the door to go out but stopped.

"Babe, you should've stuck with those commercials you were making. You were halfway to stardom with those."

"Going into medicine has worked out fairly well. But why are we talking about this right before you go to the altar?"

"Because it's the last time we'll ever talk as two single women."

June chuckled. "Yeah, single."

June found the small bouquet of gardenias that Amy would hold during the ceremony. She touched them lightly, thinking of her moment in the Oval Office for the hundredth time that day. Gardenias had always been a favorite of hers. She took them back to Amy. Outside, they weren't quite as ready as what they'd been told, so Amy sent her out to find out what the holdup was.

June discovered Mick and the girls were just coming in. Mick was dressed in a sandy-colored suit, his necktie tied snug around his neck. The girls, one the flower girl, the other the ring bearer, were dressed in tiny taffeta dresses that had Amy's eye for design all over them.

"You girls sure look pretty today! But no playing outside until after Mommy's ceremony, okay?"

"Mommy said if we don't play rough or make noise, we can stay at your house tonight!"

"And have dinner with you!"

"And you'll take us to the beach tomorrow!"

"Auntie, do you have a new house?"

June crouched down, realizing just then she had neglected to have a long talk with her nieces. She never had told them directly she would remain behind when they went home.

"Yeah, honey. I'm gonna live here now."

"Why?"

"Because I want to live here," June said quietly.

"Can we come for sleep-overs?"

"You'll have to fly on the big airplane. But you sure can! Any time you want!"

"Auntie…" Ruka started to say, but was interrupted by her grandmother's touch on the shoulder.

"Honey, we have to get your mommy's ceremony started, okay? But we're gonna talk and play all night long at my house, okay? But be good girls for Grammie."

She watched as they went to their proper positions, getting a refresher of what to do from their grandmother.

***

The ceremony went off perfectly. Women blotted their eyes, men shifted uncomfortably in their seats, Koemi and Ruka behaved themselves, and most of all, Amy was the living image of bridal perfection.

Then came the reception line-up, the last big task of the day before June could finally relax and get a meal. The first order of business was to congratulate the bride and groom. June had no idea of what to say, and couldn't remember what she had said at Amy's first wedding, also an extravagant affair. But the big moment was coming, and she needed to think of something.

Words came to her mind. 'Deserve the best', 'the perfect life', 'Heaven forever', all of it sounded contrived and lame.

The right words came to her just in time. She smiled brightly when their eyes met. June could tell Amy's eyes were just as wet as hers.

"Try to get this one right, Sis!" She smiled even more broadly and leaned in to kiss Amy's cheek. "I'll miss you," June whispered in her ear.

She stepped over to face Mick and stuck her hand out. A smile appeared on her face as if by magic.

"Congratulations, Mick." She leaned in to touch cheeks with him, giving him a polite but meaningless one-handed hug. Close to his ear, she whispered, "Just remember, if anything ever happens to my sister or the girls, I'll hunt you down like a rabid dog."

June took her place in the line, shaking hands, receiving compliments, holding back warm emotions that insisted on welling up. Photographers' bulbs flashed, and fashion and gossip magazine journalists wrote on pads and whispered into small recorders.

During the reception, music played softly, and a few couples were dancing. It wasn't until mid-way through the meal that June's phone rang with a call from the movers. They were at the house waiting to for her to come and sign for her things.

"They're here," she whispered to her dad.

"Who?"

"The truck drivers with my stuff. They're at the house, waiting."

"We need to go there now?" he asked.

"It's Sunday and they're union, Dad."

He practically leapt from his chair. Ten minutes later, they were at her little house. The delivery truck was there, lowering the container to a gravel pad next to the kitchen door of the house.

She paid them for the delivery service by credit card, and off they went. With a set of keys, she removed both padlocks from the rear doors. Once her father had the doors open, she saw her household belongings from LA.

"Can't really unload anything right now," he said, looking at the tight pack job that the LA movers had done.

"Not that I want to, but we should get back to the reception. It's up to me to make some sort of clever but raunchy toast."

In the half hour they were gone, they weren't missed.

The reception lingered on, and by the end of the afternoon, June felt as tired and whiny as what her nieces looked. Amy looked even worse. June barely ate, having only a salad and a piece of cake, washed down with iced tea and one sip of champagne for the toast. Having two left feet on the dance floor, it was pointless to pursue that, just to prolong the day.

"Amy, I gotta go. I'm taking the girls for a drive, but we'll stay in Mom and Dad's suite tonight. My stuff from LA came today, so I can finally start playing house tomorrow. If you want, the girls can stay with me for as long as you want."

"Sure?"

"Take a vacation, have some fun."

"I already have little bags packed for them."

"I saw them in Mom's room. They'll be fine."

They used Tak's rental sedan for the scenic evening drive, June driving. They got to a popular beach and resort area called Kihei on the other side of the island. What served as beach and tourist activities support in the daytime turned to entertainment and restaurants in the evening, something a little too mature for the girls. Still dressed in their formal taffeta dresses, they found a small homestyle restaurant to eat at, a place June had discovered on a previous visit.

Walking in, they were out of place. The other patrons were dressed in T-shirts and shorts, definitely a local crowd. A tiny Filipina waitress beamed when she saw June in her gown and makeup, and the girls in their dresses, before showing them to a table.

"You just get married?" the waitress asked. "Where's the groom?"

"Ha! No, my sister."

"My mommy did!" Koemi said.

Ruka stepped forward. "My mommy, too!"

June ordered bowls of noodle soup for them all, and a plate of vegetarian sushi, popular items at the little restaurant. June layered several napkins over the girls' dresses with the hopes of keeping them clean.

"Sleeping with you tonight, Auntie?" Ruka asked.

"If you don't mind sharing a bed with me?"

Both the girls squirmed with excitement.

"Grampy will be there and he can snore pretty loud. Is that okay?"

"Daddy snores loud, too."

Koemi meant Mick.

"He sure does."

"How you know Daddy snores loud?"

"Oh, uh, your mommy told me once. But guess what? Starting tomorrow, we get to stay in my new house for a few days! Won't that be fun?"

They both nodded, slurping long noodles from bowls.

"You girls will have to help me, though. You can pick out your rooms."

"Is it a big house, Auntie?"

"Not as big as my other one, but it sure is pretty."

"It's your princess castle, right, Auntie?" Ruka said.

"It sure is!"

"Is your prince in it?"

"Not yet but maybe someday."

"And then you'll be king and queen, huh?"

"That's the idea."

"Is it a pretty castle?" Koemi asked.

"You'll see it tomorrow, okay?" She dabbed her lips and pushed her bowl of cold noodles away. "Ready to go?"

The girls slept in the car on the way back to the resort. Letting the kids into her parent's suite, June got them undressed and into bed, before flopping down in the TV room with her father.

"Mom's in bed already?"

"Not much of a night owl these days. Nice ceremony."

"It couldn't have gone any better."

"Think any further about your mom and I visiting for a while?"

"A little. It's a good idea. Can you let me settle in first?"

"Do you have anyone who can help unload the truck tomorrow? You're supposed to be taking things easy, right?"

The only people she knew on the island were Elaine the realtor and Henry, the nurse who taught her how to surf. Elaine wasn't a friend, and it had been several months since she'd made contact with Henry.

"I guess my first task is to start making friends." She made a point of making eye contact with her father. "And not a boyfriend, so don't start gossiping."

He held up his hands in surrender. "Given up on listening to gossip. It only causes me trouble."

"Can you and Mom help? The girls can carry small boxes while Mom puts things away in the kitchen. You and I can carry the larger things."

"I don't want you stressing the baby, June."

"Dad, right now the baby is about the size of a pinhead. It would be impossible to stress it. Anyway, growing up with me as its mother, the kid will have plenty of stress to endure. It may as well get used to it."

They watched the replay of some baseball game on the TV for a while, giving her time to think.

"You know what? I'll take you up on your offer of moving in for a while. But you'd have to promise to do things my way and not to take over the house."

"We don't want to interfere. Just help out a bit. Your mother and I looked earlier at the house and think an extension off the back for a master bedroom and bath would be perfect."

"That's what I've been thinking."

"I'd be glad to do it for you, and I promise I'd get help whenever I needed it."

"Fine. In the next few weeks, I want you to learn everything you can about construction methods in Hawaii, and county building permits or whatever is needed to build something like that. If you can plan it all out, all the lumber and pipes or whatever that's needed, I'll take a look at it."

A smile broke across his face, and June couldn't help but smile back at him.

***

At the end of the week, June ferried her parents to the airport while Mick drove Amy and the kids. It was an extra-hard moment for all of them, since June was staying behind.

"Dad, send me those plans once you have them finalized. Mom, brush up on contemporary maternity stuff. I'm going to need your help a lot more than you think."

"Everything's going to be fine, Dear. Just keep a good attitude and don't work too hard."

June saw a group coming toward the terminal. "Amy is here with her entourage. Time for you to go."

Mick had found a baggage cart and was loading it to take into the terminal. They all said their goodbyes, but June reached out and clung to Amy's arm one last time.

"This is it, I guess," Amy said to her. "We're all grown up now."

"Seems so."

"We all like your house and approve of the hospital, but you got to promise to quit keeping secrets from us, okay?"

"Yeah." June's lip began to quiver, and when she saw Amy's eyes tear up, the flood gates broke. "Take care of the girls, okay?" June said through sniffles when they pushed back from each other. "And when next Christmas comes around, send them here. It would be great to have them for a while."

"Me and the kids will make time for visits. Christmas on Maui sounds like a good idea."

"Mick too."

"Sure?"

"A week ago I wasn't so sure. But it's okay now. It's all just more Kato family history." She watched her nieces tag along on each side of Mick, their natural father, and newly wedded to their mother. "He's right where he belongs."

"What about you?"

Even though the sun was shining, a few raindrops fell on them from a dark cloud tumbling across the tropical sky. She thought of Jack in DC, running the country from the Oval Office, and remembered her wedding ring in the drawer of the Resolute Desk. June touched her tummy with the palm of her hand.

"I'm exactly where I belong, too."

Sinister Intent

The old car pulled into the loading dock at the end of the dead-end driveway. The driver maneuvered the car in the truck parking area, tires caroming off the curbs, until it was aimed back out. Unsure how long his errand would take, the driver quietly nudged the car door closed and went to the back entrance of the hospital.

With a simple wave of his hand, he made his way past the sleepy desk clerk in the Receiving Office, just inside the loading dock. He knew it was close to quitting time for the nightshift clerk, and if he worked it right, another clerk would be on duty by the time he left again. No one would see him twice, not long enough to get a good look at him.

He had never been in a hospital before. A disorienting, uncomfortable feeling crept over him in the clean and brightly lit corridor. Because of the early morning hour, the corridor was mostly empty except for a janitor buffing the linoleum floor. He walked past the whirring machine as if it wasn't there, continuing on until he got to an intersection with another endless passage. A sign hanging from the ceiling pointed him to the elevators that would take him up to the lobby. No one was there except a few early bird employees coming in the main entrance.

When he had driven by the evening before, the place looked small, simple even. But once inside, just finding his way through the maze of hospital corridors was hard enough that he considered postponing his job. He figured it might be easier to try a different way, a different time, a different place. The job was turning out to be more complicated than what he first thought.

He'd been approached a few weeks earlier, in a cheap Honolulu bar. He met two of them that night, one dressed too pretty in expensive resort clothes, the other too nervous for being on vacation in Hawaii. While the pretty boy drank expensive scotch and ogled the dancers, the nervous one barely knew scantily clad women were coming on to him. Whether they were friends on vacation or locals having a night out, they were the Chinatown bar's version of the Odd Couple.

It didn't take long before a conversation was struck up between the three of them. No names were shared. A simple job needed to be done, and the pay would be good, too good to pass up. He listened to the details for a few minutes. The Odd Couple were too eager, but as long as they kept feeding him expensive liquor, he'd listen. He had a good idea of what was coming; they wanted someone dead, and had a tight timeframe for it. They didn't care how he did it, a horrific accident on the highway, food poisoning, gang-style execution, as long as it didn't look like a hit. It would be up to him to decide.

Over his fourth glass of scotch, he gave it some thought. Five grand in cash would come in handy. As an ex-soldier dishonorably discharged in shame, he had the skills to kill. As an ex-con, he had nothing to lose. He agreed to meet them the next night at a more secluded location to talk details.

Meeting in the parking lot at the Diamond Head overlook, a place where people parked and no one cared what went on, he was given the particulars of the job. They had parked side by side, doing the deal out the windows of the cars old-fashioned drug deal style, something he was quite familiar with. The time came to know who had limited sunsets.

There was someone who worked in the hospital on Maui that needed to be dead. Sooner the better. Simple as that.

He was given a photograph, a slip of paper with a name and place, and an envelope of cash. Barely looking at the picture, he flicked his thumb through the stack of hundreds, the half now-half later type of deal. The flight to Maui and his room arrangements would be his problem, but the payday was good enough. They agreed to meet again after the job was done. Even if the Odd Couple reneged on the second payment, he still had a pocket full of cash.

It took only a couple of days to plan. He wouldn't waste money on a pistol. He wanted something quiet. He also couldn't risk making it look military, leaving a piece of evidence like that behind. It had to look gang-style, it had to be quick, it had to be easy, it had to be cheap. Most of all, it had to work the first time. There was no screwing up a job like this.

Not again.

He took his flight to Maui empty-handed. Getting off the plane, he went straight to the airport's long-term parking lot and jacked a 'Maui cruiser', an old junk car no one would ever notice on the road or care was missing. The fenders were rusted, the paint oxidized, the windshield cracked, and the door didn't close right. But it was easy to hot-wire.

His next stop was to find a knife worthy of doing the job, and easily tossed away later. By late afternoon, he had a room in a backpacker's inn in old town Wailuku, a small place hidden away and shaded beneath a giant banyan tree. At twenty bucks a night, he could stay for a few days and wait out the fervor of heightened security checks at the airport.

When the morning came, it was the sound of cooing doves outside the window that woke him. He was already late, but if he hurried, he could get to the hospital before too many people were around. The old Maui cruiser struggled to life with a backfire, but it got him to where he needed to go. Now, here he was, pacing through endless corridors, looking for one particular room, kicking himself for not doing at least a walk-through of the building the day before.

After one last pantomime to gain directions from someone who looked officious, he found the door marked LA-137, matching what was written at the bottom of the crumpled piece of paper in his hand. Not knowing what to expect inside the door, he hoped no more of the silly charades would be necessary. He just wanted to get the job over with. That far in, he felt more compelled than ever to go through with the scheme that had been laid out in front of him, what he was getting paid handsomely to do.

He hadn't done anything like this in a long time. The last time hadn't gone so well. His knees felt weak and his chest was tight. He reached forward, yanked open the door, and stepped in, all in one single motion.

Facing him were several old metal filing cabinets, a desk with an empty chair, with a single plain chair set next to it. Taking the slip of paper from his pocket, he was reluctant. He had two names on his list, two separate jobs to do. The pretty boy in resort clothes had returned alone the night after their meeting, tacking on the second name, doubling the payoff in the process. Dollar signs appeared in his mind, a solid reminder of why he signed on. He compared the name on the slip in his hand with the nameplate at the front of the paper-cluttered desk. Finding a match to the second name, he crumpled the paper into his fist.

There was another door in the opposite corner of the room tucked in between filing cabinets. He stepped over to it, cracked it open and peered through the gap. A man in a white jacket worked alone, his back turned, looking down at the task in his hands. The black slate table he was standing at was layered with racks of small plastic dishes, all in tidy rows and columns. The whirring and clicking sounds of several machines made a cacophony of noise that echoed throughout the room. Worst of all was the stink that hit his nose.

After watching the employee work for a moment, the man quietly swung the door closed again. He took the extra chair from the desk and jammed it up under the knob of the outer door to the corridor. He then locked the door. Assured no one could disturb him, he took a few steps to inside the lab to be alone with the man working at the table.

There was a stink of chemicals and something earthy. He had never before smelled either and could only describe it as disease. There was enough ambient sound that his slow breaths were hidden. He took a few steps forward to just behind the man, his footsteps completely lost in the noise of the room. It was the crunch of something under his last footstep that made his presence known.

The man in the white coat looked startled when he turned around.

They looked each other in the eyes, both as startled as the other. The man looked at his crumpled paper and compared the name to what was on the white jacket of the employee. One of the names matched.

"Arthur Silva?" the visitor asked.

"Who are you?" The man in white pressed his back against the high lab table behind him, a fruitless effort to back away. "You don't belong here."

"You Arthur Silva? Arthur Silva?" insisted the intruder.

The lab worker wore a forced smile. "Oh, you want the boss. I'm not Doctor Silva. He'll be back in few minutes. But brah, you really not supposed to be back here in the lab, especially dressed like that." He tried to motion the man back out to the office.

The man took the crumpled paper from his jacket pocket again and unfolded it. He looked at the name on the bottom. He pointed a bent finger at the name, then tapped it on the embroidered name on the worker's white lab coat.

"Arthur Silva," the intruder stated again with conviction.

With a nervous laugh, the technician tried stepping away. His path was blocked by the intruder.

The technician's speech picked up, telltale warbling sounds of frayed nerves in his voice. "Oh yes, good eye! I'm wearing his jacket today. But you see, I spilled some coffee on my own jacket this morning. It's still drying since I rinsed it out." His voice firmed up then. "But brah, really, you're not supposed to be in the…"

His explanation fell on deaf ears, or at least uncaring ones. With a movement as quick as it was natural, the intruder reached to his back pocket. With a click, a long slender blade snapped open. The lab technician stared silently at the blade with saucer eyes and a hanging jaw. With a half step, the intruder got to within arm's reach of the white-jacketed man.

"Oh my…" uttered the technician.

The technician tried to raise his hands, but with one quick swoop, the man slashed the blade across his neck. In a laser-fast backhand, he slashed back across the victim's neck on the other side. Blood gushed forward, even before the man could grab his throat. The dazed, confused look on the face of the technician told the story as he dropped to the floor. Thick, crimson fluid continued to flood between his struggling fingers.

The man stepped over the bloody body to a bank of sinks. He washed his hands, letting the water splash over his knife at the bottom of the sink. Yanking paper towels from the dispenser on the wall, he realized he had already spent far too much time on this part of his job. Carefully drying the knife and his hands, he went back to the door.

He hurried through the office, replacing the chair in its original position next to the desk. Unlocking the outer door, he passed unnoticed into the corridor. As quickly as that, his errand for the day was complete.

***

The stretcher thudded against the double doors of OR Room 4, guided in by Dr. Miller the anesthesiologist, an ER nurse named Henry, a respiratory therapist, and an orderly. Even Connie, the Operating Room charge nurse, hurried her way down the hall to be a part of the rushed parade.

With gloves on his hands, Henry pressed large wads of blood-soaked gauze firmly on both sides of the man's neck. The team moved the patient to the operating room bed before the stretcher was removed. Without a surgeon anywhere near, it was the ER nurse running the show right then. The community hospital was small enough that employees knew each other personally, and knew something about each other's jobs.

"Connie, be sure Doctor Soseki knows we're here in the room with the patient!" Henry called out, just as the stretcher was being pushed out the door past her.

Henry was no rookie when it came to trauma; he'd paid his dues in an LA hospital for several years before returning home to Maui. But on the quiet, cheerful island of Maui, a gang-style slashed throat was completely out of the ordinary. He looked around at the other nurses working frantically to get equipment set up and surgical instruments arranged, and he instinctively knew they were overwhelmed with the sudden arrival of the emergency patient.

He called out to Connie again. "And while you're at it, find someone to help him."

"I've already called Soseki, and he's on his way in from home," Connie shouted from the door, never actually entering the room. She was vigorously sucking on a lemon drop in her cheek. "So early in the morning, I can't find any other surgeons in house right now to assist. But where's Doctor Cabrera? She could help with this."

"Just as we rolled out with this guy, a massive heart attack rolled in the door unannounced. Plus, there was a school bus accident, some kids coming in. It's mayhem in the ER right now and Cabrera is focused on that, just like I should be."

"What do you want me to do?" Connie asked.

"I'm a little out of my element here. Just try to find someone to help in here, please."

With that, the OR supervisor turned on her heel and went back to the front desk and her lemon drops, leaving the clamorous room behind.

"Ahh, trauma," the anesthesiologist said. "You gotta love it."

"Maybe you have to," Henry said. "I sure don't. That's why I live here."

Busy keeping the flow of blood in check, Henry watched Dr. Miller quickly apply vital sign monitors. After that, the anesthesiologist gave syringes of medications in the intravenous line to prepare for his next task. With his scope in one hand, he slid the endotracheal tube into the patient's windpipe. He inflated the cuff, hooked up the circuit tubing that lead to his anesthesia machine, and squeezed oxygen into the man's lungs. Watching the chest rise, he turned on the anesthetic gases and taped the tube securely in place. As Miller worked, Henry pressed mounds of blood-soaked gauze on the patient's neck, quickly scrolling through his mental list of any surgeon that might already be at work that early in the morning. An extra pair of hands were needed, and now.

"Henry, what's the story on this guy again?" Dr. Miller asked. He took another look at the patient's pupils before closing his eyelids.

"Lab tech working alone in the lab, found down in a pool of blood by one of his co-workers. They called a Code Blue, and he was brought to the ER for treatment on a spare stretcher. It's anybody's guess who slashed him, but he has wounds on both sides of his neck. The carotid on the right looked transected. Cabrera tried getting clamps on. No other injuries. Unknown medical history. We typed and cross-matched him for four units of blood."

"Any word on his labs?"

"H and H were both low, crit at twenty-eight the last I heard. Want to transfuse?" Henry asked.

"Not yet," Miller said. "He looks Hawaiian. Not that it has anything to do with transfusing him."

"You probably know him, or at least have seen him around the hospital. Kekoa Baxter. Worked here since the place opened five years ago. Old family on the island. Everybody knows the Baxter family."

"The Baxter Family? That big house in town with the museum?"

"One and the same, only nobody lives there anymore," Henry muttered, watching Dr. Miller start a second intravenous line. "I wonder where Soseki is?"

Meredith, the other nurse in the room, spread antiseptic skin prep solution on the patient's face, neck, and shoulders. Whenever Henry let up on the pressure, a new flood of blood would well up. One of the clamps that had been placed in the ER wasn't doing its job.

Dr. Miller watched. "Just reclamp it, Henry."

"You suppose Soseki would mind? He's pretty fussy about who does what with his patients."

"What he doesn't know won't hurt him. Anyway, he's not here in the room. Until he gets here, this isn't his patient, he's ours. If it keeps the patient from bleeding to death, who cares who puts it on?"

Henry hesitated.

"Consider it a doctor's order."

Henry carefully lifted the wad of gauze, opened the useless clamp, dabbed with the gauze again, then replaced the small clamp in the correct position, closing the vessel, stopping the rapid pulsations of blood coming from the heart.

He heaved a sigh of relief.

"Thanks, Henry. Saved the day for us again," Meredith, the OR nurse, said. After Henry stepped away, Meredith began positioning the patient's head, continuing to prep the surgical site. "See if you can find Soseki out there."

Outside the room, he found Dr. Soseki already at the scrub sink vigorously washing his hands and forearms with a bristle brush. He was getting more of the disinfectant soap on his shirt and floor than on his hands.

"He's here, already scrubbing," Henry told the others when he went back into the room for a moment.

"He's not coming in to see the patient?" Miller asked. He was still new at the hospital and hadn't learned staff idiosyncrasies yet. "He could at least do some sort of evaluation."

"Yeah, well, wait till you work with him," Henry said quietly to Dr. Miller. "I don't know what he's like here in the OR, but in the ER, he's a real piece of work."

"Isn't he retirement age?"

"Beyond. But he's the only vascular surgeon we have right now. Between you and me, West Maui Medical Center would be better off with someone right out of training than Doctor Neal Soseki. Maybe what he did in New York years ago with a team of residents helping him might've worked, but it doesn't work here."

When he saw through the little window Soseki rinsing his arms at the sink outside, Henry began to excuse himself again. He was done there, and only wanted to get back to his real work in the ER.

"Here comes His Excellency." A glance at Dr. Miller made him make a double take. Henry and Dr. Miller, "Millertime" to his surf buddies, were good friends away from work, instantly becoming friends with their dry senses of humor and abilities to ride shoulder-high waves. "What in the world are you laughing at, Millertime?"

"I'm just keeping a list for your boss of all your improprieties. But I'm running out of paper!"

When Soseki eventually strode into the room with his wet hands raised before him, soapy water draining from his elbows, he looked around. "Where is everybody?" he demanded in less than a jovial tone, and without a greeting. He looked down at the patient's neck. "What's the big emergency? The patient is barely bleeding."

"Both carotids are clamped. We were hoping you could tell us who's assisting you. Connie is on the phone trying to find an assistant, but is somebody coming from your office?" Miller demanded.

"I'm supposed to have an assistant. I can't do this alone! Someone find me an assistant!"

"You have Tiffany to help until someone else gets here." With a quick salute to Millertime, Henry left.

As soon as he was at Connie's desk, Henry could tell she hadn't found an assistant surgeon yet. At dawn on Maui, surgeons were either just getting up, or out on a surfboard catching the first waves of the day.

"Connie, I know someone that might be able to assist."

"Who?"

"There's a new neurosurgeon at the hospital, just moved here from LA. I saw the announcement in the hospital newsletter about her starting to work here."

She looked up from what she was doing. "People actually read the newsletter?"

"Aren't we supposed to?"

"What's his name?" Connie asked.

"Her. June Kato. I bet she'd love to have a case to do, to do some work."

Connie found the number listed for June and made the call, asking if she could come and help with an emergency case in the OR.

"Right now, I'm sitting here in an empty clinic. What's going on?"

"Fifty-something-year-old Hawaiian man, well-loved on the island, lab tech at the hospital, found with his throat slashed just a few minutes ago. Right now, our one and only vascular surgeon is hopefully getting control of carotid bleeding, but without an assistant."

"The thing is, this is my first day. I'm supposed to be in meetings starting at eight o'clock. You can't find anyone else?"

"The ER is swamped," Connie said. "It's that magic hour, when most surgeons are still on their way in."

"It's nearly seven o'clock! How late do people sleep here anyway?" she asked, hurrying for the door.

"Welcome to Maui time, Doctor Kato."

***

June went into OR 4 with a headlight on her head, her loupes settled on her nose, and a surgical mask across her face. From where she stood, she could see blood welling up from the patient's neck. Water continued to drip from her elbows as she held her hands aloft, waiting for a towel. She had already spoken to the nurse in the room about getting a sterile gown and gloves out for her to wear. She dried her hands and got ready for her surgical garb.

"Your assistant is here, Doctor Soseki," Meredith announced.

He looked over his shoulder at June, then snapped his head back to the bloody neck wound in front of him. "I don't want some nurse to help me! I need a doctor."

June's and Meredith's eyes met only briefly.

"My name is Doctor June Kato. We haven't met yet. I'm new here at West Maui Medical Center."

"Who are you? Some gynecologist just out of residency? Not enough pregnant women on this island to keep you busy, so you're branching out into vascular surgery?"

June had her gown and gloves on by then, and went to the table where Soseki was working. The nurse attached the light cord for her headlight and switched the light source on. What was created was an intense spot of light wherever June aimed her vision. She made a quick assessment of the injury and what the other surgeon had already accomplished. The more serious injury was directly in front of her, two clamps already in place and controlling the blood flow. Soseki was working at the opposite side, the less injured artery.

"Actually, I'm a neurosurgeon, ten years out from residency and a fellowship." She got a gauze sponge from the scrub nurse and took the suction tip in her hand to begin assisting. Soseki had clamps in place and had already dissected down and exposed the thick artery, the largest that went into the head. With each beep of the EKG machine, the vessel bounced. "I'm only new to Maui, not to surgery, and certainly not to invasive carotid procedures."

"Bully for you." Dr. Soseki held his hand out to the scrub nurse and asked for a vascular clamp. "I'm the busiest vascular surgeon on the island. I'm in someone's neck at least once a week. How many carotid procedures have you done recently?"

"I was averaging just over two hundred a year in LA. But I had a bigger population to pull from there."

"Well, we finally have a neurosurgeon on staff here," he snarled as he worked. "That will certainly help improve consumer base. One thing that is lacking around here is a sound financial base of operations."

June tried to recall if she had read any medical journal articles authored by Soseki, anything on carotid surgery, anything at all. The name Soseki was unusual enough that it would stand out in her mind, Japanese like her name, but it didn't sound familiar.

Soseki positioned one of his clamps, June dabbing the blood away with her gauze sponge. With her move to Maui, she'd been hoping to leave behind slashed throats.

She looked at the clamped artery, no blood flowing past it into the brain. Soseki's hands were busy positioning a clamp at the opposite side of the patient's neck. If he closed that clamp, the patient would get little blood flow into his brain, certainly not to the most important parts. It was a simple method of controlling bleeding, an archaic technique best left in the history books. June kept her face silent, but cringed internally.

"You don't like using a shunt until you get the artery repaired, Doctor Soseki? It could be placed on this side while you repair that side."

"Trying to take over my case already? You just got here."

"No, not at all. I noticed you have this side clamped already. If you clamp that side also, this man won't get much blood to his brain." June knew she had just crossed a line by telling another surgeon how to do his case. It was, in fact, a supremely bad way to start her first day at a new hospital. She didn't know the man's reputation, couldn't remember seeing his name on journal articles she'd read, if he had much clout at the hospital, but somehow she needed to backpedal a bit. On the other hand, the patient needed blood flow into his head, something critically important to a neurosurgeon and tantamount to the patient's survival. "I guess I'm just looking at it from a neurologic, and survival, paradigm."

Temporarily placing a plastic tubular shunt in the vessel would allow blood to continue to flow into the patient's brain while they worked, and give the surgeon more time, providing for a better repair of the damaged vessel. Both arteries, one on each side of the patient's neck, were injured, one severely. By using a temporary shunt, blood could continue to flow into the patient's brain around the area they were working.

Soseki shifted in his hand the small clamp meant to close off the vessel. He opened the clamp a bit, and lowered it into its proper position. Just before squeezing it closed, he set it aside.

"We should use a shunt for this," he said to no one in particular. Meredith heard him, and got one from a cupboard. The scrub nurse Tiffany prepared it before handing it over to Dr. Soseki. Winning the skirmish, June set down the suction tip and took a slender pair of forceps in her hand, ready to help place the shunt.

The tubular shunt was set in position, gauze sponges were placed nearby, soft rubber tapes passed around the large vessel, and clamps were set but left open. Everything was ready for possibly the trickiest part of the surgery: opening one of the largest and most important arteries in the human body and sliding in the shunt. If it went well, they'd breathe a sigh of relief. If it went poorly, disaster could strike. Because they were so tricky, some surgeons didn't like using shunts, June's assumption about Soseki.

June controlled her breathing into long, slow breaths that started deep in her belly. With a suction tip in one hand and forceps in the other, she was ready for Soseki to place the shunt.

"Meredith, watch the time for us, please," June said.

As soon as she said that, Soseki loosened the clamp on the vessel at the base of the neck, then opened the clamp where the vessel entered the head. Everything in position, he held his hand out.

"Forceps."

June set the shunt into place, tucking one end into the end toward the heart. Opening the clamp there, they filled the shunt with blood before tucking it into the upper end of the injured artery. Sending an air bubble into the man's brain would be disaster, the biggest risk at that point, and it had to be done without losing control over clamps and bleeding. Tips of forceps functioned in sync competently and silently, as if the two surgeons had worked together many times before. As one led the way, the other followed, performing the delicate and exact maneuvers needed for success. Elastic bands were used to hold the shunt tight inside the vessel. Once everything was in place, June stood ready with her suction tip. Dr. Soseki removed both clamps.

'Hallelujah,' June breathed silently to herself when there was a rush of crimson blood through the shunt and not out the artery.

"Does that make the neurosurgeon in the room happy?" Soseki asked with a hint of snark.

"Very," June said back, trying to keep her tone of voice even. "Blood flowing into the brain makes me very happy."

"Two minutes of clamp time, Doctor," Meredith announced.

"I've never liked those," Soseki said. "Too clumsy."

"Seems like it sometimes, huh?" June said back, trying to be diplomatic. She was still working on salvaging her start at West Maui.

As Soseki repaired the traumatic defects in the artery with slender monofilament sutures, June glanced up at the clock. She had already completely missed her first meeting, and was late for the second.

"Meredith, I hate to ask you for a favor, but can you make a phone call for me?"

June told her who to call and the message to give, and listened while the nurse made the call. Satisfied the message was delivered that she would be at her next hospital administrative appointment a little late, she turned her full attention back to the surgery.

"Only Monday morning, and you're late for meetings?" Soseki asked, still with the unpleasant hint in his voice.

"First day at the hospital and I'm already missing appointments."

His thorny eyebrows bounced. He had the long eyebrows that many Japanese senior citizen men had. "This really is your first day at the hospital?"

"Except for a quick walk through last week, this is my first real day of work. First case in the OR, first time to meet anybody, first time to miss scheduled meetings with administrators. Although that part doesn't bother me so much."

Soseki finished repairing the injured artery, and the team focused on the other side of the neck. "What was your name again?"

"June Kato. K-A-T-O."

"Well, Doctor Kato, why don't you take over and repair that side. I'd like to see your fancy LA technique."

It was another little jab at her and she knew it, but she went ahead and started the repair. As soon as the clamps were in place on the more seriously injured vessel, a thin strand of blue suture and needle clamped to an instrument was set in her hand. At one end, she began suturing the vessel closed again.

"You just moved here from Los Angeles?" Tiffany asked.

"That's right. In the last two weeks, I've bought a pickup truck, had my new but very old house updated, filled it with furniture, found new appliances, acted as maid of honor at a wedding, and started a pea patch in the back yard." June kept the fact to herself she was also a newlywed and recently discovered she was pregnant. In time, that would divulge itself. "I've been looking forward to starting work, just so I can get some rest!"

"Whose wedding?" Tiffany asked.

"My twin sister's."

"That wedding at that big estate last week?"

"Yep, that was my sister."

"I saw the pictures in the newspaper. There was even something on the local news about it."

June finished with one strand of suture and began working with the other. "Where Amy goes, cameras tend to follow."

"You gave up a practice in LA to come here?" Dr. Soseki asked. "Couldn't compete with the big dogs there?"

"I think she was one of the big dogs," Dr. Miller said from behind the screen that separated him from the surgical site.

"Oh?" he asked.

Miller noticeably ignored Soseki. "We've been expecting you, Doctor Kato. I've been reading some of the journal articles you've published these last few years. Good stuff."

"You had nothing better to do on a day off on Maui than read neurosurge articles?" she asked.

"I have a strong neuroanesthesia background, one of the reasons the hospital recruited me," Miller said. "It looks like we'll be working together quite often."

"Me too," said Tiffany. "And Meredith. We'll be your primary team for neuro cases."

June got another instrument with a new needle and suture attached, and began the repair of the vessel from the other end. Slowly, she made tiny railroad track stitches, meeting up with her first stitch in the middle of the damaged artery.

As she focused on her task, they shared their backgrounds, training, and educations. They had a few things in common, that Miller had done his training in Los Angeles also, just at the competitor training program to where June had trained. They traded a couple of good-natured raspberries about each other's universities, and had a good chuckle.

"Looking forward to our new team," June said.

By then, she had the vessel closed, and it was watertight when the clamps were off again.

"Six minutes of clamp time for this side," Meredith said. "That must've been some wedding."

"Who cares about a wedding at the beach?" Soseki said. "There must be a dozen of those every day of the year."

June tried her best to ignore him once again, but this time. "For most people, wedding day is the biggest moment of their lives. Why not hold it in a beautiful place like a Maui beach?"

"Good for the island economy, if nothing else," he muttered.

Once Soseki started to suture the wounds closed, June begged off to go to a meeting. She stepped away and removed her surgical gown.

"Does your husband like Maui?" Tiffany asked before June left the room. It was obvious she was digging for gossip.

"I'm here alone, actually." June shrugged. "It was time for a change, so here I am."

"Oh, so you really were a failure in La La Land and landed here to start over?" snapped Soseki.

"People who have lived and worked their lives there have earned the right to call it that. Others do not." With that, June left the room. Before the door closed, Meredith went out with her.

"Doctor Kato, never mind Doctor Soseki. He has that old-school mentality that doctors are men and women should be at home making babies."

"That would make for a pretty boring workplace, Meredith." June couldn't help but smile for a moment. "But who doesn't like a wedding?"

***

With no further meetings to attend or patients to see in the clinic, June went to lunch early, finding a place on a shady patio. She hadn't brought much, just fruit and salad in Tupperware, and coffee from the cafeteria urn. Wondering how she was going to fill the rest of her day at the hospital, and how she was going to earn money in the next few weeks or months, at least until patients started coming to her clinic, someone came to her table.

"Mind if I join you?" Meredith asked, a lunch tray in her hands.

"Of course." June pushed her things aside. "How was your morning?"

"Much better once we got rid of…once we were done with that first case with Doctor Soseki. Not much of a welcome to you on your first day here. Sorry about that," the nurse said.

"Never mind. Just two surgeons marking their territory. Just out of curiosity, is there some sort of backstory about him? I've read his hospital bio and a few things online, but that's never the real story."

"He's okay, I guess. He's a good surgeon, but his attitude gets in the way of his work."

"What about his attitude?" June asked.

"Well, for as poorly as he treated you, he's even harsher on the nurses. The patients are real happy with him, either." Meredith ate slowly, looking like she was trying to decide how much she wanted to divulge. "Apparently, years ago, he was big stuff in New York City, and everybody swooned over him. But he's here now, and we're not swooning. I guess it's a cultural thing, that big shot doctors in New York get swooned over for all the fancy education and things they've done, but here in Hawaii, we swoon over people who are nice to each other."

"That's the impression I've got, and one of the reasons why I moved here. People here are just plain nice to each other, and with no strings attached. Pretty different than what goes on in big cities. But tell me about Kekoa Baxter?"

Meredith smiled. "Kekoa is about the sweetest man you could ever meet. That's what's so strange about him getting slashed. Everybody likes the guy."

"Could he have turned on someone, maybe got threatened somehow and threatened them in return?"

"You saw him. Kekoa is a big guy, but he's so gentle. He's just a big Teddy bear."

"What exactly is his job?" June asked.

"Officially, he's a phlebotomist. He's been working here since the day the place opened. I've heard he also works on special projects for the lab director. But his real job is spreading his good mood all over the hospital, especially with the kids. Their faces light up in giant smiles when they see him."

"That is odd that someone would want to attack him."

"Do you know how he's doing?" Meredith asked.

"I saw him in the ICU a little while ago. He's in a sedation coma, something Soseki did to keep him calm and quiet for a couple of days to give his body a chance to start healing, and his brain a rest. Otherwise, things seem okay."

Meredith leaned forward to speak quietly. "When you say give his brain a rest, what do you mean?"

June wondered if she had said too much and needed to do some damage control. "Oh, not much to it. With both of his carotid arteries open like that, his brain got a reduced amount of flow to it for a few minutes. That's back to normal now, but keeping him sedated allows his brain to recover from the minor and temporary insult. I do the same thing with all of my carotid patients, in fact, with all of my craniotomy patients."

They talked for a few more minutes about what June was expecting in the OR, and how Meredith would be one of the nurses often working with her. When the nurse returned to work in the OR, June took herself on another lonely tour of the hospital, once again wondering how big of a mistake she'd made in moving to Maui.

***

The day wasn't long, but by the end of it, June had had enough of meeting administrators, department heads, and nurses while touring the hospital. Even with the unexpected surgery to start her day, she still had enough time to stop in at a supermarket. With all of her tasks in the last two weeks, she was still learning her way around her new community.

Carrying a bag of groceries in one hand and her briefcase in the other, she got in the back door just as a soft afternoon sprinkle started. She kicked off her shoes, letting the screen door clatter closed.

"I thought it didn't rain on this side of the island," she said, setting the groceries on the kitchen table.

Almost immediately, her phone rang with a calling number that seemed familiar. Answering, it was Henry, the nurse at the hospital. They caught up on a few pleasantries about the house and her move.

"Do that case with Soseki?" he asked.

She began putting away the things she had bought. "Yep. Did my first case at West Maui Medical Center. First crack out of the box, and I'm working on an attempted murder victim. I thought I left all that behind in LA."

"It went well?"

"Surgically, yes. I'm not so sure I made any friends today, though."

"Something happened with Doctor Soseki?" he asked.

"I almost slapped him, but otherwise, the patient survived and that's what matters. Not the first time two surgeons didn't bond in the OR."

"No ideas on who might've done it?" he asked. "Slashed Kekoa?"

"I never heard anything. But there were almost two attempted homicides today at the hospital. Same victim, too."

"What else happened?"

"Soseki was going to cross-clamp both carotids at the same time, then repair them one at a time. Not so good for blood flow into the brain, you know?" June finished putting away the groceries and sat at the table with a glass of juice. "He's the best vascular specialist the hospital has to offer?"

"He's the only one. He's waiting until the hospital can bring someone on board before he retires."

"That might be a little overdue," June muttered. "I met the neuro team I'll be working with."

"Millertime, Meredith, and Tiffany? They'll be dedicated to you?"

"I ate lunch with Meredith, and then chatted with Millertime or whatever you call him while checking out the ICU. He said you guys go surfing occasionally."

"He's been trying to get me on a wind board lately. Have you been out since that lesson I gave you?"

"Not yet but I want to learn. Maybe just on some gentle waves at first." June took her empty glass to the kitchen sink and ran water in it. "Henry, explain the concept of Maui time to me."

He laughed. "Maui time means whenever someone can get to it. Your priority list might not be the same as mine, but it's mine that matters to me. We'll get to something whenever."

"Does that mean surgical start times are somewhat ambivalent?"

"Start times, appointments, store opening and closing times, everything. And don't try and change it or you'll run into a brick wall. Mauians are fiercely loyal to our way of doing things."

"How in the world can the hospital function like that?"

"Somehow, it does. Maybe not always efficiently, but the work gets done."

"That's going to be hard for me to adjust to. Is there anything I can do?" she asked.

"To maneuver people into doing things your way? I doubt it. Just make friends with the people you work with. Once we decide to like you, we'll bend over backwards to help. But heaven forbid we don't."

"Why?"

"Those ladies at the hospital can be brutal with their gossip."

"Great," June sighed. "I heard you had a baby?"

"I've become a family man since that time we met. Other than spewing formula for distance and accuracy, the baby's fine. For as much as he brings up his meals, he somehow grows. Complete medical mystery to me."

"Well, don't ask me for advice. Anything maternity is a mystery to me."

Once she was off her call, June grabbed a brochure she found in the OB clinic, 'What to Expect When Expecting,' and settled into a chair.

***

An ancient nervous quirk that she'd never completely overcome, June bit at the tip of a fingernail, then set her hand at the side. Stirring her bowl of ramen, she took her first slurp of noodles, her dinner that evening. A gecko squirmed out from under a picture on the wall and dashed around the corner to the screened back door.

"At least I have a pet to keep me company."

It was the first time she'd heard it in a few days, but the sound of a creaking floorboard came from down the hall. She went to where she thought it was and checked doors and windows. Finding nothing but a breeze that was fluttering the simple curtains she'd put up, she stepped here and there on floorboards in the bedrooms and hallway. She stood still for a moment, waiting to hear it again. Completely unsatisfied, she went back to her dinner.

June sighed when she heard it a second time, almost as if it was mocking her. "And a ghost."

She watched as the gecko stared at a moth fluttering around the back porch light outside. It lost interest when an ant crawled along the doorframe. Dashing forward, it flicked its tongue once, getting an easy meal.

"The great outdoors, right here in my kitchen."

The gecko went back to watching the moth while June continued eating her noodles.

"I suppose you deserve a name, since you're keeping ants out of the house."

The gecko repositioned.

"I don't even know if you're a boy gecko or girl gecko. How do I tell that? Lift your tail and take a look?"

The gecko squeezed through the gap to go outside, taking up a new position on the screen to stalk the moth.

"For some reason, you look like a Herman."

While June watched the hunt, the gecko crept closer to the moth one or two steps at a time, until the moth fluttered off.

"Well so much for the wildlife safari," she muttered, taking her bowl to the sink.

***

Following her ancient habit of turning on the coffeemaker and putting a bowl of instant oatmeal in the microwave to cook while she showered, June started Tuesday morning with a yawn.

Wincing at the flavor of the oatmeal, she checked the box for freshness. Getting rid of that, she put two slices of bread in the toaster and drank coffee while waiting.

"So, when does all this fun of living on Maui start?" she muttered when the toast popped up. Taking a bite, she shoved it back in the toaster again and adjusted the burn setting.

Waiting another minute, she took her blackened toast back to the table where she read another brochure about the early stages of pregnancy.

After eating only one slice of the burnt toast and reading half the brochure, she left the table.

"This really is pathetic. Almost forty years old, single, living alone, no foreseeable money coming in, and taking crap on my first day from a workmate. Really good idea coming here, June."

She washed her dishes and drove to work.

"Time to start cutting back on the caffeine and taking in more protein. I should find a high-risk OB one of these days. It won't be cheap, either. Just exactly who do I ask about that without divulging I'm pregnant? The last thing I need is gossip going around about me on my first week at work."

When she saw the sky beginning to lighten over the ocean, she pulled to the side of the road and watched, delaying her trip to work.

"Maybe this is what they mean by Maui time."

Once she was at work, she looked through the hospital directory for names of obstetricians that specialized in high-risk pregnancies. She was expecting to be labeled as that, because of her age and previous gynecologic problems. Seeing only one, she called that office.

"Doctor Borwin's schedule is completely filled, over-booked, in fact," the scheduler said. I could get you on his schedule for a year from now."

"Fine with me but I think my baby might not want to wait that long before being born."

"Maybe I should schedule you now for when you have your next baby?"

"Let's just take this one kid at a time, shall we? Is there anybody else at West Maui Med that takes high-risk patients?"

"There's a new one at the hospital, Doctor Gill," she said.

"A man or woman?"

"Woman. Nobody knows much about her. Gossip has it she just finished her training and did some sort of fancy fellowship in difficult deliveries. The hospital worked pretty hard to recruit her. West Maui Med is trying to compete with the other hospital on the island."

"So I've heard. What's her full name?"

"Divya Gill. Has her clinic in the hospital. I'm sure she's accepting new patients. It's so hard for new doctors to get patients, especially in a small place like Maui."

"Tell me about it. She's right out of training?" June asked, one hand stroking her flat tummy. She knew it wasn't going to stay that way for more than a few more weeks. She got the phone number for the office before hanging up.

"Do I want to trust my one and probably only baby to someone right out of training?" she muttered as she went through the list of doctor's names again. "A gynnie residency training is four years. Mine was nine years. Plus, two more years in a fellowship. So, pardon me if I get a little picky over who delivers my baby."

Instead of calling for an appointment, she let the idea percolate through her decision tree for a while longer. By the end of the morning, June had finished the last of the welcome meetings at the hospital, mostly clearing away the remainder of administrative details. With one final handshake, she was a full-fledged member of the West Maui Medical Center ohana, such that it was. It left her with just enough time to get a bite to eat in the cafeteria.

She found a set of elevators that would take her down to the cafeteria on the ground level. Waiting along with a pair of Filipina nurses, both with lunch bags in their hands, June wondered what might be served in a Hawaiian community hospital for lunch.

When one elevator door opened, she stepped forward and held the door for the two nurses to enter. They both smiled and waved her off. June shrugged and went on her way down. She grabbed a tray and got in line at the food steamers. By the time she was through the line to get food, the cafeteria seating area was busy.

"Is the pancit vegetarian?" she asked the serving lady behind the counter.

"Chicken kind pancit," the lady said. She was small, dark, and her chef's smock was smudged with illustrations of the lunch offerings. "Ono today!"

"Ono?"

"Tasty!"

With a scoop of steamed rice and soggy spinach on a plate, along with a large glass of lemonade, she made her first trip into the sunny dining room. At first glance, she could see all the tables were occupied. With nowhere else to go, she took a lap through the room, hoping to land a spot. No empty tables were available, but she saw a chair at one. Perched at the table were the two Filipina nurses that waited for the second elevator.

"Mind if I join you?" June asked, approaching the table.

They cheerfully nodded her to take the empty chair and chatted with her a moment. After introductions, June learned they were both nurses and had been at the hospital right from the opening day, even leaving old jobs at the other hospital on the island to work here.

The two nurses finished their meals and prepared to leave.

"But better be careful about that elevator you took before," one said to her quietly.

"Oh? Why?"

"Haunted."

The other one took over with the explanation, in a hushed voice. "What she means is, it was the place of the first death at the hospital."

"Really? In an elevator?"

"Story goes, they were taking a guy from ER to ICU. The elevator got stuck between floors for a while. He coded in there. You know, Code Blue."

"When they finally got to a floor and the door opened, the guy was dead. Never got him back again."

"That's sad," June said, not entirely believing the tale.

"These days, that same elevator still works funny, you know?"

"Doesn't always stop at the right floor, especially around lunch time."

"That was the time the guy died, right in the middle of the lunchtime rush."

"I see."

They departed, leaving June alone. Once she was finished, she looked at her watch, and still had time before her next appointment, something new that had been made only that morning. She stowed her tray on a cart and walked back through the dining room, keeping a small bag of pretzels in her hand for later.

She saw one person dressed in a lab coat sitting alone at a table meant for four. Long glossy black hair was draped over a young woman's chest. Slender and dark-skinned, she didn't quite fit in with all the other dark-complected women in the cafeteria. Suspecting who the young woman was, June smiled, getting one in return.

"Mind if I sit here?" she asked the young woman with a smile. "Not many tables available right now."

"Sure, please," the woman said, politely aiming her hand at a chair. She folded her newspaper and set it aside.

As soon as June sat, she saw the embroidered name on the woman's white jacket.

"Oh, you're Doctor Gill. I've heard about you."

"You have? Really? I've just started working here recently," she said with a hint of singsong to her voice, entirely different from the local accent many people had on Maui. "Nobody knows me."

June introduced herself and they shook hands.

"Let's see, this is August, which means you just finished training this summer, right?" June asked.

"Right. I've only just started last month. But how did you know?" Dr. Gill asked.

"Believe it or not, you're an old-timer here compared to me. This is only my second day."

They chatted about where they had trained in Los Angeles, discovering they had trained at the same institutions, only a decade apart, and compared notes on old professors. They shared a good laugh over a couple of their medical school instructors.

"Have you been busy?" June asked, getting around to the next point in her mind.

"I have a lot of competition from the larger hospital in town. They took me here because of my background in difficult deliveries. Otherwise, I'm just another obstetrician on the island waiting for girls to get pregnant, and doing basic gynnie stuff in the OR. As busy as these island ladies are in the bedroom, it's so hard to get a client base here."

"I suppose women are pretty faithful to their obstetrician, one baby to the next?"

"Unless something goes wrong. Pretty morbid idea, that my practice involves high-risk women and their pregnancies." She lowered her voice to a mumble. "At least I'm not working in a clinic for women who were forgetful about birth control, if you know what I mean."

June could feel her face warm up, and knew she was close to blushing. "Yes, well, that would be me."

"I'm sorry! I meant…"

"I know what you meant," June said with a smile. "It's not trouble, just a surprise. I never really thought I'd be in this position, at least not so easily."

"Nature often has ideas of its own."

June chuckled. "It sure does." She could tell her tablemate was looking her face over, at crow's feet and laugh lines, the tell-tale signs of middle age that could no longer be hidden with simple makeup.

"How long have you been married?"

"Time to tell a secret or two," June said quietly. There was no way she was going to explain about Jack at a lunch table in a hospital cafeteria. "Exactly for as long as I've been pregnant."

"From the looks for your figure, that hasn't been very long. Congratulations on both."

"Thanks. I' not entirely sure I'm married, though. It's a strange situation that's difficult to explain."

"You're not the first lady that's told me that. How far along are you?"

"Three weeks. Twenty-four days, to be precise." June tore open her bag of pretzels and offered some to her tablemate, watching the face of Dr. Gill. "This is my first, and even though it's hitting me like a freight train, I'm pretty excited.

"It's a joyous occasion then?"

"Of course! But before we go any further, are you interested in having me as a patient? Fair warning, I'd be coming in with a few issues."

"Who doesn't anymore?" At the end of lunch, Dr. Gill handed over a business card. They already had an appointment for that afternoon in her clinic for June's first maternity checkup. It turned out that Divya Gill wasn't any busier in her clinic than June was in hers.

June learned her way around the clinic she would be sharing temporarily, until there was space for her own neurosurgery clinic at the hospital. She saw four patients, all of them laborers with bad backs. Two had decent insurance, while the other two could barely manage to pay for that visit, let alone diagnostic tests and procedures. With them, she relied on old-fashioned diagnostic tests and skills she could perform right there in the clinic at no cost. The tests weren't perfect, but good enough to give her a good idea of the problems the men faced with their backs. She gave them instructional sheets that included exercises and basic physical therapies they could do on their own at no cost, with the hopes of getting back to work without costly surgery. By the time she plowed through several assistance programs that might be able to help pay for further hospital care, it was time for her own appointment with Dr. Gill.

Divya did a quick basic exam, impressed with June's level of health.

"You're definitely pregnant," she told June.

"I've done enough of those dipsticks, they should give me stock in the company," June muttered back.

"You get a lot of exercise. You should consider eating more. But let me guess, you're vegetarian?"

"Easy to tell, huh?" June answered. "My mother is already harping at me about eating more. But I run each morning, not as much as back home in LA, but some. I've actually gained a couple of pounds since moving here."

"You'll be gaining at least twenty-five more pounds in the next few months. And don't fight it. Just let it pile on." She covered June's lower body with the paper sheet and lifted her gown up to expose June's abdomen. "These scars…"

"Yeah, some history there. First, I had an ectopic pregnancy a few years ago, so I'm down to only one ovary and tube. That's the surprise I was talking about."

"I see. But back to the ectopic. What happened then?" Dr. Gill asked while palpating June's abdomen.

June swallowed, dryly. "Left over from a rape."

"I'm sorry," she said quietly. Dr. Gill covered her again and stepped up closer to the head of the narrow exam table. "Did they catch the guy?"

June stared at the ceiling, wondering how to answer. "It took a team effort."

"I hope he went to prison for a long time."

"Not long enough. Actually, it's a long story, something few people know. Maybe you should come over for dinner sometime. I could tell you the story and save some clinic time?"

"You seem very strong, at least about that. I think if it were me, I'd cry my eyes out every time I thought about it."

"That was me for a long time, but I'm done crying. I figure the jerk doesn't deserve the satisfaction of having a victim cry over what he did."

"That's a healthy attitude," Divya said.

While June dressed, they decided that evening was as good of a time as any to meet for dinner. June gave directions to her home, not far from the hospital.

With nothing else to do, June went back to the ICU to see if she could get in to see Kekoa Baxter, her emergency surgical patient from the day before. She had made rounds on him the evening before and again that morning, both times having a hard time getting past the police guard posted at the door. As she was walking into the department, Dr. Soseki was just walking out, seemingly in a huff.

"Doctor Soseki, good to see you. How is Mister Baxter?" she asked, trying to get his attention.

"And you are?" he asked, looking at her face.

"Doctor Kato. I assisted you yesterday with his surgery."

"Oh, yes. He's not doing as well as he should."

"Oh?"

He took her to a corner where they could talk privately. "I'm limited, you see, in his care. It turns out, he selected the cheapest insurance the hospital offers to employees, that state insurance plan. Garbage, if you ask me."

"That doesn't mean he shouldn't be doing well. But I heard he comes from a wealthy family here on the island."

"You're new here, Doctor," he said to her. "To these people, wealthy means something different than to the rest of the world."

"These people?" June asked.

"Native islanders. They just don't understand that healthcare costs money, and they don't take good care of themselves. And when they get in trouble like this, they expect to get things for free. It becomes a burden for the rest of us."

"A burden?"

"You've been a doctor long enough to know what I mean."

Hearing the words 'these people', and how he said it, got her ire up. "If you like, Doctor Soseki, I'd be glad to assume the burden of his care."

"Would you?" he asked, almost in disbelief.

"I wouldn't mind at all."

He turned on his heel and went back to the patient's chart. June watched over his shoulder as he put a note in it, turning Baxter's care over to her.

"He's all yours, Doctor," Soseki said as he left the unit. "Have a nice time."

June watched him leave, going directly for the elevator. She looked at the unit secretary sitting at the main desk. "Well, that takes care of that. I have my first patient."

"Good riddance," the secretary muttered.

June went to the police officer stationed just outside of Kekoa's cubicle. He must've overheard the exchange because he waved June right in.

She explained to the nurse at the bedside about the change in care providers, and introduced herself. A respiratory therapist was there, working with the breathing tube and ventilator machine.

"We've heard about you, Doctor."

"Oh?"

"We've been gearing up and doing continuing ed related to neuro patients."

June was impressed. "Well, thanks. But why is Kekoa still intubated? It's been almost thirty-six hours since his surgery. He should've been off the vent last night or this morning at the latest."

"Talk to Doctor Soseki about that," the nurse said.

"It's his lungs. We've been wanting Soseki to get a pulmonologist in here to see Kekoa, but he wouldn't order the consultation," said the respiratory therapist, the person mainly in charge of the ventilator, the breathing apparatus that fed oxygen to the lungs. "Every time we've tried to get him off the vent, he wouldn't take a breath on his own."

"That's the sedation," June said, scanning the medication sheet. "How much is he getting?"

"Just at night, our usual ICU protocol. Otherwise, he's off the sedation."

June put on a pair of exam gloves and pulled back one side of the neck dressing. "How long has this been red?"

"Since this morning. We told Soseki about that also, along with a small fever."

"And?"

"He just grunted," the nurse explained.

"He didn't order antibiotics or blood cultures?"

"The antibiotics he's got were in the OR," the nurse said. "I tried talking to him about that also but he blew me off, saying I should mind my own business."

"That is your business. The patient's health and recovery is your primary concern."

"To him, I'm just a nurse."

"Well, forget about him. We're all on the same team now, and that's Kekoa's team," June said.

June felt as though she'd fallen through some medical time warp, that nurses were expected to keep quiet and nod a lot when the doctor was in the room. She changed the dressing, and while doing so, ordered antibiotics to be given IV. She knew right then and there she would have to spend a fair amount of time going through all of Soseki's old orders for the patient, renewing everything. At the end, she hated to do so, but she looked in the very back of the chart, at the business page. Sure enough, the patient had the bare bones insurance program, something that paid the basics of hospitalization, and almost nothing in provider care. She took a copy for herself and left once she was satisfied the nurse was following all of her new orders.

She stopped at the police guard outside the door.

"Do the police have any idea of who did that to him?" she asked, peering down at the seated man.

"Absolutely none. But I'm just his guard, extra duty," he said. He mentioned the name of the police detective in charge of the investigation, and she made note of the guard's name, another Hawaiian name that was unusual to her.

***

June was just going in the back door when Divya Gill came up the driveway.

"Quite the adventure finding your house, June," Divya said, following June to the back door.

June laughed. "This far off the road, I won't get many door-to-door solicitors."

Divya got a quick tour of the freshly redone house. "Well, if I didn't know you were going to have a roommate in a few months, I'd try to figure a way of moving in here with you."

"Sooner than the baby coming, I'll have two other roommates," June said, getting dinner started in the kitchen. "My parents have talked me into having them here to help out for a while."

"That's good, right?"

"Mostly. I know so very little about anything maternity, I'll be leaning on you a lot. Hopefully my mom will take up some of that slack. Or at least not interfere."

"You're a doctor, June. You know a lot more than what you think. And I bet anything you were a lot more involved in your sister's pregnancy than what you let on."

"Speaking of that, what's the likelihood of me having twins?"

"Pretty high. You're a twin and your twin had twins. It might be a good idea to get two of everything." June brought two bowls of ramen to the table, along with stir-fried vegetables. "I noticed the bedrooms are small. Are you planning on keeping the baby in the room with you?"

"Somehow I need to cram a lot of stuff into one small room. But my dad has offered to add-on a master bedroom and bath onto the back of the house."

"Can you afford it?"

"I sank just about all my money into buying this place and in the move to get here. I'll have maternity bills coming up, and patients aren't standing in line at my clinic door. I lie in bed at night wondering if I've bitten off more than I can chew."

"You weren't expecting to be pregnant. What about the father? Is he able to help financially or is he out of the picture?"

"He was the one responsible for bringing this place up to date. You should've seen it a few weeks ago. What a wreck."

"But what about helping out with the baby? Is he taking responsibility?"

"He doesn't know yet. Other than you, only my parents know. I want to make sure…well, you know."

"I usually don't do ultrasounds until week eight, but since you're slender enough to get good resolution on the images, I want to do one sooner, just to see if we can determine if it's tubal. We might also be able to see if there are twins."

"Knowing either one would take a lot of worry off my mind."

"For something more fun to talk about, tell me about your man. Or maybe it's not so much fun? I didn't see any masculine touches in the house on the tour, nothing in the bathroom that indicated you share it with someone."

"It's a little complicated," June said.

"It usually is for women in your position. I'm guessing he's back in LA unwilling to leave his job to be here with you? His job is more important than you are to him?"

June had lost her appetite for the remainder of her meal. "It's something like that. He's in Washington DC for the next few years."

"That's certainly a long distance relationship. You didn't want to join him there?"

"I guess it was the DC lifestyle I wouldn't have been able to tolerate." June watched as Divya struggled using chopsticks to eat noodles. "Maybe I should explain."

June told the story about her relationship with Jack Melendez, how they met, dated, were engaged, broke up, and renewed the relationship only recently. As proof of her not being psychotic, June found a few photos of the two of them in various places, LA, DC, Seattle, the desert house in the Mojave. The clincher was a picture of her and Jack posing in the Oval Office in front of the Resolute Desk, the Presidential seal on the floor in front of them, a small bouquet of gardenias in June's hand.

"Yes, that really is more complicated than the usual girls in my clinic," Divya said, still flipping from one picture to the next. "This is all real, right? Not some weird Universal Studios gimmick?"

"All very real. I bet you never thought one of your first patients would be high-risk and the First Lady. You're not going to bail on me, right?"

"Most OBs would avoid you, just because of the potential liability. I'm glad to have you. Not because of your status or that of the baby, but because you're so willing to start a family under such circumstances. When I meet a woman like that, I'll do anything to help her. Very inspiring."

"Well, Divya, hang on tight, because the next few months could turn out to be a bumpy ride. There is one more thing."

"Keep all of this quiet?"

"If at all possible, I'd rather not have that part of my life exposed quite yet. I think you can see how it could make things difficult?" June asked.

"For all of us. I was going to say something stupid like we all have our secrets, but yours in giant. It's safe with me."

June relaxed. "Thanks. I've had enough trouble with the papparazi."

The noise of a door slamming shut echoed through the house.

"What was that?" Divya asked, looking startled. "Is someone here?"

"Every now and then, a bedroom door slams shut or a floor board creaks somewhere. I have a draft in the house that I can't find. Either that or I have a ghost."

Divya had a natural cheerfulness about her, something June picked up on at lunch, one of the reasons why she wanted her to be her obstetrician. The conversation changed to hospital work, and June's expectations for working at the hospital. It wasn't long before they got around to Kekoa Baxter, and the little bit of gossip either of them had about what had happened in the lab the morning before.

"It's so weird," June said. "Why would anyone attack a lab tech?"

"And especially him," Divya said. "I've heard it would be hard to find someone more liked than him on this island."

"Since I took over as his doctor, I've been reading about the Baxter family. Old time Hawaiian family with ties to other prominent families all over the islands. What I can't figure is why someone from a family like that has to go out and get a job as a tech in the hospital?"

"Maybe all the family has left is their good name? It would be a shame to think they might've squandered their wealth on bad land deals or trusting the wrong business associates."

"Whatever happened, he's getting a lot of pro bono care because of the insurance he has pays for almost nothing. When I've done that in the past in LA, it was always gang-bangers that had been shot up, not what seems to be a kind-hearted Hawaiian man."

"How's he doing? Will he be out of the unit soon?" Divya asked.

"Oh, HIPAA regulations. Can't really talk about it." She had to be careful how she proceeded. "But I did assume his care today. Doctor Soseki wanted to move on to other patients, and seemed glad to turn his care over to me."

"Because of funding?"

"Trying to be diplomatic, but yes, because he would earn nothing from his care."

June cleverly shifted the topic over to Divya's practice, giving her the third degree about why she wanted to be an obstetrician, how many patients she had, how busy she wanted to be, all the usual. She asked just enough personal questions to satisfy her appetite, but left more for another time. Once the dishes were done, Divya knew how to be a good guest and found the door.

No sooner was she gone than June's phone rang. She'd seen the local number enough to know it was from Henry.

"I heard you took over Kekoa's case today. How's he doing?"

"Without divulging too much, he could be better. Some of his family came in, spent much of the day with him. There are leis all over the ICU nurse's station, but they can't be in the room with him. Somebody set up some little rock altar in the waiting room, some sort of religious thing."

"The old Hawaiian religion is pretty interesting. Maybe a little like the native Indians in North America, that there's spirit in rocks and things from nature."

"Same as Shinto in Japan. That's what I thought when I saw the rock."

"Often, the Hawaiians use what looks like a simple rock as an amulet. I really don't know much about it, but I think sometimes it can attract good spirits, and other times it can keep bad spirits away."

"Spirits, as in ghosts?" June asked. "The hospital hasn't been there long enough to be haunted, has it?" Then she remembered what the two Filipina nurses told her about one of the elevators in the hospital. A patient had tragically died in it, and ever since, they avoided using that elevator. "I heard about the haunted elevator. Is there anything to that?"

"Employees were calling it the Ghostavator until someone from admin told people to knock it off," he said. "Not much to it unless you're superstitious."

"The last thing a hospital needs is a rumor going around that the place is haunted."

"I think what his family is doing in the unit with the rocks and leis has more to do with spiritual practices and taboos. Just trying to get the best environment for him."

"The best things for him right now are heavy doses of antibiotics and a pulmonology consult," she said. "He's still on the vent, and his incisions don't look good. I checked and Soseki didn't order any antibiotics for him."

"That guy is such a jerk. We really need a new vascular surgeon at West Maui Med."

.

"I was thinking about that. Maybe there's a way I could weasel my way into doing all the carotids there?"

"Would he let you have them?" Henry asked.

"Yesterday he made it sound like he couldn't care less about doing them. I kind of enjoy them, actually. And it would bring a little more business my way. Fifty cases a year, according to Soseki."

"Good luck. I hope you can manage it. Check with admin and see what they have to say. But June, one word of warning."

"Yes?"

"Try not to cross swords with Soseki. He can be pretty devious."

***

A steady breeze blew, night turning to dawn. Over the ocean, white clouds tumbled through the purple sky in ever-changing shapes. One moment there would be a dog with its tail in the air, the next a mountain, followed by a dragon wearing a hat. It was how a day should start.

June was walking from the parking garage to the main entrance of the hospital when she noticed something new. In the small courtyard garden near the front door was a large lava rock, mounds of cheerful flower leis draped over it. There were so many leis, the scent was heady as June passed by.

"I wonder if this is a holiday?" she asked herself going in the front door. Not only hadn't she seen leis there before, but hadn't noticed the rock either. It looked big enough to require at least two strong men to move it into place. "I'll have to ask Henry about Hawaiian holidays the next time I see him."

Her first stop was in the ICU to see Kekoa Baxter, her one and only patient admitted to the hospital, the one she picked up from Dr. Soseki the day before. She got one call in the middle of the night about his condition, a spiking fever. She had ordered aspirin, a new antibiotic to treat the patient's infection, and had him put into isolation. After ordering blood cultures to find the exact bacteria causing the infection and fever, she dressed in cover garb and went in to see him.

217

"Mister Baxter? Can you hear me? Are you waking up yet?" she asked him, gently tapping his shoulder with a gloved finger.

"He had his pain meds about an hour ago, so he might not come around," the nurse said. She had followed June into the room with glass tubes for drawing new blood samples.

"Has he come around at all since his surgery?" June asked.

"Not yet," the nurse said, filling a lab tube with blood. "Not even when his family comes to see him. They're getting pretty upset."

"Well, I would think so." She went about changing the dressings on the silent man's neck. What had originally been one large gauze dressing that encompassed both sides had turned into two smaller ones. The one side that had been simpler to repair in the OR looked as though it was barely inflamed. But examining the other side, the edges of the wound were bright red, the stitches pulled taut against the swollen flesh. "These infections are getting worse."

"They're not upset about his infections, Doctor. They're upset about the care he's been getting here," the nurse said.

"Oh? What's bothering them? Everything I've done has been according to usual medical protocol based on best practices," June said, putting new layers of dressing gauze on the wound. "The infection wasn't from the surgery, but from when he was attacked. The knife was probably contaminated with something. That being said, his initial post-op care could've been managed a little differently, but Kekoa is getting what he needs now."

"The thing they're upset about is Doctor Soseki," the nurse said quietly. "The local people don't like him much."

"I see." June wanted to add her own opinion of the man wasn't very high either. Although he had good ability, his techniques were old-fashioned, almost archaic. His lacsidasical approach to Kekoa's post-op treatment had been appalling. Withholding necessary and important medications and treatments, just because of insurance, bordered on malpractice in June's book. That was from a purely medical point of view, and the way the nurse spoke, it sounded like there was more to it than that. "What is it about him they don't like?"

The nurse stepped over and stood next to June, pulling strips of tape off a roll and handing them to June to secure the dressing. "It's the way he talks to people, like we're dumb. Nurses are supposed to stand for him when he walks into the department, even if he doesn't bother saying hello. And he barely even visits with the families. Some people think it's that old New York attitude, that he's the doctor and the doctor is God."

"Jeesh. What century is this?" June muttered.

"Personally...never mind."

"No, not never mind. What is it?" June asked quietly.

"Just another chauvinist prick."

June had got a heavy dose of male chauvinism from him on her first day in the OR. "Oh? As in male chauvinist? Or something else?"

"Probably all kinds. Yesterday, the family asked if a kahuna could come in and see Kekoa, that maybe the kahuna might be able to help. Soseki wanted no part of that. Actually forbade it, as if he has control over something like that. That was right before you took over."

"Sorry. I'm new in Hawaii. What exactly is a kahuna?" June asked.

"Something like a Hawaiian priest or healer. There are different kinds. Some treat pregnant women and babies. Others treat sick people using native plants and herbs. And others can sense if someone's mana has been, I don't know the right word, maybe broken or disrupted?"

"And mana is?"

"Wow, you really are new here. Mana is a person's spirit, sort of their divine power or essence. Everybody has it. In Hawaiian beliefs, someone that is sickly has poor or weak mana. That's what Mister Baxter's family thinks, that his mana was disrupted when he got, well..."

"Injured. I see," June said to complete the idea. "And they want to bring a kahuna in to check him out?"

"Right. Maybe to do some little ritual."

"Would the hospital allow something like that?" June asked. The nurse was white, but spoke with the soft accent most people on the island used.

"Most of the administrators here are snooty white people from the mainland, or they came from Oahu's business world. I doubt they care much about local traditions."

"If there's no specific rule against it, it's not prohibited, right? Which means what administrators don't know, won't hurt them."

"I like your way of thinking, Doctor."

"The problem is that he's in isolation right now because of his infection. The kahuna would have to either suit up like we have or stay out of the cubicle. The less traffic in and out of his room, the better. If the family comes in, give me a call in my office. I'll come and talk with them."

They were both done with Kekoa's care right then, but June kept the nurse in the little cubicle to talk privately.

"Tell me about Soseki. How long has he been here?" June asked.

"I've heard he retired here to Maui right about the same time the hospital opened. Lives in some giant luxury townhouse condo at the beach. When the hospital needed a vascular surgeon, they heard about him living on the island, not far from here. Somehow, they got him in here to work part-time."

June wondered how she was being received. She was bringing some baggage with her from the mainland, including a baby in a few more months. She was also beginning to recognize how two distinct groups of people on Maui were viewed, those born and raised here and those from the mainland.

"It sounds like his attitude is getting in the way of his work." They stepped out of the cubicle and removed the protective layer of clothing from themselves. June pulled off her gloves last, dropping them in the red bag trash bin. She washed her hands in a sink nearby. "And the administration is afraid that if the media or the general public found out we had kahuna coming in to treat patients, it might look bad?"

"Exactly. Some people still get pretty nervous about things like that."

"It's just another religion. Is there anything else they're upset about?"

"That more people can't come in to see Kekoa," the nurse said. "He has a big family here on the island."

"I've heard he's quite popular. But we can't risk turning the place into a zoo, with endless streams of people coming in to see him, especially while he's in infectious isolation."

"He also needs his protection from whoever did that to him," the nurse said. "The more people that come and go, the less protected he becomes. All of us nurses here in the ICU are afraid somebody might come back and try to…you know…again."

"I get the idea a lot of people in the hospital are feeling the same way. I know I am." June went to a desk to do some charting and write new orders for Kekoa's care. When she finished, she found that same nurse. "Don't forget to let me know when his family comes in. I'd like to talk with them for a while." June turned to leave, but stopped to ask one more question. "Do you suppose they'll take to me any better than they did to Soseki? A brain surgeon from LA instead of a vascular surgeon from New York?"

"Anybody would be an improvement over him."

On her way out, June nodded and smiled at the police guard at Kekoa's door, the same man as the day before. Her next stop was in the cafeteria. Cruising past the steamer pans of breakfast foods, there was little she had an appetite for. She went to the far end where the breadstuffs were located and dropped two slices into a toaster. While those cooked, she got a cup of decaf coffee. At the last moment, she spilled a little out and topped it off with regular coffee. When she got back to the toaster, the slices had popped up, which she turned around in their slots and rammed down again to blacken them. Finally, with her toast on a small plate and her coffee, she went to the checkout register with her coin purse in her hand, ready to pay.

"You're new here?" the Filipina asked after looking at the name embroidered on June's white lab jacket.

"Yes. Why?"

"You're Doctor Kato?"

"Yes."

"No need pay for you. No pay for any of the doctors. You should go back and get some mo' bettah toast. Bacon is good here."

June dropped her little purse in her white jacket pocket. "I saw that. This should be enough for today. Thanks."

June took her tray into the brightly lit dining room, scanning for a place to sit. There were quite a few empty booths, but she saw the perfect place to eat her breakfast.

"Doctor Soseki, mind if I sit with you?" she asked cheerfully, and with her brightest smile. If there was one thing she knew how to do it was produce a fake smile. Having been a fashion model in the past, she had a repertoire of smiles and facial expressions a mile long and was willing to pull them all out of storage to work the guy into submission, if she had to.

"Oh, yes. Doctor Kato, isn't it?" He made space at the table for her to put her tray. His New York accent seemed stronger than she had heard previously. "Finding your way around the hospital?"

"Slowly but surely."

He looked at her minimalist breakfast of two slices of burnt bread and frowned.

"These people can't even make proper toast," he said, pushing his plate away. He sipped something that looked like tea.

"I've just been to see Kekoa," June said.

"How is he? On the mend?"

"Not exactly." June gave a quick report on Kekoa's condition, including the infectious process that had started, sure to add a soft editorial about the lack of post-op antibiotics. The next part was trickier. "I heard you were restricting his visitors?"

"The family wants every Tom, Dick, and Harry on the island coming for a visit. Along with the family witch doctor."

"You mean a kahuna?" June asked.

"Whatever they're called."

"Would there have been a problem with that? I mean, do other docs here allow that?"

"This is a medical facility, doctor. We have educated, trained, and licensed physicians here, along with nurses, therapists, and technicians. If people want black magic, they can go to the neighborhood voodoo clinic."

June wasn't sure why, but she found the man insulting. Probably because of the condescending attitude. "The family is quite upset. Would there be harm in allowing someone to come see him?"

"Maybe they could make a poultice of dead leaves and butterfly wings to stick on his neck?"

"Or just to appease the family. They're not very happy with us, and it's only been a couple of days since his injury. It would simply be a gesture of good will toward Kekoa and his family. You were the one that only yesterday said the hospital is trying to broaden its consumer base. By showing the public we're open-minded and willing to embrace, or at least consider, alternative therapies would be one way of accomplishing that."

"And as soon as you bring a witch doctor in here, the paying clientele will disappear, leaving us with providing free services to homeless beachcombers." His voice got louder as he stood to leave the table. "Doctor, I don't know about where you come from, but if this hospital wants to be a marketable success, we need to rely on proper medical standards of conduct."

"No, you don't know where I've come from. But one thing is quite obvious, we've come from vastly different places."

He glared down at her. "Pardon me?"

"Our families might've come from the same place in the past, but somewhere along the way, yours took a wrong turn to produce someone like you." June returned his glare. "Kekoa, and all my other patients, will get exactly what he needs medically. And if that includes bringing in spiritual help along with ordering antibiotics for post-operative patients to prevent infections, so be it. Fair warning, Doctor. Don't get between me and my patients."

"Go ahead and take your ridiculous ideas to the Board of Directors. See what they think of them!" With that, Soseki stomped out of the cafeteria.

June looked around at others nearby and noticed she was the center of attention right then. She suspected it was exactly what Soseki had intended, to make her look foolish in front of others, just by saying the right things in a raised voice.

Steamed after the argument with Soseki, June choked down the last of her coffee and left her second slice of toast alone. Taking her tray, she left the dining room. "Ridiculous my rear end."

The wide corridor that led from the cafeteria to the main lobby was decorated in a cheerful tropical motif. Pastel pink and green wallpaper clung to the walls, and a bright casino style of carpeting covered the floor, deadening the sound of her footsteps as she stomped toward her clinic. Along one side of the corridor were tall windows, letting in natural light, with a lava rock garden outside. On the other wall were framed photos of the board of directors and the head of each specialty department. June slowed just enough to look at each portrait, reading the names, trying to remember them for future use. It was one of the last pictures that surprised her. Not only was Neal Soseki the head of vascular surgery at the hospital, but he was also on the hospital Board of Directors.

"Now isn't that cozy," she muttered sarcastically. "Only my first week here and I've already pissed off the ivory tower."

***

June had already met most of the doctors and nurses in the Ear, Nose, and Throat clinic where she was stationed temporarily. She saw the first of her patients for the day, and then with nothing else to do except worry about earning a decent living in her new hometown, she logged onto her desktop computer.

"Okay, what exactly is a kahuna?" she said, typing the word into the search bar.

She found several sites, all with a similar literal definition of 'to take care of cooking', and with a more figurative meaning of 'to take care of something important', or by extension, to be a caretaker. Mostly it meant to be a leader of a specific group, something like a priest is to a community. One site went on to explain that ministers, experienced craftsmen, magicians, wizards, and doctors, the people of the community most responsible for making sacrifices, were considered kahuna. Any of them could be men or women, without prejudice.

There were numerous and different levels of kahuna, more than twenty just in the healing professions. June discovered that they were specialized, the same as doctors. Some were bonesetters, others dealt with conditions of the skin, while others focused on healing wounds. Some of the busiest were concerned with the health of pregnant women and babies. Training of kahuna consisted of many years of apprenticeships, often starting in childhood while under the guidance of an elder practitioner. If a child seemed especially adept at recognizing health problems, they would move in with that type of kahuna to learn the trade, often spending decades learning from the master.

"Wow. They really had a lot of responsibilities," June said as she went from one website to another. She read about the various levels of medicine practitioners, drifting to her own obstetrical concerns. "Kahuna hoohapai keiki was someone that induced pregnancy. Nope. Too late for that." She scrolled down. "Kahuna hoohanau keiki was someone that delivered babies. No, too soon for that."

She continued reading beyond the mother and baby practitioners until she found what she wanted. She got out a pad of paper and pencil to make notes on the new terminology.

"Kahuna la'au lapa'au were the general practitioners, and kahuna haha were the diagnosticians." She read further down the page. "Then there were the kahuna aloha that induced love, and the kahuna ana'ana, which induced either healing or death, something of a witch doctor in modern parlance."

She quit taking notes and sat back in her chair. Staring at the computer screen, she re-read the last few sentences about witch doctors.

"No, we're not going there, June," she said to herself. "That looks like trouble."

She went back to a page about basic kahuna practices and read further, trying to cram study for when she met with Kekoa's family later. It was right then that she got a call from the ICU nurse taking care of him.

"And just so you know," the nurse told June in a hushed voice. "When they learned Kekoa has a new doctor taking care of him, and that you're sticking up for him, they started calling for more people to come in. There's already a dozen of his family here, and they're still making calls."

Sighing, June slipped into her white lab coat. She still had three hours to go before her next patient, not giving her an excuse to get out early if the meeting turned ugly. While she walked to the ICU, she called her sister Amy in LA.

"Sis, do me a favor, okay?"

"Yeah. What's up? How's the new job?"

"Never mind that. Just text me at my new number if you don't hear from me before I call you back. I have a big family meeting to go to, and it may turn ugly."

"And you need an escape call. Got it."

"And if I don't call back after the text, call me ten minutes later."

"Got it. But what's up?" Amy asked.

"Not much. My first patient here is nose-diving into a serious infection, I've alienated another surgeon, who also happens to be on the Board of Directors. And to top it off, my patient's family wants to bring in a kahuna to try and heal him."

"Typical for you. What exactly is a kahuna?"

"Not sure. Just don't call them witch doctors," June whispered into her cell phone before ending the call.

The waiting room at the intensive care unit was swamped with visitors. If June hadn't known they were all related, she never could've put the group together as a family. Tall, short, heavy, skinny, dark-skinned, pale and freckled. Hair colors ranged from senior citizen white to blond, to every shade of brown and black. Some wore aloha shirts and slacks, others in T-shirts and shorts, one man was in a sports coat and necktie. They looked like the usual crowd waiting to get into a football stadium to watch a game. One older petite woman was dressed in a colorful mu'u mu'u, wearing a necklace of large brown nuts, and a leafy green lei, woven tightly into itself. In spite of her demure size, she seemed to stand out in the crowd.

"Wow, so many people here to see Kekoa," June said as a way of greeting them all. Mostly they stared back in silence. Trying to break the ice again, she introduced herself and handed out her new business cards to anyone that would take them.

"Aloha," the old woman in the mu'u mu'u said in a deep, quiet voice.

June looked at her, and handed over the last of her cards. "Hi. Thanks for coming. Kekoa has a big family. It's nice you all came in for him."

"There's a lot more than this," a man in front of the group said. He was broad-shouldered, narrow-waisted, dark-skinned, and his dry curly hair was marginally under control. He had the same eyes as the old woman. "My name is Leonard. I'm Kekoa's cousin."

He did a quick introduction of the others, some names familiar, others had Hawaiian names June wouldn't be able to remember.

To keep from making too much noise in the ICU, they went out into the hallway to talk there. She explained how she had taken over Kekoa's care the day before, and had done some tests on the infection. She went through as much of his care as she could, even though she'd had him as a patient for less than a day, and only assisted with his surgery. For the most part, the group stood quietly and listened until she was done.

"You're from mainland?" the older woman asked. June tried to remember her name, something like Auntie Haunani or Haunana.

"That's right. This is still my first week here at the hospital."

June heard a round of grumbles, but they stopped when the old woman spoke. "I'm sorry my nephew has been so much trouble for you."

June was surprised the woman apologized for Kekoa. She had been expecting quite the opposite, to get some hint of blame that he wasn't recovering. She had no idea of what to say to this family that felt so foreign to her. "Kekoa? I wish he was waking up better so he could see you. I'm sure he misses you as much as you miss him."

They all beamed. Whatever she said, it was what they needed to hear right then.

"I heard from one of the nurses that you want a kahuna to come in and see Kekoa?" June asked. "Being new here to Hawaii, I don't know how to respond. I just don't know enough about that yet, or how to find a kahuna that might be able to help."

The old woman stepped forward, a teenage boy at her side. For the first time, June noticed an old plastic shopping bag in her hand. "I like some time with him, alone," she said in her heavy accent.

"Now?" June asked back, looking over her shoulder back through the glass double doors of the ICU. Late morning was a busy time in the ICU, with treatments and visitors for every patient.

"Mo' bettah than latah," the old woman said back in her heavy accent.

"For?"

The old woman took another step forward and opened her bag for June to see the contents. Inside was a green leafy garland similar to what she was wearing, and a small black lava rock at the bottom. "To put on Kekoa. Bettah mana for him."

June looked the old woman in the eyes, and figured she was the family kahuna, the way she had read a few minutes before. The old woman looked back, her wet eyes steady, unwavering. "Are you the kahuna for the family?"

She nodded in return.

June wasn't sure of what to think or how to respond. This culture was all new territory for her, and she was in the position of plying politician. She wanted to be gracious to the family, but also needed to be an ambassador for proper health care. With no better idea on how to proceed, she figured it would be best to go with it. "Just those things?" she asked.

She got a nod back. "And short prayer."

"Let me go check with Kekoa's nurse."

"You in charge of Kekoa, yeah?" the old lady kahuna asked.

"Yes, but there might be something the nurse needs to do. We try to be a team. Anyway, we get kind of picky about things in the ICU."

June went back into the department and found the nurse. She could almost feel the family's collective set of eyes pinned on her as she negotiated with the nurse to allow the leafy lei and dusty stone to come in.

"Flowers are normally not allowed here, Doctor Kato. And the stone…I'm not so sure…" the nurse said, glancing beyond June to look out at the family in the hallway. "What does she want to do with that?"

"I don't know what's she's going to do with the stuff, but maybe we could put them on a tray and cover them with something?"

"That might work."

"She wants to say a prayer also."

"As long as it's quiet, it's okay with me. We have ministers in here all the time praying for patients. I can draw the blinds so she can have privacy," the nurse said as June went back to the family. "But I insist she dresses in isolation cover-ups."

"Okay, so just one person at a time," she told the family when she returned to them. She looked at the old woman with the bag in her hand. "You want to go first?"

As soon as June got the woman dressed in isolation gear and at Kekoa's bedside, June's cell phone rang with the text message from Amy.

"You need go?" the woman asked, the green lei in her hand.

"I should. Do you need anything else from me?" June asked her.

The woman shook her head while looping the lei on a pillowcase that covered Kekoa's chest. It was obvious June was no longer needed. She went out to the nurse's station where Kekoa's nurse was watching his vital signs on a remote monitor.

"Have we got the blood cultures back yet?" June asked her. She was pointed to a computer screen to read. "Nothing terribly unusual. The usual kind of bacteria, and not a lot of them. But he sure is having some sort of reaction to a minor infection."

June left the department again, nothing else she could do there. She was instantly absorbed by the family in the hall.

"So, that lady…what was her name again?" June asked one of them.

"Everybody knows Auntie Haunani," a middle-aged woman said. She had a batch of freckles across her nose and cheeks that didn't go with her Polynesian features. She spelled the name for June.

"And she's your family kahuna?"

"For the whole island," Leonard told her. "Auntie wants you to come see her at home."

"Oh?"

"It's okay," said a woman with a cheerful smile. She re-introduced herself as Judy, another cousin, and had nearly the same voice and accent as the old woman. "It's good kind occasion to tell you 'bout."

June mentioned something about being busy, and instantly scolded herself for telling them a lie. The family seemed like good people, and deserved something better than what they had been getting from the hospital so far in Kekoa's care. "Just call that number to remind me. Maybe I can meet with her after work sometime."

When June's phone rang with a call, she excused herself from the group and tried rushing off to look busy. She looked at her phone, and was surprised it wasn't Amy's call, but an unknown caller. It wasn't the OR or her clinic, and with Kekoa being her only inpatient, nurses on the wards had no reason to call her. It had a hospital prefix, but that was all she could tell from the number.

"Hello, this is Doctor Kato."

"Doctor Kato!" said a pressured but cheerful man's voice. Whoever it was had already had too much coffee that morning. "Have you been avoiding me?"

"I'm sorry?" June asked as she went quickly down the hall to the elevators. She had no idea who was calling her.

"This is Robert Townsend, the chairman of the Board of Directors at West Maui Medical Center."

"Oh, yes. Hello. We were supposed to meet the other day but…"

"You jumped into your new job with both feet, I hear. That's how we like it here. But I'd still like to meet with you, if you have the time right now?"

June looked at the time on her phone. She had two hours before her next clinic appointment, which gave her plenty of time to meet him and grab lunch, or at least take a walk outside. One thing she had never liked was meeting administrators, or anyone in charge of something that held closed meetings. With no excuse, she begrudgingly agreed to go to his office.

When both elevator doors opened in front of her, divulging several passengers each, June went to the one on the left. Her rational mind said either elevator car would take her wherever she needed to go, but she was just superstitious enough to buy into what the nurses had told her about the haunted elevator on the right.

Five minutes later, she was shown into his office. Already there and seated was Dr. Soseki. She forced an insincere smile and shook hands with Townsend before taking the other seat.

"You come to us highly qualified, Doctor Kato."

She smiled, not knowing what to say. This was one of the hard parts of meeting with administrative types, that there was always some ulterior topic just below the surface. With Soseki in the room, she had a pretty good idea of what was coming. "Thank you."

Just then, her phone rang with her sister's number.

"You need to take that?" Townsend asked.

"No, it's okay. Just a reminder call." She put her phone back in her pocket. "So, is there anything in particular that we need to discuss? I'm always a little uneasy in these types of meetings."

"Not unlike going to the principal's office during lunch hour. But there is something I'd like to discuss. Doctor Soseki here has a concern or two."

"Oh?" June looked at Soseki's unmoving head. He didn't even blink, but stared straight ahead.

"He doesn't like the way you stole a patient from him, and believes it's to practice some voodoo rituals?"

"Voodoo? Stole?" She looked at Soseki again, confused. "Who did I steal? Kekoa Baxter?"

"Exactly," said Townsend.

June raised her hands, palms up in a surrendering motion aimed at Soseki. "I don't understand. I thought you wanted me to take over his care?"

"Surely there is a sense of sarcasm in Los Angeles?" Soseki said.

"You didn't want me to take him on my service? You even wrote a note in his chart indicating as much."

"I can transfer him back if you like. But the family might be…"

"Keep him. Consider him a gift from the Department of Vascular Surgery. Don't spend your twelve dollars of reimbursement all in one place."

"I'll be sure to put the same value on his reimbursement as I do with any other patient." June was still confused, but being pissed was taking over. Soseki's attitude had gone beyond being passive aggressive to downright asinine. On the one hand, he was complaining about June supposedly stealing his patient. On the other hand, he clearly was disinterested in Kekoa and his care, most likely because of inadequate insurance. Kekoa was being used in some hospital pissing match, something June had no interest in. It was, in fact, she had wanted to leave behind in LA. She looked back at Townsend. "But what's this about voodoo?"

"It's come to my attention that the Baxter family wants to perform unusual rituals in the hospital. That can't happen."

"Oh?" She wanted to impulsively rub his nose in the fact that rituals had already started. Not only would it not get her anywhere, it would be a gigantic step backwards in hospital détente. "You mean prayer?"

"This is a medical facility, not a traditional place of worship. We can't allow unusual practices within the hospital. Now, if the family wants to do something elsewhere, that's fine. But not here. No amulets, talismans, or fantastical practices are allowed."

"Fantastical practices? What might those include?"

"Let me assure you, Doctor Kato, I can only imagine what might go on."

"I see." June looked down at her fingers wrestling with each other in her lap. She willed them to stop before looking up at Townsend again. She caught his gaze and held it. "If they were Catholics, would Kekoa be allowed Rosary beads? Or a yarmulke for a Jew? Would a minister be allowed to visit and pray for him?"

"Those are different circumstances."

"I think they're not. If prayer and a simple item that reflects faith brings comfort and hope to a family in a time of grief, why not allow them that much? I've just met the Baxter family, at least a part of it, and they're experiencing a lot of distress right now." June's ire was up, and getting more out of control the more she talked. "And if some old has-been surgeon doesn't give a crap about the well-being of a patient's family, or ordering post-operative antibiotics for a traumatically injured patient with a contaminated wound, an admired employee of the hospital, maybe he should retire once and for all?"

"Piss off," Soseki said on his way to the door. Once it was slammed shut from the other side, June and Townsend looked at each other again.

"Believe me, Doctor Kato, we're looking forward to seeing his backside go out the door on his last day," Townsend told her. "We have a new guy coming in July, someone just out of his training. Neal never did produce much in the way of numbers for us."

"There's more to a hospital than numbers and reimbursement, Mister Townsend."

"Not in this office. What exactly was the problem in the OR the other day?" he asked.

"In surgery? He was going to clamp both carotid arteries at the same time. Doing that would've left very little blood flow into Mister Baxter's head for an extended period of time. Maybe a few decades ago, that was how it was done. But in this day and age, we have better techniques."

"I see. Do we need to report him to the state?"

"For malpractice?" June asked. "No way I would do that, especially on my first week here. But he agreed to turn over all the major head and neck vascular surgery to my service, or at least I think he did, and I'm happy to do them. If it's true someone is coming soon to replace him, why bother reporting him? He seems like the type that could do a lot of damage to a hospital's reputation by stirring up trouble in the media. As far as malpractice is concerned, that's up to the Board of Directors to decide." That's when June recalled Soseki was on the Board of Directors of the hospital. "But since Soseki has a seat on the board, I doubt that'll happen."

She was done with the meeting, and needed to find a way out. But there wouldn't be any more escape texts or calls from Amy.

"But on the other matter…"

"The rituals the Baxter family wants to perform?"

"Yes. There really cannot be any of that."

"I see," June said, but she didn't. "I must tell you that I can't support that decision, nor will I obstruct you from enforcing it. I'm still new here, and I just want to take care of my patients and earn a living. But somehow I'm stuck in the middle of this little drama that has been perpetrated by someone else, and behind closed doors." She stood abruptly and pushed her chair back. "Don't expect me to be your cop. If a religious object happens to be in his room, I won't notice it. Just like a crucifix, a menorah, or an om sign painted on the wall."

She gladly left him behind.

As soon as she was out his office door, the small waiting area outside began to swirl. June stood still for a moment and closed her eyes to recover. Her head was pounding from the lack of caffeinated coffee, and from sitting through the meeting. She needed to blow off some steam, and get something to eat.

June knew she had to return to the ICU waiting room to tell the Baxter family the bad news about having their religious practices limited by the hospital. By telling them, she was participating in a game she wanted no part of. But not telling them, she'd leave them out on a limb all alone. Whatever came of it in the long run could be sorted out later. In the next few minutes, she needed to find a diplomatic way of discouraging Kekoa's family from being too intrusive into his care.

But first came half a cup of coffee, that was slugged back in mere seconds.

By the time she was back to the ICU, Auntie Haunani was done with her prayers, and Leonard had come in. While June had been away, even more family members had shown up. They went through more introductions, June overwhelmed with so many names.

"I guess I should've asked before, but have the police said anything about who might've done this to Kekoa?" she asked the group.

"No idea. But a witness has come forward."

"Oh? Well, that's good news."

"Maybe, maybe not. All they really saw was a man in a black leather jacket and jeans leaving in a hurry from the back entrance of the hospital at the loading dock," another cousin said.

"That's a good lead for the police," June offered as a hopeful idea.

"Or maybe not," Judy said. "He looked like a local guy. Dark skin, black curly hair, kinda tall. That's all the description they got."

June gave it some thought. She wasn't a cop but she had training in epidemiology, a way of narrowing down leading information to get to an end idea. "You know, that's more information than what you think. It leaves out all white people, right? And women of course. And maybe not a local guy at all."

"Why not local?"

She looked around at their faces, wondering how her idea would be received. "How often do any of you wear a leather jacket or jeans? Can you even buy a black leather jacket on the island?"

"Construction workers wear jeans all the time," one of the men said.

"But the witness didn't say anything about him looking dressed like a construction worker. And even early in the morning, we don't have to wear jackets, right? The weather here is just too mild to need an extra layer." June paused a moment to let it sink in. "The guy had to come from somewhere else if he was wearing a leather jacket."

"The othah crazy kind thing is," Judy said slowly. "We no can imagine anybody ever wanting to hurt Bruddah Kekoa. We think it was whatchmacallit…"

"Mistaken identity," Auntie Haunani said quietly from where she was seated. "I think bad guy got wrong bruddah."

"Yeah, maybe." June looked at Haunani, sitting deflated and alone on the couch, and went to sit with her. She looked up at the others. "Could you guys give Auntie and me a minute to talk alone?"

After they had moved away, mostly to the cafeteria or to rotate through a vigil at Kekoa's bedside, June turned her sights on Haunani.

"Auntie, while I was away, I was called into a meeting with an administrator here at the hospital, actually the top person here. He's insisting that no more things be brought in to Kekoa."

"You mean the rock and ti leaves?"

"Yes. I wanted to tell you that before someone else came by and told you."

"That stone from family heiau, bring good energy to Kekoa, strength of ancestors. Ti leaf lei keep away bad spirits."

"I know how important those things are to you and Kekoa. But unfortunately the hospital thinks they might be troublesome."

"I gotta take'm back?" Auntie asked quietly.

"I think you should leave them there. But you must understand, someone else might remove them."

"No one touches dat stone but me or Kekoa."

"Is there another place we can put the stone, so no one sees it?" June asked.

"Undah bed is okay. Or undah pillow or mattress. Needs to be near him."

"And the lei? It really shouldn't be in the room with him."

Haunani looked over at Kekoa's glass cubicle. "Outside the door?"

"That might be okay. But even so, you might have to find a new hiding place for those things each day. You know, keep moving them around."

"One housekeepah here named Lei Lei, Hawaiian wahine, maybe she could clean his room each day," Haunani said as more of a suggestion than as a question.

June smiled; she was forming a team around Kekoa. "Maybe she wouldn't see a rock under the bed or ti leaves in Kekoa's room when she cleaned? I doubt the nurses care too much, if it's meant to help Kekoa. I know it isn't perfect, but we have to be smarter than the people who sit behind desks all day."

"We figure it out," Haunani said with a smile.

There was still the other issue, something Leonard had mentioned earlier. "Leonard said you wanted to talk to me about something?" June asked.

Auntie Haunani reached and put her hand on June's tummy. "Hapai, yeah?"

June instantly blushed. It was far too early for her to be showing, and no one at the hospital knew she was pregnant. Outside of her immediate family, only her OB knew. Somehow, the old woman had figured it out. "Yes, just a few weeks."

"Married?"

"Yes, but he doesn't live here.".

Haunani's smile slowly faded, and along with it, June's. When she remembered kahuna were often trained and responsible for pregnant women, she knew something else was coming.

"Too skinny. No eat enough."

"It's still early, Auntie."

"Poi."

June knew of the starchy root food, something like mashed potatoes. "Poi?"

"Good for you. Make you big, and make baby strong."

Haunani handed over a slip of paper, handwritten notes scrawled on it. June could tell right off it was something of a list of things to eat, and simple recipes for cooking them. Haunani had already prepared something for her, almost like a prescription diet. She noticed right off that there was pork in the list.

June stood and refolded the paper, slipping it in a pocket. "I'll try cooking one of them tonight. The thing is though, I'm a vegetarian, something I won't change."

"More poi then. Anyhowz, tonight you eat with us at Judy's house."

"But…"

"Judy tell you where."

"Is it a potluck? Should I bring something?"

It was obvious Auntie Haunani was done with June, just when Judy and a couple of others returned to the waiting room. June got the address and basic directions to a place in Kahului, one of the main towns in central Maui.

As soon as June was free from the group, she looked at the time. She barely had time to get back to the clinic to see her next patient, missing lunch. What had started out as a slow day had become busy.

A Diabolical Plot

Being unfamiliar with the streets in town, and not wanting to go to Judy's house alone, she needed someone to accompany her. Calling Divya, she learned she was on call that evening and expecting a mother to deliver. Knowing only one other person on the island, she called him.

"Henry, this is June Kato. How'd you like to risk your marriage and take a woman to dinner?"

"Uh…"

"You can even bring Karen with you."

"Already feeling lonely and homesick for LA, June?"

She had to admit he was right about that. "I've been invited to a small house party in Kahului for this evening and I have no idea of how to find the place, what to bring, or what to expect once I get there."

"And you were thinking if a local took you, you'd fit in better?"

"Pretty much, and that I might actually find the place. Any interest?"

"Who is it?" he asked.

"A cousin of Kekoa, one of the Baxters. A lady named Auntie Haunani invited me, and she said to be sure to bring along my man. Since I don't have one, I thought you might want to fill in, along with Karen, of course."

"Auntie Haunani? *The* Auntie Haunani?"

"I guess. Why?"

"Other than the mayor, she might be the most famous person on the island. Maybe the most prominent kahuna anywhere in the islands. Everyone wants to meet her. How'd you get an invitation?"

"I guess because I took over in Kekoa's care."

"Might be something more diabolical than that."

"Diabolical? I didn't feel threatened by her at all, or by the family. They were rather kind to me."

"She's probably trying to get you pregnant."

June knew that wasn't the reason, since Haunani had already figured out June's secret. Still, she wasn't interested in letting on she was pregnant to anyone else. "Basic science principals dictate…"

"Word is, she's helped get more women get pregnant on this island than there are husbands for them all."

"Why in the world would she want me pregnant?" June asked. "It's not really any of her business."

"You're looking at it from your point of view. Look at yourself the way she does, a woman about to exit her prime childbearing years. She probably has some sort of idea that you are supposed to have a child and she's going to make that happen, whether there's a man in your life or not."

"And once again, basic science…"

"Better do what she says, if only to make her happy. Most people on the island would be thrilled to be invited to a party at one of the Baxters' houses, especially if Auntie Haunani was going to be there."

June took the slip of paper from her pocket and tried reading it. "She gave me a list of things to eat. Apparently, pigs are frequently on the menu here. You'll have to look at the rest of this stuff, because a lot of it doesn't look familiar to me. Several Hawaiian names."

She was just getting back to the clinic and saw a waiting room full of patients. One of them had to be waiting for her. She hurried down the hall to her tiny office.

"Hey, I got to go and play doctor. But please consider accompanying me this evening, okay?"

**

After she had seen her three patients in the clinic, June cruised through the emergency room out of habit, just to see if there was anything there for her. Finding nothing interesting to a neurosurgeon, she made rounds on Kekoa. Most of his family had left, Auntie Haunani nowhere in sight, and June breathed a sigh of relief she wouldn't have more questions to answer.

Kekoa was still the same. His lungs were being inflated by a mechanical ventilator, unchanged from the time of his surgery. June knew from experience that the longer he was on the ventilator, the more his brain relied on its help. If he didn't begin to respond and wake up soon, a lengthy process of weaning him off the artificial breathing machine would be needed. She changed the dressings again, the wounds still looking about the same: not yet healing, but at least not as red as in the morning. All in all, her two days of care hadn't produced much better results than Soseki's had. Or Haunani's lei and lava rock.

She read a note from a pulmonologist who had been there to see him, along with notes from other specialists. A medical team was beginning to form around Kekoa's care, something that should've happened from the very first moment he was treated. On that particular day, it was the best that could be done for Kekoa, along with whatever Haunani might conjure up.

"Hi," she said to the cop stationed at Kekoa's door. "You're the same guy that's been here every time I've come to see him."

"Part of Baxter ohana," he told her in a low voice. Getting a better look at his pock marked face and dark skin, she could see something of a family resemblance with Leonard. He was also a lot bigger than what she first realized.

"He has a large family. It's nice they've been coming in to see him."

"Family all over the island."

"Say, did anybody talk to you about what we were thinking? About his attacker?"

"About his clothes? And being from off-island?"

"Yeah. It seems strange that the attacker was wearing a leather jacket. Nobody here wears something like that, right?" she asked the cop. She looked at the name patch on his shirt, making a point of remembering his name of Kaleo.

"Nah. Leonard went to Sears in town today to see if they sell them. Otherwise, nobody else on Maui sells clothes like that. But I'll make sure detectives look into it."

It was the same old message from all cops, that someone's idea had been passed along to someone else, bumped along to another investigator, all of whom would 'look into it'. But maybe if he really was family, Officer Kaleo might've actually passed it along.

"Judy reminds you about dinner," he told June when she turned away.

She turned back to him. "Should I bring something? I'm not familiar with customs here."

"No need. Sistah, you just bring big appetite." He smiled at her for the first time, using the same accent as all the rest of his relatives. "Best thing to do with Auntie is do what she say."

By the time June got home, she felt like she'd worked a full day, rather than just seeing four clinic patients. She had got a call back from Henry, that he and his wife would pick her up at home, and was sure to mention several times about his wife coming along.

"Nice to meet you, too, Karen. Since this was my idea, can I pay for your babysitter?"

"No need," husband and wife said together.

"I never did figure out what to bring," she said settling into the back seat of Henry's car. June's reception by Karen was frosty at best. "We should stop at a market."

"Shouldn't need to," he said in the same way Officer Kaleo had. "They'll have too much."

"I can't show up empty-handed."

"Don't worry about it, Doctor Kato," Karen said. "You're an invited guest. You don't have to bring anything."

At the bottom of the driveway, June asked Henry to take her back to the house. Inside for only a moment, she dashed back out to the waiting couple, a gift bag in her hand.

"What's that?" Henry asked, looking at what she held.

"Candies I bought in LA before I came here, so I could send them back to my mother for Christmas. They're her favorite."

"That'll leave you nothing to send her," Karen said.

"Actually, it looks like the entire clan will be coming her for Christmas."

They rode along in silence for a few minutes, until they got to the short tunnel the highway passed through. Once they emerged on the other side, June got the business card with Judy's address on it. "You know where Kea Street is?"

"Near the mall."

"But you know where it's at?" she asked, nervously picking at the card.

"Yes!" he said, with almost as much irritation. "Not far from where I grew up."

"I'm sorry, but I just don't know what to expect this evening." She looked at the box of chocolates in the gift bag, wondering it was too small. "Maybe we should stop for flowers?"

"You're fine."

June sighed. "What's kea mean?" she asked after a few more minutes.

"White, like snow. You've heard of Mauna Kea?"

"I don't know much Hawaiian," she said, taking a look at the large hospital in town as they passed it, the competitor to where she worked.

"It means white mountain, or mountain with snow on it. For whatever reason, that one gets a bit of snow at the top each year, while the others usually don't."

"So, kea means white or snow?" she asked.

"Both. Or either one. The only thing pure white in Hawaii is snow."

"I see," she muttered, still looking out the window.

"That's why it can be either one. Or both."

"I get it."

June realized she snapped and apologized.

"I'm looking forward to this party," Karen said. "Meeting the Baxters is really something."

"They certainly seem to be a big deal on the island."

"June, you need to understand that they aren't all blood relatives. In Hawaii, we have hanai relatives, sort of an old-fashioned kanaka way of unofficially adopting someone into the family. But those bonds are just as strong as blood relations."

"Is Kekoa blood or hanai relations with Haunani?"

"Blood, as is Leonard and Judy. Most of the people you've been meeting at the hospital have been blood relatives. I imagine you'll meet a whole lot more this evening."

"There was someone there named…" June gave the police guard's name a thought, trying to remember it. "I can't think of it, but he looked a lot like Haunani and Leonard."

"How'd you meet him?"

"He was the police guard at Kekoa's ICU room. Three days in a row, actually."

"Could be anybody in the department," Karen said. "To people new in the islands, all Polynesians look alike."

June tried not to take it as an insult, but she was discovering she didn't like Karen any more than Karen was acting kindly to her.

They turned into a residential area. June knew they weren't far from the mall, near the main police station and swimming pool in town.

"You grew up near here? Can we go see the house?" she asked.

"No more. Been taken down. Someone bought two houses side by side, took them down, and put up one big house."

"Doctor Kato, Henry never did tell me how the two of you met," Karen said.

"Oh, I was a patient in his ER one night while on vacation a while back."

"Were you in an accident?"

June laughed. "Spider bite. I think I was more seriously injured when Henry said my butt was flabby than being bit by the spider."

Henry looked at June in the rearview mirror. "I don't remember saying anything like that."

"How do you know what her butt looks like, Hen?" Karen demanded.

"It was when he pulled my underwear down to give me a shot."

"You pulled down her undies?"

June had some damage control to do when she noticed Karen glaring daggers at Henry. "Just to give me a shot. Thinking about it, maybe it was when we were at the beach to go surfing."

"You went surfing with her?"

"No! Just saw each other at the beach one day!"

"It sounds like you saw a lot of her, Henry. When did all this take place?"

June was staying out of it. She'd already stirred up too much trouble and knew better than to get caught between a sparring husband and wife, even if she was the one who they were squabbling over.

"A while back."

"A while how far back? When I was fat and pregnant?"

"No, before then. It was when you were out of town…" He stopped himself.

"When I went to Honolulu that time?" she said, her voice pitching higher. "You were dating her while I was off the island?"

Thankfully, it was time to park at the curb. Both sides of the street were lined with cars and pickup trucks, forcing Henry to park the next block down. When Karen got out, she slammed the door behind her, not waiting.

"Sorry, Henry. This was a supremely bad idea to ask you to do this. I should've just looked on a map and found the place on my own."

"Forget it. She was the one who wanted to meet the Baxters."

"Some of these trucks are in better shape than the houses," June muttered as they walked to Judy's house, trying to catch up with Karen.

"Sometimes three generations of a family live in one little house, and they all have jobs to pay the mortgage. They look small, but expensive to live here."

"What kinds of jobs do they have?"

"These days it's either retail or resort work. Used to be agriculture. There's an old sugar cane processing plant near here.

Years ago, everything surrounding the town was sugar cane fields. When they burned the fields, the sky would be filled with smoke and soot. We called it Maui snow, since the soot would float down and settle on cars and in houses. My mom always had to choose, close all the windows and make it hot inside, or keep them open and clean the whole house at the end of the day."

"They don't do that anymore?" June asked.

"Not so much these days." He sounded nostalgic about it. "You know those little brown packets of raw sugar you find in restaurants? That's the only sugar that comes from Maui now."

They caught up with Karen and went up the short driveway to find the two-car garage packed with people. Music was playing and several young women were trying to get a karaoke machine to work. June recognized a few of them from the hospital that day, but most were still strangers. Judy came out, a towel in her hand, wearing an apron.

"You found us!" Judy said cheerfully.

June introduced Henry and Karen to Judy and a couple of others before they were taken away to the back yard.

"Lots of people!" June said back. She looked toward the back of the house and saw several tables set up and even more people. There were almost as many kids as there were adults. "Is this a birthday party?"

Judy shrugged. "Just easy kind potluck. People came by to meet you."

"All this is for me?"

She handed over the box of candies with an apology there wasn't more, getting in return a scolding that she didn't need to bring anything at all.

Judy's smile sank a bit. "You taking care of Bruddah Kekoa. This our way of showing aloha…appreciation."

"It's only been a couple of days since I started watching over him. He isn't improving much yet."

"We heard what you did in the operating room. Saved his life."

"Yeah, well, he still has a ways to go. Is there news from the police?" June asked, hopefully changing the subject.

"Maybe Leonard will know." Judy nodded her head off to one side. "He's in the back." Judy begged off, returning to the kitchen.

June went off in search of Leonard. Instead of finding him, she saw someone else she recognized. "Officer Kaleo, you're here, too." He was sitting by himself under a tree in a back corner.

"Call me Kaleo." He smiled his toothy grin at her. "Unless I'm giving you a ticket. Then call me Sir!"

"Ha! I'll remember that. And you very well might give me a ticket someday!"

"Maybe I let you off…the first time." He led her off to the side to talk privately. "I heard the detectives talking. They have a few more leads, and a suspect list. They have good sketches out, even to the other islands for police bulletins."

"Good. I hope they find the guy pretty soon."

"And they think the same thing as you, that it was odd he was dressed like that. That might be the most important lead they have right now."

He nudged her back toward the garage crammed with people. She did a quick count and decided there were over two dozen people at the house. When she looked back to thank him, he had already wandered off.

"How do things look with Kekoa?" someone seated in a lawn chair asked. She looked familiar to June, the woman with the freckles across her nose.

"Well, he's not getting any worse, but not any better either. There's something about his condition that I just can't figure. It's almost as if his body is refusing to cooperate with his treatments."

"Dat's exactly it," said someone from the back. June recognized Auntie Haunani's soft voice. "He no get better until someone is caught."

"Well, I think he'll get better soon," June began to say. Haunani waved it off, and called her over to a chair next to her. She pushed the teenage boy out so June could sit. Haunani shoved a glass of punch in June's hand to drink.

"Kekoa's mana is gone broke. It can be fixed again, but not so easy."

"I see. But his medical treatment…"

A small crowd was gathering around, listening.

"I no care 'bout hospital or treatments or what you doctahs say. His mana needs fix."

June wasn't sure of how to proceed. She thought she had explained that afternoon to the woman that there couldn't be any rituals or objects left in Kekoa's room. "But the administrators said today…"

"Screw them," Auntie said. "I can do it at night, when those dopes stay sleep in their beds. Tonight, and two more nights. Then Bruddah Kekoa finally get better."

"What about that rock and those leaves?" June asked, trying not to burst into laughter at Haunani's description of hospital administrators. She agreed whole-heartedly.

"That started it. To clean the place. Pohaku…rock to purify the land, lei to purify the air. Draw up bad mana like magnet. Tonight, do a little more."

"We were able to get a local nurse assigned to his care tonight, so there shouldn't be too much fuss about Auntie being there," a large woman dressed in a mu'u mu'u said. She looked as old as Haunani but twice as big. June recognized her but couldn't remember her name. The thing that really got to June right then was how the family was able to manipulate a hospital staffing schedule so easily, and quickly.

"Visiting hours in the ICU are over at nine o'clock in the evening."

Haunani nudged June's arm to take another drink of the punch, something highly botanical in flavor. She wondered for sa moment if everything in the drink was safe, or even legal.

"That's where we need your help again," the woman said.

"Oh?"

"We need you to sign a paper to extend his visiting hours."

June crunched her face, but tried not to frown. "I need a really good reason for something like that."

"Like?"

"That someone is dying, and the family wants to be at the bedside."

The group seemed to take a collective deep breath.

"It would work once, but not for the second night," June explained. "Hospitals keep track of that sort of thing. If I get caught abusing it, there'll be trouble. Not just for me, but for you guys, too. They could take away your visiting privileges altogether."

"We'll do that tonight," Haunani said quietly, nudging June into drinking more. She leaned in close to June and whispered, "Good for baby."

All June's adult life, she'd been reluctant to drink something if she hadn't opened the bottle or can herself, or made it in her own kitchen. Here she was with strangers, drinking something obviously homemade. Strong but not with the sting of alcohol. She looked around and saw other young women drinking the same thing, so she went with it. She was an invited guest, and the point of the party was to get to know her better. How would it look if she wouldn't accept their hospitality? Anyway, there would be no point in spiking her drink, the doctor responsible for caring for a family member.

"What about the next two nights?" June asked, after taking a sip. "You said you need three nights total."

"Maybe I can help with that," Henry said from the back of the crowd. "The ER called today looking for someone to fill in tomorrow night. Maybe I could take a stretcher out to the ambulance bay, put Auntie on it, cover her with a sheet and put an oxygen mask on her face. Then take her up to the ICU. If we're lucky, nobody would notice."

"But…" June began to argue.

"And you'll have nothing to do with it," Henry said to June.

"Okay, go for stretchah ride tomorrow night," Auntie Haunani said.

"And the third night?" June asked. "Maybe she could dress like a doctor or nurse and I bring her in through the main entrance?"

"You stay away from this," Haunani implored, with several people nodding their heads. "You no need more trouble."

Judy came out to the garage, banging a wooden spoon on the bottom of a metal pot, announcing it was time to eat. Several kids raced from the garage, followed by adults, Haunani, the large woman, and June bringing up the rear.

There was enough food for twice as many people as were there. June looked for dishes obviously vegetarian, and things she could recognize. Spreading just a few things on her plate, she found Karen on a low wall in the garden, already eating. Henry was being entertained by a small group of men.

"You didn't get much on your plate, Doctor Kato."

"I'm vegetarian," June said, leaning in close to whisper. "I have to be careful about eating at other peoples' houses."

"Find something you can eat?" she asked.

"I think so."

"Make sure you eat it all and go back for more later."

"What's this brown stuff?" she asked, poking at something lumpy on her plate.

"Pork."

She nudged it off to one side. "Karen, I want to apologize for the fight you guys had earlier. Nothing ever happened between Henry and me. I want you to know that."

"I know. I just get kind of jealous sometimes. And when he said he saw your butt, well, it set me off."

"You do realize he sees women patients all the time, right?"

Karen nodded. "That's why I get so jealous. When we go to the beach together, I know where he's looking, which is usually at me. But at work…I know it's silly, but I can't help it."

"For what it's worth, he didn't see much more than a few square inches, and I can guarantee he'll never see it again."

"Except you guys went surfing together. Are you going to be one of his surf buddies?"

"Not for the foreseeable future, something else I can guarantee. Don't get me wrong, I enjoyed surfing that time, and your husband is fun to hang around with, but I won't be on a board for a while."

"How many times have young wives heard that lie?" Karen asked.

"If it means anything, I have a little secret to share, but only if you promise not to tell Henry for a while."

"I can keep a secret, if it's good enough."

"My rear end, plus a lot of the rest of my body will be changing pretty soon."

Karen leaned in close to whisper. "You're pregnant?"

"Yep, but nobody at the hospital except my OB knows, including Henry. Somehow, Auntie Haunani figured it out, though."

"Which is why she's been feeding you that goopy drink. She gave that to all the pregnant girls here tonight."

"Any idea of what's in it?"

"As in should you stay close to the bathroom in the next day or two?"

"That's one way of putting it," June said, setting aside her plate.

"Should be harmless. Probably just a bunch of vitamins. I doubt she'd do anything to harm someone." They watched as Henry came up to them. Karen smiled at him. "And I'll be sure to keep your secret."

"What secret?" he asked.

"Nothing," June and Karen said together.

Judy showed up, holding a large paper bowl. "Doctor, you're vegetarian?"

"Yeah, sorry!"

"Auntie sent this to you."

June took the bowl and looked at some purple pasty stuff.

"Poi," Judy said. "Put some pounds on you."

"Thanks. It's very purple."

"Best kind on the island. Use your fingers to eat it. One finger for kids, two for women, and three for men."

June obeyed and dipped two of her fingertips into the thickly crushed taro root dish called poi. It was warm, and felt like heavy mashed potatoes. It had an unexpected flavor, also very botanical. She smiled at Judy, who promptly smiled back before leaving.

"Doing okay?" Henry asked after a few more minutes.

"Tastes good," she whispered, eating the last of the poi. Other than being very salty, June mostly liked the food. "My ankles are going to look like tree trunks tomorrow though, from all this salt."

"Cardiologist's nightmare. In the clinic again?"

"Five whole patients, and all in a row, too. I might be able to get out in time for lunch at home."

"Finding any surgical patients yet?"

That was a tough topic for June right then. Doing surgery paid much better than seeing patients in the clinic, often several times more per hour of time spent. Evaluating basic back pain didn't pay much more than doing sports physicals on high school kids. It was going to take time until she was able to get patients needing surgery on her schedule. But she needed revenue coming in soon if her transition from LA to Maui was to be successful, and if she expected the hospital to open a clinic especially for her.

Before she could answer, Leonard came by with his wife. They sat on the low wall, bookending June and Henry. His wife, Marietta, was more white than anything else, a switch from most of the people there at the party.

Marietta gave June a small plate of steamed spinach with whole garlic cloves. June ate one, the garlic hitting her taste buds hard. She appreciated the gesture, of getting iron to build her blood and the garlic to aid her digestion, both common dishes pushed on pregnant women in Hawaii. June figured Auntie Haunani was responsible.

It wasn't long before Henry figured out June's secret for himself.

"The spinach, the extra helpings of food, Auntie Haunani hovering over you like a long lost child. You're pregnant?"

"Secret's out, I guess."

June got congratulations from the small group before she was left alone with Marietta.

As Marietta chattered on about her kids, pregnancy, and imploring June to come to her for pregnancy advice, June eavesdropped on Leonard and Henry's conversation. It was mostly about sports, two of the island high schools soon going head to head in battle for isle supremacy.

Leonard's topic shifted to Henry and Karen, how long Henry had known her, when they got married, the usual gossipy things discussed at potlucks.

Another woman came up to June and Marietta, talking with Marietta as though they were old friends since she had intimate knowledge of her pregnancies. It was the same woman she had noticed in the garage earlier, the one who looked very familiar. She figured it out when she heard she was a waitress at a mall restaurant. June was discovering how small the island really was.

"You've been in Ka'ahu Restaurant, yeah?" the woman asked. June had remembered her name started with a 'K', but wasn't Hawaiian.

"That's right, for breakfast a few times. I think you've been my waitress each time." June suddenly felt embarrassed, wondering if she had left a decent tip. "I like it there."

"Didn't you come in with a large group a while back?"

"When my sister was here for her wedding a few weeks ago. We weren't disruptive, were we?"

The girl laughed. "No, but you no eat much. Just get some toast, then send it back to get burnt to a crisp!"

"Yep! That's me!" June returned the woman's smile. Her name was coming to her, something like Karissa. "And mango juice."

"Next time you come in, we'll find something more bettah for you to eat. Especially now that…" Karissa tapped her tummy in a knowing way, sending a new flush of pink into June's cheeks.

"Everybody at the party knows?" June asked.

"This is Maui. By tomorrow afternoon, everybody on the island will know."

After more conversations with other couples, June sneaked a look at the time on her phone. It was getting late, and she needed to maintain her habit of rising early.

"Henry, maybe we should go. I have an early morning," she said when another couple came up to them.

"I'll find Karen," he said, going off to the kitchen in search of his wife.

It wasn't that she was shy, and she had been looking forward to making friends on the island, but not so many and all in one night. The other side of it was, all these people were related to a critically ill patient, her first patient at her new workplace, and there was no reason to believe he would get better soon. At that point in time, she still didn't know what was keeping him unconscious and comatose. As far as June was concerned, she needed to be keeping a professional distance from the entire group, not hanging out at a potluck with them.

It took another half-hour before they were able to break loose from the grips of the Baxter family. Just as they were about to leave, Judy found them. She had a large bag of foil-wrapped plates, forcing it into June's hand.

"More poi, vegetables, and banana lumpia. And no pork."

June struggled to keep from blushing at the thoughtfulness.

"Is nothing private on this island?" June asked once they were going to Henry's car.

"Not on Maui. And you may as well get used to it. Pretty soon, you're gonna be a prominent character in our little production of life and times."

"Oh? Why?" she asked.

"Single pregnant lady brain surgeon from LA, moves to Maui, buys old local kind house, saves the life of someone from the Baxter family. Gossip doesn't get any juicier than that."

"I haven't saved anyone's life."

"Don't fight it, Doctor Kato. Learn to enjoy the attention," Karen said.

"Except that my very first patient is one of Maui's most beloved men, and that he's not doing so well under my care, in spite of all my training and best efforts."

They went another block in silence until Henry stopped.

"It would've been the one on the right," Henry said, pointing at the modern house built on the lot. He was talking more to Karen than to June. "We had a row of bananas along the back wall that kept some of the sand out, a big mango tree on the side, a rubber tree on the other. And a big fan palm right up here in the front. It got so big, the fans blocked the front walk for a few years, had to walk around it until it got taller. Now all that's left of the place is the concrete wall at the back of the lot."

"What color was it?" Karen asked.

"The house? Green. We never once painted it. Got a new roof once after Hurricane Iniki took the other one mostly off."

"I remember that. Hurricanes are unusual here, aren't they?" June asked.

"It hit Kauai the hardest. Here, it was just high winds. Maybe the storm knew it was time for a new roof."

Arm in arm, he tugged his wife into walking again, June bringing up the rear. She felt like she was intruding on their private moment, a quiet walk in the evening.

"I didn't know I married a fatalist," Karen said, not really expecting an answer.

"Oh, heck yeah! If something can go wrong, it will. To be an emergency room nurse, you have to be fatalistic. Every patient is about to die at any moment, and it's only through sheer luck and enough medication that anyone survives a trip to the ER."

"Is that true, Doctor Kato?" Karen asked June. "You were one of his patients."

"Am I in that category?" June asked, thinking of the first time they met.

"Of course! It was luck you didn't have an allergic reaction to spider venom, and you got meds to counteract the mild reaction you were having."

"I think the shot you gave me in my rear hurt more than the spider bite."

"If you could go back in time, would you do any of it differently?"

"Yes. I'd ask for a different nurse to give me the shot, if for no other reason than to have a jealous wife not mad at me."

**

June was able to sneak Haunani into the hospital late in the evening after the potluck, where she was able to perform her rites behind closed curtains. June had been curious and wanted to peek, but didn't want to risk ruining the rudimentary relationship she was forming with the family. It was beginning to look as though she needed them as much as they needed her, if Kekoa was going to pull through his medical ordeal. Leonard finally sent June away, promising Haunani's procedure wouldn't take much longer and they'd leave as soon as she was done.

On her way into the hospital the next morning, June noticed an even larger heap of flowery leis draped over the lava boulder. So many, in fact, they were tumbling to the ground. Along with the new leis, several ti plants had been planted in the small garden spot. The scent of so many flowers in one place was strong, and June lingered for a moment to take in as much of the scent as she could to start her day.

"The family is really doing a lot to honor Kekoa," she whispered to herself as she went to the ICU to see Kekoa.

His condition was the same, comatose for no apparent reason, but at least the infection was getting better. She found the nurse taking care of him, the same as usual.

"Let's draw a serum tox screen, and request specifically to look for narcotics," June said.

"I know nobody is giving him any sedation," the nurse said. "I seriously doubt anyone would slip him a mickey."

"Something's keeping him zonked." June sorted through the vials of medication on the cart in the room. None of them were labeled as sedatives. "Give me a call when you get the results back."

**

For Haunani's second late night visit to Kekoa, they had to be much sneakier than the first. A small team of Baxters assembled at the rear of the hospital in the middle of the night, once again led by

Leonard. June parked nearby and gave them the 'hi' sign before going in. The plan was for them to wait another ten minutes before June checked the ICU to make sure the native Hawaiian nurse was there taking care of Kekoa again, before slipping Auntie Haunani in through a back door and up to the ICU using the utility elevators.

The plan worked well, considering the short notice and spur of the moment planning they gave themselves. The nurse taking care of Kekoa that night was a distant friend of the Baxter family, someone in on the little scheme. She had given the faux call just after midnight, providing the phony message that there was a problem with Kekoa, requesting June to come in.

Possibly the reason it had gone so smoothly was that Kekoa was the only patient in the ICU that night, and few people were around to notice anything out of the ordinary going on in his cubicle. They got Auntie Haunani in there, drew the curtains around the cubicle, and the nurse stood watch outside. While Haunani said her prayers, June took aside the other nurse in the department to distract her. Once June could no hear Haunani's prayers, she went back to the cubicle. Haunani was already packed up and ready to leave. Scanning Kekoa's bed, June saw no sign of stones or flower leis, just a satisfied grin on Auntie's face. Minutes later, June was back home and in bed, task completed.

***

"I wonder what today is going to bring?" June asked herself in the empty Ghostavator on her way up to the ICU the next morning. "I hope Kekoa is improving and that I'm not being led around the hospital late at night on some Polynesian wild goose chase."

His medical condition was still improving, although slowly. When she asked the nurse if he was showing signs of regaining consciousness, she only shook her head. The toxicology screen also showed no narcotics in his system at all. For all intents and purposes, Kekoa Baxter was on a prolonged holiday. Her next stop was in the clinic, where she found the receptionist, scheduler, and office manager dedicated strictly to her.

"Well, you have five patients total today, all of them this morning," Jesskah told her. June wondered if her name was really spelled that way on her birth certificate, or if it had morphed into that when she moved to the island. From the very first day, June was able to catch the fake accent the twenty-something-year-old mainland transplant used.

"Are any of them here yet?"

The girl twirled a pen in her hand, oddly since she was the princess of digital devices. Whenever June saw her, she was busy on her phone or the computer. "Not yet. I'll let you know when they're getting checked in."

June turned to go down the hall toward her little office space.

"Oh, by the way," Jesskah called after her. She held up a pink slip of paper. "There's a message here from the chairman of the board of the hospital. He wants you to call him as soon as you're in."

June took the slip and went to her office. She had a good idea of what it was about. Somehow, Townsend had likely heard about the midnight doings in the ICU from the last two nights. She barely sat before dialing his number on the desk phone.

"Mister Townsend, this is June Kato. How are you today?" she said in a sweet but contrived voice.

"It's come to my attention, Doctor, that there is an arrangement of flowers…"

For some reason, the flower lei and rock that Haunani had left in Kekoa's room the night before had been discovered by someone not sympathetic to the cause. June needed to think quick to come up with some sort of explanation.

"Let me explain."

"No, let me explain to you, and one last time. Apparently I didn't make it clear to you that overt religious displays would not be allowed at the hospital, and that includes the exterior of the hospital."

"Exterior?" June asked.

"The rather large display at the main entrance to the hospital, something that seems to grow with each passing day. I noticed this morning there are now plants growing there."

"I noticed it also. But let me reassure you, I know nothing about that."

"Are you certain? The timing of it is rather peculiar, as it showed up on the day your patient was injured."

June felt compelled to protect the Baxter family, but somehow without damaging her career. "There's no way of knowing who's responsible. It would only be guesswork that the Baxters have something to do with it, rather presumptuous actually. It is rather innocent, after all. Placement of flower leis on a stone seems quite sweet to me, given the effort it required. Even if it is from that family, it's outside the hospital, well within your guidelines."

"Still…"

"Still, we need to remember who is at the center of all this: Kekoa Baxter. He's the one who needs to be focused on, not our petty little needs to win some sort of political contest. Has anyone talked with the night shift security guards? Maybe they know something about it?"

"I'll look into that. Were the séances in the Intensive Care Unit the last two nights arranged by you?"

"I know nothing about séances," June said truthfully. The religious rites Haunani had performed had been called something else, a Hawaiian word June couldn't remember right then, but not séances. "I am a medical doctor, and I use modern medical and surgical practices to treat my patients."

"Just so you know, Doctor, I'll be posting a guard outside Mister Baxter's door tonight, to prevent anything from happening."

"Good. He can keep the police guard company."

"And if Mister Baxter doesn't respond to your care soon, and by respond I mean wake up, I'm having him transferred to the other hospital on the island where he can receive the competent care he apparently needs."

What he said was much more than a simple barb; it was a full-blown insult.

"Mister Townsend, if he'd had competent surgical intervention right from the beginning, including early treatment with antibiotics and a pulmonary consult to address his respiratory needs, he would be going home soon. That's something you need to take up with Doctor Soseki, someone I'm still considering reporting to the State Department of Professional Licensing, and not try to pin on me. Under my care, Mister Baxter's condition has improved. Had he been left to Soseki, his family would most likely be planning a funeral right about now."

June tossed the phone hand-piece in the cradle. She dug through her purse, trying to remember if she got a business card from Leonard the day they met. She found one and dialed the number on it, hoping it wasn't too early to call.

"Leonard? This is June Kato, at the hospital."

She gave him a quick report on Kekoa, that he still hadn't woken, but she had ordered head scans for that day. They shared a chuckle about the caper the night before, of getting Haunani in and out of the hospital unseen. She told him about the spy in the hospital, but neither could figure who it was.

"I have a question for you," June said. "There's a flower display at the entrance of the hospital. I guess it's not really even a question, but more of a warning. When the chairman of the board of the hospital spoke with me just now, he said he's quite upset about the flowers, for whatever reason."

"On the rock? I've seen them also. Very thoughtful."

"According to the hospital administration, they need to stop. It might be a good idea, too. Whatever we can do to stay on their good side right now is best for Kekoa. Please pass the word through your family to not put flowers or plant any more shrubs in that little garden, at least until we can get all this sorted out."

"Us? As far as I know, we have nothing to do with those. It's something very Hawaiian to do, to make an offering like that, but Auntie Haunani has been taking care of that at her home, and at a nearby heiau hidden in the hills."

"The Baxters aren't putting the flowers there? Or the ti plants this morning?"

"What ti plants?"

"Never mind." June bit her lip a moment, wondering how she should proceed. She had something else to talk to the family about, and Leonard seemed to be the family spokesperson. Money was always a sensitive subject, especially in the hospital where care got very expensive and bills stacked up in a hurry. "Say, Leonard. There's something else I need to talk to the Baxters about."

"Yes?"

"Kekoa isn't married? Or has kids?"

"Poor guy has never found the right girl, even though half the island loves him."

"I see. The thing is, his care is quite expensive, and his reimbursement comes only from the state-mandated insurance."

"Which doesn't pay much. But what's your concern?"

"This is very difficult to discuss. I need to do more testing, and that gets expensive. One of the first things I heard from the hospital, and frankly Doctor Soseki warned me about this, was that there would be little reimbursement for his care. Is there a way that maybe each member of the family could chip in a small amount, something of a gesture, once the bills begin to come in?"

"Maybe there's some confusion," Leonard said. "First, I'm sorry you feel stuck in the middle of something like finances. You shouldn't worry about that as his doctor. Second, if the hospital is concerned about Kekoa's bills, they should come to one of us directly so we can manage it properly, not by going behind our backs."

"I'm sorry," June tried saying.

"Just because we're Hawaiian and we live in small houses, it doesn't mean we're destitute. In our family, we all have jobs because we want to work, to have a schedule of some sort, to be productive."

"I guess I'm even more confused than you realize."

"The Baxter family has a trust fund. It's rather large, Doctor. But we don't dip into it unless an emergency comes along, or use it for college tuition for the kids."

"Emergencies like Kekoa's injury," June said, filling in the blank.

"We've been expecting someone from the hospital to contact us, but so far no one has come forward. The Baxter family was an original benefactor of the hospital, something that isn't public knowledge. But still, there shouldn't be issues concerning reimbursement. You really don't need to be worried about that."

June was embarrassed that she had brought up the subject. She'd listened to others who knew little about the Baxters, and had guided her care of Kekoa accordingly. In a way, she was treating him as poorly as Soseki had. "You're absolutely right, Leonard. Kekoa's bills shouldn't be any of my concern at all."

June hung up the phone, already mentally exhausted, and her day in the clinic hadn't even started yet.

Getting to the Bottom of Things

June couldn't be a cop and investigate the crime that put Kekoa in the hospital, but she was a doctor and needed to get to the bottom of why he wasn't coming around. Antibiotics were relieving his infected wound and the aggressive treatments as prescribed by the pulmonologist were clearing his lungs and helping his heart function, but his brain continued to be on vacation.

There was a medical reason for him not waking up yet; it just wasn't obvious. Spending much of her time thinking of what that reason might be, in the clinic, out on runs, losing sleep at night, she considered every possible factor. She checked and double-checked the level of sedation, and every time she asked a nurse, they all denied administering anything. She had blood drawn to check for a toxicology screen, if indeed someone had been giving him narcotics on the sly; the screen came back negative, indicating there were no meds in his system that could be controlling the function of his central nervous system. She'd performed neuro exams every day, checking his reflexes and peripheral nerve function, and every time they came back nearly normal. Pupils reacted to light, feet twitched to stimuli, and he had a gag reflex. The nerves that arose in his brain, brain stem, and peripheral nervous system were all within normal limits.

Then she decided to get an EEG, to check activity within the brain itself. A portable machine was brought to the ICU and electrodes hooked up. Within a few minutes, the technician smiled while showing June the printout.

"He has the exact same EEG of a patient in a sedation coma," the woman said.

Figuring on Maui time and that it would take a few hours before a neurologist to take a look at the results, June knew Kekoa's brain was alive and well inside his head. But Townsend's expectation that Kekoa either wake up that day or get sent to another hospital for 'better treatment' loomed over the situation like a black cloud.

"Okay, fine," she said, giving the printout back to the technician as she was leaving with her portable machine. "I'll get a scan of his brain. If that doesn't show something, then I'll be up a creek with Kekoa, doing all the paddling by myself."

Two hours later, June waited in the radiology control room, watching patiently as digital images from an MRI came up on the computer screen. She'd seen scans of brains thousands of times before, and hardly needed a second glance to know Kekoa's brain was normal. Watching the nurse and respiratory therapist prepare to Kekoa take him back to the ICU, she crossed her arms and sighed with mild exasperation.

"Normal scans, June," the radiologist said, switching from normal views to blow-ups on his monitor. "No pathology that I can discern."

"Your machine has been calibrated and maintenance is up to date?"

The radiologist double-checked all the settings. "Everything up to date. Why?"

"You don't see any indication of infarct? No bubbles that might've floated, no bits of plaque or clot that might've broken loose and got caught in the Circle of Willis or PICA during surgery? Nothing at all?"

"Perfectly normal, June. I only wish my brain looked so healthy as this patient's. Were you looking for anything in particular?" the radiologist asked.

"Stroke, or an occult embolus that might've floated into his brain during carotid surgery. Fifth days post-op after bilateral carotid repairs, and he won't come around. We used a shunt and had fairly short clamp times. I've taken him off all of his sedation, and respiratory therapy and the pulmonologist have tried weaning him off the vent, but he won't take a breath on his own."

"Check his blood toxicology?"

"As in someone doping his IV? First thing I thought of. One of the oldest tricks in the book, actually, for a so-called friend to come in and dose a patient, just to keep him stoned. But I've checked each morning and there's nothing. Plus, he just isn't built like a user, you know?"

"Something is going on somewhere with him."

"Yeah, something. But what?" June rubbed her face. "Do me a favor. Expedite your impressions and get them into the chart. Administration is breathing down my neck to get his condition improved."

"Or what? It's not like doctors can snap their fingers and the patient magically gets better."

June sighed again. "Somehow, magic will need to be performed if I want to keep my position here at the hospital."

"One thing that might help is to find the guy that attacked him. If he attacked once, he will again," the radiologist said. "That might help answer a few questions."

"Which has all of Maui on edge right now. Every day there's another article in the newspaper about Kekoa and the investigation, and my name always seems to be a part of it. Not a good way of starting a new practice, being associated with a patient who was brutally attacked and not recovering as expected. I get the feeling that the news stories are being manipulated behind the scenes by someone. I've been through that in LA where I just came from, but I never expected it here on Maui."

"Like they always say, keep your friends close and your enemies closer. Who was primary surgeon, you or Soseki?"

"That's a big part of the issue with admin. He started out as primary, repairing one side while I repaired the other. He initially kept the patient on his service but did very little to treat him post-op. It was the next day when he found me doing rounds on the patient, and said I should take over his care. So, I did. A few hours later, I was sitting in Townsend's office defending myself, Soseki making snide comments the entire time."

"June, I've never met the guy, but from what I've heard about his rep, you've crossed swords with the wrong guy."

June stood, ready to go back to the ICU to see Kekoa. "I've been in a few sword fights of my own, but I'm not going to use

Kekoa as a shield, or a weapon. If Soseki or Townsend want to pick a fight with me, they can step out of the shadows and be a man about it."

June heard the radiologist say something about a breath of fresh air just as she was leaving. Back at the ICU, she noticed Judy sitting in the waiting area.

"Well, the good news is, Kekoa's brain seems healthy. He didn't have a stroke or embolus, as I told you might've happened. His EEG is normal, his reflexes all give normal responses, everything is what we call within normal limits."

"What is it then?" Judy asked. "Why won't he wake up?"

"I'm not sure. It really is rather peculiar, that he won't come around, and that his wound has been slow to heal. The signs of infection have passed, no redness or fever, no inflammation at all now. But it's almost as if his body is refusing to heal."

A tear ran halfway down Judy's cheek before it was wiped away. "Is he dead? Maybe he died and we don't know it?"

June reached forward and touched the woman's arm. "No. He's perfectly alive. His heart is beating strong and all his vital systems are working well. It's just as if he's taken a holiday, that he doesn't want to come back quite yet." June instantly knew that was the wrong thing to say just then. "Or that something is preventing him from waking up. I just need to figure that out."

Judy finished drying her eyes while they sat on the small couch. "Like Auntie Haunani said, it's his mana. It's broke."

"I guess I still don't know enough about mana."

"There's something called ho'oponopono," Judy said quietly. "It's a practice that's something like finding forgiveness for the spirit. It's something Auntie plans for tomorrow night."

"About her visits…" June began but was interrupted.

"Since the man that did the terrible thing to Kekoa can't be found, we need to do something else to help Kekoa in his healing. She needs to heal his mind, body, and spirit, and then do ho'oponopono at the end. The stone and ti lei you saw were the beginning, the healing of his mind. Last night, Auntie worked on his body. Maybe that's why your film showed nothing wrong with his brain, yeah?"

"Yes, maybe. But…"

"Tonight she works on his spirit, and tomorrow night, ho'oponopono."

"I'm all for spiritual healing, and respecting peoples' beliefs and faith, but you must understand there is a medical reason for his comatose state," June insisted. "I just need to find what it is, and make the corrections in his care. Maybe a different antibiotic, even though he doesn't really show an infectious process. Also, his body might be very sensitive to the medications I have him on at night, to help him get natural sleep. It's called narco-naive, and…"

"Been several days. The man that did this thing to him might never be caught. We have to do what we can for Bruddah Kekoa's mana. Please understand that, Doctor. We appreciate everything you've done for him, but so far, the hospital hasn't brought him back to us. That's why we do these things late at night."

"Along with the leis and ti plants out in front of the hospital?" June asked.

"That's not from us. Must be for another patient in the hospital."

"I just want your family to know that I'm not going to give up on Kekoa. I'm going to do everything I can from a medical standpoint to bring him back to the Baxters."

"Will you help Auntie Haunani come in tonight?"

"Yes, but let me figure out a plan first. Is there anything else?" June asked.

"Eating the food we sent home with you? The poi?"

"Had some for breakfast." It was true too, that June ate a little of it before coming to work, her only breakfast that morning.

"Karissa would be happy."

"Oh? Is she the one that made it?"

"Yeah, but she's also what we call a kahuna hoohapai keiki."

"Keiki means children. And I'm learning what kahuna do. What does the rest mean?"

Judy smiled. "Hapai mean pregnant. She the kind of kahuna that help women get pregnant."

June thought about it for a moment. She had been pregnant since before moving to Hawaii, and it was confirmed by several tests and by her OB. She wasn't trying to get pregnant, she already was. Something was fishy about Karissa and Haunani, working on June's pregnancy so much, but sitting in the hospital ICU wasn't the time or place to explore it.

"Judy, I need to go. But if you wait here, the nurse will come get you to visit Kekoa soon."

***

During her down time, she sat in the hospital library, pouring over medical journals, looking for any precedent on other patients in Kekoa Baxter's predicament. Finding nothing made her feel even more alone in her quest.

A light rain had started when June went out to her pickup truck for the short drive home at the end of the day. The sun was also shining just then, something June had discovered happened quite often on Maui. She watched for a rainbow over the ocean, for some sign that things were going to change for the better.

During dinner, she called Henry.

"Henry, you think Auntie Haunani is doing Kekoa some good?"

"I think it's making the family feel better. And for as long as they get to practice their rituals, they're off your back, right?"

"Mostly. I had a long talk with Judy today. She said Haunani is determined to proceed, with or without my help. I tried telling her I was doing everything possible medically, but she refused to hear it. The family insists Kekoa won't get better unless Haunani does her thing."

"So, let her."

"Which I don't mind. But once hospital admin finds out I'm helping the family, which in this case is viewed as aiding and abetting the enemy, I could be out of a job and fighting for my license to practice medicine. I've sunk too much into this to give up what I've worked so hard for in my life, just because I've upset a couple of old cronies."

"Apparently you haven't seen today's newspaper," he said.

"Why? What's in it today?"

"I'll read the front page article." June heard the rustle of paper in the background of the call. "Doctor June Kato, a recent transplant from big city mainland, struggles to keep alive her one and only patient in the hospital, reports Townsend, the Chairman of the hospital Board of Directors. In every way she has been a failure, to inadequately care for her patient, refusing to take advice from senior physicians, and in non-compliance with administrative requests."

June swore. "What?"

"It gets worse. Townsend went on to say that whatever two-bit hospital Doctor Kato came from should take her back."

June swore again. "He recruited me! He told me how much traffic would come my way if I signed on, how glad they were to get someone from the mainland, specifically from my old hospital, and someone with my reputation. So far, they haven't lived up to their end of the deal of finding a clinic of my own, or doing any promotional work, announcing to the community a new neurosurgeon is on the island. Did the reporter say anything else in the article?"

"Only that you promote the practice of voodoo and have brought in a witch doctor to treat your one and only patient. Is there some sort of witch garden at the hospital that I haven't seen?" Henry asked. "I always go in the ER entrance at work."

"Someone has been leaving leis on a lava rock at the main entrance. He probably means that. He keeps telling me to knock it off, but I have nothing to do with it."

"You think it's the Baxters?" he asked.

"Both Leonard and Judy have said the Baxters aren't responsible for the leis. There're even ti plants growing there now, something else they deny knowing about. I believe them, too."

"Planted in the ground or cut leaves in vases?"

"Planted. They looked like they've always been there. Not like someone dug a hole, tossed the plant in, and walked away. They look growing and healthy, the dirt around them completely undisturbed. Is there some special meaning in that?"

"When people plant ti at doors and windows, it's meant to keep evil spirits away. Another Hawaiian superstition but everybody has them at their houses."

"They're all over the place at my house, especially around the front and back door. I can't even use the front entrance, that it's so crowded with ti plants and hibiscus. I was thinking of chopping them back one of these days."

"Don't do it. Just use the back door. If they really are in the way, get a native Hawaiian to do some pruning. They can use the leaves for ceremonies and leis," Henry said.

"I didn't know they were so important. Do you suppose that was the point of someone planting them at the hospital? An attempt to keep evil spirits out?"

"Most likely."

"Despite what the Baxters say, I still think they have something to do with it. Haunani has ti leis at Kekoa's bedside and a lava rock under his bed. Apparently, ti leis are pretty important to Auntie Haunani."

After the call, she decided on going for a run. She left the house without stopping to put on jogging shoes. Barely looking at traffic before sprinting across the busy road down the hill from her house, it wasn't long before she was on the beach, running at a full clip. On the wet sand, gentle waves of warm seawater washed against her shins. She redoubled her efforts, bringing more pain. Not only did she accept the pain, she wanted more.

June barely noticed when she had cleared the two resort areas and had passed through the open public shoreline. It was two miles to that point from her home, and another mile to the next hotel and resort area, her usual turn-around spot for an ordinary jog.

She noticed then how hard she was running, and the sweat that was pouring off her. It was mid-evening in the balmy tropics, and she was running across sand and through water. She hadn't got lunch and barely ate that morning. But in spite of all that, she barely felt fatigued.

When the images of Divya scolding her for getting so much strenuous exercise and Haunani giving her the devil for not eating enough food floated through her mind, June pulled to a stop at the last tourist store at the resort. It was the place Karen worked at, Henry's wife, who was studying to get into a hospitality training program. She patted down her pockets and realized she'd left home in such a hurry, and with no money, not even her keys. Instead of going in, she went to a drinking fountain she knew well from previous runs.

"Howzit, June!" someone behind her said cheerfully.

She turned and saw Karen. "Hey, Karen. Not at school today?"

"Done with classes for the day. Anything new with Kekoa?"

"Not really." June used some of the water to splash on her face. "I just talked to Henry a while ago."

Karen frowned. "He just called me. That's terrible what was in that article."

"I need to keep focused on Kekoa. The rest of that stuff can be dealt with later, with a lawyer, if need be."

Karen pushed June into the air-conditioned store and stuck a bottle of cold passion-orange-guava juice in her hand, known locally as 'POG', a tourist favorite. "What's going on with Haunani?"

"I need to figure out a way of getting her into the hospital late tonight, and again tomorrow night, and past the guard the hospital administration has stationed at Kekoa's room." June cracked the lid off the small bottle and took a swig. "Any ideas?"

"I'm the wrong person to ask about cloak and dagger stuff. Something that might work is what you've done on the mainland in the past. Maybe local Maui people won't notice until it's done?" Karen asked.

"Maybe. The problem isn't with local Maui people but with a surgeon and administrator, both from the mainland, picking a fight with me, also from the mainland. They also seem to have a spy working for them, to get so much information as quickly as they do. Now that the news channels have got a hold of the story, we all look like fools, seemingly careless about Maui people, only thinking of ourselves."

"I still don't know you very well, June, but I don't think of you that way. Anyway, are you supposed to be exercising so hard in your condition?"

"Ha! That's the first time someone has used that word to describe me. Maybe I should go home at a gentler pace."

***

June ran at a jogging pace, not in a hurry to get home, but to work off the anxiety that had grown in the short talk with Karen. She stretched her run further down the opposite side of the beach, spending as much time as she thought she could manage, before returning home. By the time she was ready to cross the road for the final leg back to her house, she was washed with sweat, her legs covered with sand, and eyes stinging from salt.

Hands on her hips and panting, she waited for a long line of cars to pass, and caught a heavy whiff of exhaust from a delivery truck. Unable to blow it off, she stumbled over to a patch of crabgrass and bent over.

After the last of the POG had cleared from her stomach, she wiped her mouth with the front of her shirt, having given up on decorum a bucket of sweat earlier. When a break in the traffic came, she got across the road and up the hill to home.

"No more POG for me."

The house was dark and quiet when she went in. Her first stop was the shower. With nothing clean to wear after, she wrapped tightly in the bath towel and went to the laundry pantry to find something to put on. After dressing, she went to the kitchen to start dinner, with a taste for saimin salad.

She boiled the noodles, then set them in a tray on the windowsill to cool. After that, she began making the oily sauce. Shredding lettuce and chopping spinach came next, followed by draining the lumpy tofu. For some reason, it didn't look like enough. Just as she sat down to eat, her phone rang.

"Hi Leonard."

"We're on for tonight, right?"

"Haunani going to see Kekoa? I suppose. I just haven't figured out a way of getting her in there without being seen."

"Yeah, there's a guard posted outside his little room today. Somehow, we need to distract him."

"Any ideas?" she asked.

Leonard outlined his idea of dressing Haunani in housekeeping clothes to get her through the hospital undetected.

"What about the guard?" June asked.

"Idea for that, also. Just as Auntie gets to the ICU, someone pulls a fire alarm. That makes for mass chaos in a hospital, right?"

"Pretty much. But it's also a felony, too much trouble for any of us." It wasn't a bad idea. Giving it some thought, June came up with a similar idea that wouldn't cause so much trouble. "On the other hand, there's a code system which includes a baby abduction code. I think they call it a Code White. When that's announced, security is supposed to rush to the maternity ward, and employees watch exit doors and elevators for anybody that might have a baby. Hospitals have practice drills for that all the time."

"Not so much trouble?" he asked.

"Not felonious, anyway."

"Who would steal a baby?" he asked.

"I don't know. Not our problem. Just bring your aunt to the back door of the hospital tonight at midnight, with whatever she needs. I'll take care of the rest."

As soon as she was off that call, she called Henry back.

"Henry, I need to ask a favor and you can't ask why."

***

At five minutes to midnight, June drove through the parking lot, looking for Soseki and Townsend's cars. Seeing their assigned parking spaces vacant, she took a deep breath and parked near the Emergency Room.

Leonard was already there with Haunani, waiting in his pickup truck. June signaled for them to wait a moment.

Finding Henry already at work, he took her to where the ER housekeeper was waiting.

"Size small housekeeper uniform," the young woman said, holding out the outfit on its hanger. "Why you want it?"

June took the hanger. "This is one of those don't ask, don't tell things." She gave the housekeeper an envelope, which disappeared into her pocket when she hurried off.

June brought Haunani in, leaving Leonard to wait in his truck. Once Haunani had changed into the housekeeper outfit, they found the spare cart abandoned by the ER housekeeper and went to an elevator, Haunani's bag of supplies hidden beneath linens. When the elevator on the right opened, Haunani refused to take it.

"We can't stand out here all night, Auntie," June said, jabbing her finger at the elevator button again. "The longer you're in the hospital, the more likely you are to be found. All of our plans would go right out the window."

"That thing have bad spirits in it. No good kind of thing to ride."

The other elevator dinged and slid open, allowing them to go to the ICU alone.

"Maybe someday you can do a cleansing on that, too."

"Not Hawaiian spirit haunting that. Some other kind. Needs whatchamacallit…an exorcism."

"I have enough trouble on my hands without worrying about that right now," June said as the door opened. She helped the old woman get the heavy cart off the elevator and guided down the short distance to the ICU entrance. "You remember the plan, right? As soon as you hear Code White being called over the PA system, and see the guard rush off, you go into Kekoa's room and do what you need to do. His nurse knows to pull the curtains and leave you alone, but you'll need to hurry. How much time will you need?"

"Five minutes is enough. Not time but power of the spirit when praying is what counts."

June left her alone. Going to a dark corner of the ICU waiting area to hide in a shadow, she called Henry. "Okay, do your thing."

His thing was to call one of the nurses in the maternity ward, a locally born and part Hawaiian nurse who was in on that night's scheme. It was her job to call in the baby abduction code, pretending it was a planned but unannounced drill. Two minutes later, the Code White was announced over the hospital paging system. Thirty seconds later, she saw the security guard assigned to watch Kekoa's door bolt for the stairs.

Finding a new position to watch Haunani, she watched as the skinny woman tried to push the cart forward on the carpeted floor of the hallway. It barely budged. Throughout all that, the Code White was repeated several times.

'Come on, just leave the cart behind and take your bag of stuff to the room,' June thought as she watched Haunani try to propel the cart forward. The message must've gone through, because the woman abandoned the cart and went into the ICU where June could no longer watch.

She watched the time on her watch when she heard the last of the code announcements.

"Three minutes," she whispered, still hiding in the shadow. "That guard will be back soon."

With each passing minute, June checked her watch.

Haunani never came out.

Another minute passed.

"Come on. Just say the prayer and get out."

The elevator door slid open. Out came the security guard, walking toward the ICU entrance, a grim look to his face.

Still no sign of Haunani.

June panicked. If he found Haunani in the room with Kekoa, she, the Baxters, and June would all be in trouble. She considered trying to call the unit secretary as another distraction, but worried her voice would be recognized. Then she saw the guard stop at the housekeeping cart in the middle of the hall where it had been left.

Haunani still wasn't around to defend it.

"What the devil is this doing here?" He shoved it to the side, parking it near the wall.

Just then, Haunani came out the double doors to the ICU, still in her housekeeper's uniform.

"Hey, keep your cart out of the middle of the hall!" the guard griped. "Don't you know it's in the way? Someone could crash into this thing if they were in a hurry!"

Haunani barely paid any attention to him, only passing by with a large smile on her face, leaving him and the cart behind.

***

June took a cold shower before going to bed that night. She had checked on Kekoa by calling in when she got home from the late night hospital visit, and found nothing new in his condition.

In bed in the dark, she tapped a number on her phone. A text message from her sister had been waiting to call her back. Discussing problems in the middle of the night was nothing new to them, ever since they shared a bedroom as kids, discussing homework assignments, boyfriends, and the issues of growing up in the big city. Maybe the topics had changed in recent years, but the problems were just as pressing.

"Amy, what's up?"

"It's four in the morning, Babe. People here in the real world are sleeping."

"Oh yeah, time difference. I'll call tomorrow, okay?"

June ended the call and set aside the phone. Pulling the sheet up to her shoulders, she settled in to wait for sleep to overcome her mind.

Just as her mind was drifting off, leaving the worries of the day behind, her phone rang.

"What's wrong?" Amy asked curtly.

"It can wait, Sis."

"You don't call me in the middle of the night, say you have a problem, and then hang up. Now, what is it?"

"Nothing. Go back to sleep."

"Are you in jail? A patient in the hospital? Lost in the tropical wilderness?"

"No, no, and no. I think."

"I already know you're knocked up. Mom told me all about it. So, what's wrong?" Amy said insistently. "Is the baby okay?"

"That blabbermouth. Next-Gen Kato is fine. I have this patient at work, a Hawaiian guy. He got his throat slashed gang-style. There's not much of a description of the guy that did it, and the police can't find suspects to interrogate."

"Please tell me you're not getting involved in some stupid scheme to find a gangster."

"No! Not at all. The thing is, the patient isn't waking up from his surgery, and that was Monday morning. It's been almost five days since it happened."

"I don't know much about surgery, but that seems like a long time."

"He should've come around later that day or the day after. I've taken a scan of his head and his brain is perfectly normal. But his wound isn't healing and he's not even close to being conscious. He just lies there."

"There's nothing else wrong with him? Is he stoned on something?"

"That's the first thing I thought, but no. Otherwise, he's in good health. Not a marathoner, but healthy enough to survive his injuries."

"What's his family say?" Amy asked.

"His family is huge. It's like there's more of them with each passing day. I've never seen a guy so well-liked as Kekoa. They're doing these ancient Hawaiian prayer things in the middle of the night. There's this auntie, I'm not even sure if she's his real auntie or just some lady the family knows. But she's been sneaking into the hospital late at night to pray for him."

"So? If it makes her and the family happy, let her. Can't hurt, right?"

"That's what I say. But the administration of the hospital thinks otherwise."

"Oh, and here we are at your problem," Amy said matter of factly. "You're already butting heads with the powers-that-be at the hospital?"

"It's not like that. The administrator won't even go see the patient. He just hears rumors before attributing them to me and the family. The thing is, it's hit the newspaper here. Each day, there's a new story about Kekoa and his family doing what the administrator calls ancient voodoo rituals, and my name gets plastered all over it."

"That's someone you need to stay away from. And I mean very far away. You just moved there. Don't start screwing yourself first week on the job. I mean it. Don't get involved in hospital politics, and don't get involved in family dynamics. You have enough of that stuff of your own right now."

"You're right. I'm reading too much into this whole thing. I just need to focus on getting Kekoa awake and back out of the hospital."

"How's Jack? Talk to him lately?"

"Not in a while. Every time I call, he's busy with a meeting or on his way to a helicopter to take him somewhere."

"Huh, imagine that. Looks like Mom wins the wagering pool."

"What?"

"I thought you'd find a way of out-working the President in your first month on the job. Mom said you'd take it easy, at least until the baby came."

"What did Dad say?"

"He thought you'd be living in the White House by now."

"Tell everybody thanks for the support. Now I don't feel so bad about calling late."

"Why didn't you tell me about the baby sooner?" Amy finally asked.

"Oh, I just didn't want to upstage your wedding." June explained how she'd been to a high-risk OB and that everything checked out okay, so far. "She'll do an ultrasound in a few more weeks, just to make sure it's not tubal and not twins."

"What's wrong with twins?" Amy asked.

"One at a time, Amy. And I might stick with one, total. This is wearing me out."

"Wait a few more months. Then you'll know what worn-out really feels like!" Amy said. "Taking vitamins?"

"Yes, mommy."

"Eating enough for two?"

"Yes, mommy."

"Don't get smart with me, or I'll come there. And I'll bring the rest of the family with me." There was a pause. "Better yet, I'll send Mom and Dad to live with you."

"They're already coming, unless I can think of a way of preventing it."

"It's not a bad idea. Dad's been talking about what he could build on the back of your house. I'm not supposed to tell you this, but he's getting architectural plans drawn up."

"Don't I get a say in it?" June asked. "It's my house, after all."

"Apparently he wants to save you money and do most of the work himself. Mom thinks you need a nanny and has already put her name at the top of the list."

"The kid won't be born for another eight months!"

"Not for the baby. For you. She knows you won't eat right unless somebody forces you. Or get enough sleep. Which by the way, I need to do right now."

After hanging up, June made the mental note to call her old colleague and boss in LA, Fred Towns, to get a phone consult about Kekoa's condition first thing in the morning.

**

When June woke in the morning, the sun was already streaming across the bed, something she knew didn't happen for at least an hour after sunrise. She looked at the little alarm clock at the bedside, then tossed it back again.

"Is that right?" She picked up her phone and looked at the time on it. She was late. "Forget about getting breakfast this morning."

With less than an hour before she needed to be in the clinic, she went straight for her shower and quickly dressed. Barely raking her fingers through her wet hair and foregoing makeup, she was out the back door and into the pickup truck. She had only minutes to drive the short trip to the hospital and make rounds on Kekoa before getting to the clinic for her first appointment. Breakfast would have to wait until later.

"I'll have to start setting the alarm clock again," she said to the windshield as she pulled out onto the highway for the mile drive to work. "So much for Maui time."

She saw Henry in the ER doing something with a patient. Then she saw the young housekeeper from who she had borrowed the uniform the night before. Giving her a polite wave as she hurried away, June wondered if the girl was indeed Townsend's spy.

It was only a moment before she was at Kekoa's bedside. The day shift nurse was there right then, and June wondered if any of their late night shenanigans had been discovered.

"Nobody here yet to see Kekoa today?" she asked the nurse.

"Someone was earlier, I'm not sure who it was, though." The nurse moved aside so June could do a more thorough exam. It didn't take June long to find out there were few changes in Kekoa's condition.

"And he's getting absolutely no sedation during the day, right?" June verified with the nurse.

"Not from me. I was here yesterday and gave him nothing. No paralytics, no sleep meds, no sedation."

June finished her exam and wrote a note in the chart.

"Let me know if there are any changes at all. I need to be here to see them."

"What about his family?"

"I think they're getting tired of seeing me, frankly. I'll give them a call later."

June hurried out again, half that she didn't want to face the motionless Kekoa, half because there was still hope she could get to the cafeteria for watered-down coffee and maybe even a slice of toast before going to the clinic. If Maui time held up, she'd get lucky and her first patient of the morning would be late.

The savory aroma of fried pork in the cafeteria took the edge off her appetite. Standing in line to pay for her toast and coffee, her phone rang with the clinic number. She learned that sure enough, the first patient couldn't get a ride to the hospital until later in the morning. June suddenly had an hour to kill.

"I told you the other day, you no have to pay, Doctor," the young cashier told her. The girl was wearing no makeup that day, and June got a better look at her natural face. She couldn't have been more than fifteen years old, one of those family workers that Henry had told her about, someone with a part-time job that contributed to the family income at home to keep the house running and bills paid.

"Sorry, I forgot. But I can just come and get some food and take it with me? I don't have to sign for it?"

The little cashier slipped off her stool and led June to a corner condiment bar. There was a clipboard in a drawer that June hadn't known about. On it was a list of physicians' names, a calendar of sorts where she could just sign for a free meal in the cafeteria. It was a perk of working there as a doctor, something she never learned about because she had been too busy for the orientation grand tour of the hospital on her first day there. But behind her name, the area to sign had been blacked-out with ink.

"Oh, some kind of problem," the cashier told her.

"Why is my name highlighted like that?" June asked. Not that it mattered much. A slice of toast and coffee didn't amount to much, even at island prices.

"Usually that means…"

"What?"

The girl looked up at June, several inches taller than her, and blinked her dark, limpid eyes. She smiled sweetly. "It normally means you don't have the privilege. Maybe just a mistake today?"

June thought otherwise. She thumbed back through the pages of previous days, and found she had meal privileges on those days. Something was fishy in the cafeteria, and it wasn't breakfast food.

"How do I find out if there's a mistake?" June asked, sliding the drawer closed again.

"I can call the manager and ask," the girl offered. "I'll let you know at lunch time."

After paying, June took her dry toast and cold coffee to a table in a back corner and sat. Finding the maturity not to care about a sign-in sheet on a clipboard, she got out her phone and dialed a number.

"Fred, June Kato. Do you have a minute?"

She caught up on the latest news with her old boss back in LA, Dr. Fred Towns, the director of the neurosurgery program at the busy hospital she'd left to come to Maui. His deep and confident voice was a welcome sound; even the familiar sounds of the hospital paging system in the background were somehow heartwarming. Mercy Hospital in downtown LA was often a nightmare, but for an instant, she missed the pace of it. It had only been a few weeks, but she knew she missed working with him, and her busy schedule there. He had always been there for advice and encouragement, and she was hoping for a bit of that today.

"I need a consult. I have a forty-year-old native Hawaiian man, mildly obese and prediabetic, in otherwise good health. Early Monday morning he suffered bilateral knife wounds to his neck, left worse than right. His left carotid was transected completely, the right only nicked. I assisted, and eventually took over his care. We used a shunt, kept the clamp time to a minimum, and the procedure didn't last longer than two hours max."

"What's the problem?" he asked.

"He won't wake up. I've done a follow-up scan of his head to see if he threw a clot or embolus, an EEG, examine his reflexes twice a day, and his brain is perfect. He gets no sedation during the day, only light evening meds. But he doesn't fight the tube, and has had no periods of consciousness at all. And maybe the weirdest thing, his wound isn't healing. No signs of infection in forty-eight hours, but no signs of healing either. Whenever I change his dressing, it looks like we just finished his surgery an hour before."

"I don't know, June."

"It's getting kind of creepy."

"How so?"

She looked around at the tables nearby, to check if anyone could overhear. "He has this giant family, and a couple of them are what they call kahuna. Like priests of their ancient religion, or spiritual advisers."

"And?"

"And, the one has said the patient won't get any better until his spirit has been cleansed, or something like that. But I also get the idea that the guy who attacked him is a part of this."

"A part of what?" he asked.

"His healing. As if Kekoa won't get better until the police find the perp."

"Come on, June. That's a little out there, even for LA."

"Seriously! And the whole time, the family acts like I'm supposed to be patient with the process."

"Patience has never been your strong suit, June. My suggestion is to stay away from all that. Just treat the guy the way you would any other patient. Change his dressings, give antibiotics, maintain the status quo."

"Fred, you know the drill. If he doesn't come around pretty soon, I'm going to have to do a trach on him for long-term intubation, and put in a feeding tube. I'm already pushing limits with both of those. Not long after that I'll need to find a rehab bed for him." She sighed. "And this is for a guy that should be walking out of here."

"If that's what you have to do, if that's what's best, do that." There was a pause, and June knew from experience he was forming something else to tell her. "June, let your clinical expertise and judgment guide you in this, not your heart. It sounds like you're getting too involved with all the other stuff. But you can't. Been there, done that, remember?"

June knew he was right. "Yeah. As much as I hate the idea, I'll get a social worker involved."

"Why do you hate it?"

"One more person getting involved in his affairs and his family, and then billing for it."

"Is there an issue with funding?" he asked.

"He's mostly self-pay, but the family is supposedly well-off. I just hate the idea of running up a bill unnecessarily."

"That's how it works in hospitals. You know that."

"There's more to this case than what meets the eye, Fred. They deserve their privacy, but with each passing day, the media turns it into something bigger. Attempted murder and mayhem on Maui, or whatever they're saying today, and my name is being smeared all over it. Because of that, the hospital administration isn't thrilled with my presence." She noticed the time on the clock on the wall. "I gotta go. I'll call you in a few days to let you know how it turns out."

***

When she got back to the clinic, her patient was waiting, ahead of schedule. June brushed the coffee smell from her breath and got started. The first thing she discovered walking into the little exam room was how sickly the patient looked. She offered a quick greeting to the man and his daughter sitting there with him, and thanked them for being early.

"So, you've been sent here from Doctor Soseki's clinic?" she asked after a quick review of the patient's chart and history. She stuck arteriogram X-rays up on the view box, internally cringed at what she saw, and then noticed the date on them. Almost three years before. They were the most recent films in the folder.

"Dad's supposed to come in once a year to have his arteries checked," the middle-aged woman sitting with the man said. The father had a Japanese last name, but the daughter had too much pink in her cheeks and wave to her hair to be full-blooded Asian. She spoke with the local accent. "Doctor Soseki's assistant checked everything except his neck. They said you're the expert for that."

"Something like that." The man remained quiet, almost stoic, exactly what June would expect from an elderly Japanese man. She reclined him back into a comfortable position and listened for a moment to each side of his neck with her stethoscope.

"I thought neurosurgeons only worked on brains?" the woman asked once June had removed the stethoscope from her ears.

"Diagnosis and treatment of all neurologic disorders of the brain, spine, and peripheral nerves. We also do surgery on the arteries of the neck that supply blood to the brain. That really is the main focus of surgery of the brain, is to improve its function, and that relies on good blood flow."

June began with a full assessment of the man's nervous system, even what wouldn't be affected by the carotid artery blood flow. When she was done, she didn't like her findings. Excusing herself for a moment, she went out to the hallway and brought back the portable ultrasound machine.

She did a quick assessment of the man's neck vessels on both sides. It was worse than what she had thought.

June rolled a stool over and had a seat. She had already completed her exam, and now had to break some bad news.

"Mister Tanigawa, do you still work?"

"Pau hana long time ago," he said back in a low voice. His accent was heavy.

June had already learned that expression meant work was done. "What did you do?"

"Car garage."

"He was a mechanic all his life," his daughter explained. With each passing exam, her eyes had grown larger, suspecting something. "What's wrong?"

"What's your diet like? Do you eat a lot of fatty foods?"

He looked at her for the first time. "Whatchu think? I eat Japanese kind food!"

"At home with us, anyway. He still eats loco moco plates when we go out."

"Loco moco is the rice smothered with gravy and sausage or pork?"

"And egg on top." A smile crossed his face. "Best kind at Ka'ahu's in town."

"And I bet you smoked for a long time too?"

"Not at home anymore. Not since the grandchildren came. But he comes home sometimes smelling like them. Why? What's going on?"

"Mister Tanigawa, you have a large amount of build-up in your neck vessels of something we call plaque. It came from years of cigarettes and bacon, and it has got to the point that it needs to come out. I bet you get confused sometimes? Forgetful?"

"Yes," the daughter said.

June explained the procedure, but that she would also need better X-ray studies of his vessels first. She scheduled those for the next morning.

"Doctor Soseki has said the same thing, but that it could wait for a while."

"He's overdue. Honestly, I'm surprised he hasn't had more difficulties before now."

"We have to do the X-rays tomorrow, on a Saturday?" the daughter asked. "We have plans with da keiki."

"His grandchildren are important, but right now, his health is even more important. Your father has very limited blood flow through his neck and into his brain. Ideally, I'd like to do the X-rays right now, and the surgery tomorrow, but I need to check labs and have his heart and lungs evaluated. It's an extensive surgery, and there are some serious risks, so we shouldn't rush if we can help it. All the tests could be done tomorrow, and we could do surgery on Monday. Or even on Sunday, if an OR room is available."

"Doctors always in big hurry," he said, mostly to himself.

"And unfortunately, this time we have to be. If the vessels get any more clogged than they already are, you'll get almost no blood to your brain. Even worse is if even just a little piece of plaque breaks loose and goes to your brain, you'd die. There wouldn't be much we could do about that."

He looked at her again, his eyes red and wet. His face was dark from a lifetime in the sun, his head almost bald, his cheeks drawn. He had that look that older Japanese men sometimes get, of looking very much like an aged Buddha.

"Then let me go."

That's when a tear ran down his daughter's cheek, and she put her hand on his.

June almost wanted to cry also. "Your grandkids would miss you too much." He looked too much like June's grandfather had when he was the same age, not long before his death twenty years earlier. For some reason, her mind switched to the Japanese language before she spoke to him again. "Anyway, too soon for you to go. You have grandbabies to raise!"

"Oh, your Japanese is so good!" he said back in Japanese, giving her a thumb's up. "Just like a real Japanese person."

"I learned from my grandparents and at Japanese school when I was a kid."

The man looked at his daughter and smiled. "Hey, she's a good one! If she say I need surgery, then I need it, by golly!"

Instead of waiting for the next day, she scheduled the X-ray studies for that afternoon. It would be a film series in which dye would be injected into his vascular system, and X-rays taken as the contrast dye flowed through his neck into his head. It would tell June the amount of blockage on each side, and which side to do first. Only one side at a time could be done, the worst first.

"I'll be there when they do the exams," she said to them when they left the clinic, the daughter trying to keep control of her emotions while she also tried keeping her father upright and moving forward.

She saw her next two patients, before finding time for a refill of coffee and a real meal. First, she went back to the ICU to see Kekoa, and see if his family had come in yet. That day, there was only a modest showing of folks compared to previous days. Having little to share with each other, and not wanting to bring up late night activities at the hospital figuring it could only stir up trouble, she went to examine Kekoa.

Waiting outside the cubicle door was a man in a suit, odd for the usual aloha dress code. With the way he intently watched June, he looked as though he was waiting for her. Kaleo, the usual police guard, wasn't around that day.

"Can I help you?" she asked once she was out of Kekoa's cubicle.

He flipped open a small notepad, a dead give-away he was a detective of some sort. "Doctor June Kato?"

"Yes?"

"Detective Larry Atkins, from the Maui PD." They shook hands quickly, June feeling some sort of oily residue on his hand. "How's our boy in there doing?"

"Are you the detective responsible for investigating his assault?" she asked.

"That's me," he said with an East Coast accent. It was either Boston or New York, June couldn't tell, but with the way he was still wearing a suit in the tropics, it was obvious he hadn't been there long. "Along with a couple uniforms helping me with leg work."

"Yes, I think I've met one. Anyway, what can I do for you?"

He took her out of the department and down the hallway to talk privately. "What I need to know is…" He nodded his head back in the direction of Kekoa in the ICU. "…will he wake up again?"

"As in give a statement as to what happened?"

"A statement and some leads would be nice."

"There isn't any other evidence to look at? No fingerprints, nothing?" she asked.

"They keep the lab impeccably clean, but the office the perp passed through was covered in layers of prints. We still running all of them, trying to separate lab employees from visitors to narrow the field, and so far nothing has turned up. Mostly the district attorney is breathing down my neck about whether this guy's going make it or not."

"Why is that so important? The crime gets investigated either way, doesn't it?" she asked, folding her arms across her chest.

"If death is imminent, we can get more manpower on this. Maybe even the feds."

"Maybe if you spent more time investigating, and less time trying to get other people to do that for you, you might've come up with a few more leads by now."

"Well, now, wait a minute here, lady…"

"Doctor. My name is Doctor Kato." She kept her unblinking eyes glued to his, waiting for a reply. Or a challenge. She didn't get one. "Something I found out is that this might have been a case of mistaken identity."

"Oh? Why?" he asked.

"Kekoa was working alone in the lab at the time of the assault, and wearing the lab director's lab coat at the time. Quite possibly the man in the leather jacket, your perp, thought Kekoa Baxter was the lab director named Arthur Silva. Maybe your investigation should start, or should I say the next part of your investigation could include looking into that angle?"

"Maybe. And maybe you'd like to be there at the time I talk to this lab director?" he asked, making it sound like the challenge she'd been waiting for.

She looked at her watch. "I have patients to see later but have time right now."

He accepted her challenge. "You're on."

They went together to the downstairs lab. Once they were inside, June wondered in which part of the lab Kekoa was attacked. Several techs were working with analyzers and equipment, the drone of electronic machines loud. After asking where to find the director, they were pointed off to an office at the back of the lab. There they found a door labeled with 'Arthur Silva—Lab Director'. June reached forward to knock, but the cop stopped her. Instead, he gave the doorknob a turn and let himself in.

"Mister Silva?" Detective Atkins asked.

The man spun his chair around to look at his visitors. "I'm Doctor Silva. Who are you, and why are you in my office?"

"What? Is everybody around here a doctor or something?"

"This is a hospital," June muttered. "You were expecting librarians?"

"Who are you two?" Silva asked again. He shoved several sheets of paper together into a neat stack before minimizing the window on his computer screen. He seemed uptight about something, maybe being interrupted in his work.

"I'm Detective Atkins from Maui PD." He handed over a business card to the lab director before looking at June. "This is…a doctor."

June tried to smile when she shook Silva's hand. "Doctor June Kato. I'm taking care of Kekoa Baxter upstairs."

"Poor boy. How is he?"

Silva looked genuinely concerned, and the way he used the endearment 'boy', he made it sound as though they had been on good terms with each other. Silva had only a splash of silver in his hair, and couldn't have been much older than Kekoa.

"About the same. The family is quite worried about him. Frankly, so am I."

"We came to your lab because there are a few questions," Atkins said loudly to get their attention back on him. "First, your where-abouts early Monday morning?"

Atkins took notes while Silva gave his alibi. He got a phone number of someone to call to verify what he'd been told. "I went through all this on that terrible morning."

June saw beads of sweat along Silva's hairline, odd for being inside an air-conditioned laboratory. If she saw it, Atkins the detective was sure to notice also.

"Now, I understand Baxter was wearing someone else's lab clothes at the time. Is that correct?" Atkins asked, still with his notepad in hand.

June watched Atkins write, and then gave him a broader look. The image to her was almost humorous: an old-fashioned gumshoe chasing a perp down a palm-lined beach, dressed in his suit and polished leather shoes. As a new transplant herself from LA, she knew she was still pretty rigid, but she also knew she was further along in the relaxed 'Maui time' continuum than he was.

Dr. Silva's voice brought her around again. "That's what I was told by the police on Monday, when they were here investigating. Apparently he was wearing one of my lab jackets."

"Have you checked to see if yours is missing?"

"I have several. I wear some while I work here in the lab. The others are dressier, for meetings. It was one for working in here that's missing. I suppose that's the one they found him in."

"And it had your name on it?"

"Yes, that's right. Embroidered in blue, just over the pocket. It was an old one leftover from many years ago." He pointed to

June's jacket. "Very similar to hers. Would I be able to get it back eventually?"

"Sorry, it's evidence." Atkins made a note and June watched, trying to read what he was writing. "Now, any idea of why he was wearing it? Didn't he have one of his own?"

"He did. All the lab employees do. Required for when they work here in the lab, or go out on specimen collections. We found his jacket in his locker later, coffee stains on it. He must've spilled coffee on it and changed into something available. Apparently, it was mine. Really, I don't mind that sort of thing at all, as long as they take care of it."

"I'll have to take a look at it."

"I believe the police took it from his locker that morning, as evidence you see, along with everything else in his locker," Silva said nervously. "Surely you must know that. You are with the police, aren't you?"

"As much as you're with the hospital. And as long as we're on the topic of employees, I'll need the names of every employee here in the lab." He tossed his head toward the door that led back out to the lab. "I may as well get started interviewing them right now."

June knew she was no longer needed, not that she ever was. Meeting Silva had been her intention all along, and that much was done. Nor did she want to hang around for police interviews of employees that likely had nothing to do with Kekoa's attack. She glanced at her watch again, saw it was just about time to see her last patient of the day in the clinic, and bade Silva goodbye. As she turned to leave, she was sure to ignore the detective.

Walking away, she wasn't entirely convinced Atkins was a detective. Getting a start that he might actually be the perpetrator returning to the scene of his crime, solely to find possible witnesses, she went back to the lab door, but didn't go in. Staying outside, she listened for a few minutes as Atkins continued to ask questions of lab employees, getting simple 'I don't know' answers in return. When he began sounding frustrated and started badgering one of them, June went in, purposefully blocking the door.

"Detective Atkins, when we first met a while ago, you didn't show me your police ID or badge. Isn't that something you should show each of these people giving your statements?"

He looked at her, his ire obviously rising. "You're a cop now?"

"No, but it seems to me that to make this official, you'd need to identify yourself right?"

"Hey, that's right!" the current lab tech being questioned said. "Where's your badge, man?"

Atkins took out his credential wallet and flashed his badge and official MPD ID to both the tech and to June. Seeing that, she left them behind.

"Rats," she muttered as she hurried along. "I thought I was on to something."

Her patient in the clinic had symptoms that were easy to diagnose: back pain, leg numbness, and a foot drop on one side that made him limp and often catch his foot while walking. For good measure, June sent him for X-rays and a CT scan of his back. Slowly but surely, surgical patients were showing up in her clinic, and some of them with decent reimbursement, something that would make both the hospital and her bank account happy.

Just as she was thinking of going to the cafeteria to see if any hot lunch food was left, her desk phone rang. "A meal sometime today would be nice," she mumbled, reaching for the phone.

"Doctor Kato, this is Mister Townsend."

"What can I do for you?" she asked with a sigh. She hadn't come in through the main entrance that morning, but figured the mounds of flower leis had grown, and she was about to be scolded once again.

"I'd just like to thank you for managing the, um, expressions of love at the main entrance."

She couldn't tell for sure if there was a sound of sarcasm to his voice, but decided it was best to pretend there wasn't. "I haven't been through the front door today, so I have no way of responding."

"All of the old leis have been removed, leaving only one behind. The plants are still there, only now two hibiscus have been planted in the back corners, and the other things…"

"Ti plants?"

"That's right. Those are still there as well. But at least the leis are gone."

"Let me assure you, I had nothing to do with that. I really do have better things to do with my time than managing hospital décor and landscaping. And one of them is getting a late lunch before a new patient goes for studies in interventional radiology. Something that would make you happy is that he's a paying customer, and will require at least one surgery, probably two. So, if you don't mind…"

"That's the spirit, doctor!" he announced quite cheerfully. "Glad to know you're coming aboard!"

She hung up, but stared down at the phone. "I don't know what ship you're floating, but don't include me as a passenger."

Most of the food was gone by the time she got to the cafeteria. The line server cleaned out the rice bucket into a bowl for her, then ladled poached carrots over top. With some decaf coffee, a secret splash of regular in it, June had just enough time to eat before going to radiology to watch Mr. Tanigawa have his neck vessels X-rayed. Once the contrast dye was injected into his upper body vascular system, deformities and narrow areas caused by blockages would be easy to spot, and she could decide on the extent of the surgery needed. Studies of both sides were planned, and whichever side was more occluded would have surgery first.

Mr. Tanigawa was already in the suite being worked on, and with a glance, June could see where they were in the process of taking his film. It would be only a few more minutes until some images could be viewed on the computer screen in the control room. In the meantime, June sat with Tanigawa's daughter, learning her name was Alice, she had two kids, and had lived on Maui all her life.

"Do you have any more questions?" June asked her.

"When would you do the surgery?"

"I've checked with the OR schedule, and there's plenty of time available tomorrow, if his lab tests and his medical doctor okay him for it."

"So soon," Alice said with resignation to her voice.

"He'll be much healthier, and he'll feel better too. I think you'll be surprised how much more alert he'll be."

"If he's so bad, why wasn't the surgery done sooner? We've been bringing him to Doctor Soseki's office for several years, always hearing the same thing, that it wasn't time yet."

June tried muscling out a sincere smile but failed. "I don't know. But it's time now. I know it's frightening, but this is a good thing we're doing for him."

June thought of her grandfather who had died many years before, from the exact same issue that she was trying to prevent in Mr. Tanigawa: part of the clog breaking free and floating into his brain, causing a rapid but excruciating death. She explained it to the woman once again, using less personal terms.

She stepped away and found a lead apron and jacket to wear before entering the control room. There was a thick pane of glass between that room with control panels and computer and the room where the films were taken, the walls and glass leaded to prevent radiation exposure. She wanted the extra layer between her and the X-ray equipment, to protect the baby in its earliest stages of development, just to be sure.

June watched as the radiologist injected the contrast dye, waited for the right amount of time to pass, before taking several films in succession. June watched the hazy gray-scale image on the live monitor as he worked, and didn't like what she saw. It was only moments later that the images began to appear on the computer screen, sharp digitally-enhanced images of white pathways against a black background. It was the right side of the man's neck. The radiologist joined her at the computer.

"That's ugly," she muttered.

"Must be eighty percent occlusion," he said back. He made several prints of the squiggly white paths and stored the rest.

"Looks like I'm starting with the right side." June made some notes in the patient's chart.

"I'll give him a flush and do the other side."

The radiologist did some work with the sedated Mr. Tanigawa. June watched the monitor as he flushed his vessels with plain solution. Then he injected the opposite side with contrast dye.

June watched on the computer screen in live time as the white trail of contrast flowed up Mr. Tanigawa's carotid artery, coming to an almost complete stop. She looked through the glass window to see what was going on. The same monitor screen that the radiologist watched was aimed at June. It was the same for him. He still held the syringe in his hand, attached to the injection line.

She looked back at the screen on the desk in front of her. Looking closer, she could just make out the tiniest trail of contrast dye leaking past the blockage in the man's left carotid artery, barely anything getting through.

She stood in a hurry and rapped her knuckles on the glass window, giving the time out sign with her hands. She went around the corner and into the room.

"Hey, he's probably ninety-five percent occluded on that side, so don't force it," she told the radiologist and the tech with him. "I can't risk a piece of plaque breaking loose."

"Ninety-five is optimistic. I was thinking more along the lines of ninety-nine," he said back, shutting down some of his equipment. "What do you want to do?"

"Surgery. And now."

"Want me to balloon him? Try and open him a little?"

"That might stir up more trouble than what it's worth." She picked up the desk phone, tried to remember the right extension number, but had to ask to be connected to the Operating Room. As soon as she was done scheduling the emergency surgery, she went out to Alice, taking films with her.

She broke the bad news in a hurry. She had no time to waste, and did her best to explain that to Alice. She held up an X-ray to the ceiling light.

"You can see here where there's only about twenty percent of the usual amount of blood flow into his brain," June said tapping her fingernail on the film. "And that's the better side. There is almost no blood flowing through the other artery into his brain at all."

"What's that mean? You want to do his surgery soon?"

"Today. Now. There really isn't much choice. Frankly, I'm rather surprised he was able to walk and talk today."

It was only moments later that Dr. Miller showed up, the anesthesiologist that would be working with her.

"Millertime, I have his medical records coming from his primary's office, and his daughter is here for you to get a history. Can you make it happen for me?"

"Did he eat today?"

"Not since breakfast, and that wasn't much," Alice told him. "He hasn't been feeling well the last few days."

"How are his lungs?"

"Okay, I guess."

Miller listened to Mr. Tanigawa's lungs with his stethoscope. June watched his face for a reaction. She remembered from her morning exam that his breathing was okay, but nothing to brag about. A lifetime of cigarettes did that to a person.

"And?" she asked once he had the earpieces out.

"Could be better, but we've done surgery on worse. When was his last cigarette?"

"He hasn't been out of the house in a month, so that long I guess. Why? Are cigarettes really that important?"

"For breathing, circulation, blood pressure, healing. Everything is affected by smoking both in the short term and in the long run. That's why we ask so often at the hospital."

Once Miller and Alice agreed to allow the surgery to commence, June went to the front of the stretcher and pulled, while Miller pushed from the backend. Alice brought up the rear. A thick folder of X-rays went along with them.

By the time June was done teaching Alice the last of what she needed to know right then, and getting the signed consent from her to proceed, the lab blood tests were back. Miller was stone silent as they looked at out of whack numbers, and June internally cringed.

"Still want to proceed?" he asked.

"I'm game if you are," she said quietly. "A gifted anesthesiologist like you should be able to fluff up some of those values, right?"

"And some magic."

Ten minutes later, they wheeled him into the operating room where nurses were busy setting up equipment. All she had left to do was find someone to assist her. There was one man she wouldn't bother calling.

***

Of the four operating rooms in the department, she was the only one working. She'd gone down the list of surgeons, none of them available that afternoon. Either they were out of the hospital or busy in their clinics. It wasn't until she got to the names of the gynecologists and obstetricians that she saw a friendly one. She dialed Divya's number first, her new obstetrician, begging for help.

June had already made the incision in Mr. Tanigawa's neck by the time her assistant showed up in the room.

"I'm a little out of my element in the vascular room, June," Divya said.

"You had a general surgery rotation in training, right?" June asked as soon as Divya joined her with gown and gloves on. Divya stood on a step at the opposite side of the head from where June stood. She got a pair of retractor instruments put in her hands to help hold the wound open.

"Of course, but not this kind of thing."

"Well, if you screw it up, you're fired as my OB."

June glanced up over the loupes across her nose to see Divya's response to her joke.

"Just kidding, Divya."

"Sorry, June," Divya said in her mildly Indian sing-song voice. "A little terrified right now. The last time I saw carotids exposed like this was in the cadaver lab in med school."

"Yeah, well, just wait till we open this bad boy up and start picking decades of plaque out. Your main role is to follow me with whatever I'm doing. If I work in a new spot, move your retractors there. When it gets wet, suck the blood out with that tip there. When I eventually begin to suture, you'll follow along with that also, pinching the strand of suture with the tips of your fingers and keeping the suture line taut." June stopped and refocused her gaze, nudging one of Divya's hands out of the way. "And most important, don't ever block my view of the vessel."

As June worked on getting the vessel free from the tissue around it, it bounced with each beep of the EKG. She arranged everything she'd need for the next few moments, the most crucial part of the entire surgery.

"Millertime, I'm about to clamp and open the vessel."

"Roger that. Say June, do you have a nickname?"

"Nope, and it's going to stay that way. And if you ever want to piss me off in a hurry, call me Ma'am."

With one last reminder to the scrub nurse of what she'd do and when, June proceeded with clamping the vessel, slicing it open, removing fifty years of disease, plunking large pieces of plaque into a metal bowl.

"Vitals, Millertime?"

"So far, so good. I took the liberty of putting on my handy little EEG monitor on his head."

"And?"

"It doesn't show much, only if there is activity or none."

June carefully irrigated the vessel, getting any last bits and pieces of plaque washed free before she started to close. "Yes, and?"

"There is still the same activity as before."

"That's something, anyway. His heart's doing okay?" she asked.

"Better than mine right now," he said.

"Mine, too," Divya said.

In a small bowl was the tubular-shaped plaque that had been removed, Divya staring at it. Yellow and rubbery, it was an almost perfect internal cast of the carotid artery.

"That went a lot better than I anticipated," she said once she had the artery closed and the clamps were off. "Millertime, everything still okay?"

He was looking at his monitors, jotting down vital sign numbers onto paperwork. "His blood pressure is starting to bottom out from all the extra blood flow he has right now."

"Crap." She looked over at him. "What?"

He turned around. "Just kidding."

"Hilarious," June muttered into her surgical mask. "Tell me, does Henry from the ER ever try and drown you while you guys go out surfing?"

"No, but the waves do. He has a baby now, which takes up all his previous surf time."

"Surfing?" Divya asked.

"Maui is the surf mecca of the world, Divya," June said.

"I want to try it sometime," Divya said. "Looks fun. I just don't know how to go about learning."

June set down the suture she'd been using, picking up another. "Yeah, well, maybe Doctor Miller will take you. It sounds like he has plenty of time on his hands lately." She glanced up at Miller. "If the waves aren't very good, you could talk about epidurals."

June looked at Divya's face and could see a full-blown blush going on, even with her dark Indian complexion.

"Or maybe not."

June got a new set of forceps and the last closing stitch of suture in her hand, and began to close the first layer of tissue. Her brow was damp, and a trickle of sweat ran down her back. She and the others had worn lead aprons for the two-hour case, so she could do some intra-operative X-rays. Once she was satisfied there was good flow into the patient's brain on that side, she knew the case was successfully done. But wearing the extra eighteen pounds of the full-body lead gown was heavy and cumbersome, and had brought a heavy sweat to June for most of the case.

"You do many of these, June?" Divya asked.

"Back in LA, about two hundred a year. Here, this is my first. Except for Kekoa, on Monday. What we did for him wasn't much different than this."

"How's he doing? He's been quite the talk of the hospital. Everybody seems to know him, or at least heard of him."

"Not bad," June said, almost done stitching. She wasn't sure of how to answer. There was only so much she could share because of patient confidentiality laws. "Actually…"

She was saved from saying anything more when her phone rang. The circulating nurse held it up to June's ear so she could talk while she worked.

"Mister Townsend, I haven't heard from you in several hours. What can I do for you?" she said once she heard the caller's voice.

June had the nurse put the call on speaker so she could keep working.

"It's come to my attention that, once again, someone has been visiting Kekoa Baxter after visiting hours were over."

"Oh?" June said, trying to inject a bit of an innocent little girl's tone of voice. Occasionally it worked.

"Again last night. It seems there was some sort of emergency code called, which drew hospital resources away from the Intensive Care Unit to other places. Do you have an explanation for that?"

"Absolutely none. What was the emergency?"

"I don't know. Something about a baby abduction."

"Oh my," muttered Divya.

"A baby was kidnapped?" June asked.

"No, just a false alarm. We're still trying to determine if it was a drill or a false alarm."

"Did it work?" June asked.

"What it did was draw Mister Baxter's guard from his post to elsewhere."

"Well, it sounds like it worked, if the guard responded appropriately. Security is supposed to respond to calls like that, right? Isn't a baby abduction a priority over someone sitting outside a patient's door all night?"

"That's not the point, and you know it, Doctor. I just spoke with the nurse manager in the ICU. She also denied knowing anything about it. Are the two of you working together in some sort of scheme?" His tone of voice was getting irritated.

"You mean Sandra? No. I barely know her. Anyway, why should she know what happened during the night? She works during the daytime, right?" Behind her surgical mask, June was smiling over the fact her was chasing his tail. "Whatever your investigation is about, you seem to be going in the wrong direction with it, Mister Townsend."

Once again, he ignored her plaint. "I just got off the phone with the night shift nurse that took care of Mister Baxter. She told me…"

June slapped the stitch and forceps down. "You called the night nurse at home? After working all night, and now trying to get sleep?"

"I don't care about that. I need to get to the bottom of…"

"And I don't care about you," June said to interrupt. "Nor about your petty little problems. Now, if you don't mind, could you please leave the care providers of the hospital alone and let us do our work? We are the reason patients come to the hospital, after all, not you."

June nodded at the circulator to end the call, and began cleaning the patient's neck.

"Making friends on the island, June?" Dr. Miller asked with a chuckle.

"That's a two-way street. Seems to me, the administration needs to make friends with the providers. We are the ones that bring patients, and business, to the hospital."

"Why was he asking about someone visiting the patient late at night?" Divya asked. "Aren't family members allowed to visit during late hours if the patient is in serious condition? I don't see any problem with that."

"Normally it's not. His condition has been stable, just not improving. But for some reason, Townsend doesn't want Kekoa Baxter to have visitors, especially at night."

"Do you know who the visitor has been?" Miller asked.

To not lie to her new friends and workmates, June had to choose her words carefully. "Whenever I've been in Kekoa's cubicle, only the nurse has been there with me."

"But…" Miller led.

"All I know is the family wants to practice some traditional Hawaiian rites. Apparently, someone has been going in late at night to do that. Townsend also seems to think the leis at the front entrance have something to do with Kekoa and his family."

"Why is Townsend calling you? Other than being his physician, what do you have to do with his family?"

"Not much, but just to keep all of you out of trouble, I'll keep my big trap shut." She sighed, finished applying the dressing, and pulling away the sterile drapes. She was done with the surgery. "All I can say is that there's something really fishy about Kekoa being knifed the way he was. There's way more to it than someone randomly attacking a lab tech in a hospital, or a case of mistaken identity."

"And there's still no word on who attacked him?" one of the nurses asked. "That's what the nurses are worried about, that if a big guy can get knifed in the hospital, what about the rest of us?"

"I don't know. But Townsend seems to think extra security here at the hospital is better used in watching one patient rather than watching over the rest of us. Otherwise, I've heard nothing about extra guards being posted in or around the hospital."

"That's why the nurses are so concerned."

"I'd like know what happened to Kekoa. I have the feeling that once his attacker is caught, he'll begin to recover. And I bet you anything there's more than just one person behind it."

"I've been following it in the newspaper," Miller said. "If nothing else, the island has found out there's a new neurosurgeon on the island with all the times your name is mentioned in the articles."

"Not exactly the kind of exposure I was hoping for. A detective from the Maui PD visited me today. He said there are no leads." June pulled off her gown and gloves and tossed them away. "I'd just like to see Kekoa start to improve, and soon."

June rolled her head in circles, trying to loosen tight muscles. Maybe the rest of the world didn't recognize it right then, but she proved herself worthy of the title 'surgeon', in spite of the circumstances. Once again, she enjoyed the deep sense of satisfaction it brought.

***

Just as June was getting home, Henry called her.

"Hey, we're going to have to stop calling each other so much or people will start to gossip. Does Karen know you called me?"

"She's at work. What she doesn't know, won't hurt her. Last night seemed to go well."

"With Haunani? Perfectly, but as far as I'm concerned, I'm taking myself out of that loop. They supposedly want to go back tonight and do one last ritual. They'll have to do it without me."

"Why?" he asked. "I thought you were all in with whatever it took to treat him, even if it meant smuggling in an old lady with sacred leaves and rocks in a bag."

"Except I have a hospital administrator breathing down my neck, a police detective popping into my office, and my name and reputation being dissected by news reporters who haven't even bothered interviewing me." What she thought she had left behind in LA with the media trying to figure out the identity of the White House mistress was starting all over again on Maui. "Other than going to work every day, I'm going into hiding."

"Remember Leonard from the party?" Henry asked. "I saw him this morning. He said that according to the police, there might be a break in the investigation."

"Oh? They know who it was that attacked Kekoa?"

"Not yet. Only that there's another witness, and a better description. Apparently, TSA has been on the lookout for anyone that matches the first description, and so far nothing. Police are hoping he's still on the island."

303

"If I had my preferences, I'd rather he was ten thousand miles away. What else did Leonard say?"

"They think the guy is Hispanic rather than Polynesian or Filipino."

"I forgot to tell you that a police detective came to my office and we went to talk with Doctor Silvers in the lab. Apparently, there was some big mistaken identity, that he was the intended target and not Kekoa."

"That's what the police told Leonard. At least they have another direction to investigate. How is he today?"

"Kekoa? I just saw him on rounds, and for the first time, his wound looked as though it's starting to heal, quickly too. He isn't waking up yet, but at least there's some change in his condition."

"That's good news for his family. Maybe what Haunani has been doing is working for him."

"But I also got a message from administration that I need to find long-term care placement for him unless he shows even more improvement, a place that takes vent patients. If he isn't breathing on his own by Sunday, I'll have to trach him and put in a feeding tube for long-term care. Something about taking up bed space unnecessarily."

"What?" Henry asked. "It's an eight bed ICU!"

"And until this afternoon, Kekoa was the only patient in it. Right now, both my patients are the only ones in there, which is sure to raise a few eyebrows in administration."

"Aren't they insured?" he asked.

"Yes, but it seems anything with my name attached sets off alarms in second floor offices. And try talking to a family about packing a loved one off to long-term care with breathing and feeding tubes."

***

Later, when her phone rang, the bedside light was still on, the journal on the floor along with her pillows, the bed sheets in a mess. The time on the little bedside clock betrayed her hopes for a peaceful night. She recognized the calling number on her phone as the ICU at work.

"Doctor Kato, there's been a development with Mister Baxter," the nurse told her right off.

June sat bolt upright in bed. Just when he was starting to show some improvement. "Oh? What's happened?"

"For the last couple of hours, he's been showing a few signs of consciousness. He's a bit restless, opening his eyes, gripping my hand when I talk to him."

"That's great! Is he trying to speak? Agitated at all?"

Often when patients first stir from long periods of unconsciousness they are confused, leading to agitation. It wouldn't be the first time June had to order a sedative to medicate a patient that was just emerging from a long sleep.

"Not concerned with his tube, or agitated. Just as though he is trapped somewhere between awake and asleep."

"Sounds good." June got out of bed. "I'll be right in."

It took only a few minutes to dress and get to the hospital. Oddly, or maybe not so much, she saw Leonard leaving the hospital parking lot in his pickup, with Auntie Haunani in the passenger seat.

"They came in anyway, even without my help," June said, parking in her space. "Surely they being here doesn't have something to do with Kekoa waking up all of a sudden?"

In the middle of the night, the hospital was quiet. Passing through the ER, the only entrance open that late at night, she gave a quick wave to Henry.

Not wanting to wait for any elevator, she ran up the stairs to the ICU. She saw Mr. Tanigawa at one end of the department, uneventfully sleeping, his nurse perched on a chair next to his bed. June went straight to Kekoa's bed.

"What's up?" she asked the nurse, who was busy talking to Kekoa. His eyes were slightly open, his arms secured with straps at the side of the bed so he couldn't reach up and pull loose his breathing tube or the IV lines. His eyes shifted to June when she spoke.

"He started getting rather ambitious with his hands, so I secured them. But he's fighting his tube and the vent. Maybe it's time to take the tube out?"

A respiratory therapist, the person mainly responsible for maintaining the tube and ventilator, showed up just then. "Yep. Looks like it's time."

While they unhooked the circuit tubing that led from the ventilator to the tube in Kekoa's throat, June began talking with Kekoa, telling him not to fight, to take deep breaths, and if he breathed well, the tube would be removed from his throat. There was a hallelujah moment when Kekoa made eye contact with June and nodded his head slightly.

It all went as planned. Kekoa was able to breathe on his own when detached from the ventilator. After a few minutes of showing he could comply, they removed the tube from his throat. It was a landmark moment in his recovery, now almost six days along. After another hour of trying to orient Kekoa to where he was and what was going on, June left him. Having a huge sense of satisfaction in her heart, she went to see Mr. Tanigawa. There was a window near his cubicle, the sky just starting to lighten, a new day beginning.

She called Leonard with the good news.

"He's awake and alert and having something to drink," June told him. "I noticed you and Auntie Haunani leaving the hospital earlier."

"Yes, she performed the last of her things for him."

"Well, it must've worked. From what I could see, I'll have him transferred to a regular ward bed in the afternoon and he should be able to go home by Wednesday. I just have one question. How did you get Auntie up to his room without being stopped by the guard?"

"Remember that idea we had the other night, about the fire alarm?"

"You didn't!"

"No. When I took Auntie up there, we planned to just talk our way past that guard. But just as we got to the ICU, there was a fire drill. Alarms going off everywhere!"

"Who pulled the alarm?" June asked.

"We have no idea. It was only the two of us in the hospital. We didn't have any real plan or help. It just sort of happened at just the right time."

A Major Discovery

By the time she was home, June was finally hungry. She looked in a bag of chips and decided against them. She found a packet of instant ramen noodles and boiled water. While she waited, she diced up some green onions and crumbled some tofu. By the time her simple meal was ready, she barely had an appetite for it.

Slurping some of the limp noodles, she called the ICU. Learning both Kekoa and Mr. Tanigawa were both sitting up and drinking juice, she still wasn't satisfied. She liked seeing her patients in person. She dressed in loose clothes and went back to the hospital. It was almost noon when she got there.

"Mister Baxter, my name is June Kato. We met early this morning, but you might not remember much of then."

He reached his hand up from his bed, the IV tubing falling away from his arm, the needle taped in place at the back of his hand. "They told me you were the doctor that did my surgery. Thank you," he said with a dry voice.

She pulled up a stool and sat next to his bed. "I was only the assistant."

"You've been watching over me all week. My family told me about that." His voice was raspy from the tube that had been in his throat for several days, catching on the occasional word. For a change, his family wasn't there, not even one representative. "They told me how much you've done...and what you did for the whole family."

"My pleasure. You sure have a large family, and they're very concerned for you." There was a subject she was still curious about, and maybe right then wasn't the best time to bring it up. But she had to know. "Someone brought a lot of leis to the hospital and created a little shrine out front." She scooted her stool closer to him and lowered her voice. "And Auntie Haunani came in every night to see you. I think maybe all of that did you more good than anything I did."

"Leonard came in this morning, said what Auntie did." He reached for his cup of water, and June helped him drink from it. "The nurse told me about the leis in a garden someplace, asked Leonard if they were for me. He told her, No way! Too expensive."

"I thought that's what someone said once, maybe Judy, that they didn't know anything about all the leis or the new plants. But someone went to a great deal of effort to put them there."

"Probably for another patient here." His head flopped back as if he were tired.

"Did the police come and speak with you?" she asked.

"For a few minutes. A man in a suit. I told him what I could remember." His eyes rolled closed.

"Kekoa, you need your sleep. Would you like a sleeping pill for that?"

"I'll sleep good." He lifted his head again to look at her. "Thanks again."

June visited the sound asleep Mr. Tanigawa. She decided they both looked good enough for transfer out of the ICU to regular ward beds in the morning. Writing notes to that effect in their charts, she sat at the nurses' station for a moment, still reluctant to go home and face the evening alone.

The department was quiet, not much activity at all. She leaned forward, resting her head on one hand, her elbow on the desktop. She found a position that was comfortable for her chest and settled in. Only a moment passed before her eyes got heavy.

There was a noise, and some bickering. The bickering got louder, some words were said, and it came from the area of the patient cubicles, not from the locker room. When she looked back in Kekoa's direction, his nurse was looking at her hand. What was surprising, or alarming, was that a tall man was hurrying from the department. June just barely got a glimpse, but he was wearing dark clothes, odd for Maui, even late in the evening.

Now wide-awake because of the ruckus and the activity, June got up from her chair and went over to where the nurse was on the phone.

"Who was that?" June asked the nurse, expecting the reply that it was another relative of Kekoa. She listened as the nurse talked to the hospital operator, asking for security to come to the department. "What happened?"

"I don't know who that jerk was, but he came in here, went straight for Kekoa's IV, and started messing with it. I told him to knock it off, but then it looked like he had a syringe in his hand. I yelled at him, and just before he could inject something, I tried to take the syringe away." The nurse was rubbing her hand and wrist then, obviously red. June took it in her hand, giving it a better look. "Then I thought he was going to break my arm until I pushed him away. That's when he left."

"He was messing with Kekoa's IV?"

"He had a syringe of something, and..."

June didn't need to hear any more than that. She took off out of the department, almost at a gallop. Out in the corridor, she saw no one, except for the security guard that was hustling to the ICU.

"Did you see a tall guy in dark clothes, heading out?" June asked him in a hurry.

"No. What's going on?" the guard asked, barely slowing down.

June pointed him to the nurse, before leaving again. The guard had just come from the elevator where the door was closing, so she took the stairs down. Inside the stairwell, she listened for a moment, heard a few footsteps echo up from a lower floor, a door creak open, then slam shut again. She took off down the stairs at a run.

Halfway down, she slipped her cell phone out of her pocket and tried to dial at a full speed descent. Unable to recall the Emergency Room number right then, she tried the number for the detective she'd met two days before. Told he was busy by a police answering service, she dropped the phone back into her pocket and rushed her feet even faster.

Once she was at the ground level, she pushed open the door, but stalled for a moment before rushing out. When there was no commotion, no swinging billy club, no thrown punch, no kicking foot, she went out and peered into the night air. It was just a small seating area used as the smoker's corner at the back of the building, only one small light overhead, and a dimly lit parking lot beyond. She watched for movement, listened for a car door that might slam shut, waited to see if an engine started up. Nothing but the sound of crickets and her gasping breath greeted her senses.

Knowing better than to go any further alone, she turned back into the stairwell and started upstairs again.

"It had to be him," she said to the empty stairwell. "Tall man, dark clothes, looking for Kekoa."

When she got back to the ICU, a second guard had joined the first in talking with the nurse. June gave her account of the situation, and learned that one guard would remain in the department, while the other took a longer look outside. Once the police had shown up to investigate, and June gave her account of what happened, took one last look at Kekoa, and turned for home.

She was exhausted when she went out the ER exit, watching all around. Locking herself inside her pickup, she put it in gear and made the quick drive home. It was there that she got her next big surprise.

"Now what?" she grumbled when the headlights flashed across something next to the front porch. Her landscaping efforts hadn't started yet, except for the small vegetable patch in the back yard. She parked in the usual place next to the back door by the kitchen, and saw something unusual there also. A large lava boulder had been placed near the back porch, a lei draped over it. "What the…"

She picked up the lei, felt the freshness of the flowers, gave it a sniff, and laid it down again.

"Did Leonard and Haunani do this and I didn't notice it before?"

June went inside and locked the back door, putting the security chain across. After kicking off her shoes, she went to the front door and flicked on the porch light. Looking outside a front window, she saw nothing moving or unusual. She went out to the porch to have a look around.

Several ti plants had been planted along the old front walkway she rarely used. Another lava rock was set into the heavy red dirt at the front steps, with yet another flowery lei draped over it.

"What's going on? Why would they do that? Is it a thank you gesture?"

She locked herself in and turned out all the lights. Tired of mysteries for the day, she went back to bed, not even taking off her clothes.

***

The next morning started much too early when June heard her phone ringing. Answering, it was her mother.

"Trying to catch up on sleep, Mom. What's up?" She kept her eyes closed as she listened.

"We have our airplane reservations."

"For where? Taking another trip to Europe? Or is it to Scandinavia this time?"

"To there. Maui. We'll be moving in with you."

June's eyes popped open. "What?"

"Next week. We arrive next week."

"Already?" June sat up on the side of her bed. "Mom, we never made definite plans."

"Amy said you were looking forward to us being there, that you needed our help."

"Oh, really? Well, I'll just have to talk to Amy about that."

"Dear, the sooner your father starts on the addition, the sooner it's done. Then you and the baby can move in there."

"Which is something else that hasn't been discussed to completion."

"It's the best thing and you know it."

June flopped onto her back. "What day do you arrive?"

After getting their arrival time, she went to the kitchen to start breakfast. While a pan with water for oatmeal heated, she made coffee. By the time coffee was done, the oatmeal was hot. Having no interest in that, she burnt two slices of toast.

June used the kitchen phone to call the hospital. Learning Silva, the lab director, wasn't taking appointments, she tried to get his home number. When she couldn't get it, she left a message for him to call her as soon as possible.

"Should I go in and try to get his home number?" she asked her cold bowl of oatmeal.

She took it to the sink and ran water in it, before pouring another cup of coffee. She took one sip and poured it out.

"No, as in forget it. Might not be able to get it even that way. But what about that detective I met the other day? Maybe he has more information about what happened last night at the hospital."

June went to her purse and got Detective Larry Atkins's business card. Using the kitchen phone again, she called him.

She could tell she got him at home, that it was Sunday morning fun time with the kids. It took only a quick explanation of her ideas over Silva's safety before she got some action from the detective. Surprised at how willing he was to be helpful that day, she pushed her luck with another question.

"Did you hear about the incident at the hospital last night?" she asked him.

"The man that tried to inject Baxter with something? Yeah, I did. I already have copies of the reports, and went in as soon as I heard about it. I know this will sound absurd to you, but the good thing is we know he's still on the island. Now we can surveil the airport even more closely for anyone even close to matching his description. It won't be long now."

"But what about Doctor Silva?" June asked. "Is he safe?"

"As soon as I hang up with you, I'm sending a car to check on him." There was a pause, something June had discovered was common with detectives in their phone conversations. "I took note that you ran after the guy last night. I wish you wouldn't do that."

"But…"

"Please leave the chases and apprehensions to the police, Doctor."

June was too tired to argue. "He's right. I need to let them chase the bad guys. I have enough to do."

Back in bed, June got into a comfortable position on her side. It wasn't long before she was half asleep, daydreaming of Jack several thousand miles away. She had been so busy, even with as few patients as she'd had, that she rarely got the chance to think of him, let alone miss him. She grabbed her phone and dialed, hoping he'd have some time for her on a Sunday.

"June, I was just thinking of calling you. How's life on Maui?"

"Not nearly as relaxing as I thought it would be."

She gave him an update on her patients, the police involvement, her name in the news so often, and the trouble with the hospital administrator.

"That's a rough way to start at a new job. Any regrets leaving LA?"

"About a dozen times a day. What's new at the White House?"

"Oh, just the usual Mad Hatter politics. There is something that involves you, though."

"Oh? Something juicy, I hope."

"You know that chaplain that married us?"

"Reverend Gustafson. What about him?"

"It turns out his licensure for DC lapsed a while back."

"And this concerns me how?" June asked, wishing she'd gone back to bed instead of calling.

"It turns out he performed our wedding ceremony there in the White House Oval Office while he was unlicensed. We're not actually married."

It was the second surprise of the morning. "Wait. What?"

"He performed the service without having a valid license. We're not married."

"Ministers have to be licensed to hold a wedding?"

"Who would've thunk?" he said. "Now, if you like, I can fly you here to DC one of these weekends. Or if you can wait a few months, I can stop there on my way to an Asia diplomacy trip."

June touched her tummy. "We're not married?"

"Not legally, but try and keep up, okay?"

"Let's think about this for a moment, Jack."

"Think about what? Having the wedding there or here? Do you want to go ahead with the large wedding sooner?"

"Think about not having one at all."

"No wedding? Where's this coming from, June?"

"Are we supposed to renew our vows to each other? We barely did the first time, which evidently didn't happen at all, legally. Don't you think the whole idea of us being secretly married for the next several years before having a public wedding later is a little absurd?"

"It's possible to start and have a family in the White House, June. I'm sorry you don't see that."

"I'm sure it is. It's just as easy to start one on Maui."

"It could be a few years before I'm out of office to make that kind of move," he said. "You want to wait that long?"

"I'm not waiting at all. It seems biology has interceded into whatever we want to decide."

"What do you mean?"

"I had a little surprise when I got here. It seems we're going to be parents whether we're married or not."

"Parents?"

"Yes, Jack. Parents. Your first Presidential scandal was officially confirmed by my OB earlier this week. Congratulations. The White House Mad Hatter is running wild through the East Wing and there's not a thing the Secret Service can do about it."

June ended her call and tossed the phone aside. She rather enjoyed the idea of hanging up on the President.

***

After two more hours of staring at the wall, watching the clock, and waiting for the phone to ring, June slipped out of bed. In the kitchen, she poured a glass of lemonade, which she wished was whisky. Calling the hospital, she told the ICU nurses she would be there in an hour to write her patients' transfer orders for an ordinary ward bed. While she talked on the phone, she peeked out the front window at the porch and front steps. Sure enough, the ti plants really were there, along with the boulder and flowery lei. Only now, there were several more leis on the rock. A hundred yards off the main road and up a driveway, it would've taken quite the effort for someone to leave them there.

"Great." She sighed. "Patients' families are turning into prowlers, leaving gifts behind. What's next? Text messages and creepy phone calls?"

Now that Kekoa was on the mend, the late night visits by the Baxter family should stop. That would also bring an end to the harassment from Townsend in administration and maybe mend the bridge between her and Soseki. She would even allow him to take credit for saving Kekoa's life, if it allowed their little hospital soap opera to end. As far as she was concerned, it was time to move on.

Pulling into the hospital parking lot, she noticed two four-wheel drive police vehicles with single blue lights on top parked near the entrance, Maui police vehicles. "Must be here to investigate what happened last night. Maybe they'll finally get somewhere."

In the outdoor alcove that had turned into a garden shrine in the last few days, June noticed the boulder had only one lei on it. There were more hibiscus bushes in the back, blooming cheerfully with red and yellow flowers. More ti plants had also been planted in the space, now crowded with cheerful greenery and life. It was the perfect greeting for an entrance to a hospital.

"I'm sure I'll hear about those flowers in some memo from administration," June said walking into the main entrance. "For Heaven's sakes, we can't have cheerful flowers growing at a hospital?"

She was quickly in the ICU, where both Kekoa and Mr. Tanigawa were sitting up in their beds, drinking juice.

"So, ready to get some of these monitors off and go to a regular bed, Mister Baxter?" June asked while changing his dressing.

"Ready to go home."

June smiled, and sincerely, for the first time in a days. "A couple more days, okay? But today you'll at least be getting out of the ICU for a more comfortable bed on the ward. Believe me, that's a big improvement."

She had the same routine with Mr. Tanigawa, of changing his dressing, inspecting the wound, and offering reassurance. Then his daughter herded in two young grandchildren, her husband, a sister, and a neighbor, all to meet June. Instead of Mr. Tanigawa being the center of attention, she was.

The son-in-law took June aside.

"How long until we wait for the other side of his neck to get cleaned out?" he asked.

"Oh, several weeks. What I did the other day needs to heal completely. But he's getting good flow into his brain, and that's most important."

"Why did Doctor Soseki wait so long?"

"I don't know. But I'm planning to ask a lot of questions in the next few days about that."

"It's okay if we come back to your clinic?" the son-in-law asked.

"I hope you bring him back to me for his follow-up appointments. My office will send out a reminder when the time comes."

"No, I mean all of us. You know, for physicals or whatever? None of us have been to the doctor in so long. We never knew there were good doctors like you working here. Maybe we should come in?"

She took it as a compliment and assured him she'd find the name of a qualified family practice doctor for them to see. Two hours earlier she'd been complaining about her move to Maui, how it wasn't working out well at all, how much she missed living in LA, and was seriously considering returning. Now, with one or two simple compliments from patients' families, she felt good about her decision. Once again buoyed by life and good cheer that she was doing something right as a physician and as a woman, she went to the cafeteria, ready for a meal.

She waited at the elevators. When the one on the right opened, she took a hesitant step forward, then waved it off. A bed with a patient was inside, along with two nurses. With a second glance, she could see it was Kekoa on his way to the general ward. She gave them a quick wave.

An odd feeling swept over her, which she brushed aside with an impatient jab at the elevator button. She was relieved when it left again. Something just didn't feel right about it. Maybe it was the gossip she had heard from the two nurses on her first day at the hospital, about the one elevator car being haunted, or maybe it was something else. She hated the idea that she was believing in such a silly superstition, and so easily.

'Simple as that,' she told herself silently, as more people gathered at the elevator to wait. 'Nothing more than hospital gossip.'

More people gathered at the elevators, each giving the down button an impatient whack. Something other than impatience bothered June though, and she couldn't quite shake it. It had something to do with the other elevator, or Kekoa, or maybe the police cars she had seen earlier, she just couldn't think of what. She watched the numbers change over the doors, both of them closing in on the second floor where she was.

When there was a *ding* and a door slid open, June shook her head, turned and walked away. Finding a quiet spot in a waiting area, she retrieved her phone from her pocket, scrolled around through the saved numbers, and made a call. Her meal could wait.

"Detective Atkins? This is June Kato at the hospital. I noticed two police cars at the hospital when I came in this morning. Is there something new about Kekoa Baxter's case?"

"Not since last night. Not directly related to him anyway."

She could hear other voices talking in the background of the call, and wondered if he was at some crime scene somewhere or at the station. She didn't care what; she only wanted more information. Something was digging at the back of her mind, and she was sure it had something to do with Kekoa Baxter and Dr. Silvers. "What's that mean, not directly?"

"You didn't see the newspaper this morning?"

"No, why?"

"Front page article about the investigation. We've figured out what the motive was for the attack."

"Who did it?" June asked, glad the search was coming to an end.

"We only know why. Who is what we're still trying to figure out."

"I don't understand. If you know the reason why, you must also know who."

"Not quite yet. But you'll be happy to know I'm here at the hospital right now, making an arrest in the case."

"That's good. But I'm still confused. Who are you arresting?"

"A member of the Board of Directors, Robert Townsend."

"What?" She thought she'd heard wrong.

"It's all in this morning's newspaper," he told her. "After questioning that Silva fellow a couple more times down at the police station, we learned a little more about what's been going on around here. It seems Mister Townsend and Doctor Silva have known each other for quite a while." He paused for a moment to answer a question at his end, listening to loud voices in the background. "Doctor, I need to get going."

After the call abruptly ended, June dropped her phone into her pocket again, and stood frozen in place. Right at that moment, the chairman of the Board of Directors for the hospital was being arrested for something related to Kekoa's attack. It made some sense then, all the push-back she'd been getting from him during the week, and the antipathy toward the floral displays and shrine outside the hospital. All of the flowers and late night visits by the family only brought more attention to whatever Townsend was trying to hide. There had been almost a hateful attitude from him toward Kekoa. But still, it didn't make sense. What grudge could a hospital administrator hold against a lab tech and popular citizen of the island?

June decided to look for a newspaper to read. Finding they were sold out at the hospital gift shop, she went to the lobby to look. In the waiting area were the usual ancient magazines, torn and tattered. Mixed in with them was the local newspaper, one section folded to the half-complete crossword puzzle. She sat on a chair with the front section of the paper. Across the bottom was a long article about Kekoa's case, everything she already knew.

On page five, she found the remainder of the story that the detective hadn't told her. Townsend and Silva had known each other for years, working at an Arizona hospital before coming to Hawaii. They had been investigated in Arizona for charges of graft and embezzlement, neither of which stuck. After those lengthy investigations in Arizona, they both lost their positions at the hospital and quietly fell off the map, only to re-emerge on Maui with a new scheme.

The lab director Silva had won a large national grant to work on a research study, evaluating new medications in the treatment of arthritis. Maui was to be the tropical location for the study population, with other study sites on the mainland. For a while, everything seemed quiet, both Townsend and Silvers remaining under the radar of law enforcement or the media. Both had been hired at the opening of the hospital, and the journalist of the article questioned if their backgrounds had been properly looked into during the hiring process. Once police detectives started to piece things together during the Kekoa attack investigation, they looked into Silver and his study. That's when they found that money was being diverted from the study into pockets, mostly Townsend's.

"But what's that got to do with Kekoa and the Baxter family?" she whispered, scanning the remainder of the article. Then she found it halfway down.

The Baxter family had been major partners in funding the construction of the hospital. When it came to the research project, they got interested in becoming funding partners of that also. But when Kekoa looked into the project as an employee of the hospital, using the inside edge of working in the lab, he discovered funds were being siphoned off, just vanishing. Lab equipment and machines for use in the research hadn't been purchased, the part-time employee meant to assist in the project hadn't been hired, and data wasn't being collected. When Kekoa confronted Silva about it, the lab director got nervous and went to Townsend. That's when someone was hired to kill Kekoa and eliminate the threat of the Baxter family from pulling project funding, and ultimately going to the authorities about the diversion activities, which would expose Townsend and Silva's fraudulent scheme.

"Those jerks. There never was a mistaken identity. They sent someone after Kekoa, just to shut him up. But was Doctor Soseki involved?"

She read through the article again, looking for the vascular surgeon's name, but there was nothing.

June folded the newspaper closed and tossed it down.

"Maybe Townsend has been paying off Soseki to help in killing Kekoa, maybe not. Just like Amy and Atkins say, it's none of my business. Crime solved."

***

June went back to the elevator. When she got there, she wasn't sure if she wanted to go up to see Kekoa or to the cafeteria. If she went to see Kekoa, she knew she'd only get more involved in his family's drama and the police investigation, something she had promised herself to stay away from. If she went to the cafeteria, it would be like shrugging her shoulders, as if she didn't care.

One of the elevators *dinged* and opened in front of her. She glanced at the button for the direction, and saw it was going up. She decided to let fate make the decision for her.

Three nurses stood toward the front, chatting. Just as June stepped inside the elevator, she noticed one of the passengers, a man in the back corner.

She froze. The elevator wouldn't wait. She looked at the nurses, who had stepped aside to let her in. Even her face felt frozen. The man stared back at her. She shook her head, and pointed her finger toward the floor, pretending she wanted to go down instead.

As soon as the elevator door was closed, she got her phone and dialed.

"Detective Atkins, I just saw the man you're looking for. At least, I think it was him!"

"What are you talking about?"

"Your perp, in the Baxter investigation!"

"Where? Here in the hospital?"

"In the main set of elevators, the one on the left. He was going up, along with three nurses."

June watched the numbers over the elevator door change. It had made a stop on the next floor up, before continuing up. Worried about the nurses, June hit the stairwell and took to the steps two at a time, trying to catch up.

"Just exactly how do you know it was the same guy?"

"I saw him last night, remember?" she said, breathing hard. "Tall, dark features, sunglasses, dark clothes."

"Leather jacket?"

"No. But everything else matches."

"That describes half the men on this island. The other half aren't tall. So?"

"Most people here don't wear dark clothes, at least not during the daytime. It's the same guy, I know it."

She burst out onto the next floor up, looking to see if the nurses had got off on that floor. Not seeing them, she looked at the numbers over the elevator door. The elevator made one more stop, then started to descend again. She hit the call button for it. The other elevator seemed stuck at the lobby level, the lowest floor.

"Okay, fine. Where did it stop? Did you notice?" he asked with a disinterested voice.

"On the third, fourth, and fifth floors. Now it's coming back down again." The elevator *dinged* its arrival, the doors sliding open. No one was inside. "It just got here on the third floor, and it's empty."

"Fine. I'll send someone to check out those upper floors. But I want you to go to the cafeteria."

"I'm not hungry," June said. She considered taking the elevator to the next floor up to see if she could spot the man.

"I want you where there're lots of people. I'll want to talk to you later."

"Yeah, sure," she said before quickly ending the call. She got to the elevator just before it closed. Hitting the button for the fourth floor, Kekoa's new floor, she waited.

Instead of going up, it continued its slow trek downward.

"Come on," she muttered, watching the floor indicator change from two to one. It stopped at the main level where the lobby and cafeteria weren't far away. Several doctors and nurses got on, and each button got pushed. Standing next to the control panel, hitting the 'door close' button several times, June was going to have to wait until she got back to the fourth floor.

She was the only passenger after the third floor. "Come on," she insisted, jamming her thumb repeatedly on the 'door close' button. "Get going."

Finally, the door slid open. June hadn't been to the fourth floor except during a quick tour on her first day at the hospital. Other than the nurses' station, she had only a vague recollection of where anything was on the ward. She hurried down the long corridor to the centrally positioned nurses' station, locking eyes with the first person she saw there.

"Hi. I'm June Kato. Kekoa Baxter was just transferred here a few minutes ago. Can you tell me where his room is?"

"Yes," the woman said. She pointed to the area just behind June. "Four-Twelve, just across the hall there. We like to keep the new transfers from the ICU near the nurses' station."

June didn't bother listening after the room number. Turning, she hurried into the room. Kekoa was the only patient, in the bed next to the window. On one side was a nurse adjusting his sheets. On the other side of the bed was someone in a white lab coat. He had the IV tubing in his hand. Kekoa looked at June, and waved with a smile on his face. He seemed to be enjoying the attention.

June went over to them. Looking at the man in the white lab coat, she was lost in confusion again.

"I'm sorry, who are you?" she asked the tall man. He was the same one as she'd seen on the elevator a few minutes before. Only now, he was wearing a white hospital jacket over his dark civvie clothing. At least she thought it was the same man.

"This patient's doctor. Why?"

"Pardon me? I'm Doctor Kato, and I just happen to be his doctor." That's when she saw a syringe in the man's hand, the IV tubing in his other hand. "What are you doing?"

"Giving him his medication."

June glanced at the nurse, who only shrugged back. "We didn't know who Doctor Kato was," the nurse offered.

The man's thumb was on the plunger of the syringe, just beginning to push.

June rushed forward. "Stop that!"

She tried grabbing the syringe away, but the man was too quick. Fighting off her first attempt at blocking him from sinking the plunger, she went back more aggressively.

She locked his hands, twisting them upside down. She was able to pry his fingers loose from the syringe, but it remained attached to the IV tubing, swinging wildly as they grappled over Kekoa's bed.

The nurse shouted for help, calling out for a security code to be called on the hospital loudspeaker. Kekoa simply lay there, looking stunned at all the activity.

June and the man continued to fight, and she finally got him away from Kekoa's bed. Shoving him back, he fell onto the empty bed nearby. Instead of going after him, she turned back to Kekoa, who had a look of fear in his eyes. As big as he was, he was helpless in his bed. June grabbed the syringe and pulled it loose from the tubing, and tossed it into the corner of the room near the nurse that had stepped back. Once it clattered to the floor, she spun on her heels to face the intruder.

Even before she could face him, he planted a heavy fist in her ribs, knocking her back into the side rails of Kekoa's bed. Bouncing off them, she doubled over to the side, trying to take a breath.

By the time she could right herself, the man was headed for the door.

"Hey!" she shouted after him.

By the time she got to the door, the overhead paging system was announcing the call for security to the fourth floor, mechanically repeating the message continuously. She got out to the hall just in time to see the stairwell door swing closed. She ran there and burst through, slipping on the linoleum floor.

Catching herself on the steel banister just before she tumbled forward, she propelled herself down the stairs. She heard the sound of rushing footsteps echoing from below her somewhere. Not knowing how much further ahead he was, she hurried even more.

"You can't out run me!" she shouted as she took the stairs two steps at a time. She went as fast as she could in her cork clogs.

She heard a door slam just as she approached the second floor landing. He had already exited out the ground floor doorway, by now racing through the lobby toward the main entrance.

June slammed chest first into the first floor door, unable to stop herself completely, her shoes skidding on the floor. Yanking it open, she rushed out. His white lab coat had been tossed into a corner, left behind by the fleeing man.

Getting to the center of the lobby, she was panting hard and in pain from where she had been slugged in the chest. The lobby was almost completely empty, except for one volunteer at his information station and a small patch of visitors seated in a waiting area. By the time she got there, the security alert for the fourth floor had ceased. New alerts started, one for security to the lab, along with a Code Blue. Something was going on in the lab, but she didn't care right then. She had her attention set on the man fleeing out the main entrance and wasn't about to give up.

She wasn't sure, but she thought she saw the man in black heading for the double glass entrance doors where a group of people was just coming in. June started running again, her cork clogs clomping on the carpeted floor.

At that time of day, the sky was bright with sunshine, and light was glinting off car windows in the drive-thru at the front of the hospital. The contrast between the subdued lighting inside the lobby and the bright natural light of outside was almost blinding to

June when she rushed out. Shading her eyes with her hand, she scanned the immediate area.

The tall man was lost in the busy crowd in front of the hospital. With the clogs on her feet, she hadn't been able to keep up. June tried seeing past several people going into the lobby, others waiting for their rides, some getting into cars at the curb, patients being discharged with the help of nurses, all of the various people that can be found at the front of a busy hospital throughout the day. Squinting as she looked around, she saw the head of a tall man between cars in the parking lot. He was too distant to be sure it was the same man, but he had dark hair, which was good enough for June to continue chasing.

"Hey!" she shouted again, running as hard as she could.

He was struggling with the car door. It gave her time, allowing her to catch up. Just as he was swinging the door open, she ran into it, slamming it shut again. She bounced off, falling back against another car.

He yowled in pain and tumbled back. When she saw him, he was holding one arm, bent unnaturally mid-forearm. By slamming her body into the door, his arm had been caught in the door, snapping his forearm bones. She didn't care about his arm though, but instead took a long look at his face.

June was sure it was the same man, from the elevator and from Kekoa's bedside.

"What were you doing to Kekoa?" she screamed at him. She never noticed as others passed a few cars away.

"Screw you. What do you care about that guy?"

With his good hand, he reached behind his back, and pulled a knife. Hitting a button, the blade flipped open. Aiming it at her, his hand shook, his face turned inside out with pain.

June stood her ground, only a couple of steps back from him. She knew half a dozen ways of disarming a man with a knife. "What are you going to do with that? Murder me like you tried to do with Kekoa? Then go to prison for the rest of your life?"

"If I have to, I'll cut you open from ear to ear, just like I did with him." He raised his hand higher, but it still shook.

She ignored his warning. A knife she could deal with. A maniac holding it was another matter, though. She needed to proceed carefully and lead him into the direction that was best for her. "That arm must be pretty painful. You think you could actually drive with it like that after knifing me? And drive in a hurry?" She tried to grin at him, but she wasn't fooling herself. She was scared then. A desperate man in tremendous pain was capable of almost anything. She'd faced them before. "You won't get off this island, not with your arm like that. Every cop and TSA agent will be looking for you, and both hospitals will be alerted to watch for a tall man with a broken arm."

He swore at her, once again trying to control the shake in his knife hand.

She stared him in the eyes, trying to keep her attention off his weapon. "Just give up."

Instead, he took a step forward, his hand raised, ready to swing the blade.

June lost her patience. To keep from being slashed, she turned slightly. As quick as a cat, she swung her foot up and caught the man square in the crotch. She'd kicked hard enough to feel her toe sink, taking something with it.

The knife clattered to the ground, which she kicked beneath a car. Positioning her feet on the ground again to take another kick if needed, June heard footsteps trotting up from behind her. She spun around. It was Detective Atkins and an officer in uniform. Both had their weapons drawn. When they saw the man on the ground writhing in pain, clutching at his crotch, they took aim.

"Raise your hands!" the officer shouted.

He raised his hands, but slowly. Atkins pushed past June, took the knife from the ground, and shoved it in his back pocket.

"Step back, Doctor," Atkins said to June gruffly.

When she did, the uniformed cop stepped forward, and slapped a pair of cuffs on the man. He yowled again when his broken arm was manipulated, the deformity obvious at a glance. He got patted down after.

"Careful," she said. "He's got a broken arm."

"Shall we take the cuffs off and give back his blade?" Atkins said to her derisively.

"Okay with me. I'm the one who disarmed him of it."

She watched as the over-sized uniformed cop pull up the man and lead him away, reading him his Miranda rights as they walked. The man was bent forward in pain because of his arm. When June looked toward the main entrance, two more police cars had arrived, blue lights flashing.

"Didn't I tell you to wait in the cafeteria?" Atkins said to June in a scolding tone. "To not get involved?"

"Yes, but…"

He began to lead her away also, back to the hospital entrance. The people milling out in front of the hospital had their attention on the man in cuffs, and on June and Detective Atkins. Her little chase scene in the parking lot had become a spectacle.

"What part of 'don't get involved' is confusing to you?" he asked, this time with a smile growing on his face.

"Basically, all of it." She hesitantly returned his smile. "Telling me to not get involved in something is an engraved invitation to be disobedient. Anyway, it's a good thing I got involved. He was ready to inject Kekoa with something."

"That's what the nurse said, that you chased the guy out of his room. The first part, of going to his room, I don't mind. But chasing him out of the building…seriously? What were you thinking?"

"I don't know. I guess I wanted the guy that's caused so much trouble for so many people this week."

"We knew what he looked like from hospital security cameras. We have profiles and a full-face image. Those would've been distributed to police departments all over the islands and TSA, along with the media."

"A lot of good the media has been this week."

"I saw what they printed about you the last couple of days. I'm sure that if I lean on them a little, they'll print a retraction."

"Thanks. How'd you find us out here in the parking lot?" she asked

"That nurse said you took off running after him down the stairs. When we got outside of the lobby, people pointed toward the parking lot, saying a woman was chasing a man, and she looked mad."

June blushed, not knowing what to say. "Yep, that was me."

The uniform cop took the man to the emergency room for his arm to be put into a splint. While that happened, June gave a statement to Detective Atkins in the lobby. After she had gone through it all, he had her tell the story again.

"Okay, that should take care of it," he told her, flipping his little notepad closed. "But count yourself lucky, that I'm not citing you."

"For what?"

"Oh, I don't know. Obstruction of justice, interfering with police activity, something." He stood from where they sat on a couch in the lobby waiting area. She stood along with him. "I should go find my partner and our perp. Looks like I have a long evening of questioning ahead of me."

Now that the excitement had died down and her adrenaline rush was leveling off, her ribs were beginning to throb where she'd been punched. She did her best to stand up straight.

"I guess I should ask if you're okay? Did he injure you in the chase, Doctor?" Atkins asked.

"Me? No, I'm fine. I need to go upstairs and check on my patients."

"You haven't had enough for one day?" he asked. They had stopped near the elevators.

"Not till my patients get tucked in, safe and sound. Whatever that is here on Maui."

***

Mr. Tanigawa was eating rice, steamed cabbage, and seared mackerel that had been brought in for him by his daughter, ignoring the simple meal June had ordered for him. Kekoa Baxter was deep into a bowl of poi, pulled pork, and sweet bread rolls, brought in by Judy and Leonard. Judy was dressed prettily, and Leonard was once again in a pressed aloha-style shirt.

Kekoa was understandably curious about what had happened earlier with the man and the syringe. June tried to make a quick explanation, but couldn't think of what to tell him except a simplified version of the truth.

"I think there are a lot of details I still don't know. It looks like the police finally got the guy, though. Too bad it took so long, but that's good news, right?"

"I hear you're expecting?" he asked.

Just then, Auntie Haunani and Leonard came in, eliciting the happiest face June had ever seen on a man.

"You still eating poi Karissa send home?" Haunani asked, setting her sights on June.

"I think I'm all out."

Haunani's eyes narrowed. "Ate it all?"

"Yes, Ma'am," June said.

Haunani smiled. "Good. Takes care of that. No more worries about baby."

"I thought it was to put more weight on me? Should I eat more poi?"

"Karissa's special kind, for girls like you. Any kind poi or potatoes are okay now."

"What's the difference between hers and ordinary poi?"

Leonard told them to go out in the waiting area to talk about 'girl stuff' while he and Kekoa could visit.

"Karissa special kind of kahuna," Haunani said once they had some privacy.

"Yes, Judy told me about her. She's the kind that helps women get pregnant, but I already was before I came to the island."

"Pregnant but not right way. Your baby stuck in wrong place. Her poi special kind, to make baby…what's it called?"

"Implant?"

Haunani pointed in agreement. "In womb instead of tube."

June felt the blood drain from her face. "How'd you know it wasn't in my uterus, my womb?"

"Remember at the party, I touch your tummy? I know then. That's why all the special poi from Karissa. My kind, Judy's, no one else's work for you. Must be Karissa's. You eat any kind of poi now, just to make yourself fat." Haunani gave a thumbs-up sign. "Baby okay now."

"But why didn't you explain that before?" June asked.

"Would you have believed me?"

"Probably not." June thought of all the running she'd been doing that week and rushing around the hospital, chasing after a criminal. "I have been worried. I should be taking better care of myself."

"Your baby grow up big and strong. One part you, one part papa, one part Kekoa."

"Kekoa?"

"You saved Kekoa's life, caught the criminal. Because of that, big kind spirit in your baby, big kind.

When June took Haunani back to Kekoa, he beamed happily, and it wasn't long before he was on the phone with other relatives.

With nothing else to do but make notes in both patients' charts, June went downstairs to the ER. It was busy, and instead of bothering an ER doctor about looking at her ribs, she found Henry just coming on duty.

"What happened?" he asked quietly. "You look frazzled."

"Only frazzled?" She gave her a brief recap of what happened in Kekoa's room, the chase through the hospital, and the knife aimed at her in the end.

"Oh, him. The cops just took that guy out of here with a splint on his arm."

"I'm the one that broke it for him."

Henry laughed. "I should've known you had something to do with it."

She playfully punched him in the midsection. "But I think he broke one of my ribs. Can you check for me?"

"Let me get a doc."

She grabbed his arm. "Just check. You've seen my butt. You may as well see my chest."

After closing the privacy curtain, she removed her white coat. He helped her recline back on the stretcher while she opened her blouse. That's when she remembered she had worn one of her prettier and skimpier bras that day. She wondered what Karen might have to say if she happened to see them right then.

"Just keep focused on the task at hand, Henry. I want to send you home to Karen worthy of her love and adoration."

As he gently palpated her ribs, she couldn't help letting a few tears trickle down from the corners of her eyes. When he found the one that was tender, she winced and grabbed at his hands to stop.

"Want me to get the X-ray tech for a film?" he asked.

"No, just get me a binder."

He helped her sit up on the side of the stretcher and she left her blouse off while she waited. She listened to the chaos of a busy ER, sounds she'd heard a thousand times before. A familiar voice pierced through the rest of the din, someone calling for Henry. Try as she might, June couldn't place whose voice it was.

After he brought a rib binder, Henry looked around at their little cubicle while June removed her bra. "This is the same bay as when we met, huh?"

"One and the same," she said, feeling self-conscious covered only by her little bra.

The same voice called Henry's name again, June recognizing it this time.

"Just a minute, Karen," he said.

June wasn't sure, but she thought his face was turning as red as hers right then.

"You forgot your lunch," Karen said from the other side of the privacy curtain.

"Just a minute. I'm with June Kato right now."

The curtain was flung back, Karen standing there looking at June and Henry. June was still only in her bra, Henry's arms around her trying to wrap her chest with the binder.

"Henry!"

Karen turned on her toe and rushed off.

"Maybe you should go after her," June said, taking the binder from him.

Once he left, June was able to get the binder around her chest and the Velcro straps tight. Getting her blouse and white jacket back on, she tried to laugh off what had just happened. Just as she was easing down from the stretcher, Henry and Karen returned.

The three of them apologized to each other, and Karen finally left, looking very dissatisfied.

After her talk with Haunani, June was concerned about her pregnancy and called Divya Gill to come see her. Once again, she gave a quick re-enactment of what had happened the hour before, keeping quiet about what Haunani had said.

"I told you, no strenuous exercise, June. I saw you running through the lobby earlier. I even called your name, trying to get you to stop. I'm terribly disappointed with you," the obstetrician said, while sweeping an ultrasound probe through the gel on June's belly.

June was stunned. Not for being scolded; she expected that much. Divya had always been so sweet in their earlier meetings. "You're right. I shouldn't have chased after him."

"And you have the baby coming. If he would've punched you in the belly instead of the ribs, well…"

"You're right about that, too. I should've been more careful."

"You really need to think about these things. I'm not a miracle worker. If you don't take care of the baby, nobody else can do much for you if things go wrong. And you know what I mean by that."

"I'm sorry. I forgot." June grabbed a handful of tissues to dry her face. "I'm less concerned about that than I am about it being tubal. Can you see anything on the ultrasound?"

"Still looking. Divya adjusted settings on the machine and continued to search for any sign of a fetus with her slimy probe. "What about your other new friend?" she asked, still with the interrogation, but with a softer tone.

"I have friends here?" June asked, surprised by the question.

"I was being facetious. What about Neal Soseki? Going after him now?"

"Ha!" June blew her nose. "I think Soseki's days are numbered, and he did it to himself. There's plenty of stink going around about him already. Even Townsend said he wasn't bringing in much revenue, likely because patients hate him. After the way he treated Mister Tanigawa so poorly these last few years, he won't have a license to practice medicine much longer."

"Which leaves West Maui Medical Center without a vascular surgeon. We're trying to bring docs in, not get rid of them."

"We have someone…well, me…that can do the carotids. I talked to my old boss a few days ago, and he knows of someone there that's looking for a job after her vascular fellowship in LA. What better place than Maui for a young woman to start her career as a surgeon?"

"Enough of that."

"Is it tubal?"

"If it was, there would've been some thickening in the fallopian tube. I followed your remaining tube a couple of times and there was nothing. So early in your pregnancy, it's hard to see, but look here." Divya turned the ultrasound monitor to face June and tapped at a place on the screen. "Say hello to Baby Kato."

June cried all over again when she saw the tiny speck that Divya pointed to. Once the gel was cleaned from her belly, Divya helped her sit up on the side of the stretcher. She set her hand on June's shoulder. "Will you do me a favor when you get home?"

"Sure, what?"

"Eat dinner. Order a pizza to be delivered, eat a tray of lasagna, five packages of ramen, whatever it takes to put some weight on you. You look like you've lost weight since the last time I examined you."

"Maybe a few pounds. But I promise I'll do my best to eat myself into maternal obesity."

"That's the spirit!" Divya helped June down off the stretcher and walked her to the exit door to the parking area. "And go to bed early."

"There is good news, or at least it's supposed to be good news," June said, looking at the printout of her ultrasound as they walked.

"On a day like today, we all could use some."

"My parents are moving in with me next week. Between you and them, I'll be towing the line in no time. Once my sister gets involved, and she will, there's no hope for me."

Divya laughed. "Reinforcements!"

***

The cheesy casserole June baked that evening filled the house with the aroma of garlic and cheese. She got a bowl and spoon, ready to dig some out. Putting the bowl away, she took the entire casserole to the kitchen table with the spoon and lemonade from the fridge.

"Divya and Haunani want me fat."

For a change, she flicked on the television in the living room, positioned so it could also be watched from the kitchen table. She found a local news channel before sitting at her meal.

"Police were called to West Maui Medical Center late this afternoon, when a laboratory employee shot himself, an apparent suicidal gesture," said the anchorwoman at the news desk. A stock image of the medical center was just over her shoulder in the background.

"Now what happened?" June asked, taking her first spoon of the sticky noodle casserole. That's when she remembered there had been some sort of security code announced, followed by a Code Blue, just as she was racing through the hospital in pursuit of Kekoa's attacker.

"After almost an hour of resuscitative efforts in surgery, Doctor Arthur Silva was pronounced dead."

"No kidding. But why didn't they call me? After fifteen years at an LA County trauma center, I think I'm fully qualified to treat head injuries," June muttered, assuming Silva had shot himself in the head.

"The scene unfolded when Doctor Silva was approached to be questioned by police about proceedings at the hospital. Witnesses

told our station reporters in exclusive interviews that in the heat of the moment, Silva removed a pistol from his desk drawer, placed it against his chest, and pulled the trigger. Before police or onlookers could react, Silva drooped from his chair, tumbling to the floor in a heap."

"That's nice to think about while eating my dinner." June pushed the casserole away after only three spoonfuls, having lost her appetite. "A blowout gunshot wound to the heart."

"Stay tuned for updates as more details of this tragic event come to your evening news sta…"

June flicked off the television. "Well, isn't that a nice little hospital staff I've joined. In my first week, there was an attempted murder, a suicide, surgical incompetence, and corruption and embezzlement in the Board of Directors. Not to mention a kahuna and lei flower memorials inexplicably coming and going in the middle of the night."

June put the casserole in the fridge and poured more lemonade. Sitting in the living room with her feet up on the coffee table, she grabbed the romance novel she had hidden in an end table drawer. The trouble at the hospital was winding down, she had a free evening, and she planned to put it to good use. Solitude and fantasy were exactly what she needed.

Barely two pages in, her smart phone rang.

"Doctor Kato?"

The masculine voice was familiar but she couldn't place it. "Yes?"

"I hope you don't mind I called so late."

"It's not late. But who is this, please?"

"I'm sorry. This is Leonard Kalihi, of the Baxter family."

June sat up. "Oh, yes! How are you, Leonard? Is there a problem with Kekoa? I just saw him a short while ago and he looked good."

"Not at all. That's just it. He looks great, sitting up, eating his dinner. We just, the entire family wants to thank you for your efforts, for your care for Kekoa."

"Not at all. I'm sorry it took so long though, before he came around." She was, too. It was a rough start to her career at West Maui Medical Center, her very first patient having been slow to respond to her treatment plan.

"He said he'll be able to go home in a couple of days?"

"That's right, as long as he continues to improve."

They chatted for a moment about Kekoa, what his care at home would be, and when he could potentially go back to work. Through it, something tickled at June's mind.

"Leonard, I have a question for you, or maybe more of a request. First of all, I really do appreciate what your family has done at my home these last couple of nights."

"Sorry?"

"The rock, with the flower leis on it. And the ti plants you've planted. I'm sure it must've been quite expensive," she explained.

"I don't understand."

She was confused. Maybe she wasn't explaining right, or using the wrong words. "At the doors of my home on the last two nights, someone has placed large lava boulders and draped colorful leis over them. Not only that, but several ti plants have been planted. It must've been terribly difficult, but whoever did it, was absolutely silent."

"Just a moment, Doctor." June listened as Leonard talked to someone else. She thought she heard Judy's accented voice in the background of the call, along with several others before he came back to the call. "Let me call you back in a few minutes, okay?"

She set the phone aside after the called ended, going back to her book with a shrug. Only a few lustful pages passed before her phone rang again.

"Doctor, I've talked to the family here at the hospital, and no one seems to know anything about your leis. Then I called Auntie Haunani, thinking that maybe she arranged for something. She also knows nothing about them."

"But it's just like the display at the hospital, near the front entrance. You guys did those, right?" June asked. She tried to remember if she'd asked him about it earlier in the week, but couldn't think of the answer right then.

"We saw those. Also, we had nothing to do with those." Leonard answered a question from someone at his end of the call. "But we did get a letter in the mail yesterday from the hospital asking us to stop the activity."

"Really? And it wasn't your family?"

"No one in the Baxter family has enough time. We all have jobs, and by the time we get home from work, we're too tired to do much landscaping, especially at someone else's house."

"What about Officer Kaleo? Could he have done something like that?" She had wondered all along if he was a relative of some sort.

"Officer Kaleo?"

"Yeah, the police officer that was assigned to guard Kekoa those first few days in the ICU. He had Kaleo on the name patch on his uniform shirt."

"I never saw him," Leonard said flatly, almost hesitantly. "Kaleo is a given name. On uniforms, they put the family name."

"Really? He was there the whole time, every time I went on rounds to see Kekoa anyway. I know Judy saw him there one day."

There was another pause, and June listened to a muffled conversation at Leonard's end of the call.

"Doctor, how did you know we had someone in our family named Kaleo?" Leonard asked when he came back to the call. "And that he was a police officer?"

"It was on his shirt, on his uniform."

"I ask, because we had an uncle in our family, a police officer, who perished many years ago. His name was Kaleo, but it was his first name."

"But…"

"Auntie Haunani has said he comes for visit, mostly when there's trouble, or someone in ohana needs help."

"So…wait. You mean that officer at Kekoa's door, the one I talked to a few times…"

"Was probably our Uncle Kaleo."

"And you said he…"

"Perished many years ago. Good for you to meet his kind soul."

June didn't know what else to say, letting only a timid 'okay' slip out.

"Welcome to our ohana, Doctor. To the Baxter family ohana!"

"Maybe you should just call me June."

***

June turned the television back on, hoping to find a gossip show of some sort to distract her mind from conjuring up images of ghosts. Instead, the local news was just ending.

"And as we wrap up this evening's newscast, we have one last report from West Maui Medical Center, where an apparent suicide took place today. Doctor Arthur Silva died tragically by his own hand today, at almost the same time as his partner in crime was being placed under arrest by local authorities. Robert Townsend, head of the hospital's Board of Directors…" An image of Townsend shot up on the screen just behind the news anchor's head. *"…was arrested for attempted murder, embezzlement, and complicity in medical research fraud. When asked by reporters at the scene outside the medical center, he had this to say:…"*

A film clip of Townsend started, his arms cuffed behind his back, his head hanging down, being led out of the building by two uniformed officers, Detective Atkins bringing up the rear. Several reporters thrust handheld microphones in his direction, one woman shouting out, "Why'd Doctor Silva have to die?"

Townsend looked at the camera aimed in his direction instead of the person that asked the question. "He didn't have the guts to go on."

"Seriously?" June asked the TV.

"Our research team here at the Maui Tele-Media Center has discovered that Doctor Silva and Mister Townsend were no strangers to law enforcement. Both were working under false identities, and had old warrants out for their arrest for previous crimes in Arizona. It will only be a matter of time before more questions arise, begging for difficult answers. And possibly the

biggest question might be why Doctor Arthur Silva shot himself through the heart, on this warm and breezy day on Maui."

June flicked off the television. Others were under arrest, one had died, and the hospital would look bad in the press for a while. On the other hand, her patients were recovering, their families happy. That was most important. So what if she needed the help of a ghost? She was beginning to discover there was a spirit to the island, something very indefinable but also quite undeniable.

Her phone rang. She recognized the number and answered. "Detective Atkins, what can I do for you?"

"Doctor Kato. Mostly I just wanted to let you know the ADA will need a formal statement from you about what happened today. His office should be contacting you later in the week."

"I figured as much. But can you fill in a few blanks for me?"

"Such as?" he asked impatiently.

"Just exactly who tried to kill whom in this deal? It really is quite confusing."

"Yes, quite the little soap opera. Piecing together what the perp has said, along with what Townsend confessed to, two men were supposed to have been murdered, something of a contract hit."

"Oh?"

"Townsend must've watched one old movie too many. Both he and Silva went to a Honolulu bar to find a guy that would kill Kekoa Baxter, because Baxter had learned too much about their little fraud scheme of skimming money from research grants. They were worried he'd go to authorities, and that their backgrounds would be discovered."

"So, the guy with the broken arm, the perp or whatever, tried to kill Kekoa on Monday morning, but failed," June summed up. "But who was the other?"

"Not exactly. The perp went looking for Silva on Monday morning, but just happened to find Baxter instead. You see, Silva was the other intended victim. Townsend had added his name to the list he gave the hit man, figuring he was getting too nervous and was about to spill. In a twist of irony, it just happened that Baxter was wearing Silva's lab clothes that day."

"Townsend wanted both Kekoa Baxter and Arthur Silva dead to hide his embezzlement, hired some guy in a bar, and then thought he was going to get away with it? How cliché is that?"

"Or just plain stupid," the detective said. "But he succeeded in Silva's death, anyway."

As far as she was concerned, June was done with it. She would give her deposition to the district attorney and walk away, taking her broken rib with her. Once again, just as both Henry and Atkins had warned her not to do, she had got too involved in something that didn't belong to her. This time, however, she was lucky enough to get out of it intact. Now, all she really needed to know was who was responsible for the leis and ti plants.

Murder and kahuna and leis didn't matter that evening. Maybe with her recent news of carrying a baby, and the move to Maui, she really was turning over a new leaf in life.

She picked up her phone again and dialed a number. Finding Jack was too busy to talk, she called another number, one she had saved in her favorites list.

"Yes, hello. I'd like to make an appointment for a massage with Dalene, for this evening if at all possible."

...

About Kay Hadashi

Kay Hadashi is a former surgical nurse who turned to writing suspense and adventure novels, weaving medical drama into many of her plots. Third generation Japanese American and born and raised in Honolulu, her stories include strong women characters and are steeped with Hawaiian and Japanese culture.

Most of her books span three generations of the Kato family, and the adventures they share. Hadashi has written more than twenty books and has contributed to several mystery short story anthologies. David VanDyke, best-selling author of the Plague Wars and Stellar Conquest Series, calls her character June Kato, a 'kick-ass heroine'. Toby Neal, author of the Lei Crime Series, says, "Here's an author whose heroine mine should meet." She has also teamed with Nick Stephenson of the Leopold Blake private detective series to write "Ratio", a cross-over novel including both of their characters.

Readers who enjoy exciting stories filled with suspense and drama like Hadashi's novels. From the thrills in the original suspense series, to the trials of a daring young woman in the Melanie Kato Adventures, the writing team at Kay Hadashi Novels hopes you find something fun to read!

Made in the USA
Monee, IL
29 March 2022

93772061R00204